THE TWENTY-FIFTH HOUR

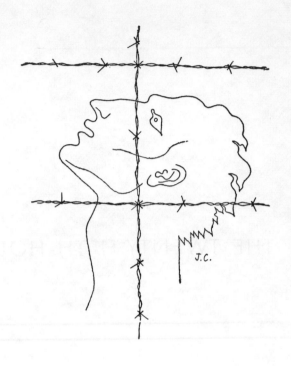

Translated from the Romanian by

RITA ELDON

the twenty-fifth hour

C. VIRGIL GHEORGHIU

Henry Regnery Company, Chicago

First published in France by Librairie Plon as LA VINGT-CINQUIÈME HEURE, *translated from the Romanian. Copyright by Const. Virgil Gheorghiu, 1949.*

The following passages are reprinted with permission and thanks to

Harcourt, Brace and Company, Inc.: on page 8, from *The Rock* by T. S. Eliot, copyright 1934 by Harcourt, Brace and Company, Inc.; on page 282, from *Murder in the Cathedral* by T. S. Eliot, copyright 1935 by Harcourt, Brace and Company, Inc.; on page 319, from "Gerontion" from *Collected Poems of T. S. Eliot,* copyright 1936 by Harcourt, Brace and Company, Inc.; on page 108, from *The Condition of Man,* copyright 1944 by Lewis Mumford; on pages 48 and 319, from *The Travel Diary of a Philosopher* by Count Hermann Keyserling, copyright 1925 by Harcourt, Brace and Company, Inc.

Random House, Inc.: on page 85, by W. H. Auden, and on page 320, from "New Year Letter" by W. H. Auden, copyright 1945 by W. H. Auden.

The Macmillan Company: on page 10, from *The Meeting of East and West* by F. S. C. Northrop, copyright 1946 by The Macmillan Company; on page 50, from *Purposes of the Acts* by W. Burnet Easton, Jr.

(CONTENTS)

THE TWENTY-FIFTH HOUR

(FANTANA)

⊂⊒ ⊂⊒ ⊂⊒

"I just can't believe you're going," said Susanna, snuggling closer to Johann Moritz. She put her hand on his head and stroked his black hair. He drew back.

"Why don't you believe it?" he answered harshly. "The day after tomorrow, at dawn, I'll be gone."

"I know," she said softly.

They were standing near the hedge. The air was cool. It was past midnight. Johann caught hold of her hands and pushed them away.

"And now good-by!"

"Stay a little longer!" she begged him.

"Why do you want me to stay?" His voice was steady. "It is getting late. I've got a lot to do tomorrow."

She did not answer, but held him more closely. Half opening his shirt, she pressed her cheek against his bare chest and looked up at the sky.

"Look how bright the stars are," she said.

He was expecting something important. He thought that

was why she had made him stay. But she was only talking about stars. He turned to go. Then he remembered that he would not see her again for at least three years. And so, just to please her, he, too, looked at the stars.

"Could it be true that every man has his own star in the sky? And that it falls when he dies?"

"How should I know?" he answered. He had now made up his mind to go.

"Good-by!"

"Do we, too, have our stars up there?" she asked.

"Like everyone else," answered Johann. "Up there or within us."

He took her head in his hands and gently pushed it away. Then he went. She walked with him as far as the path, holding his hand. She looked at the stars, then at him.

"I shall expect you tomorrow night," she said.

"If it doesn't rain."

She would have liked to run after him, to beg him to come even if it did rain, but he was striding rapidly away. He disappeared round a corner of the garden. For a while she stood still, smoothing out her dress and brushing away the bits of grass that had stuck to her hips. Before going into the yard she looked at the trampled grass beneath the walnut tree where they had lain side by side. The smell of Moritz's body still lingered about her—a smell of crushed grass, tobacco, and cherry stones.

Johann crossed the field and made for his home, whistling as he went. He was wearing black army trousers and a white open-necked shirt. He was barefooted. Several times he stopped whistling and yawned. Then he thought of the woman he had just left—Susanna—and he felt like laughing. "All that nonsense about stars. Women are like children. They think up all sorts of silly questions," he said to himself. Then he thought of his journey to America, which was to start the day after tomorrow. Then he stopped thinking altogether. He began whis-

tling again. He was sleepy. He wished he were already home
and in bed. He had to get up very early. It was to be his last
day's work. And already it was nearly dawn. Johann Moritz
quickened his pace.

🙚 🙚 🙚

THE next day, at dawn, Johann stopped by the village well and,
opening his shirt wide, took some water in his hands and rubbed
his face and neck with it. There was no one about. The villagers
were still asleep. Walking down the middle of the road, he
dried his hands by passing them through his hair. He straightened his collar, leaving his shirt open, and contemplated the
village as it emerged from a milk-white, early-morning fog. This
was the village of Fantana, in Romania. Twenty-five years ago
Johann Moritz had been born there. Now, as he stood gazing
at its low houses and its three churches—Catholic, Protestant,
and Orthodox—he remembered that Susanna had asked him
whether he was not going to miss living there. At the time he
had laughed at her question, answering that he was a man.
Only women felt homesick. But now that the time had come to
go, he somehow felt sorry and rather sad. He resumed his whistling and stopped looking at the village.

Father Koruga's house stood on the main road, not far from
the Orthodox church. The gate was locked. Johann bent down
and picked up the key that was kept hidden under the gate so
that he could get in when he came to work in the morning. He
took his time opening the heavy oak gate. The dogs came
bounding toward him and jumped up in greeting. They knew
him well. Johann Moritz had been coming to work for Father
Koruga every day for the last six years. He felt quite at home
there. But today was his last day. He would spend it picking

apples. Then he would collect his wages and tell the priest he was leaving. As yet the priest knew nothing about it.

Johann went into the barn and fetched the baskets that he piled up in the cart. The priest came out on the veranda. He was wearing nothing but a coarse white shirt and trousers. He had just got up. Moritz greeted him with a smile. He put down his basket, rubbed the dust off his hands, stepped onto the veranda, and took the white jug of water out of the old man's hands.

"Let me pour it out for you, Father."

Johann poured the water into the priest's hands. He looked at the tapering fingers as white and delicate as a woman's. He enjoyed watching the old man as he soaped his beard and neck and forehead. He watched so intently that he forgot to go on pouring out water. The priest waited, his outstretched hands covered with lather. Moritz felt guilty and blushed.

Alexandru Koruga was the Orthodox parish priest. Though he was only fifty, his hair and beard were silver white. He had the long, slender, emaciated body of a saint painted on an icon, the body of an old man. But the look in his eyes and his way of speaking betrayed his youth. When he had finished washing, the priest wiped his face and neck with a coarse towel. Johann stood beside him, jug in hand.

"I would like a word with you, Father," he said.

"Let me get dressed first," answered the priest. He took the jug out of Johann's hands and went toward the house. When he reached the threshold, he turned round.

"I also have something to tell you. Something that will please you. Meanwhile, put the baskets in the cart and harness the horses."

All morning Johann and Father Koruga picked apples and filled the baskets. They worked in silence. When the sun touched their shoulders, the priest stopped and stretched himself. He was tired.

"Let's have a rest."

"Very well," said Johann.

They went toward the sacks filled with apples and sat down on one of them. They were silent awhile. The priest felt in his pockets for the packet of cigarettes he always brought for Johann and handed it to him.

"You have something to tell me."

"Yes, Father, I have."

Johann lit the cigarette. He threw the match into the grass and watched it go out. He found it hard to tell the priest he was leaving. He wished he could put it off.

"I will tell you my news first," said the priest.

Johann was glad that he would not have to speak first.

"The little room next to the kitchen is empty," said the priest. "I thought you might like to have it. My wife has whitewashed it, hung up curtains, and put out clean sheets. In your house there is only one room. It is not enough for you and your parents. When you come to work tomorrow, bring your things."

"I am not coming to work tomorrow."

"Then the day after tomorrow," said the priest. "From now on the room is yours."

"I won't be coming at all any more," said Johann. "Tomorrow I am sailing for America."

"Tomorrow?" The priest opened his eyes wide.

"Tomorrow at dawn."

His voice, though steady, was tinged with regret and embarrassment.

"I've had a letter. The ship is at Constanta and is only stopping three days."

The priest knew that Johann wanted to go to America. Many young peasants were going to America. Two or three years later they would come back with money and buy land. They had the finest properties in Fantana. The priest was glad that Johann was going. In a few years' time, he, too, would own a fine property. But he was surprised that he was leaving so soon. Johann had never mentioned it, and every day, all this time, they had been working side by side.

"I only received the letter yesterday," explained Johann.

"Are you going alone?"

"With Ghitza Ion. We are signing on as stokers. We'll work in the engine room. That way we only had to pay five hundred lei each. Ghitza has a friend in Constanţa who works in the docks. He has arranged everything."

The priest wished him good luck. He was sorry to lose him. Johann was young and worked well. He was kindhearted and honest, but he was poor. He had not an inch of land.

All that day the two men worked together. The old man talked about America, and Johann listened, from time to time heaving a sigh. Now he almost regretted his decision. In the evening, after taking his wages, he stood before the priest with downcast eyes. There was no further need for him to stand there, but he had not the courage to leave. The old man patted him on the shoulder.

"Write to me when you arrive," he said. "Tomorrow morning you can come and fetch the food I promised you for the journey."

He gave him five hundred-lei notes on top of his earnings and said:

"Come at dawn. Knock gently on the windowpane. It would be better if my wife did not hear. Women are sometimes stingy, you know."

"I have to meet Ghitza Ion at the other end of the village before daybreak."

"Then you will just have time to call in here on the way. Otherwise I would have told you to come round this evening."

"I'd rather come tomorrow," said Johann. He was thinking Susanna would be waiting for him that night. Then he went.

❦ ❦ ❦

FATHER KORUGA stood the knapsack against the wall by the window. He put out the light. Then he got into bed. Before closing his eyes to sleep he thought about Johann Moritz's journey to America. While packing the sack he had had a curious feeling that it was really he who was going. He, too, thirty years ago, had packed up his baggage for that very same journey. It was when he had just received his doctorate in theology and had been appointed a missionary to the Orthodox community of Michigan. A week before his departure he had sent a telegram resigning the post . . . he had met his future wife and had got married. Ever since, he had been the priest of the Orthodox church in Fantana. The village was small and life difficult. He had often regretted changing his mind. But then it was too late. America had remained an unfulfilled dream. Every time one of the peasants was ready to make the crossing, Father Koruga gave him cigarettes, food, and money for the journey and asked him to write from over there. He kept all this from his wife. Not that she would have objected, but every time the old man thought of America he felt he was being unfaithful to her. It was for her that he had given up America. But deep in his heart the old conflict still smoldered.

Johann meant more to him than the other peasants. He had been more than a hired man: a valued helper, a friend. So he felt that with him a part of his own self was setting out for the New World.

That night there was a full moon. The priest could not sleep. He got out of bed and lit the lamp. Crossing toward one of the bookshelves, he took down a book. Before opening it he stood and looked at the rows of well-stocked shelves that lined the walls on three sides of the room. There were books in English, German, French, and Italian. Further on were the Greek and Latin classics. During the thirty years he had spent in Fantana, these books had come to be old friends. Sometimes he used to wonder why he had never followed the advice of his friends and taken up a university career at Bucharest or Iaşy. Twice he had refused the offer of a chair in the History of the Church, and he had not regretted it. In Fantana he celebrated Mass on Sundays and holy days, and the rest of the time he spent looking after his land, his bees, and his orchard. In the evenings he read. He was prepared to accept what the future held in store for him. Only once had he tried to force his destiny, and that was when he had planned to go to America. He had done everything humanly possible to get there and yet he had never sailed. Something unforeseen had happened. After that he had given up making plans and believing in their inevitable fulfillment. The priest opened his book and read at random: . . . *The nature, not merely of human affairs but of all things, is in part indeterminate, and consequently a wise man, an informed man, will never absolutely commit himself. One loses face when one has committed oneself to a specific, definite future course of events. . . . A person in the Orient who puts himself in such a position is covered with shame, because he has disregarded what the East teaches man to believe is one of the most elementary facts about human experience and of the nature of things generally: namely, their indefiniteness and their contingency.*

This belief also makes the traditional Oriental suspicious of moral codes that lay down determinate, specific lines of conduct which must hold valid under all circumstances. Determinate things in the world are transitory. Hence, any rules based upon them can never be expected to hold good in all circumstances; and consequently the dying of man or the sacrifice of human beings for determinate, concrete, moral precepts shows a lack of religious as well as of philosophical and scientific wisdom. *

* F. S. C. Northrop.

The priest closed the book and returned it to its place. Am I really sure, he wondered, I don't regret having decided not to sail for America thirty years ago? And if I don't regret it, then why all this strange excitement today, now Moritz is going? Drawing the bedclothes round him again he thought: What I feel is not regret at having stayed behind, but rather a nostalgic craving for a thing that exists only in our imagination. If ever it were to come within our reach, we should discover soon enough that it was not at all what we had hoped. Perhaps America is not really what I am looking for, but only something that serves as a pretext for my restlessness. America is the invention of our nostalgia. "*America is a Utopia.* . . . *Before being discovered it was present in the dreams of the poets and in the investigations of the scientists.*" * Not to have known America may be less painful than to have known it.

And still the priest was too agitated to sleep. He was as eager for the day to break as if he himself were meeting Ghitza Ion at the other end of the village and going to Constanţa, where the ship that was "stopping only three days" was waiting for him.

It was still dark when he woke up, but the cock was already crowing. The priest opened the window. The road was deserted and the village lay shrouded in morning mist. He undid the sack and put in the packet of cigarettes from off the table. If Moritz goes, there is no one else to whom I can give cigarettes. I bought them for him, he reflected. Light was beginning to filter through the window. He heard footsteps approaching along the road, but they passed by the house and faded into the distance. If he didn't hurry, he would keep Ghitza Ion waiting. The priest went out on the veranda and washed in cold water. But Johann was not there to pour it out for him.

The sun had risen and there was still no sign of Johann. The priest waited till noon. Then he came to the conclusion that Johann must have awakened too late to call for his sack. "It's a

* Alfonso Reyes.

pity he didn't come. I had packed supplies enough for at least three weeks. There would even have been some over for his first days in America."

"Dinner is ready, Alexandru," said his wife, who had appeared on the doorstep.

"I'm coming," answered the priest. With a pang of regret he stuffed the sack away under the bed. It was the final gesture of renunciation of an ideal reluctantly abandoned after thirty years. He went in to dinner.

"If only Moritz had taken this sack, I should have felt that it was I who was going. *Qui facit per alium facit per se.* What a pity he did not come."

V V V

AFTER taking leave of the priest, Johann walked over to the well at the side of the road and washed. Making his way through the village, he headed toward Nicolae Porfirie's house. Nicolae Porfirie had some land for sale by the edge of the wood.

"I'm sailing for America tomorrow," he said when he reached the yard of the house. "When I get back I'll have enough money to buy that field of yours, but before I go, I'd like to leave you a deposit on it, so that you won't sell it to anyone else."

"How long do you expect to be away?" the peasant asked.

"Till I've saved up enough—two or three years."

"That's plenty of time. In three years you'll do it easily. No one has ever taken longer than that. Money's easy to come by in America."

"How much shall I leave you?" Johann asked.

"I don't need money. Come back in three years' time with fifty thousand lei, and the field is yours. I won't let anyone else have it; I'll wait for you."

But Johann pulled a bundle of notes out of his trousers pocket and counted them out on the doorstep.

"Here's three thousand," he said. "I'd rather leave a deposit, all the same."

Johann shook hands with Nicolae Porfirie to seal the bargain and went off. It was not yet dark. He wanted to have just one more look at the field on which he had just paid the deposit. He knew it well, for he had already looked at it countless times before, but this time it was different. The field belonged to him now: all he had to do was to bring the money.

☙ ☙ ☙

Johann struck out across the fields. His shirt was damp with sweat and stuck to his skin, for he was too impatient to walk slowly. When he came to a spot not far from the oak wood he stopped. From where he stood to the edge of the wood stretched his field. It was sown with corn that stood shoulder-high. It was not a big field but it would take a house and a yard, a kitchen garden and a small orchard. His eye ran over it, measuring its length and breadth. He could see the roof of his house rising above the green corn; and the long balancing pole of the well, the great oak gate, and the stable. Often enough, looking over that same field, he had seemed to see all these things, but never more clearly than today; everything seemed real, just as he had planned it. Looking at the waves of green corn rustling in the breeze, he smiled. Bending down, he scooped up a handful of earth in his left hand. It was like taking hold of a living thing— warm, like a young sparrow in his palm. He bent down and scooped up more with his other hand; this handful, too, was warm. He squeezed it tight in his fist and then scattered it over the field. Then he pushed on through the corn toward the wood, but in the middle of the field he stopped again to pick up another handful of earth. "This is warm, too," he said to himself. "The whole field is warm and alive." He rubbed the earth against his cheek and breathed in its fragrance. "It's a good strong smell, a smell of tobacco." He lifted his head and filled his lungs again and again with the sweet-scented air of his field. Then he went back the way he had come. Susanna'll be waiting by now, he thought, and began to whistle.

ꟷ ꟷ ꟷ

JURGU JORDAN, Susanna's father, lived on the outskirts of Fantana, in a large house with a roof of red tiles. Johann made his way through the garden to the bottom of the yard and looked through a gap in the fence. He watched Jurgu coming out of the house and treading heavily onto the veranda, closing and bolting the shutters, then carefully locking each one. Johann followed every movement. When Jurgu had finished, he glanced suspiciously behind him and then went down the steps, which creaked under the weight of his giant body. He wore his usual green jacket, short boots, and riding breeches. He crossed the front garden, double-locked the gate, and ferociously shot home the bolt. Then he swung round and made a tour of the house, peering suspiciously in all directions as if he were searching for someone hiding in the shadows. Finally he went in by the back door. There was the sound of a key turning twice in the lock, and then there was silence. Jurgu went into his bedroom, whose walls were covered with hunting trophies and the stuffed heads of deer, wolves, and bears. Shotguns, pistols, and cartridge pouches hung between antlers and stuffed eagles. On the floor beside the enormous bed were spread two black bearskins. Jurgu lifted a gun off its hook and stood it against the bed. Then he took a revolver, a candle, and a box of matches out of a drawer and arranged them neatly on the bedside table. He sat down on the edge of the bed to remove his boots and set them down side by side on the black bearskins, breathing heavily all the time. He always put his boots in exactly the same place so that he could find them in the dark merely by stretching out for them. At last he undressed and got into bed, sinking into the white pillows like a bear into snow. From behind the fence, Johann saw the light fade, flicker, and finally go out. The window became a black blot in the darkness.

There was still a light on in Yolanda's room, but it was a soft, subdued light, screened by a silk lampshade. People said that Yolanda, Jurgu's wife, was an unhappy woman. One night, twenty-one years before, she and Jurgu had come riding into the village and put up at the inn. Nobody knew where they had come from, but it must have been from far away. She was Romanian, but he was not. Later it turned out that they had come from Hungary. They had both been wearing long, fur-lined cloaks. When they had made a meal of grilled steak and wine— he devouring like a wild beast, she scarcely pecking at her food —they had gone to bed in the innkeeper's room. Three days later people learned that they had come to stay, and a few weeks after that they had bought the inn. When Jurgu first came he had known not a word of Romanian, but now he spoke it well. They had made no friends in Fantana. They had even sent their daughter, Susanna, to a school in town so that she would not make friends with village children. The villagers caught glimpses of Yolanda only when she was on her way to the Orthodox church or when Jurgu drove her to town. His gigantic frame towered over her in the carriage and made her look less than half his size. She had fair hair, like finely spun silk, and blue eyes, and Susanna was the very image of her. That was all that was known about Jurgu Jordan. One winter night he had killed a man who had tried to break into the house. He had aimed straight between the eyes with his rifle. The police had maintained that Jurgu had been in the right to shoot a man who had broken in by night to steal his money. The villagers thought otherwise. Murder, they muttered, was always murder. But gradually the whole story was forgotten; it had all taken place so long ago.

Now Johann watched Yolanda's light grow dim, flicker, and go out. He cupped his hands to his mouth and called with the hoot of an owl.

The owl cry rent the air and came back in echoes. Then there was silence, but only for a second. The shutters of the corner room flew open, and Susanna jumped lightly over the window sill. Across the yard and through the gap in the fence she came racing, on tiptoe, toward where Johann was waiting for her.

❧ ❧ ❧

"Why do you have to go on using the owl call? Why all this hooting and toowhooing? Why?" She had come through the hedge. Johann tried to kiss her, but she resisted.

"I've told you already not to call like that." Her heart was thumping with fear.

"How else should I do it?" Johann asked.

"Any way you like," she said. "But not that. The hoot of an owl is a bad omen. It means bad luck and death. That's why you mustn't use it."

"Old wives' tales!" said Johann. "There's no other bird sings both night and day, good and bad weather alike, winter and summer. None except the owl. Nightingales only sing in the spring. If I come and sing like a nightingale, your father will spot that it is a man. Do you want the giant to find out?"

"Of course not," she said, "but the owl brings bad luck all the same."

"That's not my fault," said Johann. "Why couldn't God make some other bird which could sing all the year round and all round the clock without being an omen of death? But let's not squabble about that tonight. No more secret meetings from now on. I'm off to America tomorrow morning. When I come back you'll be my wife and I shan't have to stand any longer behind the hedge, hooting like an owl."

He held her close to him, and she folded her arms round his neck and clung to him. They were underneath the walnut tree where they had met the previous night and every night since they had first known each other four months ago. Johann felt the whole weight of Susanna's body limp in his arms. He had to hold her to prevent her from falling, and, putting her gently on the grass, he lay down by her. Their bodies were entwined like creepers. Neither spoke. Hands groped for each other in the dark; they closed their eyes, and their mouths met. Somewhere at the bottom of Jurgu's garden crickets were chirping. Then they, too, were silent. Still she lay enfolded in his arms. A few paces away her blue dress lay on the grass. She had taken it off so that her mother should not find it creased and stained green. The inky cloud that had obscured the moon had now lifted, and her shoulders gleamed in the darkness. Johann had taken off his shirt and had made Susanna lie on it. Against her white body, his skin was as dark as the bark of a tree.

"Don't go away, Jani."

"Why do you have to say that?" he said, frowning. "You know that if I stay, we can't buy any land. If we have no land, we can't get married. Where do you expect us to live if we have no house and no land? In three years' time, I'll be back with the money, and then we'll get married. Or perhaps you don't want to marry me any longer?"

"Of course I do, but I don't want you to go."

"What do you expect me to buy the land with, then?" Johann smiled. "You know, I've already paid a deposit on Nicolae Porfirie's field. I'll pay him the rest when I come back."

Johann told her how he had talked to Nicolae about the field and had gone to see it afterward, and how he was going to build the house and stables.

[17]

"Jani, if you go, you won't find me alive when you get back!" said Susanna without listening to what he was saying.

"What's the matter with you all of a sudden?" Johann was really annoyed with her this time.

"Nothing," she said. "Just a feeling inside. You needn't believe it, but when you get back, I'll be dead."

"Nothing of the sort," said Johann. "You'll be living at home with your father and mother, same as you are now. I'm not worried about you. After all, you won't be alone."

She started crying softly.

"What is it?" he asked, and kissed her. Her lips were cold and salty with tears. "What's come over you?"

"You'll only say I'm being silly. I'd better not tell you."

"All right, I won't say you're just being silly."

"I think my father will kill me," she said.

"Who on earth put that idea into your head?" he said harshly. "Why should he kill you?"

"There, I knew you wouldn't believe me! But I'm scared to death. I'm sure I'm right. Father has found out something—I don't know how—and that is why he'll kill me."

"What has he found out?"

"About our love," she said.

Johann drew away from her. Susanna's naked body gleamed like marble in the grass.

"Has your father said anything to you?"

"No."

"Has he scolded you?"

"No."

"Then how do you know he has found out?"

"Something tells me he has." Her tears were flowing freely now. "But it's not only a feeling. When I brought the dishes in at dinnertime today, Father glared at me with hatred in his eyes. 'Turn round and face the wall!' he roared, and though I had my back turned, I could feel his eyes on my hips. Then he said: 'Turn round to the window!' Again he stared at me, sideways this time. He marked the outline of my belly and hips the way he does with horses. Then he shouted wildly: 'Get out, you dirty slut!' He wouldn't eat anything more. I went out, and that was when I knew for certain that he had found out everything. When I was small, Father often used to scold me; he even beat me till he drew blood, but he never called me a dirty slut. Today at dinnertime, he said: 'Get out, you dirty slut!' "

"How could he have found out?" Johann asked. "He has never seen us together."

"He has never seen us, but he knows everything."

"But how can he tell?"

"Just by looking at me."

Johann laughed and gave her a kiss on the forehead.

"Even if he had looked at you through binoculars he could not have told anything," he said. "Do you think it shows when a woman has been making love? That's all your fancy."

"I know as a rule nothing shows, but with my father it's different. He can tell with mares, just by looking. He can tell when a mare is in foal. His friends can't make it out."

"Do you think you're pregnant?"

"No, I'm not."

"Nothing to worry about, then," he said. "In two or three years' time I'll come back with the money, and we'll get married at Father Koruga's church. We'll build a fine house and be happy, won't we, Susanna?"

She was trembling as if she were afraid, clinging to him with all her might.

"If you were here, I wouldn't be afraid!" she said. "But when you're gone, I'll die of fright. Even if Father doesn't shoot me, you still won't find me alive. I shall die of fright while you're away. Every night I bolt and lock my door, and when I hear Father's footsteps outside, I bury my head under the pillow, I'm that frightened."

Johann stroked her gently and drew her nearer to him. They were silent. She was happy because she was close to him, and he was happy because she had stopped trembling and crying. When the cocks began to crow, they got up. Susanna slipped into her dress, which was cold and damp with dew, and Johann put on his shirt. They went back hand in hand as far as the fence, and he watched her vanish through it into the yard. Suddenly she gave a sharp cry. Johann bent forward to see what was up, but Susanna was no longer in the yard: she was clinging to him desperately. She was there before he had even seen her coming, and her body was burning, and trembling like a leaf. Johann looked through the gap in the fence.

Through the wide-open window of Susanna's room came a stream of light. Jurgu was pacing up and down in his nightshirt, holding up a lantern as if he were looking for something. Johann pressed Susanna's head to his chest and stroked her hair to prevent her from seeing what her father was doing. But Susanna had seen, and that was why she clung to him. She was too terrified even to cry. They could hear Jurgu swearing. At his side appeared the slender silhouette of Yolanda for a second: a second later it was gone. Jurgu turned his back to the window, and she vanished behind his massive frame. Then they heard Yolanda's screaming—long-drawn, piercing screams that tore at the very marrow of their bones. The light went out. The open window framed nothing but the dark. Ever more despairing came Yolanda's shrieks piercing the night. Then they began to die down, becoming more and more muffled, until they ceased altogether. She had fallen to the ground. In the unlit room, Jurgu was stamping on her with his boots.

"Mother," Susanna cried, "he's killing Mother!"

She tried to wrench herself free and rush into the yard, but Johann kept her held fast, trying to soothe her. Several times, driven by the impulse to save Yolanda from her assailant, he all but let go, for the cries had now died down and Johann knew that it would soon be too late. Throughout his body, every muscle went taut—and yet he never moved. He was unarmed, and the giant had a gun and was as strong as an ox. His instinct forbade him to take on a fight he was bound to lose.

Johann locked Susanna in his arms, holding her tight to prevent her from struggling free. Blindly, he started running across the fields, lashed on by a vision of the giant, gun in hand, setting out in search of Susanna. He wanted to hide her, to take her away, far, far away from the house with the red tiles. Behind him, so it seemed, crashed the echoing footsteps of the giant lusting to kill the woman whom he held in his arms.

🐾 🐾 🐾

JOHANN cut across the fields, avoiding the path. Several times he stumbled against molehills and almost fell. He felt himself growing tired. He must have been walking for a very long time, for his arms were limp with exhaustion. Sweat ran down his forehead and into his eyes, obscuring his sight. In the middle of a corn field he stopped and put down his burden. He could not carry the girl one step further. Kneeling, he laid Susanna on the damp earth, wrapped the blue dress round her bare knees, and stretched her arms out by her sides. He tore off some large leaves from near-by stalks and made a pillow for her head. Then, stripping more stalks, he made a soft bed of leaves and laid Susanna on it. She had not uttered a word. Johann gently stroked her cheeks, her forehead, and her hair and then stood up. Pain tore at his whole body; he felt as if long needles were piercing his shoulders and the muscles of his arms and legs.

"I must have run a good way," he said to himself. He looked up at the sky already streaked with blue. Turning round, he caught sight of the oak wood a stone's throw from where he stood. At first he refused to believe his eyes, thinking it was a dream. Then slowly the truth dawned on him. He started trembling in every limb. It was no dream—Susanna and he were actually in Nicolae Porfirie's field. This was where their blind flight had accidentally brought them. The corn leaves he had torn off and laid on the ground for Susanna were leaves from the field for which he had bargained the previous day.

Tears mingling with sweat rolled down Johann's cheeks and fell to the ground, the ground that—Johann understood now —would never belong to him because he would never sail for America.

⚜ ⚜ ⚜

THE entire village of Fantana could be seen from Nicolae Porfirie's field. Johann's gaze strayed from house to house, then to the woman lying at his feet, and back to the white houses. Where could he take her? There was no answer. And yet he knew that he had to find shelter for her. He had given up his journey, he had given up the field, all because the woman he loved needed him. He could not abandon her. But that alone was not enough: he had to bring her to safety. Of all the houses in the village only two were open to him: his own home and Father Koruga's. Johann knew the other peasants would turn her away. They were afraid of Jurgu Jordan, every one of them. His own parents had only one room; he could not ask them to put up Susanna; nor could he go to Father Koruga's with a woman to whom he was not married. He did not want to cause him any trouble. If the priest were to take Susanna in, Jurgu would come gun in hand to demand an explanation. Johann did not want this to happen; and yet Susanna could not be left lying there in the open. After a moment's reflection, Johann lifted Susanna once more and made for the village. She was so pale that he thought she was sick with fright. Now and again he listened to her heartbeats—they were faint and slow—and he hurried on as fast as he could toward the village.

🕮 🕮 🕮

THE sun had already risen by the time Johann Moritz reached his home. He put Susanna down on the veranda against the wall. He looked toward the east. At that very moment Ghitza Ion was waiting for him at the far end of the village. He clenched his teeth to keep up his courage, turned his back on the rising sun, and went into the house. He wanted to ask his parents to receive Susanna. They were asleep. Aristitza, Johann's mother, was a cantankerous woman, and he would rather have spoken to his father first, but as soon as he appeared on the threshold Aristitza's head bobbed up from the pillows.

"Have you come for your bag?" she asked. "It's by the door." Johann did not answer.

"What are you doing, standing there like a sheep?" she asked. "Kiss your mother, say good-by to your father, quick. Don't go spending money over there, bring it home."

"I'm not sailing for America," said Johann.

"Not sailing?" The old woman leaped out of bed.

"No."

"Isn't Ghitza going either?" she asked.

"He's going," Johann answered.

Aristitza sensed that something queer was up. She slipped her dress over her head.

"Why aren't you sailing?" she asked. "Has someone stolen the money for the journey?"

"No!"

"Have you quarreled with Ghitza?"

"No, I haven't."

"Well, what's the matter, then?" Aristitza had reached the middle of the room and was bearing down furiously on her son.

"Nothing's the matter," he said. "I want to get married—that's why I'm not sailing."

His voice was unsteady. He did not know where to begin or

how to explain things to them. Aristitza dug her nails into his shoulders and shook him.

"I want to speak to Father," said Johann. "I am not going to discuss it with you."

"Oh, yes you are!" she flared up. "I brought you into the world, I did, not your father."

"Quiet, woman," said the old man, raising his head from under the bedclothes. He tried to conciliate her, but she would have none of it and went on shrilly:

"It's my womb that you tore out"—slapping her belly—"it's my milk that you sucked, you thankless dolt. And now you dare tell me you don't want to speak to me."

"All right, I'll speak to you, too," said Johann.

His mother was sobbing and he tried to calm her.

"I'll speak to you alone, if you like, but please don't get excited."

The old woman sat down on the edge of the bed and buried her face in her hands. Her maternal pride had been wounded, but not even sorrow could keep her quiet. Nothing on earth could induce Aristitza to hold her tongue.

"Whom do you want to marry?" she asked.

"I'll tell you in a minute," said Johann, "only please don't get worked up."

"I want to know whom you're going to marry. I'm your mother. I have a right to know."

"Tell her, Jon, it'll stop her talking," said the old man.

He could see that Aristitza was going to flare up again. Johann knew very well that the girl's name would in no way calm his mother; on the contrary, it would provoke her further.

"I am going to marry Jurgu Jordan's daughter, Susanna," he said.

Aristitza bounded toward him like a tigress, not to tear him to pieces but to throw her arms round his neck in delight.

"Now I see why you aren't going!" Aristitza kissed his eyes tenderly, his forehead, and his cheeks.

"You aren't fool enough to go to America and work like a cart horse, and then come back a few years later worn out and ill, with nothing but a few thousand lei in your pocket. You're doing what I always told you, you're marrying a rich girl." Aristitza's eyes glittered with satisfaction. "From now on I shall be rich, too," she said. "I shall have velvet dresses and a carriage of my own. I'll move into Jurgu Jordan's house—I have a family right to—because I, Aristitza, made my Jon so handsome and clever that he has won the richest girl in the village. He will be the husband of a girl with a house, a stone cellar, land, a carriage, and horses."

"Be quiet, woman," said the old man, but his voice was unsteady and betrayed his own feelings. The prospect of so much wealth overwhelmed him. Without getting up, he rolled a cigarette.

"I shall go and live at Jurgu Jordan's house," said Aristitza. "I shall leave you here," she said to the old man. "My place is at my son's side. Who is to give the young wife the advice she needs, if not I?"

"Mother, I haven't finished yet," said Johann.

"Say whatever you like, my dear," said Aristitza. "Mother's listening."

"Promise you'll hear me out quietly," said Johann.

"Anything you like." Aristitza patted his cheek.

"Mother," Johann went on, "I am marrying Susanna without Jurgu Jordan's consent."

"The main thing is that you're marrying her," said Aristitza. "I shall be the mother-in-law of Jurgu Jordan's daughter, a rich man's daughter, and I don't care whether he agrees or not."

"You'll be her mother-in-law, but you won't be rich."

"And who else will get her money? Jurgu has only one daughter—surely he won't marry her off without a dowry, when he has bags and bags of gold coins buried in his cellar. Just you leave the question of the dowry to me, dear, I'll see to it. You don't know how to deal with it."

"I'm marrying Susanna, not her money, Mother," said Johann.

"Are you trying to tell me that you'd rather have the girl than the money?"

"Yes, Mother."

"What rubbish! But all the same I understand you. Leave it to me. Nobody can make a fool of me." Aristitza could already see herself bargaining over the dowry with Jurgu, determined to hold her own over every coin.

Meanwhile Johann was telling them about the events of the previous night. Suddenly Aristitza gave a start and asked:

"What? She doesn't ever want to go back to her father?"

"She'll never go back to him," answered Johann. "Jurgu will kill her if she does."

"He will, too," said the old man. "There's no joking where he's concerned. The girl is right, her father's a brute. When he gets wild he pulls out his gun and shoots. That's what happened to some of his finest horses when he got mad with them, and yet, God knows, he treasures them as the apple of his eye. He'll kill the girl, too, if she goes back, especially after she has run away at night."

"I'm glad you understand, Father," said Johann.

"If it comes to that, it's not hard to understand. I know Jurgu well enough."

"Still, the girl could be sent home in a day or two," said Aristitza. "I'll go with her."

"Susanna's not to go back home!" said Johann. "I won't let her."

"Then what are you going to do if she has no money?" asked Aristitza. "Starve to death with her? A woman is easy enough to come by. Don't be such a fool as to take her without a penny to her name."

"I'm going to marry Susanna without a dowry," he said.

"Have you gone out of your mind, to give up America, to give up everything, for a penniless little runt?"

"Your mother's right," said the old man. "Don't be a fool. Go to America, and when you get back, you can buy your land, build your house, and get married. There are always plenty of women around, you know."

"I am not going," said Johann.

"It's not too late," said the old man. "Ghitza'll still be waiting at the far end of the village; the sun has only just risen. If you hurry, you'll catch up with him."

"Have you the heart to ask me to abandon the girl and go to America, Father?"

"Where is she?" asked Aristitza.

"Outside the door," said Johann.

Both his parents started, and their faces fell. Aristitza got up to have a look at Susanna. Johann barred her way out.

"I'm going to ask you something, Mother," he said. "Let Susanna stay here a day or two, till I find some place for her. She's your daughter now."

"You want to have her live with us?" Aristitza was livid. "Do you want Jurgu to come and kill your father and me?"

"Can't you see that we hardly have enough room for ourselves?" said the old man. "Where do you expect her to sleep? No, Jon, it can't be done."

"I suppose you would like us to feed her, too?" asked Aristitza. "And go hungry to keep her fed."

Johann lowered his eyes. He had reckoned with his mother's opposition, but he had not expected his father to side with her.

"Then Susanna will stay here only till this evening," said Johann. "There's nowhere I can take her now. Tonight we'll set out for the town, and I'll look for work there. She's not well and needs a rest before she can walk all that way. The shock she had last night has made her ill."

"There's nothing to eat today," said the old woman. "If you want her to starve, she can stay here."

"I'll bring her some food," said Johann. "What she needs is a rest; she can't even stand up."

[27]

"Your father is ill and must stay in bed," said Aristitza. "Where do you expect her to sleep—in bed with your father?"

"If there's no room in the house she can sleep outside in the hay, where I usually sleep," said Johann.

"Let her if she likes—but I won't give her anything to eat, because there isn't anything."

Johann made as if to go. On the threshold he stopped and turned to the old man, who was rolling a fresh cigarette.

"Father, I want you to be kind to her the few hours she stays here. She's wretched enough as it is."

"How dare you teach your mother and father how to behave, you shameless ninny!" Aristitza cried. "When did the egg start teaching the hen how to lay? Instead of going away to earn a decent living you dump this girl on our hands and expect us to feed her into the bargain, and on top of that you come and tell us how to behave."

Aristitza bent down and reached for a piece of wood to strike him. Had she struck him he would not have flinched. He was accustomed to hard words and bullying. His childhood had been one long round of hidings and abuse.

"You'll be kind to her, won't you?" He smiled at them. "I'm going to the village to get her some food. I won't be long." He left the room. Outside, Susanna was sitting motionless, exactly as he had left her. Johann stroked her hair.

"I'm going to the village, I'll be back in a minute," said Johann. "Try to sleep for a bit. When you wake up, you can have some food, and then we'll set out for the town."

"Aren't we staying here?" she asked, scared at the prospect of further walking.

"No," he said. "Come along." He lifted her up by the arms and led her round to the back of the house, where he helped her to lie down in the hay, pulling the flimsy dress down over her knees.

"Now go to sleep," he said. "If you don't, you'll never be able to walk to town. It's a good thirteen miles."

Susanna smiled gratefully; it was so kind of him to leave her alone to sleep. She was burning with fever and her ears were buzzing so loudly that she could hardly catch his words.

"If Mother comes and tries to pick a quarrel with you, pretend you don't know what she's talking about! Mother's upset."

Johann left her. When he had reached the road he looked round and smiled at her, but she had already closed her eyes.

🌷 🌷 🌷

AS SOON as her son had gone, Aristitza came out of the room and went round to the back of the house. Arms akimbo, she glared at the form of Susanna in the hay. Susanna opened her eyes and saw Aristitza with her hooked nose sharp as a vulture's beak and her withered, olive-colored cheeks. Then she closed her eyes again, appalled.

"I am Jon's mother," said Aristitza. Susanna moved her head slightly in acknowledgment and greeting. She pulled down her blue dress as far as it would go, for the old woman was staring at her hips and legs as if she had found her naked.

"So you want to get married, eh?" said the old woman, twisting her face into a leer.

"Yes," answered Susanna.

"I can well believe it. You're round-bellied as a mare."

Susanna buried her face in the hay. Aristitza came closer and screamed into her ear.

"You haven't yet found the fool who'll take you to wife, my pretty. No one'll have you penniless. If you've been sleeping with my son, that's your business. But he's not going to marry you."

Susanna propped herself up on her elbows. She wanted to escape, but Aristitza towered over her.

"Has Jani gone?" Susanna asked timidly, trying to change the subject.

"Who's Jani?" said Aristitza, surprised, "There's no one here called Jani."

Susanna gazed at her blankly. She did not know what to say.

"Who's this Jani you're talking about?" Aristitza insisted. "Have you gone crazy? Where do you think you are?"

"Jani, your son," she faltered in a scarcely audible whisper.

"My son is called Jon," she said sharply. "That is how I, his mother, baptized him, and no one has the right to change the name I have given him. Understand?"

Susanna saw Aristitza's fist raised threateningly.

"I understand," she said, and remembering that Moritz had asked her to be conciliatory, she added: "Jon or Jani, it's all the same. At least, so I thought."

This excuse stung the old woman to greater fury.

"Are you going to teach me the name of my own son? I'll bash your head in, you filthy whore."

"I didn't mean to annoy you."

The old woman's claws fastened onto her shoulders and she started shaking her violently. Susanna screamed. The old man appeared from behind the house in his nightshirt. Susanna's cries had brought him out of bed, and his cigarette was still dangling from his lips. Aristitza let go and turned on her husband, purple with rage.

"Have you ever heard such cheek? This slut here is trying to tell me I don't know the name of my own son. I can't stand it any longer." Aristitza picked up a large stone. "I'll crush her like a snake, I will!"

The old man caught hold of Aristitza's wrist.

"Be quiet, woman!" he said, pushing her toward the door. Then he went over to Susanna. Taking her hand, he looked pityingly at her.

"Don't cry any more," he said. "It won't help you."

"Where's Jani?" Susanna asked.

"He'll be back in a minute, don't worry."

Susanna felt protected. The old man's hand was large and rough to the touch.

"Now, child, I'm going to give you some advice, and it would be as well if you listened to it," said the old man. "Go home to your mother and father."

She was crying.

"You can't stay here," went on the old man. "If you do, Aristitza will strangle you or split your head open. She will, as surely as I stand here now. It would be a pity if it were all to end in bloodshed. Then, if Jon found out he'd kill his mother, and that would be a great sin. It must not happen, do you understand?"

"I understand." Susanna's lips hardly moved.

"If I were you, I should get up and go at once. Be gone before Jon comes back from the village. You can cut across the corn field straight home to your parents. When Jon gets back, I'll tell him you've started on your way without him; he'll never find you. You'll both get over it. You're young, and it's easy to forget at your age. Come on now, get up and go!"

Susanna had hung her head. Her ears were buzzing, and she had not even heard what the old man had been talking about.

"So you're not going, then?" he asked. He felt like picking her up in his arms and carrying her home, but he knew Jon would never forgive him that. He got up.

"If there's murder, it'll be all your fault, because you wouldn't listen to me. I've done my duty and warned you."

The old man went in, and Susanna was left alone. Johann came back from the village with a jug of milk and put it on to boil.

"You never used to think of bringing any milk for us," said Aristitza. "But you'll go and fetch it for that guttersnipe out there in the yard. I'd have done better to strangle you at birth than to give you my milk."

Johann was kneeling by the hearth, watching the play of the

leaping flames. He pretended not to hear what his mother was saying. Aristitza went up to him.

"Get out of my house this minute," she said. "And take that dirty whore of yours with you, or I'll kill her. If you don't shift her out of my sight straightaway, I'll strangle her with my own fingers, look."

"We'll go as soon as she's finished her milk," Johann answered, not even glancing at his mother's hands, which would "strangle" Susanna. "We're going to town, and you'll never set eyes on her again."

"So my lady cannot leave without having her milk?" said Aristitza. "Your mother can do without milk in the morning, but she can't."

Johann took the milk off the fire. It had not yet boiled, but it was warm. He left the room without looking at his parents. At the sound of approaching footsteps, Susanna gave a start.

"It's me," said Johann. "I've brought you some warm milk." He handed her the jug.

"I don't want any," she murmured.

"Try just a little."

Susanna took the jug out of Johann's hands. He went in to fetch his bundle—the very bundle he had got ready to take to America.

"Are you going with her?" asked Aristitza.

"Yes."

"Very well." Aristitza ground her teeth.

While Johann was taking his bundle from under the bed she slipped out into the yard. Seeing her coming, Susanna froze with fear, the jug still in her hand.

"Get up quick, before I break every bone in your body. I'll show you, you dirty little bitch."

Without waiting to finish the sentence, she grabbed hold of Susanna's hair with one hand and began to hit her with the other. Susanna let out a shriek. For a moment, as he rushed out, Johann thought he heard Yolanda.

"What are you doing, Mother!" he cried. Her ferocious glare struck him like lightning. Without even looking at Susanna, she dealt her one last blow and made off into the corn.

Susanna's face was covered with blood. Her eyes and lips were swollen. On both her wrists there were deep cuts from the jug, which now lay broken in her lap. Drops of blood had mingled with the milk to form large stains on the blue dress. Johann picked her up in his arms and walked away. He stopped in front of the door to collect his bundle, then left the yard with the bundle on his back and Susanna in his arms. The two burdens were so heavy that he could not lift up his head, and so Johann staggered on with his head sunk low between his shoulders.

𝕣 𝕣 𝕣

AT DAYBREAK Jurgu watered his horses and gave them their oats. Then one by one he patted their necks. He owned eight horses, but four of them he considered too beautiful to be harnessed and kept them only for riding. They were black Arab thoroughbreds with slender pasterns. They were his friends. Jurgu told them what had happened to Susanna. He came to them with everything that weighed on his mind. He did not trust men. The horses looked at him with their large clear eyes bright as mirrors.

"And now my wife is lying on the floor in a pool of blood, with all her bones broken," he said. The horses did not even blink.

Jurgu interpreted their silence as a sign of reproach, and said:

"All right, I'll take her to the hospital, if that's what you want."

Half an hour later his carriage left the village in the direction of the town. Yolanda, wrapped in a cloak, was lying on some cushions, gazing into space. They reached the hospital much too early, and there was not a single doctor about. They had to wait outside in the carriage till eight o'clock. As they waited, he talked to his horses without exchanging a single word or even a look with his wife. At eight o'clock he drove the carriage up to the steps, picked up Yolanda, cushions and all, and carried her like a parcel in his huge arms to the consulting room. They were called in first. While the nurse was taking off her cloak the doctor looked at the blood on Yolanda's swollen face. She lay in her nightdress, which stuck to her skin with clots of blood. Jurgu said nothing.

"Who has been beating her?" the doctor asked.

"That's none of your business," said Jurgu. "Your job is to attend to her. That's why you're a doctor and that's why I've brought her to the hospital." Beyond this Jurgu would say nothing. The doctor examined Yolanda and then had her taken straight to the operating room for urgent surgical treatment.

"I'm going home, and you can get on with the job," said Jurgu. He put on his hat and made for the door. "I'll pay what is necessary. I'll even pay in advance, if you have time to make out the bill before operating, or else I could leave you something on account." He felt in his pocket for his purse.

"You can't go yet," said the doctor. "You'll have to wait."

"What for?" asked Jurgu. He did not like people interfering. He wanted to leave the hospital at the earliest possible moment. Hospital smells were nauseating to him. Besides, he felt sorry he had showered blows on her. And now that I've finished kicking her around, the doctors'll start carving her up, he thought. But in spite of feeling sorry, he was determined not to show it. All he longed for was to get out into the open and fill his lungs with fresh air.

A quarter of an hour later an attorney appeared, accompanied by a gendarme. He had Jurgu called into the office and interrogated him. He asked his full name, age, address, and whether he was the person who had beaten the woman. Jurgu answered all the questions sullenly, with a glassy stare in his eyes. Then the attorney told him that he was under arrest for assault and battery. Jurgu's expression did not change: but when the gendarme laid his hand on Jurgu's shoulder to take him away, he suddenly turned white.

"Am I going to prison?" he asked.

"You are."

"But my horses, my horses harnessed to the carriage outside, what are you going to do with them?" The attorney glanced at the gendarme.

"Haven't you anyone to look after them for you?"

"No one."

"We'll give them to the fire brigade. They've horses to deal with already. There's nowhere to keep them in prison."

The attorney smiled gratefully at the gendarme for getting him out of a mess. He had had no idea what to do with those horses. The attorney, who was called George Damian, had arrived in the town only a few days before, and this was his first case.

At midday, as he was getting ready to go for lunch, he was informed that Jurgu Jordan had tried to commit suicide in prison by throwing himself head first onto the concrete floor of his cell. The prison governor's report ran: "The prisoner declared in the hospital that he had tried to put an end to his life because he could not bear the thought that the four thoroughbreds which he owned would be left to starve and die of thirst. It appears that the prisoner is a passionate lover of horses. His condition is serious."

Another message brought at the same time notified the attorney of Yolanda Jordan's death in hospital. He felt a taste of cinders in his mouth. At the restaurant before sitting down to lunch, he spent a long time washing his hands with soap and rinsing them in cold water. "The law," he said to himself, "will punish Jurgu Jordan with several years' imprisonment for inflicting mortal injury on his wife. But his greatest sin is neither beating his wife nor loving horses more than human beings.

These are only products of a certain mentality. Jurgu Jordan's sin is barbarity. Like every barbarian he undervalues man right out of existence. For this sin, however—though all the others derive from it—no law will ever punish him. There are only a few well-defined instances when barbarity is considered illegal."

 ☙ ☙ ☙

SUSANNA walked on a few miles and then sat down by the roadside. She was exhausted and feverish.

"I can't go any further, Jani," she said, and lay down on the grass. They were halfway between Fantana and the town. He let her sleep, waiting for a cart to go by and pick them up. But the travelers on the road were all either on foot or on horseback.

At about five in the afternoon it began to rain. Johann looked up at the sky and felt the cold rain on his cheeks. He was thinking: If it had rained last night, I should not have gone to meet Susanna. She would still have been at home now and I on board ship at Constanţa. Man proposes, God disposes—that's all there is to it!

It was already getting dark, and the rain was still pouring down. Johann shook himself into doing something.

"I'm going back to the village to find a cart," he said, looking compassionately at Susanna. She was huddled up under a cover of leaves. Her blue dress and her hair were drenched; she was shivering, and her teeth were chattering.

"Just as you like, Jani."

"You won't be scared, all alone?" he asked.

"So long as you come back, I won't be scared."

He kissed her good-by and left her. By the time he reached Fantana it was pitch-dark and the peasants had all gone to bed. He knocked at household after household, but found no one to help him. The peasants simply asked the woman's name, and as soon as they heard she was Jurgu Jordan's daughter they started making excuses. They hadn't any room. They were all afraid of Jurgu. At about midnight Johann went into Father Koruga's yard. The library was lit up, and a large black car gleaming like a mirror in the wet darkness was drawn up at the front door. From within came the sound of unfamiliar voices. Father Koruga must have guests, he thought, turning away; I had better not disturb him. The rain came pelting down on the roof. For a while Johann listened to it, then, remembering that Susanna was lying all alone by the roadside, waiting, he rapped gently on the windowpane.

ᴗ ᴗ ᴗ

"YOU'VE come just when I most wanted to see you," said the priest, helping his son Traian to take his luggage out of the car, which was drawn up against the veranda, and its hood buried in creeper and wild roses. The rain was coming down in sheets. "You're not alone?" asked the priest. Another young man stepped out of the car.

"This is George Damian," said Traian, "an old college friend of mine. I met him this afternoon in our town. He's the new attorney up at the District Court."

The priest apologized for not being dressed to receive guests. He led the young men into the sitting room and withdrew for a moment. The attorney took a look round at the cuckoo clock, the oriental carpets hung on the walls, and the closely packed bookshelves.

"I know what you're thinking," said Traian, laughing. "You're wondering how it happens that the country's most up-to-date novelist, whose books are full of motorcars, planes, bars, and electric lights, could possibly have been born and bred in a house where not a single thing has been altered or improved for the last two centuries. Am I right?"

The attorney blushed.

"That is precisely what I was thinking."

Father Koruga came into the room. He lit the oil lamp with his slender, withered fingers and set it solemnly in the center of the table. Traian undid his leather suitcase, took out a few neatly wrapped parcels, and put them on the table. Then he opened a bottle of wine and called his mother in. When she appeared, Traian filled the glasses and then took two leather-bound volumes out of a gilded dust jacket.

"This is my latest novel—the eighth. As usual, the first two copies to come from the press are for you and Mother. We'll drink to it with the same wine we drank when the other seven came out. Do you remember how happy I was when I brought home the first of all?"

The priest took his son's book in his hands as solemnly as he took the holy books from the altar. His wife held hers gingerly between the tips of her fingers and put it down on the edge of the table.

"My hands are all greasy with cooking," she said. "I don't want to stain Traian's book."

"The third copy is for you, George!"

Father Koruga kissed Traian on the forehead; the attorney shook his hand. His mother kissed him on the cheek and whispered into his ear, yet not so softly that the others could not hear:

"I still haven't read the others—forgive me, Traian. Your father's told me what they were about. But I'm going to read this one with my own eyes. I'd hate to die without having read a book written by my own son."

Traian was touched by his mother's wish. He clinked glasses all round. She then asked to be excused as there were things to be done in the kitchen.

"Stay here, Mother, just a bit longer," said Traian. "There's something else I've come to see you about, too, something just as important as the new book." Traian took an envelope out of his pocket and handed it to his father.

"Here are my royalties from the first edition of this novel. I'd like to use the money to buy a plot in Fantana, if possible not far from you. I want to build a house here and live in it to the end of my days."

The priest took the envelope and put it down on the table, smiling. His wife wiped her eyes with a corner of her apron and said:

"I know you only say that to please us. You can never stay in Fantana for more than three days on end. Each time you come, you promise to stay a month and then, after two or three days, back you get into your car and drive away again. And after that we don't see you for months."

"But now I'm going to have a house," said Traian.

"Even if you have your house, you won't live in it," said his mother. "You haven't the patience to stay put. The quiet here depresses you, I know."

Traian looked at his father and at the attorney and realized that, to both of them, his plan was nothing more than an extravagant gesture.

"No one believes me capable of doing it," he said. "Obviously none of you do. But I invite you all to come to my house in Fantana, two years from this day, if I am still alive. Then perhaps you will believe me. Let's leave it at that for the time being."

❧ ❧ ❧

AFTER dinner, the priest questioned Traian about his latest literary plans. Traian hesitated for a while before answering.

"My next novel is going to be a true story. It will be a novel only as far as technique is concerned; all the characters will exist in real life. My readers will be able to go and see them—ask them questions, nod to them in the street. I have even considered giving their addresses, possibly their telephone numbers as well."

"And who are these people whom you intend to shower with so much publicity?" asked the attorney, smiling.

"My heroes are 'all people that on earth do dwell,'" said Traian. "But since not even Homer could have written a story with two billion heroes, I shall select only a very few characters, ten probably. That will be quite enough. But their experiences will be those of all other men."

"I suppose your heroes will be selected on a scientific basis so as to be essentially representative of the human race, won't they?" asked the attorney.

"No," said Traian. "My heroes will be chosen at random. There is no need for any scientific basis. The things that happen to them might happen equally well to anyone else on earth, with slight modifications of detail. There will be crises from which no human being will escape. To describe them, I don't need specially selected heroes. Out of the two billion inhabitants of the world I will therefore choose the ten I know best: a whole family, my own father, my mother, myself, my father's laborer, one or two friends, and some of our neighbors."

Father Koruga smiled as he poured wine into the glasses.

"I shall record everything that happens to these people during the next few years," said Traian. "I've a feeling strange things will happen. I believe extraordinary things will befall every man on earth during the next few years. Such things as have never been known in history."

"If these future events are likely to be too dramatic, I hope they will occur only in your novel," said the attorney.

"These dramatic events will occur first in real life and only afterward in my book," Traian replied.

"I suppose that means that I shall actually have to live through these dramatic times?" asked the attorney. "You know I lead such a bourgeois life that it could not possibly interest your reading public. I'm anything but an adventurer."

"My dear George, the vast majority of people on earth are not adventurers. And yet they will all be forced to live through adventures so stirring that even the writers of sensational literature have never dared to imagine them."

"And what is this thing that is going to happen to us?" asked the attorney, smiling ironically.

"Joking aside, George," said Traian, "I feel that something of immense import is taking shape around us. I know neither when it started nor where it first broke out, nor how long it will last, but I am conscious of its presence. We are caught up in a vortex, and it will tear away the flesh from our limbs and crush every bone in our bodies. I feel this thing coming, as rats feel it when they abandon a sinking ship. But we cannot swim ashore; for us there is no shore."

"What is this 'thing' you allude to?"

"Call it revolution, if you like," said Traian. "A revolution of inconceivable proportions, to which all human beings will fall victim."

"And when will this revolution break out?" asked the attorney, still not taking Traian seriously.

"The revolution is upon us already, old man. The revolution has broken out in spite of your skepticism and irony. Bit by bit, my father and mother, you, I, and all the rest of mankind will gradually become conscious of the danger, and we shall all try to run away and hide. Some of us are already creeping into corners like wild animals cowering before the approaching storm. I want to retire to the country. Members of the Communist party maintain that the Fascists are to blame and that the danger can only be averted by liquidating them. The Nazis want to save their skins by killing the Jews. But these are only symptoms of the terror of every living man in the face of danger. There is only one danger, though, and it is the same the whole world over. It is only men's reactions to it that differ."

"And what is this great danger threatening us all?" asked the attorney.

"The mechanical slave," answered Traian Koruga. "You know him, too, George. The mechanical slave is the servant who waits on us daily in a thousand ways. He drives our car, switches on our light, pours water on our hands when we wash, gives us massage, tells us funny stories when we turn on the radio, lays out roads, breaks up mountains."

"I had my suspicions that it was merely a poetic metaphor all the time."

"It's by no means a mere metaphor, my dear George," said Traian. "The mechanical slave is a reality. His existence on earth cannot be denied."

"I'm not denying his existence," replied the attorney. "But why bring in the word 'slave'? It is simply a question of mechanical power."

"Human slaves—that is, the exact equivalent of the mechanical slaves of modern society—were looked on by the Greeks and Romans in just the same way—as a blind force, as inanimate objects. They were bought and sold, given away and killed, and their value was estimated solely in terms of muscle power and capacity for work. We judge our mechanical slaves of today by exactly the same standards."

"There are big differences, none the less," said the attorney. "We cannot replace the human slave by the mechanical one."

"But that is just the point; we can. The mechanical slave has proved both more efficient and less costly than the human slave and is rapidly superseding him. Our ships today are no longer propelled by the efforts of human galley slaves, but by the power of their inanimate successors. And when it gets dark, the rich man—who can afford to own slaves—no longer claps his hands that they may bring in lighted candles, as his ancestor would have done in Rome or Athens; instead he puts out his hand and turns on a switch, and the mechanical slaves light up the room. The mechanical slave lights the fire, heats the house, and warms the water for the bath, opens windows, and creates a draft with a fan. His supreme advantage over his human brother is that he is ·better trained, hears nothing, and sees nothing. The mechanical slave is never there, save when he is called. He delivers your love letters in a second and carries your voice over land and sea to the very ear of your beloved. The mechanical slave is a perfect servant. He tills the soil, wages war, manages political complexities, keeps order, and runs the administration. He has mastered every human activity and carries it out to perfection. He sits in an office and calculates, he paints, sings, dances, flies in the air, dives down beneath the sea. The mechanical slave has even become executioner. He carries out death sentences, he stands beside the doctor and cures diseases in the hospitals, he helps the priest to celebrate Mass."

Traian broke off for a moment and raised the glass to his lips. From outside came the even patter of rain.

"I'll soon come to the end of this digression," he said. "Personally, I must say, I always feel I am in company even when, to all appearances, I am alone. I can see these robots hovering around me, ever in attendance. They light my cigarette, they tell me what is happening in the world, they show me the road home in the dark. My life has taken on their rhythm. I am more constantly in their company than in that of my fellow men. Sometimes I love them like human beings and am prepared to make sacrifices for their sake. That is why, as Mother just said, I can never stay long in Fantana. My mechanical slaves are waiting for me in Bucharest. We are so much wealthier than our colleagues of two thousand years ago, who owned no more than a dozen or two slaves apiece. We have hundreds, thousands. Now I want to ask you: how many fully active mechanical slaves do you think there are at this moment upon the face of the earth? Several million million at least. And how many are there of us?"

"Two thousand million," answered the attorney.

"Precisely! The numerical superiority of the mechanical slaves is therefore overwhelming. And, when we realize that the mechanical slaves hold all the key points in the organization of contemporary society, the danger becomes self-evident. To use military terms, the mechanical slaves control the strategic positions of our society: the army, transport, and communications, food supplies and industry, to mention only the most important. The mechanical slaves form a proletariat—if by that we mean a group which, at any given moment in history, exists within a society without being integrated into that society. Man wields the controls. I am not going to write a fantastic novel and so I won't describe how, one fine day, these millions of millions of mechanical slaves rose up in revolt, herding the human race into concentration camps and prisons and liquidating it on the scaffold or in the electric chair. Revolutions of that sort are achieved only by human slaves. I will keep to facts. And the factual truth is that this mechanical proletariat will bring about its own revolution, without the barricades so essential to its human equivalent. The mechanical slaves form a crushing majority in contemporary society. That is a concrete fact. They exist within the framework of this society, but they function according to their own laws, which are different from human laws. Of the laws governing mechanical slaves, I will mention only three: automatism, uniformity, and anonymity.

"A society which contains millions of millions of mechanical slaves and a mere two thousand million humans—even if it happens to be the humans who govern it—will reveal the characteristics of its proletarian majority. In the Roman Empire the slaves spoke, worshiped, and loved according to the customs they had brought with them from Greece, Thrace, or other occupied countries. The mechanical slaves of our own civilization retain their characteristics and live according to the laws governing their nature. This nature, or, if you prefer it, this technological reality, exists within the framework of contemporary society. Its influence is becoming more and more dominant. In order to make use of their mechanical slaves men are obliged to get to know them and to imitate their habits and laws. Every employer has to learn something of the language and habits of his employees to be able to give orders. Conquerors, when they are numerically inferior to the conquered, will almost always adopt the language and customs of the occupied nation, for the sake of convenience or for other practical reasons—and that in spite of the fact that they are the masters.

"The same process is working itself out in our own society, even though we are unwilling to recognize it. We are learning the laws and the jargon of our slaves, so that we can give them orders. And so, gradually and imperceptibly, we are renouncing our human qualities and our own laws. We are dehumanizing ourselves by adopting the way of life of our slaves. The first symptom of this dehumanization is contempt for the human being. Modern man assesses by technical standards his own value and that of his fellow men; they are replaceable component parts. Contemporary society, which numbers one man to every two or three dozen mechanical slaves, must be organized in such a way as to function according to technological laws. Society is now created for technological, rather than for human, requirements. And that's where tragedy begins.

"Men are suddenly being forced to live and behave according to technological laws that are foreign to them. Those who do not respect the laws of the machine—now promoted to social laws—are punished. Man, living in a minority, gradually develops into a proletarian minority. He is excluded from the society to which he belongs but in which he can no longer be integrated. As a result, he grows an inferiority complex, a desire to imitate the machine and to rid himself of those specifically human characteristics which hold him at a distance from the center of social activity.

"This slow process of dehumanization is at work under many different guises, making man renounce his emotions and reducing social relationships to something categorical, automatic, and precise, like the relationship between different parts of a machine. The rhythm and the jargon of the mechanical slaves, or robots, if you like, find echoes in our social relationships and our administration, in painting, literature, and dancing. Men are becoming the apes of robots. But that is only the beginning of the tragedy, the point where my novel begins—my novel, that is to say, the life of my father, and mother, your life, George, and mine, and that of the other characters."

"And so we are developing into men-machines?" asked the attorney in the same ironic vein.

"That," said Traian, "is precisely what we cannot do. Therein lies the tragedy. The clash between the two realities—the technological and the human—has already come about. The mechanical slaves will win their revolution. They will conquer their freedom and become mechanical citizens of our society. And we, the human beings, will become the proletariat of a society organized to suit the necessities and characteristics of the majority of its citizens—the mechanical citizens."

"In practice, though," asked the attorney, "what form will all this take?"

"I should be as interested to see as you. But at the same time the thought of it terrifies me. I'd rather be dead than have to witness my own crucifixion and that of my fellow men."

"Have you anything specific in mind?" asked the attorney.

"Everything happening on earth now and in the years ahead is but a symptom and phase of this same revolution—the revolt of the mechanical slaves. In the end men will no longer be able to live in society and yet keep their human characteristics. They will be treated as equal and uniform, and the laws of mechanical slaves will be applicable to them. No allowances will be made for the fact that they are human beings. There will be automatic arrests, automatic condemnations, automatic amusements, automatic executions. The individual will come to be as absurd as a piston or a machine part that demanded to lead a life of its own. The revolution will spread over the whole earth. Neither among the islands nor in the forests will there be a place of refuge. There will be nowhere to go. No nation will fight on our side. All the armies of the world will be composed of mercenaries fighting for the consolidation of their robot society, from which the individual is excluded. Up to now armies have fought to conquer new lands and new riches, to satisfy their national pride or the personal interests of kings and emperors; the ultimate aim was loot or glory. All these ambitions were human. But now armies fight for the interests of a society which scarcely tolerates the proletariat, humanity, even on its most distant borders. It is perhaps the blackest period in world history. Never before has man been so utterly despised. In barbarian societies, for example, a man was rated lower than a horse. This can still happen today with certain peoples and individuals. You were telling me just now about a peasant who felt no regrets at having killed his wife, but who tried to commit suicide at the thought that his horses would not be fed and watered while he was in prison. That is the way primitive societies undervalued man. In their day human sacrifice was an accepted thing. In contemporary society human sacrifice is no longer considered worth mentioning—it is commonplace. Human life is valuable only as a source of energy; the criterion is exclusively scientific. That is the terrible law of our technological barbarism. It will reign supreme after the total victory of the mechanical slaves."

"And when will this revolution of yours break out?" asked the attorney.

"It has already begun," said Traian. "We shall witness its progress. Most of us will not survive it. That's why I am terribly afraid that I shall die before I get a chance to finish my book."

"You're taking rather a gloomy view of things," said the attorney.

"I'm a poet, George," said Traian. "I have a sixth sense that enables me to catch a glimpse of the future. Every poet is a prophet. I am only sorry my prophecies are so pessimistic. My mission as a poet compels me to shout them from the housetops, even when they are unpleasant."

"Surely you don't seriously believe what you've been telling us?"

"Unfortunately, I am convinced of it."

"I thought it was all poetic license."

"It isn't poetic license," said Traian. "Every night I expect something to happen to me."

"What could happen to you?" asked the attorney.

"Anything. The moment man has been reduced to the single dimension of his technico-social value, anything may happen. He can be arrested, sent to forced labor, exterminated, made to do any sort of work—for a Five-Year Plan, for the betterment of the race, or for what purpose you will, dictated by the Moloch Technocracy—and all without the slightest regard for his individual aspirations. The Society of Technological Civilization works exclusively according to technological principles, abstractions, and plans, and has only one moral precept: production."

"Could we really be arrested?" The attorney had dropped his ironical tone. He questioned Traian in the half-frightened way in which we question fortunetellers about the future, even when in theory we do not believe in them.

"Nowhere on this earth will there be found one free man," said Traian.

"So we shall all die off in prisons, without being guilty of any crime?"

"No," said Traian. "Man will be fettered by technocracy for a very long time to come—but he will not die in chains. Technological Civilization can create comforts, but it cannot create the Spirit. And without the Spirit there is no genius. A society without men of genius is doomed. This new Civilization, which is now superseding Western Civilization and which will eventually conquer the entire world, will perish in its turn. . . . 'The great Einstein asserts that a break of not more than two generations in the line of first-class brains specially gifted for physics would be enough for the whole fabric of that science to crumble.' *

"The downfall of technocracy will be followed by a rebirth

* Count Hermann Keyserling.

of human and spiritual values. This great light will probably come from the East, from Asia. But not from Russia. The Russians have bowed down and worshiped the electric light of the West and will suffer the same fate as the West. It is the Orient that, at length, will conquer this technocracy of ours and will keep electricity for lighting streets and houses instead of building altars to it and bowing down before it as Western society, in its barbarism, is doing today. The men from the East will not try to floodlight the hidden ways of life and the soul by means of neon tubes. They will subdue and control the machines of Technological Civilization by the power of their own spirit and genius, as a conductor controls his orchestra by means of an instinctive sense of musical harmony. But we shall not live to see those times—in our age man worships the electric sun like a barbarian."

"So we shall die in chains?" said the attorney.

"We ourselves almost certainly shall—as prisoners of the technological barbarians. My novel will be the epilogue of this phase of man's existence—this chapter of man's history."

"What will it be called?"

"*The Twenty-fifth Hour,*" said Traian. "The hour when mankind is beyond salvation—when it is too late even for the coming of the Messiah. It is not the last hour; it is one hour past the last hour. It is Western Civilization at this very moment. It is NOW."

🐾 🐾 🐾

THE priest sat on in silence, his face buried in his hands.

"Father Koruga, if Traian's prophecies come true," said the attorney, "and if man is to be annihilated or enslaved, cannot the Church do anything to save contemporary society? If the Church fails at such a critical moment, what mission can it still have to fulfill in the world?"

After a moment's reflection, the priest answered: " 'The *New Testament has always said that there would be an end and that the end would be pretty rough, to put it mildly. For the New Testament, this world, societies, and indeed life itself are but temporary experience. Moreover, the success of the Christian Church and the validity of its faith does not depend, and never has depended, on its ability to save societies or prevent physical death.*

" '*The Church did not save Roman society, but it saved Romans who were in a doomed society;*

" '*The Church did not save Feudal society, but it saved men and women who were in Feudal society.*

" '*There is no guarantee that the Church can or will save Modern Society, but if it preaches its gospel it can save men and women who are caught in this society.*' " *

"So you think Traian's prophecies may come true?"

"I usually believe what the poets say," answered the priest, "and in my opinion Traian is a great poet."

"Thank you, Father," said Traian, blushing. He felt flattered by the compliment.

There was a moment's silence.

"I think I heard someone on the balcony," said Traian.

The three men listened attentively, but could catch no sound save that of the pouring rain.

"If there had been anybody in the yard, I should have heard the dogs," said the priest. "Only my farm hand, Johann Moritz, can pass without their barking, and he must be in his bunk on board ship by now."

"I am sure I heard someone come up the steps," said Traian. "My hearing is very keen."

"One of your robots must have slipped out of the car," said the attorney, laughing. "Perhaps they have unleashed this revolution of theirs and are coming to take us prisoner this very

* W. Burnet Easton, Jr.

night. How many mechanical slaves are there employed to propel your car, Traian?"

"Work it out for yourself," said Traian. "Fifty-five h.p.—and one h.p. equals seven men."

"The active strength of several companies," said the attorney. "And we are only three. In case of attack we shall be forced to surrender unconditionally."

"Deprived of the complicity of man, the mechanical slaves are powerless to attack human beings," said Traian. "But, aided and abetted by a 'citizen'—and that is by no means the same thing as a 'human being'—the mechanical slaves can become the very beasts of the Apocalypse."

"What do you mean by a 'citizen'?" asked the attorney. "Aren't we all citizens?"

"The citizen is a man who exists only in one dimension: the social," said Traian. "Like a piston in a machine, he is capable of one movement only and repeats it ad infinitum. The only difference is that the citizen sets up this activity of his as a symbol and requires all mankind to imitate it. The citizen is the most dangerous wild beast that has appeared on the face of the earth since the cross between man and the mechanical slave. Theirs is the cruelty of man and beast and the cold indifference of the machine. The Russians have created the most perfect type of the species: the commissar."

Someone rapped twice on the windowpane.

"I told you I had heard footsteps," said Traian. "A poet's senses never let him down."

☙ ☙ ☙

THE priest went out on the veranda, leaving the door open behind him. A wave of cold air swept into the room. He came back with a young man. The newcomer was wearing only a shirt and trousers. He was bareheaded and completely drenched.

"This is Johann Moritz," said the priest. He offered him a glass of wine and asked him to sit down. Johann declined and stood by the door, not wishing to leave wet marks on the carpet and chair. Water was pouring from his hair as out of a spout. It was evident that he had been walking in the rain for some time.

"Would you like to have a word with me alone?" asked the priest.

"I could as well speak to you here," Johann replied.

"I was sorry you did not come to fetch your bundle this morning," said the priest.

"I'm not sailing for America any more, now," Johann explained. He looked at the two young men, then turning toward the priest, he added:

"Yesterday you said you would allow me to sleep in the room next to the kitchen."

The priest now understood why Johann had come knocking at the window in the middle of the night.

"The room is yours," said the priest. "Move into it whenever you like."

"May someone else sleep in it tonight?" asked Johann.

"By all means," said the priest, again puzzled. He felt that something extraordinary had happened to Johann. "If someone needs shelter it's a good thing you're doing, finding it for them."

"It's Susanna, Jurgu Jordan's daughter. She has run away from home because her father was going to kill her."

Johann remembered that when he had mentioned the girl's name to the peasants they had all refused to take her in. He looked straight into the priest's eyes.

"If it's cold in that room, light a fire," said the priest. "You know where the logs are kept."

Johann remained standing by the door. He did not want to go without first telling the priest, as though at confession, everything that had happened. When he had come to the end of his story and told them that he had left the girl in an open field halfway between Fantana and the town, Traian got up and put on his overcoat. He drove off, taking Johann with him. Half an hour later they were back.

The car drew up at the same spot by the veranda. Johann took Susanna in his arms. The attorney watched the scene from the veranda. The priest's wife walked on Johann's left, the priest on his right. The three of them came up slowly through the rain. In Johann's arms, the girl lay limp like a sleeping child, and the attorney noticed how her wet blue dress clung to her hips. Traian went into the sitting room, and the attorney followed.

"You're soaked," he said.

Traian blushed. He glanced down at his muddy shoes and dripping clothes. He had gone out and got wet quite uselessly, for Johann had lifted Susanna and put her into the car without his help; yet all the time Traian had stood beside him in the rain. Analyzing his gesture, Traian knew that, if he were to find himself in a similar situation again, he would act in the same way. "I felt the need to share in my neighbor's suffering, though my help was of no practical value whatsoever."

The priest came back. He, too, was drenched through and water was dripping off his forehead onto his cheeks and beard. Like Traian, he had followed Johann through the rain and just as pointlessly.

Just the sort of pointless things God did when He created the universe, thought Traian. He made so many things of no practical value, and yet they are the most beautiful of all. Logically speaking, for instance, the life of man is a useless creation. Just as useless and absurd as my gesture or my father's toward Johann. But it is the enthusiasm of life that is magnificent. Despite its uselessness, its beauty remains unsurpassable.

"You mustn't catch a chill, Traian," said the priest.

"Don't worry, I shan't," he answered. "How's the patient?"

"She's got a temperature," said the priest. "Your mother has made her some tea and is nursing her. God will reward you,

Traian, for bringing her in your car. The poor wretches badly needed our help."

The cuckoo clock struck midnight.

ᵂ ᵂ ᵂ

JOHANN knocked at the door. He could not wait till the following day to thank the priest and Traian. With all the misfortunes that had overwhelmed him in the last twenty-four hours, he felt only gratitude toward those who had helped him. He was glad that Susanna had found shelter and that things had not turned out worse.

Traian was looking intensely at him, with wide-open eyes. He cut him short in the middle of a sentence.

"Father, whenever I come to Fantana, I can always stay with you," he said. "Give Johann the money I left with you. Let him build a house; he needs it far more than I do."

The priest took the envelope and handed it to Johann simply, without fuss, in the manner of all great actions. He offered no suggestions, no advice, but just handed him the envelope. Johann opened it. He was not sure he had understood. When he saw the wad of bills, his eyes opened wider and wider like the eyes of a man witnessing a miracle. He tried to speak, but in his heart there was no room for words. He gripped the envelope with both hands and was silent.

"Thank Traian," said the priest after a while. "Then go to bed. Give the money to Susanna. Women are better at looking after it."

"Perhaps Moritz would like to have a glass of wine now that he is a landowner in Fantana," said the attorney.

The priest's wife came into the room. Johann lowered the glass from his lips and looked at her. She said Susanna was better. Then she took the priest aside and whispered something in

[54]

his ear. The old man frowned, then broke into a smile. Johann watched him closely.

"Don't worry, it's not bad news," said the priest. "My wife has just told me you're going to be a father. You'll have to get married first."

Johann shook hands with Traian and the attorney and went out. It was still raining. On the veranda he paused and tucked the money under his shirt to keep it dry. The envelope was warm and soft. Holding it close under his arm next to his skin, Johann saw his house and hedge, well and garden, rising up before his eyes, exactly as he had dreamed of them. He found Susanna asleep in her room. He put the money under her pillow and went off to sleep in the hay.

As Johann passed under the library window, whistling, the priest was saying to Traian:

"I shouldn't have spoken to him about marriage just now. Susanna's mother is lying in the hospital morgue and her father is in prison with her blood on his hands. It was not the right moment to talk of getting married."

"They don't know anything about it," said Traian. "They are busy scheming for the future. They have their love for each other and the money they have been dreaming of. They are happy."

"Yes, they are happy. And all the time, in actual fact, they should be mourning."

"True," said the attorney. "For us who know, their present happiness seems a profanation."

"All human happiness, on analysis, is an act of profanation," said Traian.

The cuckoo clock struck one. The three men in Father Koruga's library at Fantana listened to the clock and the rain.

ᴄ⇉ ᴄ⇉ ᴄ⇉

TWO years later Jurgu Jordan was set free. He was to go back to
the country whence he had come twenty-three years earlier.
Before leaving, he went to Fantana again to sell the house. The
local chief of the gendarmes, crossing the village street that day,
noticed that the windows had been thrown open at the house
with the red tiles where the shutters were always closed, so he
went in to see what was going on. Jurgu was round at the back,
crating his things.

"I can see you're a rich man, Mr. Jordan," said the Sergeant.
"It must have cost you a pretty penny to get out so soon."

The giant glared up at him.

"I don't understand," he said gruffly.

"I was asking what sort of sum you had to pay before they
let you out—you were sentenced to ten years."

Jurgu put down the hammer, took a paper out of the pocket
of his green jacket, flung it at the Sergeant, and went back to
his hammering. Then he said emphatically:

"That's to show you who you're talking to. In a few days I shall be wearing the uniform of a noncommissioned officer in the SS. I'm a German citizen and I'm off to do my duty to the Fatherland. And now you know why I've been released. It wasn't what you thought."

The Sergeant read Jurgu's mobilization order. He knew that German citizens could get their sentences rescinded on condition that they returned to their native country to enlist. He folded the paper and handed it back to the giant, smiling.

"Read that, too," said Jurgu, taking out another paper. It was a letter of thanks. The giant had donated his entire fortune to the German Army to pay for a Panzer. The Ambassador of the German Reich in Bucharest had sent a letter of thanks to him in prison. The Sergeant unfolded it, but, as it was written in German, could not read it. However, he examined the crest with its swastikas and eagles and the official stamp at the end.

"Are you selling the house or keeping it on?" asked the Sergeant.

"The Panzer bought with my money has already had its baptism of fire," said Jurgu, ignoring the question. "And I'll be following soon: I am no longer young, but the mighty German Reich needs me just the same."

Jurgu folded the papers and put them in his pocket. Then, picking up his hammer, he went on nailing up crates for the journey. He took no further notice of the Sergeant. When the latter began to say good-by he mumbled some phrase in his own language without even looking up.

🌾 🌾 🌾

UPON leaving Jurgu's yard the Sergeant made for the inn. It was the middle of May. He strutted down the village street, trying to keep the dust off his boots. He liked his boots to shine like a mirror. He also liked women—and brandy. The brandy he now got free of charge from the Jew at the inn. If they didn't make new laws from time to time, he thought to himself, sergeants would die of thirst. But the state took good care of that. In January he had received an order to assemble all the Jews in the village and dispatch them to labor camps. In Fantana there was only one Jew, Goldenberg, the innkeeper. The Sergeant showed him the order, which was secret, and immediately regretted it. Later on, he thought it over and realized that he had done the right thing. Every three months he sent off a medical certificate stating that the Jew Goldenberg was ill and unfit for work in a labor camp. In return he received three thousand lei a month from the innkeeper. This doubled his pay and enabled him to live comfortably. Besides, he felt he was doing a good deed. Old Goldenberg stayed at home and got on with his business instead of slaving in a camp.

When he had emptied a glass of brandy, the Sergeant drew aside the curtain and looked through the windowpane into the Jew's living room. He wanted to see Rosa, the innkeeper's daughter, and say good morning to her as usual. Rosa's skin was creamy white and soft. When the Sergeant pinched her arm he felt he was touching velvet. Rosa's skin was not like that of the peasant girls. As a rule she would be sitting at the window, reading novels. But today there was a young man at her side, talking to her.

"Who's that man?" he asked in a harsh tone. Old Goldenberg was not sure whether to tell the truth or not. Finally he made up his mind.

"It's Marcu, my son. He's been in Paris all this time."

"I'd like to meet him," said the Sergeant. He had never met a young man who had lived in Paris and he thought he might pick up a thing or two. But Marcu Goldenberg was a surly young man. You had to force the words out of his mouth. The Sergeant was disappointed. He hadn't expected young fellows who had studied in Paris to be like that, but there was a sulky sort of reserve about this fellow. He would not even drink the glass of brandy the Sergeant had offered him. A disagreeable young man. However, as the Sergeant was leaving the inn he said to Marcu:

"Come to the post tonight—we'll have a game of cards." Then he went off thinking the Jew had wasted his money in sending his son to Paris.

❦ ❦ ❦

ON HIS way past Johann Moritz's house, the Sergeant stopped. In the yard Susanna was treading clay to make bricks. In two years Johann had built a house. He and his wife had worked at it night and day. It was a beautiful tall house and had a veranda.

"What are you still making bricks for? You've finished the house, haven't you?" said the Sergeant. He tried to get into the yard, but the gate was locked.

"We're building a cowshed," she answered, and went on kneading the clay with her feet. The Sergeant could see the whiteness of the calves of her legs.

"Your husband's not at home?" he asked.

"Jani's down at the mill," she answered with a laugh.

At the bottom of the yard Johann's two children were basking in the sun. The younger one was in his cradle, the elder playing on the ground. From time to time Susanna would glance up at them before pouring fresh water over the clay under her feet and going on kneading. Her dress was too tight for her and emphasized the rounded contours of her hips. The Sergeant tried the gate again, forgetting that it was locked.

"Won't you let me in?" he asked.

"You're just as well off where you are."

"I never find you alone. And for once that your husband isn't here, you won't even unlock the gate."

"I should think not!" she said. "And now you've been standing at that gate long enough, anyway. It's time you were getting along."

"Come on, open it just for a bit, don't be so unfriendly."

"Jani'll be back any moment," she said. "If ever he finds you here, he'll be after you with that ax."

"Would you be sorry?"

"Can't you ask questions with more sense to them? You'd do better to stop it altogether and get on with your rounds. Jani'll be here any minute."

"I'll ask you one more thing and then go."

"Well?" She stopped kneading and stood waiting with her hands on her hips.

"If you weren't expecting your husband, would you unlock the gate for me?"

"There's too much you want to know," said Susanna, going back to her kneading. Up to now she had never thought what she would do if Johann were somewhere far away and the Sergeant came to see her.

"You're a married woman now," he said. "What are you afraid of?"

"Go away and leave me alone," she said angrily.

"I won't go till you answer me. If it weren't for your husband, would you still keep me outside the gate?"

"I don't know, Sergeant," she snapped.

"Answer yes or no, or else I won't go." He settled his elbows on the gate and leaned over, waiting.

"Why do you want to know?" she asked. "Jani never does go away."

"Supposing he did?"

"That remains to be seen," she said. "But Jani's not going. First we've got to build the cowshed, then the well. Why should he go away when we've got so much to do here?"

The Sergeant's eyes glistened. He drew away from the gate, saying:

"I knew you were a fine girl."

The Sergeant left her. Susanna could hear him whistling as he walked away. Frightened, she stopped working. She wrenched her feet free of the clay and ran toward her children. Taking the bigger one in her arms, she pressed him to her breast. She felt as if she had committed a sin, as if she had done some awful thing she should not have done, something that would bring down evil on Johann and the children. And yet have I really done anything wrong? she wondered. I'm all worked up over nothing. She put the child down. "Nothing wrong at all," she said to herself, and started working the clay once more, with her dress tucked up above her knees.

🐾 🐾 🐾

A WEEK later a gendarme from the post knocked on Johann Moritz's door. Johann was eating his dinner. He looked out of the window and, catching sight of the gendarme's cap, said:

"I'll go and see what he wants." He came back into the house, holding a document in his hand. When he had sat down and had begun eating again, Susanna asked him:

"What's that paper he's given you?"

Johann swallowed the piece he was chewing and answered:

"A requisition order. We'll wait till after dinner to see what the state wants this time." He appeared calm enough. He knew that all the peasants were getting similar requisition orders for horses, carts, and cattle. But he had neither horses nor a cart. He was glad now that he had not bought any. If he had, the state would have requisitioned them, and he would still have had to walk. Perhaps the state wants me to hand over a sack of corn or wheat, thought Johann. They had begun to requisition wheat, too, he knew. When he had finished eating, Johann wiped his hands so as not to soil the paper the gendarme had brought, unfolded it, and began to read. Susanna kept her eyes on his face, which turned first red, then white, and then scarlet again.

"What do they say?" asked Susanna. In silence, the children watched their father. Johann stretched himself out on the bed with his hands behind his head.

"Aren't you going to tell me what it's about?" asked Susanna, uneasy about Johann's silence.

"It's no good telling you, you wouldn't understand," he said. "I don't understand it myself."

"Bad news, Jani?"

"The quartermaster's clerk must have made a mistake," said Johann. "These regimental clerks are always thinking of something else while they're working!" He handed Susanna the order. "What do you make of it? It's a requisition order, I can tell that much. We've already had two. Once for wheat and once when they requisitioned the sacks we bought from Nicolae Porfirie. But this time it's not an order for wheat or for sacks, but it's for me. How could they requisition a man? Do you understand it?"

Susanna was slow at reading. Johann became impatient. He snatched the paper out of her hands and read it out to her. Then he said:

"How can they requisition me? After all, I am a man. You can requisition horses, houses, cows, and sacks, but not people. And yet look, there's my name. Those clerks must have gone mad."

"So what do they want you to do, then?" asked Susanna.

"I've got to report to the post tomorrow morning at seven o'clock."

"You must be right," said Susanna. "The clerks must have slipped up somewhere."

"That's it, of course," answered Johann. But a doubt had crept into his mind. He was thinking, suppose the clerks were not wrong. He made ready for the journey as if he were off for his military service. If, after all, the order was not a mistake, they might perhaps keep him a month or two.

※ ※ ※

ALL afternoon Johann tried to pick a quarrel with Susanna. She let him be, knowing that he was furious because of the order. Toward evening, Johann took the order, wrapped it in a sheet of newspaper so as not to get it dirty, and put it in his pocket.

"I'm going to show that order to Father Koruga," he said as he went out of the yard.

Father Koruga was not at home. His wife, who was in the yard, told him he had gone to town for the day and would not be back till late.

Johann thought of telling her about the order, but changed his mind, kissed her hand, and left.

In the street the dogs were barking. It was already beginning to get dark. Stumbling against a stone, Johann muttered an oath and strode home quickly.

※ ※ ※

THE night passed in an agony of restlessness. As soon as Johann had got into bed, forbidding thoughts came swarming into his head. Susanna crept close to him and slid her arms round his neck. She wanted to make him forget his troubles. But he was too preoccupied. He shook himself free of her embrace and turned his back on her. But that did not stop him from thinking. A thousand worries kept chasing through his mind. On a farm there were always so many jobs to be done that it was impossible to get through everything even by working all day and all night. But to have to go away like that, suddenly, without knowing for how long, and to have to leave everything just as it stood, was terrifying. He felt desperate. It was like suddenly dying and leaving everything in a muddle. There was so much that just had to be settled before a departure.

These and similar thoughts tormented Johann. A few days before, he had bought a load of timber. He had paid for it, cut it, and left it neatly stacked in the forest. All he had to do now was to carry it home. And now he must leave it there and go. It was good oak for building and had cost him a lot of money. He could hardly wait to see it in his yard. He had even decided where he would stack it—near the hedge, for the trunks were large. And now he must leave everything and go. All that timber, paid for and ready cut—just left in the forest.

Johann turned toward Susanna. He could not abandon all that timber. She did not even know he had bought it, let alone where it was. She would have trouble finding it in the forest. Susanna was asleep. Johann touched her shoulder.

I shall have to tell her that the timber is away up by the parish boundary, a couple of hundred yards from the stream. There are other piles round there, too. If I don't explain clearly, she won't find which is ours, thought Johann. Susanna felt his arm on her shoulder and smiled in her sleep. There was a full moon and everything in the room stood out clearly. Johann knew Susanna could never bring home all that timber alone. It was no woman's job. But at least she must know I've bought it and go and have a look at it. I must tell her that.

Johann pressed more heavily on Susanna's bare shoulder. Again she smiled. He saw her face clearly in the moonlight. She was smiling and moistening her lips with her tongue. Johann had not the heart to wake her. She slept soundly like a child. He decided instead to get up earlier in the morning so as to explain to her how and where to find the timber. He withdrew his arm and turned over onto his back. As a rule he fell asleep easily lying like this, but tonight he could not keep still. That order came back into his mind. While worrying about his tim-

ber he had forgotten about it. He was furious. Johann had done
his military service as a frontier guard. That was where he had
learned Serbian. He knew his army regulations, and they could
not have changed overnight. Men were never requisitioned like
carts, cattle, plows, or trucks. Johann rubbed his temples and
decided not to puzzle over it any more till he found out in the
morning what had happened. Perhaps it was a mistake and all
his worrying in vain—or perhaps it was one of the company
clerks playing a dirty trick on him by sending a requisition order
instead of his call-up papers.

Hardly had he grown a bit calmer and started hoping at last
to fall asleep when he suddenly remembered that Anton Balta
owed him five hundred lei. He had no idea how long he would
be away, and Susanna might need the money at home. He
turned toward her to tell her about it in case he forgot in the
morning. Susanna was sleeping on her left side, hugging her
pillow.

I wonder what she's dreaming about now, he mused, and
again could not bring himself to wake her. He would tell her
that, too, the next morning.

It occurred to him that, unless he finished building the wall
of the well, it would cave in as soon as the rains came. Perhaps
I'll be back before the rainy season, he thought, and stopped
thinking about the well. Instead he remembered the bricks for
the cowshed. That was a job he could not leave half done. So
far he had molded eight hundred bricks and had stacked them
one on top of the other to dry against the wall of the house.
Now they needed firing. If they were left to dry too long they
would crumble and all the work would be wasted. Restlessly he
tossed about in his bed. He glanced at Susanna, wanting to ask
her advice. She had uncovered herself in her sleep and lay with
her head buried in her pillow. Johann realized that she could
not help him; he would gain nothing by waking her. Once
again, it was a man's job. He went over all the men in the village with whom he was on friendly terms. Not one that he

could think of would fire his bricks for him; they all had their own houses and their own work. Had it been daytime he would have tried one or two, but now it was the middle of the night and they would all be asleep. He could not wake them up to tell them about his bricks. "I'll cover up the bricks with straw. They won't dry so quickly and maybe keep a few weeks longer," said Johann to himself. "By then I'll perhaps be back." Johann got up. The door was open, and he went out on the veranda. He had nothing on. He felt like going back and putting on his shirt and trousers, but he was afraid of disturbing his wife and children. He picked up a brick and looked at it by the light of the moon. Then he felt it carefully. It would have to be fired in two or three days at the very latest.

He turned toward the well. Then he surveyed the whole yard, completely unaware of his nakedness. He looked at the walls of the house, at the roof. Everything stood out as in broad daylight. The moon had not shone so brightly for a long time.

Johann forgot that he was leaving. He worked out how to build the cowshed. He was going to buy two oxen, a cart and horses, and then a cow. He had reached the bottom of the yard near the stack of rushes. He picked up an armful, carried it across the yard, and deposited it alongside the bricks. He knew that Susanna would be covering them up the next day, but as he happened to be near the stack he thought he would do the carrying: It'll be easier for Susanna if she has it handy. Then he brought over the straw, and he began to cover up the bricks. Soon he was warm, for he had worked rapidly. Hearing the cocks crow he gave a start. He looked toward the road, and everything suddenly came back to him. He became conscious of the fact that he was standing stark-naked in the middle of the yard and felt ashamed. He had finished covering the bricks. He went in and stopped in the middle of the room. Susanna's naked body sprawled across the bed. Johann lay down by her side without waking her. She was still unaware of his presence. Then she stretched out her leg over Johann's. He fell asleep al-

most at once. A few moments later he woke up again with a
start. He looked about him. Susanna was still asleep. The moon
was hung over the edge of the window sill like a gendarme's cap.
Johann Moritz stared at it and could not shut an eye till daylight.

❦ ❦ ❦

THAT same morning Johann made his way to the gendarmery.
As he walked he met various peasants on their way to the mill
or the fields or the forest. He avoided their eyes; he, too, should
have been starting out for the mill and the forest. But he had
orders to leave everything and go. He had been requisitioned.
He darted a hostile glance at the gates of the gendarmery. The
idea of running away flashed across his mind. If he hid in the
forest the Sergeant would never find him and he would not be
requisitioned. But yet he never stirred from the gates. He had a
wife, children, and a house, and there could be no running
away. Johann passed through into the yard. The Sergeant was
shaving in his office. Johann decided to wait until he had finished before asking him whether there had not been some mistake with the order. In the yard there was a smell of burned
milk. Someone laid a hand on Johann's shoulder. He turned. It
was a gendarme, not the one who had brought the order, but
another. On the gendarme's right was Marcu Goldenberg, the
son of the village Jew. Johann had not seen them come. They
had suddenly appeared at his side, and their looks were cold
and unfriendly. Johann had been sitting on the grass. The gendarme caught him by the collar and hauled him to his feet like
a sack of potatoes. Johann made no objection, thinking it was
only a gendarme's joke. Then he noticed that Marcu's hands
were tied behind his back.

"Shoulder to shoulder," commanded the gendarme.

If Marcu has his hands tied, then it can't be a joke, thought

Johann. He put his shoulder against Marcu's. He was frightened. Seeing men with bound hands always frightened him. Behind him the gendarme was loading his gun. Johann knew without having to look, because he had been a soldier himself. The gendarme fixed his bayonet. Johann understood what was happening and shut his eyes. As he was going out of the yard he glanced at the office window. The Sergeant had propped the mirror up against the windowpane and was still shaving. The peasants in the street stopped to watch them go by. The women came out on their doorsteps to see them.

In front of Nicolae Porfirie's house a group of women on their way back from the village well put down their buckets in the middle of the road and made the sign of the cross as the men passed by. Johann shut his eyes. Something had snapped inside him. He knew that the women always crossed themselves when they saw men with their hands tied walking in front of fixed bayonets. Johann could hear the gendarme's boots crunching along behind him. Apart from this measured tread he heard nothing. His very flesh seemed to be his no longer. Even his body and his thoughts were not his; everything seemed to belong to someone else—he had nothing left that was his own.

❦ ❦ ❦

THE chief of the gendarmes finished shaving and went out into the yard, whistling. It was a fine morning. A gendarme poured some water out for him, and he washed. The gendarme knew his chief was going to see a woman. He had watched him shave carefully, once and then all over again.

"A new one, eh, sir?" asked the gendarme with a laugh. The Sergeant glanced out of the corner of his eye and winked, but made no reply. When he had wiped his hands, he put on his new uniform and sat down at his desk. He reached for a file, took out a carbon copy of the report he had sent to barracks that morning together with the prisoners, and read it through.

"We have the honor of sending you under escort the individuals Marcu Goldenberg, doctor of law, aged thirty, and Moritz Jon, farmer, aged twenty-eight, who fall into the category defined by the law as instanced in your previous orders concerning the rounding up and dispatch to labor camps of all Jews and suspicious persons in this district. Signed, Nicolae Dobrescu, Sergeant in charge of Fantana gendarmery."

The Sergeant put the report back in the file with an air of satisfaction. He smoothed his mustache and glanced into his pocket mirror. Then he straightened himself up, slung the gun over his shoulder, and set off toward Johann Moritz's house. Now at last Susanna was alone. For two years he had been waiting to find her alone.

The Sergeant began to whistle.

🙟 🙟 🙟

AN HOUR later he was back. He had left word that he would be absent all day, and here he was, back at his desk already. He was furious. He did not know what to lay his hands on to calm himself. The correspondence file on the desk caught his eye, and he opened it. He reread the copy of the report dispatched that very morning at the same time as the prisoners and became all the more furious. He felt like tearing it to shreds; he had wasted his time writing it. Although Susanna had been alone she would not let him in. When he had tried to break open the gate she had picked up a hatchet and threatened to crack his head open. She was not joking. He knew women. If he had gone in, she would have done it. That was why he had given up and had come back to his office. But he was furious. All this maneuvering to have Moritz arrested and get his wife had come to nothing. He had worked at that requisition order for a whole night.

"I've been wasting paper and ink on a wild-goose chase," he said, and began to curse Johann for all he was worth.

☙ ☙ ☙

IN THE barrack square there was a column of prisoners ready for the march. Johann looked at their fine clothes and the leather suitcases they were carrying. He felt tired and his feet ached. The whole way Goldenberg had not spoken a word, but evidently he, too, was exhausted. They were hoping for a chance to sit. The gate had been left open behind them, and the column of prisoners began to march off. An officer hurrying by with a pile of papers in his hand glanced at Marcu Goldenberg's pale cheeks. Then he looked Johann up and down and addressed the guard:

"All Yids?" Without waiting for an answer he snatched the yellow envelope out of the soldier's hand and pointing toward the outgoing column he shouted at Johann:

"Fall in!"

Johann looked at the officer. He had not understood. The officer grabbed him by the shoulder and spun him round like a top. Then he gave him a kick that sent him flying into the ranks. Johann fell into step with the prisoners at the rear of the column and vanished with them through the gate.

Turning round, he saw Marcu Goldenberg walking behind him.

❧ ❧ ❧

THEY marched till evening. By the time they finally halted, they had already reached the outskirts of the town. Marcu Goldenberg came up to Johann.

[70]

"Untie my hands," he said, and turned his back to Johann. Marcu's hands were white and slender. Round his wrists where the rope had been, there was a blood-red mark. When Johann had freed his hands, Marcu said:

"Thanks."

He did not smile and did not look straight at Johann. Then he sat down on the grass and stared into the distance with his cold glassy eyes. Johann sat down beside him. To get talking with him, Johann held out the rope he had unknotted:

"Do you still need this bit of rope," he said. "Can I have it?"

"You can keep it," answered Marcu, sounding a little less harsh. Johann coiled the rope up neatly and stuffed it in his trousers pocket.

"It's always good to have a piece of rope on you," he said. "You never know when it'll come in handy." Marcu smiled. It was the first time Johann had seen him smile.

ꕤ ꕤ ꕤ

THE same night the column of Jewish prisoners reached its destination on the banks of the river Topolitza. The river bed was completely dry. It was bordered with willows and clumps of stunted shrubs.

Here the Jews were to dig a canal. A few houses were scattered over the horizon. There were no villages in the neighborhood. Only two deserted stables, once part of a stud farm, were still standing from the days when the land had belonged to a monastery. The stables stood on the edge of the forest. An army truck was drawn up near them with a load of picks, spades, shovels, and a field kitchen. The prisoners stared at the truck. There was nothing else for them to look at.

That night the prisoners slept in the stables. Johann lay down on the grass outside because it was softer and fell asleep straightway. He woke up several times during the night. The moon was as bright as day. Each time, he thought he was still at home till his eyes fell on the sleeping men wrapped in their coats and lying on the ground all round him. Then he remembered he was not in Fantana and shut his eyes.

Next morning, the Jews were lined up in two rows and counted. Once again Johann and Marcu found themselves side by side. When Johann said good morning, Marcu answered and it seemed to Moritz that he had smiled.

An adjutant came to the front of the squad and handed out picks and shovels. Ten men unloaded the field kitchen from the truck and set it up near by, under an oak tree. Then the adjutant, who had silver in his teeth and a black mustache, made a speech. He said the Jews were to dig the canal for the good and for the defense of their country. He also said that he—the adjutant—was the God of the Jews and that what he said was the law, even for old Moses up in heaven there. Then he told the Jews that his name was Apostol Constantin and that he had two sons, one a lawyer and the other an officer.

The Jews listened intently. Some smiled, but all were afraid.

"There won't be any food today," said the adjutant. "The kitchen hasn't been set up yet. From tomorrow on you'll get tea and bean soup twice a day. And on top of that half a loaf of bread."

Then the work began. Every day each man was allotted a plot to dig up. When he had done that, he was free for the rest of the day. If he did not finish the part allotted to him, he was accused of sabotage, handcuffed, and relegated for trial by court-martial as an enemy of the Fatherland. So, at least, the adjutant declared, and the prisoners took him at his word.

Johann Moritz had fallen out of the column and had told the adjutant that he was not a Jew. The adjutant had answered that he could not deal with personal claims until he had set up his office. Johann had fallen in again beside Goldenberg and had waited. He knew that in the army one had to get used to waiting.

Ten days later, when they had finished building a new wooden hut with tables, stools, and bunks for the guards, the office was finally opened. Johann presented himself at the new door and was told to come back in a week's time. The adjutant was still too busy to deal with prisoners' claims.

☙ ☙ ☙

WHILE he was at work excavating the canal, driving his pick into the stony ground, Johann asked the neighbor on his right what his name was. Johann liked talking to people round him. Men who keep themselves to themselves do nothing but brood hatred. His neighbor looked at him crossly.

"Are you ashamed to speak Yiddish?" he asked.

"I don't know Yiddish," Johann answered.

"Shame on you." The Jew spat and turned away. Johann addressed his neighbor on the other side. He wanted to explain to him.

"Speak Yiddish," answered his neighbor on the left.

"That's exactly what I want to explain," said Johann. "I don't know Yiddish."

The Jews eyed Johann with hostility. He stopped working and tried to explain to them. But no one was listening. Johann thought: They have agreed amongst themselves to speak nothing but Yiddish. That's their business. They are Jews and they have the right to speak their own language. But why should I speak Yiddish?

"Perhaps you speak Hebrew, if you've forgotten Yiddish," someone suggested.

Johann straightened himself up and thought out an answer. They had all stopped working and were looking at him. Then they burst into fits of laughter. Johann lost control of his temper and went purple.

"If it comes to knowing languages, I'm the one to laugh, not you," he said. "I've got four languages at my finger tips. How many do you know?"

He had swung round to the neighbor on his right, who answered quickly:

"I know Yiddish."

Johann drove his pick into the ground. He could feel they were making fun of him. They all knew Romanian, but refused to speak it.

When they had stopped work, old Isaac Langyel, the leader of the column, took Johann aside and said to him:

"These are hard times for our people, and the least we can do, when we are together among ourselves, is to speak Yiddish —it is our duty to do it."

"But I am not a Jew," said Johann.

"What's the use of pretending, now that you are here?" said Isaac Langyel. "Before you got caught there was some point in hiding it and it would have been the sensible thing to do. But here it's quite pointless. If you go on trying, here, among us, you are a renegade."

"But please understand me, Mr. Langyel, I am not a Jew." Johann's voice quivered.

"Have it your own way," said the old man, "if you'd rather be a renegade."

Johann Moritz was left alone. They had not believed that he was not a Jew. One and all, they maintained that he was lying, that he was not a Romanian, and that all his insistence was aimed at getting out of the camp.

In the camp register, drawn up by old Langyel, he was down as Moritz Jacob.

"There are no Jews called Johann," Langyel had declared. "The Jewish name is Jacob, and that is your name. It isn't Jon either, that is only the Romanian translation of Jacob."

In the camp, his colleagues called him Jankl. He raised no objections. But he did find it difficult to get used to.

"You can call me Jacob or Jankl," he said. "I'm only sorry you don't believe me."

ﬞﬞ ﬞﬞ ﬞﬞ

JOHANN MORITZ found out that all the Jews in the camp had been rounded up by requisition orders. He was now persuaded that the state requisitioned not only horses, carts, and sacks, but Jews as well. Nevertheless, he was not a Jew and that was what he wanted to tell the adjutant. But the adjutant never had time to see him. At last, one day, he managed to speak to him. The adjutant was furious.

"In the four months you've been here, you've done nothing but cause trouble," he said. "Every single time I open the door of my office I find you planted on the doorstep. Every day you have something or other to complain of. The food isn't good? You can't do the work? You can't live without your wife?"

Johann had prepared a speech that he rehearsed every day. He wanted to tell the adjutant the whole story.

"Cut it short," ordered the adjutant.

"I want to go home," said Johann. "I'm not a Jew."

"You're not a Jew?" The adjutant looked ironically at Johann. He picked up the register of prisoners that was on the table, opened it at the letter M, and read out:

" 'Moritz Jacob, twenty-eight, married, two children, resident of the village of Fantana. Name of wife, Susanna.' That's you, isn't it?"

"That's me," answered Johann.

"Then what's all this about not being a Jew?"

"It's me," said Johann. "But I'm not a Jew."

"I warn you that what you are saying is very serious," said the adjutant. "At the first sign of a lie you're under close arrest! According to you, everything written here—and these are military documents—is untrue. Think out what you want to say, remember what awaits you—now, do you still persist in maintaining that you are not a Jew?"

"I do," said Johann firmly.

"Then what are you doing here?"

"I don't know."

"Why haven't you said so before?" asked the adjutant. "I've put down in the documents I signed that the two hundred and fifty men working on the canal under my orders are all Jews. And now you turn up and say you're not a Jew. That means that I have been making false statements. So I get put on a charge." The adjutant had flushed with anger. "What you want is a couple of slaps across the face that'll set your ears ringing for a week. Nevertheless, I will record your statement. This claim of yours is extremely serious. I will therefore make out a statement, and you will sign it. If it's true you're not a Jew, then whoever sent you here is going to prison. But if you are, you'll leave the camp for the salt mines. Got that?"

Johann remained standing by the door. The adjutant made out a statement and handed it to Johann to sign. It said that Johann Moritz was not a Jew and applied for his release.

"You can go now," said the adjutant. "Tomorrow morning I'll send off the paper you've just signed. Then we'll wait for the answer."

Johann was smiling. As he left the office, he felt he was going straight home. Strul, the guard, ran after him and called him back. The adjutant had something more to say to him.

"Listen, Moritz," said the adjutant. "I have twenty-five years of service behind me. I am the father of a family. I don't want to throw away my career on account of your statement. Your case is not as simple as it looks. You have a Jewish name. You're called Moritz. Why are you called Moritz if you're not a Jew? That's the first thing. You speak Yiddish. That's another. Have you ever known a Romanian to speak Yiddish? Do I speak Yiddish?"

"I learned it in the camp," said Johann. "If you know Ger-

man and if you hear Yiddish all day, you pick it up quick
enough. It isn't difficult."

"Listen," said the adjutant. "First, you have a Jewish name.
Secondly, you speak Yiddish. Thirdly: in all these documents
you're down as a Jew. Do you still expect me to believe you're
a Romanian? Judge for yourself."

The adjutant was holding Johann's declaration in his hand.
He dropped it onto the table as though it were meant for the
wastepaper basket. Johann felt tears of annoyance come into
his eyes.

"I swear before God and all the saints, sir, that I am not a
Jew."

"We'll see about that later!" said the adjutant. "For the
time being, I have recorded your statement and I am going to
add my own observations. I believe in fair play. Always have
done, all my life. Now, over and above your statement I have
taken note of the fact that you have a Jewish name whose origin
you cannot account for, and also that you speak Yiddish but
that witnesses are prepared to swear you learned it in camp.
When you came you did not know it—is that correct?"

"Yes, it is."

"Next item," said the adjutant. "What is your religion?"

"Orthodox."

The adjutant looked at Johann with suspicion.

"Do you know how Jews are baptized?"

"Yes."

"But you maintain you're not like that?"

"I do."

"Sure?"

"Dead sure, sir."

"Go over to the window where it's light and show you
haven't been baptized like the Jews," ordered the adjutant.

Johann went to the window. He unbuttoned his trousers,
letting them slide to the ground, and stood there naked, looking
at the adjutant.

"No need to blush like a girl," said the adjutant. "There's nothing to be ashamed of. Turn to the light and let me have a look. I am obliged to ascertain the facts with my own eyes, so as to know what to set down in my report."

The adjutant rose from his desk, got down on his knees at Johann's feet, and examined him with great care. He compared what he saw with what he remembered having seen or heard about. In the end, he was none the wiser. However, his report had to be accurate. He rose to his feet, red in the face, and lit a cigarette.

"You're an infernal nuisance, Moritz," he said. "Do you think that my country has sent me here now in the middle of the war to look at your . . . ? My job's soldiering, my lad, and none of this sort of thing. If I do it, it's solely because I believe in fair play. For all I know, you might really not be a Jew, and then it would not be just to keep you here."

The adjutant opened the door of the next room and called Strul, the guard.

"Examine Moritz," ordered the adjutant. "Report if he has been circumcised in the Jewish way."

Strul knelt down beside Johann. He was a bank clerk and did everything scrupulously and with mathematical precision, as with figures. He examined Johann meticulously. Then he got up, stood to attention, and reported:

"If he has been circumcised, it must have been done superficially."

"What do you mean by superficially?" said the adjutant. "Answer me clearly. Is he circumcised, or isn't he?"

"I can't say for certain," said Strul. "There seems to be partial incision, but I can't say with any confidence whether it was made by the rabbi or whether it is due to other causes."

"You can see for yourself, Moritz," said the adjutant. "Your case is very complicated. But I shall send in the report all the same. Now get out. You stay here, Strul, and help me write this up."

Johann left the office thoughtfully, buttoning his fly as he went.

🌱 🌱 🌱

SOON after Johann Moritz's arrest Father Koruga called at the gendarmery. It was about nine o'clock in the morning. The Sergeant had just returned from the village and was in a bad temper.

"I received a requisitioning order and I carried it out," said the Sergeant. "I can give you no further information. That's all I know. If you want to make further inquiries, go to town to divisional headquarters."

"Is Moritz at headquarters now?" asked the priest.

"I don't know that, either," said the Sergeant. "And even if I knew, I wouldn't tell you. It's a military secret. The men are requisitioned for work on the fortifications, and it is forbidden to disclose their whereabouts."

The priest got up and thanked him for the information. In the afternoon he went to headquarters in town. Johann was not there. Nobody had heard of him.

"Is he a Jew?" asked a young officer.

"He is an Orthodox Christian from my parish," the priest replied.

"Then he wouldn't have been sent here," said the officer. "Go back and get hold of the Sergeant and tell him to let us have the number of the batch in which he was dispatched. Yesterday and today we've been handling Jewish convoys only. But since you say that the man you are asking for is not a Jew, then he can't have been among them."

"He is not a Jew," affirmed the priest.

The following day he returned to headquarters with the number of Johann's batch. The same officer looked into a register and said:

"I am afraid we are unable to furnish you with any information. The dossier is secret. You'll have to get a proper authorization from the War Ministry."

"All I want to know is whether Moritz has been arrested and if so where he is now," said the priest. "That cannot be a secret!"

"He has been arrested," answered the officer. "But we are not allowed to tell you where he is. We don't know ourselves. He has been handed over to the regular army, and the General Staff does not inform us where they send the men we put at their disposal, nor what is done with them."

His voice was hard. He had found Johann Moritz's name in the register, and now looked at the priest with contempt. Father Koruga went away. Behind him the officer said to the guard: "He's a priest, but he lies like Ananias. Yesterday he states that the man is an Orthodox Christian and today I find his name in the Jewish register. If he sets foot in here again, throw him out!"

🐾 🐾 🐾

FATHER KORUGA wrote to Traian, telling him what had happened to Johann Moritz. He asked him to take up the matter with the War Ministry and with GHQ on Johann's behalf. Traian wrote back that he had taken all possible steps to that end and had been promised Johann's release.

After the arrival of the letter, two weeks went by, then a third and a fourth. Two months passed. Summer drew to its close, and autumn came. Johann Moritz had still not returned. One day the priest set out to see the prefect of the county. On his way to town he met old Goldenberg and offered him a lift in his trap. The Jew had lost weight.

"I've had no news from Marcu since the day of his arrest," said the innkeeper. Then he groaned: "I've spent a fortune to keep him at school and at the university in Bucharest and Paris.

And as soon as he gets his doctorate and comes home they go and arrest him. They've sent him off to dig trenches. Is that what he went to Paris and got his degree for, to dig trenches when he came back?"

Father Koruga took a fresh loaf out of his case, broke it in two, and gave one half to Goldenberg. They both ate in silence. The road wound up a hill, and the horse took it at an easy pace. When they had reached the top, the Jew spoke.

"They have taken my house. It's been requisitioned. In a few days' time I have to move out, otherwise the gendarmes will throw me out. I built that house with the sweat of my brow. First they requisitioned Marcu. And now the house. What have I done to deserve it, Father?" The Jew was silent. The horse came to a halt. "I'm going to make an end of it and hang myself," said the Jew.

The horse went on again. Just outside the town Goldenberg got out, and the priest watched him disappear down the narrow streets of the ghetto.

卐 卐 卐

WHEN Goldenberg had gone, the priest went to the prefecture. He was letting the horse amble so as not to tire it. As he passed, he looked at the many-storied houses and thought of the words of the poet T. S. Eliot:

When the Stranger says: "What is the meaning of this city?
Do you huddle close together because you love each other?"
What will you answer? "We dwell together
To make money from each other"? or "This is a community"?

The horse stopped of its own accord outside the prefecture.

The priest came here at least once a week to find out what had happened to Johann Moritz, and so the horse knew where the priest was going when he headed for town, and stopped automatically in front of that particular building. The prefect was scarcely ever in his office, and even if he happened to be there he was always busy. The priest had never managed to speak to him. The secretaries and doorkeepers knew him by now and always greeted him with smiles of sympathy. Today the secretary wore a different smile.

"The prefect will see you," he said. "Your turn will come in half an hour."

An hour later the priest was seated in front of the prefect's desk.

"Six months ago," said the priest, "a young man from my parish was arrested. I should like to know where he is and why he was arrested. I understand he is in a Jewish camp. But he is Romanian and a Christian. I baptized him myself. I should like to appeal for his release."

"I refuse all appeals on principle," answered the prefect.

"The man I am speaking of is not guilty of anything," said the priest.

"But he's been put into a Jewish camp," said the prefect. "You yourself have just said so."

"He is not a Jew."

"That makes no difference," said the prefect. "So long as he is in a Jewish camp he comes under special laws and regulations that are not within my province. So much for the first question. And now for the second, which is the main one as far as I am concerned, and for which I granted you an interview. I want to point out to you that I don't like it when, instead of minding their parishes, the priests in my county keep on pestering the authorities with all sorts of petitions. We are in a state of war, and everyone must stand by at his post. Consider this as an official warning. I don't want to be forced into taking steps against you."

"To work for the good of mankind, for justice on earth, is to work for God and His Church," said the priest. "In interceding for Johann Moritz, I am interceding for the Church and for God. That is my mission as a priest. Moritz has suffered a great injustice."

"The injustice exists only in your imagination," rasped the prefect. "There's a war on. We are fighting for our country and for the Church against the Antichrist. Do you maintain that it is unjust if some individual or other is sent to serve our sacred cause by working on the fortifications?"

"This individual is a human being," answered the priest. "This human being was arrested and sent to forced labor, not only being innocent, but without even a trial."

"Don't be ridiculous. If we started bothering about every individual, the tide of Bolshevism would sweep over us in no time, and before we knew where we were, we'd all be swinging on the end of a rope. You, Father, would be number one. We have the certain knowledge that we are fighting for Christendom."

"Those who set no store by the individual cannot be fighting for Christendom," said the priest. "It is impossible to be the defender of the cross and at the same time its enemy."

"I suppose you would rather we released your Moritz and had the Bolsheviks descending on us, burning our churches, raping our women, and putting us in chains? Is that what you mean by fighting for the Church?"

"Nothing, not even the highest national, social, or religious ideal may serve as an excuse for injustice toward a single individual. 'Accusatio ordinatur ad bonum commune quod intenditur per cognitionem criminis: nullus autem debet nocere alicui injuste, ut bonum commune promoveat.' * The enslavement of human beings in the name of Christ is a crime against Christ."

"Are you absolutely sure the man is not a Jew?" asked the prefect.

* Saint Thomas Aquinas.

"Absolutely certain."

"In that case a most serious crime has been committed against him," said the prefect. "The culprit will have to be punished. Who gave the requisition order?"

"I don't know," answered the priest. "For the last six months I have been making inquiries among all the authorities, the civilian police, the military police, the army, and no one will give me an answer. In each case I am told it is a secret."

"Of course you would be," said the prefect. "All such operations are secret. I can't tell you anything, either. You'll have to go to army headquarters. When you've received proper authorization, come back and we'll look up the files to see who signed the requisition order. If there has been an error, I can assure you that the person who committed it will be made an example of. But until you produce a signed document authorizing you to go into this matter, there is nothing we can do for you."

The prefect got up to put an end to the interview. The priest did not move.

"Is it possible that man should have been brought to such a degree of insensibility that, like a machine, he remains deaf to the voice of his fellow beings? I cannot bring myself to believe that you do not understand my appeal. After all, you are a human being. Man is created with feelings. With a soul. Man is not a machine or a mechanical slave. In all honesty, are you left totally unmoved by the injustice done to Johann Moritz?"

"Father Koruga," said the prefect, "to be quite candid, I am very sorry I am not in a position to help you. I think you are right. I tell you that because I am the son of a priest. But simply as a matter of principle, I just don't go near the dossiers either of Jews, or Freemasons, or Iron Guards. They are dangerous explosives and are liable to go off at the merest touch. I'm a servant of the state and have no wish to ruin my career. I just keep away."

The priest stood up. As he was leaving, the prefect shook hands with him and said: "I am very sorry there's nothing I can do for that fellow of yours—what was his name again? Moritz, wasn't it? If anything else crops up, I'd be pleased to help you."

☙ ☙ ☙

ON THE road leading out of the town there was a church. As the priest was passing in front of it he pulled up. His thoughts turned to the Sergeant in Fantana, to the prefect and the young officer at divisional HQ and to all the police and officials who had kept him waiting in their anterooms and were holding Johann Moritz prisoner. He took off his hat and began to pray in the words of W. H. Auden: "*Let us pray especially at this time for all who occupy positions of petty and unpopular authority, through whose persons we suffer the impersonal discipline of the state, for all who must inspect and cross-question, for all who issue permits and enforce restrictions, that they may not come to regard the written word or the statistical figure as more real than flesh and blood . . . and deliver us, as private citizens, from confusing the office with the man . . . and from forgetting that it is our impatience and indolence, our own abuse and terror of freedom, our own injustice that created the state, to be a punishment and a remedy for sin.*"

The priest covered his thin white hair with his hat and resumed his journey to Fantana. At the crossroads he met old Goldenberg, who was also returning from the town. Recognizing him, the horse drew up level with the Jew, for it knew well that the priest always gave him a lift.

❦ ❦ ❦

THE Sergeant in Fantana received orders to draw up an inventory of all property belonging to Jews. He made a list of everything old Goldenberg possessed. But he did not send it off. He knew that Johann Moritz was also in a Jewish camp. When he had sent him to divisional headquarters he had not put him down as a Jew. He could not have done so without being guilty of misrepresentation, because Moritz was a Romanian. But the regulations for the requisitioning of man power applied to two categories: Jews and undesirable elements. He had Moritz requisitioned as an undesirable, which was legally justifiable. Anybody could be considered an undesirable by a sergeant of gendarmes; there were no specific regulations about it. At the divisional HQ he had been entered as a Jew. That was their fault, or rather Moritz's for having a Jewish name. The Sergeant was beginning to regret the whole thing by now: he had reckoned that Moritz would be kept for a few weeks. But six months had passed, and now an order had come for the requisitioning of Jewish houses. In all fairness, Moritz's house should not have been requisitioned. But in the official registers two Jews were entered for Fantana: Goldenberg and Moritz.

The Sergeant racked his brains for a solution. If he announced at HQ that Moritz was not a Jew and that for this reason his house could not be included on the list of property to be requisitioned, there would inevitably be an inquiry into the reasons for Moritz's removal to a camp. He would then have to declare that Moritz was an "undesirable." But the Sergeant did not want an inquiry. The fewer investigations the better: Susanna might give evidence against him. Some other way out had to be found. The Sergeant asked Goldenberg for advice.

"If Susanna divorces Moritz, she has the right to retain the house. There is no mention anywhere of her being Jewish. At any rate, that is how Jews with Christian wives managed it in town," said Goldenberg.

The Sergeant reflected that Susanna would never agree to a divorce. She knew her husband was not a Jew and might bring the whole scandal into the open, especially if it came into her head to consult a lawyer.

"A divorce is easily obtainable," said Goldenberg. "All you

need is a statement in writing from the woman setting out her wish to be separated from her husband for 'motives of a racial character.' The divorce is granted automatically upon presentation of the petition. No interview is required. Everything is done through administrative channels. Those are the new laws."

ﬁ ﬁ ﬁ

THE Sergeant made out an application for a divorce in Susanna's name and went round to persuade her to sign it.

"Your husband is in a Jewish camp," said the Sergeant. "I have just received instructions to confiscate your house. The documents say your husband is a Jew. I know perfectly well he isn't. It's his name that's the trouble; why the devil did he have to go and call himself Moritz?"

Susanna listened, leaning with her chin on the gate. She was staring fixedly at the Sergeant. Suddenly tears started rolling down from her wide-open eyes.

"You've taken my man from me," she said. "And now you want to take away my house. I'll kill you with my own hands first, for all that you're a Sergeant. You'll not get my house!" Susanna lifted up a large stone and hurled it over the gate. The Sergeant ducked.

"I don't want to take your house," he said. "I've brought you this paper to sign so that you can keep it."

He handed Susanna the application for the divorce and his fountain pen. She took them but could not read. Her eyes were brimming over with tears.

"What does it say?" she asked.

"It's an application for a divorce!" said the Sergeant. "But it's a mere formality to allow you to keep your house."

"You want to make me get a divorce?" she cried. She leaped up like a tigress ready to tear him to pieces. He caught her wrist over the gate and tried to calm her.

"It's only a formality," he said. "It's not like a real divorce. If you don't sign, I'll have to turn you out of the house in a few days' time. And then where will you go, with winter just round the corner and the children on your hands?"

Susanna would not hear of it.

"Jani is my husband, and I'd rather kill myself than ever be separated from him."

The Sergeant stood talking at her for over an hour. Susanna was tired out with weeping. She went indoors, then came out again. She threw more stones at the Sergeant and threatened him with the hatchet. Then she decided that after all it was better to sign a piece of paper than to be turned out of the house. When Johann came back, he would understand and forgive her for signing. He would see how faithful she had remained, and how hard she had worked, looking after the house and the children. That she had remained his and his alone. And so she signed.

The Sergeant put away Susanna's application in the breast pocket of his tunic and departed. Now he might sleep soundly at night; for now there would be no inquiries. Had the captain come, he might have put him under arrest for a couple of days. But the danger had blown over. He smiled and began whistling.

 ☙ ☙ ☙

THE prisoners in Johann's camp could all have escaped without difficulty. There were only five soldiers to guard them. But they knew that sooner or later they would be caught and brought back, and so no one even tried. Marcu Goldenberg alone had made an attempt. But whilst at large he had run straight into the adjutant and now he was back in camp again.

The adjutant assembled the prisoners before work began and put it to them:

"Am I to stick Marcu in irons and send him up for a court-

martial or am I to leave him in your charge? Will you under-
take to keep an eye on him and stop him from making a fool of
himself a second time?"

The prisoners assumed responsibility for Marcu. Until then,
he had not done a single day's work on the canal. He had
always been ill and had therefore been used as a clerk in the
office. But now old Langyel handed him a pick and showed him
the area allotted to him. Marcu Goldenberg refused point-
blank. They might cut off his hands rather than that he should
dig up a single inch of the canal.

"This work goes against my political convictions," he said.
The prisoners gathered round him. No one worked on the canal
out of political conviction and therefore they were interested
to hear what else Goldenberg was going to say.

"The object of excavating this canal is to hold up the advance of the Red Army," said Marcu. "I'm a Communist. I
flatly refuse to assist in obstructing the path of my comrades."

The prisoners appreciated Marcu's courage. They saw his
point. But when they found out that if Goldenberg did not do
his share of digging, the other prisoners would have to do it for
him, their enthusiasm rapidly died down. Old Langyel gave the
signal to start work and promised to deal with the matter himself.

As soon as work was well under way, Langyel came over to
Marcu, who was sitting at the edge of the ditch with his hands
in his pockets.

"We Jews possess one quality to a degree unequaled by any
other people in the West," said Langyel. "We know how to
come to terms. Our race is wise enough to understand the value
of compromise and to steer clear of categorical absolutes. We
inherited this virtue from the East. You understand me? 'He is
a wise man who can deal with the goat and the cabbage,' says
the Romanian proverb. You have set aside this wisdom and
adopted principles that admit no compromise, forgetting that
this attitude is characteristic of barbarians and nations of sol-

diers. Civilized and cultured peoples can afford the luxury of holding several views simultaneously, so that they can act according to the one most nearly suited to any given situation. If you wish to ignore this wisdom, that is your personal affair. We have understood that you do not wish to dig the canal."

"On no account," said Marcu.

"Your share has nevertheless to be done by someone as long as you are in the camp. So far you have been on sick leave. But from now on . . ."

"I know. But I am not going to dig," said Marcu emphatically.

"If you don't, we have to do it for you. We are doing it for you today," said Langyel. "But we can't just let you sit there with your hands in your pockets while we do your work."

"I never asked you to," sneered Marcu. "If you enjoy digging for me, by all means get on with it."

"You know perfectly well we don't enjoy it. All the same we can't simply go to the adjutant and ask to have you handcuffed and sent up for court-martial."

"Go and tell him I'm a *saboteur*," said Marcu. "Why not?"

"You are a qualified lawyer," said Langyel. "Surely you understand the position. We cannot demand your arrest and have you escorted out of the camp between fixed bayonets. We cannot do it. All over Europe today Jews are being tracked down like wild beasts, hunted and caught and made captive. But it is the Fascists who do it, Goldenberg, and they are our enemies. We Jews cannot join in the hunt. We cannot demand that a Jew be handcuffed and sent before a court-martial. But neither can we do your work for you. We are hard enough put to it to do our own."

"What's the good of preaching this sentimental sermon at me?" asked Marcu sarcastically. "Are you trying to persuade me to work on the canal?"

"I am not that simple-minded," said Langyel. "You are a fanatic. Fanatics behave like raving beasts, and it is dangerous to go too near them. Nevertheless, you have a father and mother, though I know you never think of them. But we all do. They are at home, waiting for you. You are a Jew, and we cannot forget that. You are our brother, our own flesh and blood, even if you have forgotten it. That is why we are trying to find a compromise between your fanaticism, the interests of the community, and our own sentimentalism, ridiculous as it may seem to you."

The other prisoners had formed a circle round them and were listening.

"You refuse to work on the canal because it represents an obstacle in the way of your comrades in the Red Army," said Langyel. "Rather than do this work, you are prepared to lay down your life. We will not force you to it, but instead you will have to do some other job, something that has no political or military significance. What about cleaning out the camp latrines, for example? We do it by rotation. If you are prepared to take it on regularly, whoever is on duty that day can dig up your section of the canal. But I must warn you that it is a hard and filthy job."

Old Langyel was convinced that, faced with this alternative, Marcu would decide in favor of the canal. He knew that no one could stand up to that sort of fatigue for more than two or three days on end, least of all an intellectual.

"You needn't give me an answer now," said Langyel. "Think it over till tonight."

"I don't have to think it over," said Marcu. "I've already decided."

"Well, what is it to be?"

"The latrines, of course," replied Marcu. "It is constructive activity of benefit to all. The excavation of the canal is criminal, reactionary, and Fascist. I would rather clean out the latrines every day than stir a finger to set up obstacles against my comrades."

Old Langyel turned pale. His plan had failed.

"Think it over again before making up your mind," said the old man.

"My mind is made up," said Marcu, and turned his back on him.

After that the prisoners had not the courage to address Marcu again. Johann Moritz was the only one who dared approach him.

"Have you gone crazy, Marcu?" he said. "Do you mean to do the shithouses every day? It's worse than the mines."

"Go to hell!" Goldenberg flared up at him. "I know what I'm doing."

"Nobody would think so," said Johann. At that moment he realized that the look in Marcu Goldenberg's eyes was exactly the same as that he had seen in Jurgu Jordan's. And so Johann Moritz walked away.

彡 彡 彡

THE following day old Langyel's conscience worried him over the way he had dealt with Goldenberg. He was a softhearted old man. That very evening he approached Goldenberg, determined to make him change his mind. At all costs he wanted to get him out of cleaning the latrines. He felt that he personally had condemned Marcu to this work.

Marcu was still at it. The whole day long he had carted bucket after bucket from the pit that served as the prisoners' lavatory to the edge of the camp, where he emptied them in a field. It had been raining all day, and the constant flooding of the holes made the work even worse than usual. Marcu was worn out. He was not strong and suffered from lung trouble.

"I think you'll give up," said Langyel. "This is no job for you." Marcu went down into the hole and refilled the buckets. Then he stood up and shoveled away the mess.

"A whole day in all this stench and filth," said Langyel. "I couldn't stick it if I had your job."

Marcu again gave no answer. He could hardly stand on his feet, but he went on. He lifted the buckets and passed in front of the old man to go and empty them. When he came back, Langyel went on:

"From now on your clothes and your skin will reek of this place. You won't be able to sleep because of the stench."

The old man was on the point of telling Marcu that as from tomorrow he could go back to his job in the office. But Marcu could stand no more. He had reached the limits of his endurance. The shovel was in his hands. He lifted it high in the air, shut his eyes, and brought it down. The sharp edge of the shovel caught Langyel a full blow on the head. The old man staggered, but Marcu no longer saw him. His hands gripped the shovel handle, and he struck again—and yet again. The blows were now falling in space. The old man had collapsed on the ground. Marcu was left standing, shovel in hand. He opened his eyes and saw old Langyel lying crumpled up at his feet, with his skull split open. He had not meant to kill the old man. He had acted in sheer despair. But he did not regret it.

❦ ❦ ❦

SINCE that day, four months had gone by. Johann Moritz could still see the old man's head split in two by the shovel and Marcu being escorted out of the camp between fixed bayonets, but it seemed to him that all these things had taken place many years before. The dead are soon forgotten. Marcu was not dead, but convicts are forgotten as quickly as the dead.

On this particular day it was snowing. The adjutant informed them that a general would be coming to inspect them.

"We are also expecting a visit from the King," said the adjutant. "The King wants to see the canal you have been digging.

The King drew up the plans for it with his own hand. That is why he wants to see it."

Johann thought of Marcu working somewhere at the bottom of a salt mine. Then he thought of the King, who had designed the canal with his own hand. He could see the King, sitting at his desk and sketching plans with a pencil, as in the pictures. The canal was very long—over seventy miles, according to some. Hundreds of thousands of prisoners were working on it. But each prisoner could see only his own sector and a bit beyond to the right and left. It was ten feet deep and had steep banks. It was to be flooded with water. Johann tried to imagine what it would be like with water flowing over the spot where he was standing at that moment. He had heard it said that after the war it would even be used for ships. Meanwhile it was being excavated to stop the Russians from invading Romania. That was why the work was secret. Only the King and a few generals knew about it. The adjutant had said so. In his dreams, Johann had often seen the King holding whispered consultations with his generals about the canal that he, Johann Moritz, was helping to build. Now he knew the reason why the prisoners were not allowed to write home to their wives and parents. It was so that the canal would remain a secret and the Russians would not find out about it. The adjutant said the Russians had spies everywhere, trying to take photographs of the canal Johann was digging, but the police caught them every time. Prisoners could not be released because they might give away the secret when they got home.

Johann felt he would like to come back here one day when the war was over and show Susanna and his boys the canal he had been working on. It would be filled with water then. But he now made a mental note of the exact spot where he had done his share so that he should recognize it even then. His children would marvel at it. They would never believe that the canal had once been a meadow with grazing cattle in it. They would tell other children at school what their father had done

and they would be proud of him. The other children's fathers
would not have accomplished such extraordinary feats.

At first, thoughts of home had preyed on his mind. He worried about the bricks gone to waste in the yard, the timber that
Susanna could not have brought home from the forest, the
corn rotting unharvested in the field. But that was only at the
beginning. As time went on he fretted less and less. Susanna, he
supposed, must have managed everything. What she had been
unable to do, being a woman, he would do when he got back.
Since the day the adjutant had examined him, had made him
take off his trousers and had seen for himself that he was not a
Jew, he had been expecting his release at any moment. He believed the papers had already come through but that they could
not let him go till they had completed the canal. Now that the
general and then the King were coming to see whether they
liked the canal, he would certainly be allowed to go home.
Johann bore no grudge against the state for sending him here.
Right at first he had been furious with the gendarme who had
escorted him from Fantana to the town. Later on with the sergeant. He believed that the sergeant was responsible for that
requisition order. He still thought so now. But the worst of his
fury had subsided. Every day petty annoyances kept him busy.
If, when he came back, he were to meet Sergeant Dobrescu in
the village street, he would touch his cap to him, as of old. Had
he been released six or seven months earlier, he would have cut
him dead. He might even have sworn at him for making a fool
of him with that requisition order. Time is a great healer, and,
gradually, the passion of anger had gone out of him. He knew
he would soon be home and he was longing for Fantana and for
his wife. The children must have grown. Petru would come out
to greet him at the gate. Johann lulled himself with daydreams.
He could already see himself going in through the gate, lifting
Petru in his arms and pressing Nicholae close to him. It was all
as vivid as though he were hugging them already. He would tell
Susanna what he had done and where he had been, not men-

tioning that they had beaten and starved him. Why make her unhappy? But he would tell her how he had learned Yiddish and how no one in camp, not even the Jews, would believe that he was Romanian. Susanna would laugh. Then he would go on to tell how the adjutant would only believe him when he had taken off his trousers and let him see for himself. Susanna would roar with laughter, especially about Strul's being ordered to look, too. He would tell how both the clerk and the adjutant had simply gaped and said: "We must release you, Johann; you are not a Jew, and the King ordered that the canal was to be built only by Jews." Susanna would be glad that it was all over at last and that he was back home, and she would come close to him and embrace him lovingly and say, "You are my husband and you are dearer to me than the sun that shines in the sky."

These were Johann's dreams as he stood waiting for the general. Then word came that the general had postponed his visit to the following day. The prisoners, who had been paraded in three ranks with their picks and spades, now dispersed.

Moritz was summoned to the office.

"The adjutant wants to see you," said Strul. Johann could hear his heart thumping. He was sure he had been called to be told of his release, but he refrained from asking Strul any questions. He could hardly control his joy. He had not expected to be set free until the canal had been completed, and this good news had come like a bolt from the blue.

The adjutant was wearing his new uniform. The floorboards had been freshly scrubbed in readiness for the general's inspection. The office table had been covered with clean blue paper and the files on it stacked in neat little piles. Johann halted by the door and saluted. He could hardly wait to hear the news, but he pretended not to know why he had been called. He did not want to show that he was as happy as a boy. On a chair next to the adjutant sat Dr. Samuel Abramovici. He, too, was a prisoner but he had made friends with the adjutant and spent all the day in the office with him. Strul sat down at his table in a corner. They were all very serious as they looked straight at him.

Finally, the adjutant said:

"Moritz, my boy, your wife has divorced you!" Rubbing his mustache, he went on: "We have been sent the divorce certificate, which you have to sign to show you have been notified of the fact."

The adjutant flicked a piece of paper toward the edge of the table and handed Johann the pen. But Johann remained rooted to the spot.

"The divorce was applied for on racial grounds. She no longer wishes to be the wife of a Jew." The adjutant added reproachfully: "You with all your tales about being a pure Romanian and a Christian! You thought you were fooling me, did you? But I'm an old hand at that game. I never sent off your petition, and obviously I was right. Your wife has divorced you because you are a Jew, and who should know better than she?"

The adjutant smiled. But when he caught sight of Johann's distorted face, which was going waxen, his smile vanished.

"Women are all the same," he said. "The moment you're out of the house they find another man. All whores, every one of them. Come on, don't let it get you down."

Johann could have torn him to pieces: hearing his wife called a whore was more than he could stand. He gnashed his teeth. In spite of his efforts to restrain himself, he could feel the fury boiling up inside him. His throat contracted, and he clenched his fists as if to strike.

"My wife is not a whore," he said.

"Perfectly true," said the adjutant. "You are a man whose wife is not a whore, because you no longer have a wife. You had one up till the . . ." The adjutant reached for the piece of paper and read the date. "Till the thirtieth of January. That was when the divorce was granted. Since then you have been a bachelor again." The adjutant smiled. Dr. Abramovici, too, was smiling faintly.

"My wife has not divorced me," said Johann. "I know Susanna."

"What you think you know is your business," said the adjutant. "Now sign here to the effect that you have been notified of the divorce and that you are once more a bachelor."

"I am not a bachelor," said Johann.

"Very well then, you are not a bachelor, but you must sign all the same."

Johann looked at the pen the adjutant was holding out for him and said:

"I refuse."

The adjutant flushed with anger. He had remembered that he was an army man and that Moritz's answer constituted a breach of discipline.

"Sign," he ordered. "Have you forgotten where you are?"

Johann took the pen and signed. This time it was an order: he had to obey. When he had signed on the dotted line in the bottom right-hand corner, at the place the adjutant had indicated with his finger, he put down the pen and made a move to leave the room. His eyes were blurred with tears and his head was swimming.

"Read it," said the adjutant. "So that you know what you have signed."

"I don't have to read it," he answered. "I know it's not true anyway."

He tried to open the door, but, as though it was pitch-dark, his hand groped helplessly for the handle.

"Stay and have a smoke," said Dr. Abramovici, holding out his cigarette case. Johann turned back from the door, took a cigarette, and began to smoke. The exact instant Dr. Abramovici had held out his lighter for him escaped him entirely. He struggled to remember, but there was nothing before his eyes but the dancing flame. It was the yellow flame that kept growing larger and larger.

"Have you any children?" the doctor asked. Johann woke up

as from a dream. He answered, but it was as if someone else were speaking. Somehow or other he managed to leave the office. The whole of that day he sat on the frozen ground beside the canal. He did not feel cold. All kinds of thoughts flitted through his mind. From time to time he remembered the document he had signed, and a spasm of anger shook him.

The next morning he went again to see the adjutant, asked for the document, and read it. Until that moment he had not believed it was true, but now he was convinced. Susanna had divorced him because she, too, thought he was a Jew and because she had found another man. He no longer felt angry with the adjutant for calling him a bachelor. It hurt him, but he did not feel angry, because he knew it was true. He had read it with his own eyes.

🎋 🎋 🎋

THE following morning the adjutant appeared again in his new uniform. The prisoners waited till noon on parade along the canal bank, but the general never came. The third day the adjutant reverted to his everyday tunic. He announced that the general had got annoyed and was not coming to see the canal.

For a whole week they did not work. Then Johann's camp moved farther north. Till then they had been digging in soft yellow clay. From now on the canal had to be cut through rock. The adjutant went off in the truck to fetch new tools, since the old ones were suitable only for soft earth. He was away for three days. Then two trucks arrived with tools for rock drilling and splintering. The work was exhausting, and it was bitterly cold. Johann toiled all through the winter. The food was bad. Men fell sick by the score. Many died. Johann did not fall ill. He caught nothing but a sore throat, and that only for a week. But the work progressed very slowly. By April, they had scarcely moved from where they had been at Christmas and they had excavated only a few dozen yards of canal. It was said that five hundred thousand men had worked at it all winter. The work was to go on throughout the summer and be completed by the following autumn. The water was to be let in about October. But at the beginning of May they received orders to cease work. The adjutant announced that the General Staff had given up the idea of the canal. King Carol II of Romania had been dethroned and had fled the country. And all the generals who had helped him with the plans for the canal had fled with him or had been dismissed. Their places at the palace had been filled by other generals, who maintained that the plans for the canal the King had designed with his own hand were no good. They had given the order to stop. The Jews were packed into trains and taken to the western frontier of Romania to build fortifications against the Hungarians.

As he said farewell to the canal, Johann felt sorry the King had designed the plans badly. All that work in vain.

🐦 🐦 🐦

THE new camp was in a forest on the frontier between Romania and Hungary. They had traveled by train three whole days and nights. All the tools they had used on the canal had been brought along with them. The adjutant had had his entire office, which was a wooden hut, taken up and put on the train. Strul had brought the registers. They had left nothing behind in the old camp. The prisoners had even kept their same lice, of which each man had his fair share. But in the new camp they could no longer use the canal tools. Here they had to fell trees for the fortifications. Johann had no idea what fortifications were like. But he and thousands and thousands of others felled trees by the acre and carted them down into the valley.

Johann strained his eyes to catch a glimpse of the fortifications from a distance, but he could not see them. He imagined

that all this wood was being used to erect a gigantic wall between the Hungarians and the Romanians. Perhaps, indeed,
this was the General Staff's idea: he did not know. But he was
looking forward to seeing this wall which was to separate the
two countries. When it was finished, he would be able to see it
from where they worked, high up in the forest. The Hungarians,
so he had heard, were building defense works of their own, on
their side of the frontier. He was interested to see which was to
be the higher. He was pleased when he heard the adjutant say
the Hungarian fortifications weren't worth a cent, and that the
Romanians could walk over them in a single night if they
wanted to. But they did not. Johann often imagined the Romanian soldiers passing into Hungary. He would have liked to
see them. If he were still in the camp when fighting broke out
he would be able to watch them from the top of the forest. The
adjutant told them that the Romanian fortifications were so
high that even the birds could not fly over them, and that is
why Johann imagined them to be very high indeed. There were
some birds which flew so high that they could hardly be seen
from the ground. If even these could not fly over the Romanian
fortifications, then it meant that the top of the fortifications
would not be visible, either. It would be hidden in the clouds.
Johann wondered where they would put the trees he had felled
himself. He would have liked to mark them with a special sign
and when the fortifications were complete he would perhaps
have been able to catch a glimpse of his trees right at the very
top.

    Every day as he felled the trees in the forest, Johann mused
to himself in this way. It made the time pass more quickly. He
knew that many of his ideas were childish and silly and would
make anyone else roar with laughter. And yet he was attached
to them. But he tried never to think of home and Fantana: it
made his blood boil.

    One day Strul came for him in the forest and told him he
was wanted in the office. He had not set foot inside it since the

day of the divorce certificate. Seeing the desk and the adjutant reminded him of the corner where the document had lain and the way he had leaned on his elbow to sign it. That is why he had refused to go into it again, or even to look at it from a distance. But now that he had been summoned, there was no help for it.

The adjutant was not in the office. The only people in the room were Dr. Abramovici, Strul, and the camp cook, Hurtig. Johann saluted. They acknowledged it amicably and offered him a stool. Johann looked round, expecting the adjutant to arrive. If they had sent for him from the forest, the adjutant must have had something important to tell him.

"The adjutant is not here; we can have a quiet chat and won't be disturbed," said Dr. Abramovici. He offered Johann a cigarette. Dr. Abramovici always had cigarettes, expensive ones.

"Jankl," said Dr. Abramovici, "your wife has deserted you." Johann changed color. He turned pale.

"And what has that to do with you?" he replied. "That is nobody's business but my own."

"All I meant was that there would be no one waiting for you when you came out of camp," said Dr. Abramovici. "Though personally I don't think anyone will be released before the end of the war. And the war can go on for another ten years yet."

Johann gave a sigh. If he had to spend another ten years in camp all his hair would have turned white.

"Would you like to go to another country?" asked Dr. Abramovici.

Johann remembered his plans to go to America with Ghitza Ion. If only it had rained on that day I should have been in America at this moment. I would not have gone to meet Susanna that night, he reflected. If he had not met Susanna that night, he would have been far away by now. He would not have been in the camp.

"Yes, I would," said Johann, and his face lit up. "Once before I wanted to go to America, but somehow it didn't come off."

"This time it will come off," said Dr. Abramovici. "If you agree to go, you'll be in America in a few months."

Johann looked at Abramovici, Strul, and Hurtig, and they looked back at him. Obviously they were not joking. They would not have sent for him all the way from the forest for a joke.

"I am willing," said Johann.

"Then come with us," said the doctor, "with us three. We mean to escape across into Hungary. Are you afraid of making an escape?"

"No," said Johann.

"In Hungary," said the doctor, "there are no anti-Semitic laws. I have a married sister in Hungary, and she is expecting me. Mr. Hurtig has relations there, too. But we need somebody to give us a hand with our luggage. I have a lot; six suitcases. I am taking all my valuables. Once we get over the frontier, we shall have to do ten miles on foot on Hungarian territory. I can't carry them all alone. And besides, none of us can speak Hungarian. We thought of you."

"How do we get out of here?" asked Johann.

"The adjutant will take us to the frontier by truck," said the doctor. "Otherwise, we could never get out. There are patrols guarding all the roads. But we'll be safe in an army truck."

"The adjutant knows we're escaping?"

"Of course he does," said Hurtig. "He has a large family and needs money. Wouldn't you do the same if you were in his place?"

Johann did not answer.

"Have another cigarette and then go and pack up your things," said Dr. Abramovici. "But watch out that none of the other prisoners get wind of anything."

"Right away?" asked Johann.

"As soon as possible," said the doctor. "At nine o'clock the adjutant will be waiting for us with the truck outside the gate. Come to the office as soon as you've collected your things. We'll be waiting. Don't take too much luggage; remember you have to carry my bags."

Johann went off and came back with a small suitcase into which he had stuffed a shirt, a pair of trousers, and half a loaf of bread. At nine o'clock they went out through the gate. The adjutant was waiting for them, packed them into the truck, and drove them to the frontier. At three o'clock in the morning, Johann Moritz was carrying Dr. Abramovici's cases in Hungarian territory.

By dawn they reached a railway station. Dr. Abramovici gave Johann some money and sent him to buy four second-class tickets to Budapest.

✠ ✠ ✠

AT A reception given at the Finnish Legation in Bucharest, Traian Koruga met General Tautu, the Romanian War Minister. A few days later he went to see him at the Ministry and laid before him the case of Johann Moritz. The General listened with interest. He took down details of his surname, Christian name, date of birth, date of arrest, and then said:

"Within a week at the outside, your man will be back in the village. I will order an immediate inquiry into his case and have his release papers made out. Today is the"—the General glanced at his calendar—"the twenty-first of August. If you call here on the twenty-eighth I will personally hand over his release papers to you."

"Is this Moritz your father's servant?" was the General's next question.

"He helps my father on the farm. He isn't exactly a servant—"

"There is an acute shortage of labor on the land today," said the General, not waiting for the end of the sentence. "I quite understand why you have taken so much trouble over the poor devil. Every extra hand counts, especially now in the middle of harvesting."

The conversation continued on this line. Traian tried to explain to the Minister that he was not appealing on behalf of Moritz because his father needed him in the fields, but simply because he had been unjustly arrested.

"My coming to see you is merely humanitarian in motive. It is a free and disinterested action."

"I get driven to actions like that, too," said the General. "Every time I go down to my estate I have to baptize or marry off some of the peasants. Nowadays one has to use every means at one's disposal to get the people to work. You have to get them to believe that you are their friend and even sit at table with them. I quite see what you are trying to say. Your father is in the same position as I am."

Opening a drawer, the General took out Traian's latest novel and put it down on the desk. It was a brand-new copy, and the pages had not even been cut.

"I sent my ADC to the bookshop just now to buy it," said the General. "Would you be so kind as to inscribe it to my daughter? She is called Elizabeth. She is eighteen and is simply crazy about your novels. You are one of her favorite authors. At dinner today, when I tell her you've called on me, she will ask me all about what you were wearing, the tie you had on, and what cigarettes you smoked. Such is youth, isn't it?"

Traian went down the steps of the War Ministry certain that, this time, he would succeed in obtaining Johann Moritz's release. He called at the florist's to collect a bunch of white roses he had ordered earlier in the day and then went into the post office to send his father a telegram: "Arriving Fantana August 29 with fiancée and release papers of Johann Moritz."

❦ ❦ ❦

"SO, ON August twenty-ninth, we'll be with your father in Fantana?" asked Eleonora West. She was thrilled. "Only a week to wait! I'm just dying to get there." She took the white roses out of Traian's hands and arranged them in a vase. As she stood with her back to him, Traian gazed at the russet-colored curls that fell on the shoulders of her black silk dress. He looked at her tall, slender silhouette and at her legs clothed in fine smoke-colored stockings.

"Nora," he said, "do you know what I keep wondering every time I look at you?"

She turned and smiled.

"I ask the same question as Tudor Arghezi, the poet: 'Most assuredly was thy mother a nymph, or a hind or a reed by the waters. But what was the seed that grew within her womb? Perchance that of a wood-sprite, or perchance that of a Hero? Surely thou art not of mortal descent. Among thine ancestors there must have been a hind, else couldst thou not move so lithely. And among thine ancestors there must have been sea plants, for thy body has in it still the harmony of life in the deep waters. Thine eyes are startled like the eyes of a squirrel and thy ways are changing as the ways of a Persian cat.'"

Eleonora West stood with her back to him, burying her face in the white roses.

"Have I upset you?" asked Traian.

"No," she answered.

"You have suddenly become sad," he said. "Though I can't see your eyes, I know they are clouded over. Is it because of what I have just said?"

"No!" she said with the ghost of a smile. "I am not sad. I was only thinking of my family tree with its hinds, Heroes, sea plants, and squirrels."

They sat down to dinner all alone in the huge dining room

with its antique oak furniture and wrought-iron decorations.

It was Eleonora's house, one of the most famous in Bucharest. She had designed it herself; the furniture, the carpets, everything was just as she had planned it.

At twenty-nine, Eleonora was the editor of the biggest Romanian newspaper, *The Western World*. She had studied in the greatest universities of Europe and now wrote the editorials for her own paper, ran a publishing house, edited a literary and artistic review, and played a leading role in the political, cultural, and social life of the capital. Traian had already known her for several years. Their love for each other was as great now as it had been at the very beginning; perhaps it was even greater. But they had never married. Every time Traian had asked her she had refused on the grounds that she would never make a good wife. "I am far too fond of my work ever to be able to give it up without feeling that I was throwing away an important part of my life."

"I think they are going to set Johann Moritz free," said Traian. "The War Minister promised me today that he would do it by the twenty-eighth of August. I wired my father that I was coming to Fantana with my fiancée and with the order for Johann Moritz's release. He will be as pleased with one as with the other."

"Do you absolutely insist on introducing me to your parents as your fiancée?" asked Nora.

"I'd like to very much. But if you would rather not, I won't. Father will be upset, but he always forgives in the end."

"Why introduce your fiancée and not your wife?" asked Nora. "If we get married the day after tomorrow in the morning, we'll be man and wife when we arrive in Fantana."

Traian thought she was joking. For the last two years he had been trying to persuade her to marry him. She had refused. She loved him but did not want to become his wife. She did not want to be anyone's wife. And now, suddenly, she was offering to marry him.

"Do you really mean it?" He got up and kissed her hand. "Is anything the matter? Why this sudden decision? This morning on the phone you didn't breathe a word about it."

"Nothing's the matter," she said. "On August twenty-ninth we'll arrive in Fantana already married. That's all. You have often asked me to marry you. Or have you changed your mind since? . . . I am glad you haven't."

Traian realized that some important event had taken place to make Eleonora suddenly decide to marry. But he could not guess what it was.

"For the time being let's just get married at the registry office," she said. "We can have the church wedding at your father's own church. I can see myself, already, walking up to the wooden altar in a white wedding dress, with a crowd of peasant girls following. I'll see we get the special license for the civil marriage. I'll ring up the Attorney General."

"Nora, tell me, what has happened?" said Traian. "You've been through something terrible, I can tell."

"I swear nothing has happened," she said. "Absolutely nothing. I have made a spontaneous decision and I want to carry it out as quickly as possible before anything can happen to prevent it. It means so much to me that I want to grasp this chance of happiness straight away. If there is any delay, I'm afraid I shall lose it altogether. That is all. Won't you believe me?"

ʻʻ ʻʻ ʻʻ

AFTER lunch Traian and Eleonora stayed in the library, looking at the books and paintings. Traian was sure Eleonora had spoken the truth. But they made no further mention of marriage. They both felt the need to escape from their own thoughts. He stopped in front of a picture by Picasso.

"*Pablo Picasso is perhaps the outstanding painter of our time,*" said Traian, repeating a passage by Lewis Mumford that he recollected. "More completely than any other artist, he represents both our achievements and our disfigurements. His entire work is a series of shocks: and with each shock, part of the structure of our civilization symbolically is revealed—and collapses. His maturity begins with haunting pictures of poverty and misery: the deep humanity of the blue period. Haggard columbines and famished harlequins connect him with the surviving playworld of baroque society. Then comes the primitivism of Negroid idols and masques: an effort to reassert our waning vitality by a return to primitive sources: almost synchronous with the rise of jazz. After that cubism, neo-classicism, and such empty technical virtuosity. . . . Finally a real emotion overpowers Picasso: the actual horror of the fascist uprising in Spain grips and tortures him: hence the powerful symbolization of woman's utmost misery in this study for the Guernica mural. Disintegration can go no further this side of sanity. In every phase Picasso's paintings have given a truer image of the world we live in than the so-called documentary Realists, who show only what the most superficial eye sees."

Eleonora looked at the painting, which represented a woman so disfigured by suffering that she no longer resembled a human being. It was a vision of flesh rent asunder. A portrait of the human face reduced by suffering to its essential elements. There were eyes, a nose, a mouth, and ears, but each isolated and made independent by suffering. The unity of the human body had disintegrated in its agony.

Traian Koruga turned toward Nora. For a fleeting moment he had the impression that she bore a likeness to the woman in the portrait. No photographer could have caught it. On Eleonora's face, suffering was engraved as deeply as it was on the face of Picasso's woman. It was as though there were passing through it some high-frequency current whose very tension prevented electrocution.

"Nora, what is it?" asked Traian.

"Nothing," she said. "Shall we have coffee?" Without waiting for an answer she turned her back on him, just as she had done when he had spoken of her kinship with hinds and with the plants of the sea.

卐 卐 卐

THE marriage took place at the registry office. Traian and Eleonora wore street clothes. Two friends of Traian's acted as witnesses. After the ceremony they lunched at a restaurant on the outskirts of the town in Baneasa.

"For the church wedding we'll have a proper celebration," said Traian. He began to describe the traditional custom and ways of celebrating a Romanian country wedding.

"On the way to church, peasants on horseback lead the procession—fifty young peasants in national costume and mounted on white horses. Then comes a cart drawn by four oxen holding, traditionally, the bride's dowry and the presents she has received. Instead of making a public display of our presents, we'll fill the cart with flowers. We'll have a dozen sponsors. While everybody is singing 'Isaiah dances' and the bride and bridegroom, sponsors and priests, are all dancing a round in the church, a shower of sweets comes down from the roof and children pick them up from under the very feet of the dancers. We'll scatter a whole sackful of sweets so that all the children in Fantana can eat their fill. When I was a lad I used to go collecting sweets at weddings, but I never managed to get hold of more than four. At our wedding there must be enough for the children to fill their pockets. We'll get a dozen gypsy bands with violins and guitars. Wine will flow from the barrels, and the whole village will get drunk. We'll hold the reception in a glade in the forest and we'll invite thousands of guests. The celebrations will go on for a week."

Nora glanced at her watch. She was due in fifteen minutes for an appointment with her lawyer, Leopold Stein.

"Let's go," she said. "I've got a lot to see to at the office."

Traian cut short his description of their wedding celebrations. They left the table and made their way back to town.

🌾 🌾 🌾

TRAIAN took Nora back to the newspaper office. *The Western World* building was an ultramodern block with a façade of white marble. Eleonora had had it built on the site of an old printing press. Traian looked at the six stories sparkling in the strong afternoon sunlight and smiled admiringly. All this is Nora's work, he thought.

"I'll wait for you in the car," he said. He knew that as a rule Nora drove herself home from the office, but he thought today —their wedding day—she would make an exception.

"I'll come home on my own as soon as I'm through," she said. Waiting till he had gone, she walked up the marble steps and through the massive wrought-iron doors held open by the doorkeeper, who bowed and scraped to her in his gold-braided uniform as she disappeared into the newspaper offices.

🌷 🌷 🌷

ELEONORA WEST walked into her office with an air of regal indifference. She pretended not to notice the old man dressed in black who rose to his feet as she came in. Eleonora put down her gloves and handbag on the desk and then motioned to the old man to sit down. She took out a cigarette and made an effort to light it without betraying the trembling of her hands. Then she sat back in her armchair and fixed her eyes on the man sitting opposite her.

"I am listening, Mr. Stein," she said.

The old man opened the brief case on his lap, took out a sheaf of papers, and put them down on the edge of the desk. Nora was watching him closely all the time.

"The matter is settled, Miss West," said the old man. "Here are the documents." He detached two sheets of paper from the bundle and laid them before her.

"Are these the only documents extant in the Ploesti archives?" asked Nora.

"Up to this morning, these were the only ones," answered the old man. "And now even these are lying on your desk. There is nothing further in the archives."

Eleonora cast a contemptuous glance at the papers, folded them, and put them away in a drawer.

"It would be wiser to destroy them at once," said the old man.

Nora looked at his gold-rimmed spectacles, his stiff collar, and the old-fashioned cut of his black suit.

"The moment the papers are in my desk there is nothing more to fear, Mr. Stein!" she said.

"I am not afraid for myself," he replied. "But for your own sake it would be wiser to burn them right away."

"How much did you have to pay?" asked Nora to change the subject. She had noticed that the old man was afraid. She would destroy the documents, but first she wanted to have another look at them.

"Exactly a hundred thousand lei," answered Leopold Stein.

"And your own fee?"

"It is included."

Eleonora took two bundles of bills out of the drawer and handed them to the old man. He put them in his brief case, checking a gesture that had grown into a habit—that of counting them first.

"That is all then, I believe," said Nora. She wanted to be left alone to look at the documents, but the old man remained seated.

"Have you anything else to discuss with me?" she asked.

"No, nothing," answered Leopold Stein. "The matter is settled, as far as it can be."

"Is there still some document not in order?"

"There are no further documents involved," he said. "But the whole problem is only temporarily solved by the destruction of the documents. That is what I wanted to tell you. Had I not been your father's friend and colleague, had I not held you in my arms when you were small, I would not have dared to draw your attention to this fact. But I must warn you that the burning of the documents is no final solution."

"Speak plainly."

"It is perfectly plain, Miss West. You wished to get hold of the original birth certificates of your parents, so that it should be impossible to prove that they were Jews. I have obtained them for you. I have removed them from the archives."

"And there the matter ends."

"You may destroy documents but not facts," said Leopold Stein. "In spite of everything you are still a Jewess, and if anyone tries to prove it . . ."

"If anyone tries to prove it, he won't be able to," said Eleonora. "There will be no evidence."

"But you will be asked for papers."

"I will procure them," she said. "I can get any document I want by paying for it."

"True," said the lawyer. "But then we come up against the penal code. To play with that is to play with fire."

"And was it not you who stole the documents from the Ploeşti archives this very morning?" Nora asked pointedly. "Why preach at me?"

"I am not preaching," said the old man. "I am only warning you that you are playing a dangerous game that must come to an end sooner or later."

"You know I have no alternative," said Nora, lighting another cigarette. "There is no help for it. If society forbids me to live my own life, to have a house, or a profession, or a husband, I am ready to fight back desperately and with every weapon at my disposal. I shall struggle like a wounded tigress whose every instinct of preservation is aroused."

"The main thing, Miss West, is not fighting, but winning."

"I shall win," she said, grinding her cigarette onto the ash tray.

"Do you really believe you will be allowed to carry on for long?" asked the old man. "So far you have refused to declare your Jewish origin. That was an act of youthful audacity. But you were lucky. Either through fear or through cowardice, no one has so far dared to challenge you. When there were denunciations demanding the confiscation of your newspaper and press on racial grounds, you were able to buy up those responsible for the investigations. Another victory to you. Now you have destroyed the documents proving the Jewish origin of your parents. Once more you have gained time. But the racial laws are being applied with increasing severity every day. In the end no Jew will be able to elude them. It has only just begun. That is why you are still the owner and editor of an important newspaper, whereas, according to the law, being a Jewess, you have no right to publish so much as a single article. But we must think of the future."

"I shall go on being the owner and editor of *The Western World* even in the future," said Nora.

Leopold Stein knew the faultlessly logical mind of the woman sitting opposite him. But the answer she had just given him savored of fanaticism, and the mind of a fanatic is devoid of logic. He dared not contradict her. When man abandons objective reasoning, he must not be contradicted. Every attempt to show him the truth is doomed to failure.

"At noon today I married a Christian," said Eleonora. "The newspaper will be run in my husband's name. . . . In this way no one will be able to deprive me of *Western World*, even if Romania becomes more anti-Semitic than Germany."

"Are you really married?" Leopold Stein could not get over his surprise.

"Henceforward I am Mrs. Eleonora West-Koruga," she said. "My husband is the novelist Traian Koruga, who, in a few days' time, will be owner and editor of the newspaper. And he, in his turn, belongs to me."

Eleonora gave a satisfied laugh. Leopold Stein fumbled in his pockets for nothing in particular, to hide his embarrassment, and to avoid at all costs having to confront her gaze or give her an answer. He needed a few more moments to take in the fact that it was all true.

"In other words," he said, coughing nervously into his handkerchief, "you are handing over the paper and giving up the editorship."

"On the contrary," said Nora, "not only am I not giving up the editorship, but I am even reorganizing the paper on a larger scale. I have taken on a new editor."

"That is a brilliant idea," said Leopold Stein. "A marvelous idea. And he has accepted all the conditions?"

"I don't understand," said Nora sharply.

"Has Mr. Traian Koruga, your husband, accepted this arrangement? It must be rather unpleasant for a man. It means that he has been bought by a woman for a specific purpose."

"I have bought no one," said Nora nervously. "I married for love."

Leopold Stein rose to congratulate her. She did not offer him her hand. She was fidgeting with her parents' birth certificates. Her eyes were bright with tears.

"Objectively speaking, no one deserves congratulations until he is actually dying. And once dead he is no longer in a position to accept them. Which is a pity."

The old man sat down again. He regretted his gesture.

"I thought you really had married for love," he said.

"You don't believe I am in love?" she asked. "With all your intelligence, can you fail to understand?"

"Then why are you so unhappy?" he asked. "It seems to me you are crying."

"It seems to me you are very tired, Mr. Stein. I don't know what is the matter with you. You don't understand a thing. One wouldn't think you were a Jew. I am in love with Traian Koruga. He was the first man I ever loved. I have been in love with him for several years, deeply in love. But that was not why I married. Love is no reason for marriage. I married because of the racial laws. To save the paper. To save my life. Now do you understand?"

Leopold Stein seemed not to understand. He kissed Eleonora's hand and moved toward the door. She called him back.

"This week end I am going to the country to stay with my parents-in-law," she said. "Traian's father is an Orthodox priest. I shall stay there for a few days. By the time I come back I want to find my entire property, including the newspaper, made over to Traian Koruga. I leave it to you to work out a procedure that is valid and watertight in the eyes of the law. The transfer must be made quickly."

"You're a clever woman," said the old man.

"Not at all," she said. "I am only a woman fighting with every instinct and faculty I possess to defend my right to live. Good-by, Mr. Stein."

❦ ❦ ❦

WHEN the old man had gone, Eleonora West bent forward over her desk, buried her head in her hands, and wept. She wept as only a woman can weep, not only with her eyes but with her whole being. Then she lifted the receiver and rang up Traian.

"Please come over to fetch me," she said.

"Is anything wrong?"

"Nothing, only come and fetch me. I swear nothing is wrong. Nothing whatsoever. But come quickly."

Traian Koruga got up to go. Before leaving the library he glanced once more at Picasso's woman. One half of her eye was laughing while the other half wept. It had split in two, so that the woman could both laugh and cry at the same time, and with equal intensity.

❦ ❦ ❦

WHILE waiting for Traian, Eleonora rang up Leopold Stein. He lived near by and had just reached home.

"Mr. Stein," she said, "please answer me honestly. What made me marry, do you think—love or necessity? Don't spare my feelings, I want your frank opinion."

"What do you think yourself?" asked the old man.

"I just don't know!" she answered. "If my life depended on it, I could not give an exact answer. At times I think I did it for love, at other times that I was driven by motives of expediency, and then again for both reasons together. But none of these explanations seem valid. One thing only I know for sure—that I could not have waited any longer and what I did had to be done. But I would also like to know my real motives."

"The real motive is neither one nor the other," said the old man.

"So it was not for convenience's sake that I got married, like a woman. . . ."

"No. You are too proud to marry for material interest even if the paper and your whole fortune were at stake."

"Are you sure?"

"Positive."

"Then I married for love?"

"In order to love truly, you must believe in the future," said Leopold Stein. "You must believe in happiness and, what is even more absurd, you must believe that happiness is eternal, and that the one you love can offer it to you. You are too rational to believe that. And that is why—forgive me for telling you—you did not marry for love."

"Well, then?" she asked.

"Your motive was neither love nor expediency," said Leopold Stein. "It was fear. This act of yours had all the lightning rapidity of despair."

"And so love doesn't even come into it?" asked Eleonora.

"A little," answered Stein. "But this love of yours is the love of a woman at the time when men lived in the forests and were in constant danger of being torn to pieces by wild beasts. It was only then that women flung themselves at the feet of men, demanding protection, love, and security—and all with the same intensity and passion. It is the kind of love women experience in times of earthquakes, floods, or other great cataclysms—in fact, whenever the earth seems in danger of disruption."

"Why didn't you tell me all this when you were here?" she asked.

"I did not want to destroy your apparent strength and self-confidence," he answered. "But I could see you were trembling with fright, and that your action had been prompted by fear. I felt sorry for you. Don't forget that I dandled you on my knees when you were a little girl."

Traian came into the office. Nora hung up the receiver and went toward him. She pressed close to him, laughing. Traian kissed her.

"I am glad to see you so cheerful," he said. "I thought you were crying on the phone."

ON AUGUST 28, the day before his departure for Fantana, Traian called at the War Ministry to collect the release order for Johann Moritz. As he ran up the steps, he felt as happy as if the papers were already in his pocket. The ADC, who knew that

Traian was on friendly terms with the Minister, showed him in at once. He had brought an illustrated de luxe edition of his first novel and had written a flattering dedication on the flyleaf. When he came in, the General did not rise to meet him as he had done the previous week. He pretended to be reading.

"I'm afraid I am disturbing you, General," said Traian.

"No," the General replied icily. "Sit down, please."

He did not hold out his hand, and Traian noticed it.

"I am afraid I have unpleasant news for you," said the General, coming straight to the point. "The person on whose behalf you called last week, and for whom no doubt you have come again today, cannot be released. Not for the time being, at any rate. Preliminary investigations must be held to establish whether your declaration concerning his racial origin is borne out by the facts."

Traian would have left the room there and then, but at the thought of Moritz, he remained seated.

"So that's that. And now, Mr. Koruga, there is nothing further you can do except to await the findings of the investigating body."

The General intended these words to mean that the interview was over and that Traian was expected to withdraw. Traian understood perfectly, but made no attempt to move. His father was expecting him in Fantana on the following day with the release papers for Moritz.

"Exactly a week ago you promised me these papers," said Traian. "You told me in so many words that my statement was a sufficient guarantee and that no inquiry would be necessary."

"A week ago the situation was different."

"I am unable to appreciate the difference," said Traian. "Johann Moritz is held in a Jewish camp in spite of the fact that he is a Romanian."

"That is for the commission to decide."

"But the investigations of the commission may drag on for months and months," said Traian. "It is almost eighteen months since the poor man was arrested."

"I know," said the General. "They may go on for a whole year, even two. There is no time for investigations at present. There's a war on."

"But would not my statement be a sufficient guarantee to set Moritz free and investigate afterward?"

"No," said the General.

"I am sorry to see you change your mind from one week to the next," said Traian, rising.

"I am sorry, too, but it has nothing to do with me."

"Is that a personal allusion?"

"It is not a question of allusions but of concrete facts."

"This time I think I am entitled to demand an explanation," said Traian, livid with anger.

"An explanation, Mr. Koruga? At a time when every Jew in the world is fighting hand in hand with the Bolsheviks to sub-due our country and enslave our people, you—a pure Romanian, one of the foremost writers of our land—you take it upon your-self to marry a Jewess!"

The General was purple with anger.

"As a soldier," he went on, "I consider what you have done an act of treason. Treason, that is what you are guilty of. How do you expect me, after that, to trust your word? Your appeal on behalf of Moritz even makes me suspect that in fact he really is a Jew. It wouldn't surprise me in the least to find I am right. Can you still expect me to take you at your word?"

"Evidently not," said Traian, and left the room. Going down the stairs, he grew aware of the book under his arm. He opened it and tore out the flyleaf. Then he stepped into the car.

❧ ❧ ❧

"ELEONORA is Jewish," Traian said to himself, "and she never even told me about it." He felt cheated in his love. Just outside the town he stopped his car. He opened the door and contemplated the fields. She did not tell me because I never asked, he reflected. It would have been ridiculous to ask. Whoever asks his sweetheart about her racial origin? He remembered how often, in his love for her, he had talked of her family tree, with its hinds and sea plants, its squirrels and Heroes. And every time he had mentioned these things her eyes had grown cloudy. Traian felt guilty now. Perhaps she thought I was hinting at her Jewish origin. She must have suffered so dreadfully every time. He slammed the door to and drove back to town. If only I had found out sooner. I could have spared her so much unhappiness. Poor Nora!

He drew up at the first florist's on the way and bought a bouquet of white roses for her. Because of my marriage, Johann Moritz will not be set free, he thought.

The assistant smiled as she wrapped up the roses.

ᚹ ᚹ ᚹ

"TELL me what you are writing about," said Nora. Traian had begun work on his new novel. She would hear him get out of bed at four in the morning, slip into his dressing gown, and go out of the room. He would stay in his study till breakfast, which they took together. They had been married for just two months.

"Won't you tell me?" asked Nora. She was impatient. Traian had hitherto always avoided talking about the novel, but this time he had finally to give in.

"Once," said Traian, "I made a cruise in a submarine. We spent a thousand hours under water. On board a submarine they have special instruments to indicate when the fresh-air supply is running out. But in the early days there were no such instruments and the sailors took a hutchful of white rabbits on board. When the atmosphere began to get poisonous, the rabbits died. The sailors knew that as soon as the white rabbits died they had only five or six more hours to live. It was then that the captain had to make the supreme decision: either he made a desperate effort to surface or he stayed under water and died with his entire crew. Rather than watch each other die, they generally shot each other.

"On my submarine, instead of white rabbits, they had mechanical instruments. The captain noticed that I detected the slightest diminution in the oxygen content of the air. He made fun of my keen senses, but in the end the sailors stopped watching the instruments. They watched me instead. And I would tell them, with an accuracy that the instruments invariably confirmed, whether or not there was sufficient fresh air.

"We have that gift—the white rabbits and I: we can feel six hours earlier than other human beings when the atmosphere ceases to be fit to sustain life. For some time now I have had the same sensation as I used to have in the submarine: I feel the atmosphere has become suffocating."

"What atmosphere?"

"The atmosphere in which contemporary society lives. Man cannot endure it much longer. Bureaucracy, the army, the government, central and local administration, everything is conspiring to suffocate man. Contemporary society is suitable for none but machines and mechanical slaves. It was created for their benefit. But for human beings it is asphyxiating. As yet they are unconscious of it. They believe that they are living normally as they did before. They are like those sailors in the submarine who go on working in the poisonous atmosphere for another six hours. But I know we are nearing the end."

"Is that the subject of your novel?"

"In it I shall describe the ghastly death agony—in an atmosphere destructive of life—of all people who dwell on the face of the earth. But since I cannot write about everyone, I have taken only ten, the ten I know best."

"And all the characters die?"

"Once the white rabbits have died, men have, at the outside, only six more hours to live. My novel covers the last six hours in the lives of my closest friends."

"How far have you got?"

"To the end of the first chapter," he said. "One of the characters has been torn from among us and . . ."

"And what happens to him?"

"So far he has been robbed of his freedom, his wife, his children, and his house . . . he has been starved and beaten. They have even started pulling out his teeth. Later on they will tear out his eyes and rip the flesh from his bones. And his bones will be broken, crushed. The final tortures will probably be applied automatically and electrically."

"And is it all true?"

"It is all true," he said. "In my novel I have given the names of the streets, towns, and countries in which the characters live. I have even disclosed their telephone numbers. As a matter of fact, you yourself know my first hero. You can check the truth of what I have written."

"Who is the first hero?"

"Johann Moritz."

Eleonora's forehead clouded over. The things that Traian had said about Johann Moritz were true. They had actually happened.

"I am most terribly sorry for Johann Moritz," said Nora. "So he is the hero of your first chapter. Who will be the hero of the second?"

"I don't know yet," said Traian. "Perhaps my father or my mother, or you, perhaps, or I—in any case, it will certainly be one of us."

"And will all the chapters be like the one about Johann Moritz?" she asked. "In the whole of your novel, is there not one single lucky star, one 'happy ending'?"

"Not one," he answered. "After the death of the white rabbits there can be no 'happy ending.' There can only be a few hours before all is over."

(BOOK TWO)

⊂╪ ⊂╪ ⊂╪

JOHANN MORITZ had already spent two hours in Hungary. The four of them, scared to go into the waiting room, had hung about at the back of the railway station. Then the train came in. Dr. Abramovici, Strul, and Hurtig climbed into a second-class carriage. Johann stayed behind on the platform to hand them up the luggage through the window. Just as the train began to move, he managed to jump up onto the carriage step. Hurtig caught hold of his hand, pulled him in, and shut the door. Johann was pale with fright—one second more and he would have been left behind on the platform. He had had visions of himself, stranded, all alone in Hungary, without the help of Dr. Abramovici and the others. He thanked God he had caught the train.

Dr. Abramovici and Hurtig found seats immediately. Strul and Johann looked into all the compartments, but the lights were out, the travelers fast asleep, and all the seats taken, so they sat on their cases in the corridor. After a while, a woman got out, and Strul took her place in the compartment. Johann was left alone in the corridor. Dr. Abramovici opened the door of the compartment and said to him:

"Don't go to sleep, or they might steal our luggage."

"I'll stay awake," he answered, but as soon as the doctor had shut the door, Johann fell asleep. He was dead tired. He did not open his eyes again until they were in Budapest.

By the time they got out of the train it was daylight. Johann was thirsty, but Hurtig would not allow him to go into the refreshment room for a glass of lemonade. He told him that the police might spot him and find out that he had escaped from Romania and arrest all four of them.

"You can have a glass of water at my sister's," said Dr. Abramovici. They moved on. Outside the station they paused for a moment near a row of waiting cars and cabs.

"Better to walk," said Hurtig. "The cab driver might denounce us. It would be a pity to end up at the police station now that we have got as far as Budapest."

They set off on foot. Johann had suitcases slung on his shoulders and in both hands. They were very heavy, but he found them easier to carry now than he had the night before, when they had been cutting across the fields this side of the frontier. I suppose it seems easier because I am walking on a hard surface, he thought, planting the soles of his bare feet on the cold asphalt. The trams were not yet running. Johann saw the electric streets lamps go out by themselves and asked Hurtig who had switched them off.

"Can't you stop speaking Romanian, you blockhead?" said Hurtig angrily. "If anyone hears us speaking Romanian, they'll have us all locked up."

"Aren't we allowed to speak Romanian?"

"We're allowed to, all right," said Hurtig. "But over here Romanians get put into concentration camps. Hungary considers Romania her enemy, you see."

"And what do we speak, then?"

"Yiddish," said Dr. Abramovici. "Jews are not persecuted

here as they are in Romania. To date, at least, there has been no legislation against them."

Johann took care not to speak a word of Romanian, but he could not speak Yiddish, either. He was too tired. By the time they reached the house of Dr. Abramovici's sister, who lived in Petofi Street, Johann was reeling under the weight of the cases. He put them down on the doorstep. The maid came down and helped him carry them upstairs. Her name was Julisca. Johann followed her into the kitchen. She had a blue dress on. Johann thought he had seen it before somewhere. Then he remembered that Susanna used to wear one like it.

᠅ ᠅ ᠅

DR. ABRAMOVICI'S sister was a stout woman. She was wearing a housecoat with a red floral pattern. She chattered quickly and incessantly. She called Johann into the room where Dr. Abramovici, Hurtig, Strul, and Isaac Nagy, the doctor's brother-in-law, were sitting and gave them each a glass of brandy. Johann remained standing. There were not enough chairs to go round. The doctor's sister brought in tea and put it on the table. She glanced at Johann and said:

"There isn't room for you in here. You'd better go and drink your tea in the kitchen."

"That's fine," said Isaac Nagy in Hungarian. "We have a few things to discuss among ourselves."

Johann understood that the gentlemen did not like sitting down at table with him. But he did not take offense. Julisca was glad he had not stayed inside with the gentry. She poured out successively three mugs of tea for him with plenty of sugar and lemon. Then she cut him some thick slices of bread and butter and ham. Johann was ravenous and ate like a horse. Then he wanted to have a wash, but she said:

"Come along with me to the market first. You can clean yourself up when we get back."

Johann took the basket and went shopping with Julisca. Every morning after that he went with her to market.

When he came back from shopping he chopped firewood and brought the logs into the kitchen. After dinner he helped Julisca with the washing up. She was a cheerful soul and was always making jokes. Johann liked being in the house.

❧ ❧ ❧

WHAT with the work in the kitchen and Julisca's jokes, Johann hardly noticed that he had not seen Dr. Abramovici and the others all day. At lunchtime, when he asked about them, the doctor's sister told him the gentlemen were asleep. Then he forgot to ask again. Night came, and it was only when he was already in bed that he realized he had not seen them all day long. They had, however, been in for meals. He was sure of that because he had washed up their plates after lunch. They were in for tea, too, because he had washed up five cups. But at dinner he could not remember how many knives and forks and plates had been brought out to the kitchen. Julisca had stacked a pile of plates in the sink, and he had not counted them. It worried him so much that he could not go to sleep. He had a suspicion that in the evening there had been fewer plates to wash up.

Hurtig must have gone off to his relations, he thought. He was sorry Hurtig had gone. Then it occurred to him that perhaps he had only imagined there had been less washing up at dinner. But next morning Johann found he had been right. Hurtig had left in the afternoon and had not been back to dinner at Isaac Nagy's house. But Dr. Abramovici and Strul were still there. About ten o'clock Julisca brought down their shoes to be cleaned. He worked on them with cream and polish till they shone. He was just going to take them back into the house when Julisca stopped him on the threshold. She took the shoes out of his hands and carried them in herself. Coming back, she explained:

"Madam has ordered me not to let you in. She's like that, you know. She's always afraid of having things stolen."

❧ ❧ ❧

IN THE afternoon Dr. Abramovici called Johann into the dining room.

"Take these cases and come along with me," he ordered. Johann was glad. He had been certain the doctor would send for him and had not forgotten him.

"Why do you go around barefoot?" the doctor asked with some annoyance when they reached the street.

Johann felt ashamed of having no shoes. He looked round and saw no one else with bare feet. The rest of the way he kept his head down, looking carefully at the feet of all the passers-by. They were all wearing shoes or boots. Johann was so ashamed that he wished the earth would swallow him up. He tried to apologize to the doctor, but Dr. Abramovici was walking on ahead, with his hands in his pockets, as if he had nothing to do with him.

❧ ❧ ❧

THEY stopped at the gate of an old house with a front garden full of flowers. The doctor took the cases and went in alone. Johann stayed outside and waited. He read the signboard, which said "Consulate." Then he turned his attention to the people passing in the street.

Dr. Abramovici did not stay in there very long. He came

down the steps smiling and without his luggage. But when his eyes fell on Johann, who stood leaning against the wall, waiting for him, his smile died on his lips. He stopped, put his hands in his pockets, and thought for a while, screwing up his eyebrows. He did not once open his mouth all the way home. Johann walked a few paces behind him so that people should not guess that the doctor was in the company of a man who had no shoes. Not for anything would Johann have made a laughingstock of Dr. Abramovici.

In front of Isaac Nagy's house the doctor paused, waiting for Johann to come up with him. He said:

"Jankl, your case is extremely complicated. The Jewish community of Budapest, which is obtaining papers for us to go to America, is not prepared to do anything for you. I told them you had come with us; I begged them to help you, but it was no use. Their reply was that they did not provide passports for Christians. The Committee deals exclusively with Jews. That is why it is called the Jewish Committee. And you are not a Jew, are you?"

"No, sir, I am not."

"They are quite right," Abramovici went on, "though I am sorry about it. I wanted to take you with me to America. But take my word for it, I won't let you down, I'm not the sort of fellow to do that."

The doctor took out his wallet and started counting out bills. Johann looked at the Hungarian bills and was surprised to find them so small.

"Here is twenty pengö," said the doctor. "That's for carrying my luggage. It's a lot of money. Here in Hungary you have to work for a whole week to earn so much, and you have earned it merely by carrying a few suitcases for a couple of hours."

Johann had never thought of demanding payment for carrying the luggage. He had not done it for money. But the doctor was still holding his hand out. Johann took the bills and stuffed them away in his pocket.

"The main thing is that I got you out of that camp and brought you here," said Dr. Abramovici. "Without our help, who knows how long you would have gone on rotting there? But I don't expect you to pay for that. I am not the sort of man to go exacting payment for services rendered to others when they are in a mess."

☙ ☙ ☙

JOHANN had now been in Hungary for a week. He went on doing the same work he had done from the first. He would go to market with Julisca, hew firewood, empty out the garbage, and do the washing up. In the evening he would scrub the kitchen floor and clean the bathroom and the stairs.

On Sunday morning Isaac Nagy came across Johann in the hall and said harshly:

"Haven't you found any work yet? You've been staying in my house for over a week now. I hope you don't expect to go on living on my charity indefinitely."

Isaac Nagy went off without another word. Johann wished he had looked for work before. He had not even thought of it. He had considered himself employed in the household. "How could I have been so stupid as not to look for work?" he asked himself. "These people are right. They can't go on feeding me forever."

That evening Johann spoke to Julisca about it, and she promised to find him a job. She knew somebody who worked in the chocolate factory.

"Then perhaps you'll bring me some chocolate," she said. "Unless you find some other girl to give it to."

"What other girl?" said Johann, feeling hurt that Julisca should even have thought of such a thing. "Every bit of chocolate I get I'll bring to you. I won't touch any of it myself."

That night Johann dreamed he was already working in the

chocolate factory. Next morning Dr. Abramovici came to take leave of his sister and brother-in-law. Johann carried his luggage to the station and put it in a sleeping car.

"Are you going far?" he asked.

"Switzerland," answered the doctor. "I shall have a few weeks' rest before going to the United States."

In saying good-by, Dr. Abramovici shook hands with him. Johann felt he was going as red as a beetroot. All the gentlemen on the platform had seen Dr. Abramovici shake hands with him, a man who went about barefoot.

As the train pulled out, Abramovici shouted out of the window:

"Good-by, my dear Jankl. I won't forget you. I'll do something to get you out of here."

"Good-by," Johann called back. As soon as the train was out of sight, tears came into Johann's eyes. He felt alone in the world. Hurtig and Strul had vanished without even saying good-by. And now the doctor had gone, too. He stood there on the platform for a long time. Never before in his life had he felt so completely a stranger. Then he remembered the chocolate factory. He brightened up at once and started back for Petofi Street. "As soon as I have a job," he said to himself, "I'll buy Julisca a bead necklace."

🌱 🌱 🌱

JOHANN and Julisca set out for market earlier than usual. They quickly bought the meat and vegetables and whatever else they needed for the house and then turned down a street lined with small houses. Johann carried the basket on his right arm and with his left he held Julisca. They were walking very fast.

"The chocolate factory is at the other end of the town," said Julisca. "We'll have to hurry." They were both red and sweating. If they got back too late Julisca would not have time to cook lunch. She had spoken to a man from her village, and he had told her to bring Johann along one morning and let him have a word with the boss. "If he comes, he'll be taken on at once since we are short of men," he had said.

"Maybe they'll take me on right away," said Johann, trying to force a passage through a crowd of people who had gathered at the street corner. "If they do, then next Friday I'll get my first week's wages. And perhaps some chocolate for you." He squeezed her hand tightly. They looked at one another and laughed.

"Then I'll take a room," he said. "I can't go on being a burden on your employers. I'll look for a room somewhere near the factory."

"Shall I be able to come and see you there?" asked Julisca. He did not hear what she said. He was peering ahead to find out why everyone was standing about in crowds, but he could not make anything out. Hundreds of people were crowding together, jostling against one another, and it was impossible to get by. Julisca stopped as well and tried to see what was happening. She remembered that they were in a hurry.

"Let's go another way," she said. "Otherwise I won't have time to prepare lunch."

They turned back, going even faster in order to make up for lost time. Across the end of the road there was a police cordon. Julisca glanced at the men out of the corner of her eye and hurried past them.

"Soldiers and policemen are the most vulgar men in the world," she said. "I should never marry a policeman." She turned round to see if Johann had heard. But he was no longer behind her. Julisca looked back, trying to pick him out among the crowd. She caught sight of him. He was standing by the policemen, beckoning to her. She went toward him. Now she understood why he had not followed her. They were caught in a roundup. The police had set up a road block and were checking identity papers before letting people pass. Women were not required to produce papers, and that was why she had been allowed to walk through. She remembered that Johann had no papers on him and she was afraid. She pushed her way back through the cordon. One of the policemen tried to pinch her arm, but she wrenched herself free and pushed on toward Johann. He was in an isolated group which was being shepherded in the direction of a truck by police with fixed bayonets. Johann was holding the basket up over his head so that she should see it and come for it. She saw it easily enough, but she could not get any nearer. The policemen had barred her way. By now she had already caught sight of Johann. She explained to them that she must get the basket with the day's shopping. But they either would not listen to her or else did not understand what she wanted. She shouted and swore at them, but it was no good. They still would not let her come near. Johann had climbed into the truck. He hung the basket over the side, still hoping Julisca would be able to come and fetch it. Then the truck drove off. He set the basket with the vegetables down between his knees, thinking: Mrs. Nagy will thrash Julisca if she goes home without her basket. He would have jumped out of the truck to take it to her, but it was impossible. At either end of the bench there were men with fixed bayonets. Looking at them, he forgot about the vegetable basket and began to realize that he was under arrest.

✿ ✿ ✿

FOUR weeks had passed since the day Johann and Julisca had been separated by the crowds in the street. During all this time he had had no news from the outside world. He had not even seen the sun. The windows of his cell faced north onto a courtyard with high gray walls that shut out the sky. Throughout the four weeks he had not breathed a breath of fresh air. The other prisoners were allowed exercise in the prison yard for an hour every day. He could hear them leaving the neighboring cells and coming back later. He knew they had been out in the open. He could tell it by the sound of their footsteps.

Now, however, there was silence in the corridors. It was not yet daylight. He opened his eyes with difficulty. He put his hands to his eyelids and felt how swollen they were. Blood had clotted on them, and they felt rough to the touch. He could not remember when he had come back to his cell. They must have carried me here, he thought. Every day he had been beaten. Sometimes he could not see where he was treading when they brought him back. Lately, more often than not, they had carried him back, and for hours on end he had not been able to stir. But until today he always recalled the exact moment they stopped beating him, carried him back, and stretched him out on his bed in the cell. This morning for the first time he could not remember anything. They must have made short work of it last night, he thought. It was as if he spoke of some other person, a stranger. He passed his hand over his face. He could feel a rough and bushy beard. Blood had stuck to his mustache, eyebrows, and hair. Even now the clots of it were rough and brittle to the touch, like parched earth. He passed his tongue over his lips to moisten them. They, too, were swollen and hurt like boils about to burst. He had violent toothache. So far they had knocked out four of his front teeth. This happened one day after some brutal punches on the jaw. He had spat the teeth out along with the blood, like cherry stones. He had felt the same pains then as now. "If they knocked out some more teeth last night, I won't be able to chew my bread any longer," he said to himself. But he did not bother to investigate with his tongue whether there were any fresh gaps in his mouth. The tiniest movement made him wince. He shut his eyes once more. Time passed. Along the corridor, footsteps were approaching, but he did not make his usual effort to distinguish what kinds of footsteps they were, where they were going, and whence they had come. His whole body was battered and bruised, and his very thoughts were benumbed. When they came to fetch him for questioning and he got out of bed onto the floor of his cell, he could have screamed. The soles of both his feet had swollen like fresh loaves. He could not recall having been struck on the soles. The guard knocked him toward the door, and so he left the cell. For a few brief seconds the pain in his back where the guard had hit him made him forget his smarting soles. But soon he was aware of them again. At every step it was as if someone were tearing off a strip of his flesh.

The office of Inspector Varga, who did the interrogating, was one hundred paces away. At the thought of having to walk every one of those hundred paces with his swollen feet, he broke down and sank to the ground. They had advanced only a few yards from the cell. The guard lifted him by the armpits and carried him the rest of the way. His body was as light as a little child's. All the weight there was came from his bones and skin: there was no longer any question of flesh and fat.

๛ ๛ ๛

AT THE time of his arrest, Johann had made a statement describing in detail how he had come to Hungary. The police did not believe him. They had beaten him up to get the truth out of him, but after the beating he had told the same story. And so they had begun all over again. He had been removed to the Hungarian secret-service prison. Every day he was first questioned and then beaten up.

"Why were you sent to Hungary?" asked the Inspector.

"I wasn't sent by anyone," he answered.

"You declared that an adjutant drove you to the frontier in an army truck."

"Yes, the adjutant was called Apostol Constantin; he was our Camp Commandant. He was a friend of Dr. Abramovici's and came with us so that the patrols should not hold us up."

"That was no other than Major Jon Tanase of the Romanian secret service," said the Inspector. "We know he operates in this sector. He sends agents over every month, and you are one of them. We want to know why he sent you. What is your mission?"

Johann lowered his eyes.

"I have told you the truth," he said, thinking the moment had almost come for him to be led to the torture chamber in the basement. His body was beginning to ache already in anticipation.

"Don't you realize the game is up?" asked the Inspector. "It is senseless to keep on with it. You have stated that you spent eighteen months in a Jewish camp in Romania."

"I did."

"You never set foot in one; you are Romanian."

"I am Romanian," said Johann.

"You were trying to pass yourself off as a Jew in Hungary," said the Inspector. "And to make us believe it you invented this tale about a camp. Furthermore, you have stated that you crossed the frontier in the company of three Jews."

"That is true."

"That is not true. You came alone. And you never stayed in Isaac Nagy's house. The Nagys have had no one to stay with them for the last six months. You thought we would take you on at your word, without checking up, didn't you? I have before me written statements from Mr. and Mrs. Nagy. They have never heard of you. Mrs. Rosa Nagy has no brother who is a doctor."

"They said they did not know me?" asked Johann. "Mrs. Nagy can't have said that. I used to work for her in the house, I used to go shopping with Julisca, I used to wash up . . ."

He began to cry. The Inspector shouted:

"And yet another lie. Rosa Nagy never had a maid called Julisca. If you intended to tell lies you'd have done better to have found out the name of Mrs. Nagy's servant." The Inspector was laughing. "I have questioned the servant, too. She has been in Mrs. Nagy's service for the last eight years. You have made up all that stuff about Julisca to put us off the track. Or was it Major Tanase who taught you this tale about Julisca?"

Johann shut his eyes, waiting to hear the call for the guard who took him down to the torture chamber. He wished to stop thinking altogether. But the idea that Mrs. Nagy had stated that she did not know him preyed on his mind. He could not bring himself to believe it.

He heard the door open. But the approaching footsteps were not those of the sentry who usually escorted him downstairs. He opened his eyes and found Isaac Nagy standing before him. He was dressed in a new, coffee-colored suit and did not even glance at him.

"Do you know this person?" asked the Inspector.

"I've never seen him before in my life," answered Nagy, coolly measuring Johann up and down.

"Have three Jewish refugees from Romania ever stayed at your house?" asked the Inspector.

"Apart from my wife, myself, and our servant, no one has slept in our house for some years."

"Thank you," said the Inspector.

Isaac Nagy was shown out. Immediately afterward, his wife came in. She, too, denied having known or ever having set eyes on Johann before.

"Have you a brother who is a doctor in Romania?"

"I am an only child," she said.

The Inspector gave Johann a withering look and then went on:

"Have you ever employed a servant by the name of Julisca?"

"Never," she answered. "We have had the same servant ever since we came to Budapest eight years ago, and her name is Josefina."

Mrs. Nagy went out of the room smiling. After her came an old woman who said she was called Josefina and had been the servant of the Nagy family for the last eight years.

The Inspector was once again left alone with Johann.

"Surely after that you will give in and confess you were lying," he said. "Tell me the truth: why were you sent to Hungary?"

Johann Moritz started crying.

☙ ☙ ☙

FROM Inspector Varga's room, Johann was taken straight to the torture chamber. This was the daily routine. But never before had he felt so afraid. The light hit him in the eyes the moment he came in. In this room there was always a dazzling chalky-white glare. The lamps were large and powerful. Johann shut his eyes, but the light burned his cheeks like fire.

"Get undressed," commanded the guard with a laugh.

This was one of the two fat men with a mustache whom he always found sitting playing cards at the table. Johann started undoing the collar of his shirt. When he did not undress quickly enough, one of the men would strike him over the face with a whip. He knew that. But his fingers were swollen, and he had trouble in feeling for the small buttons on the shirt. He was in absolute terror of keeping the men waiting. Never before had he felt so petrified at the thought of the whip. He glanced furtively toward the two guards. They were too engrossed in their game to notice the slowness of his movements. He managed to take off his shirt. He did not have to take off his trousers. He stood there facing a rack of iron rods rather like those used for cleaning the barrels of firearms. They were arranged in a row according to size. The ones on the left were as thick as a man's thumb—then came others getting gradually thinner. There were two rods in each size, and there were twenty sizes. He had never counted them before. The thinnest at the extreme right of the rack was as slender as a cornstalk. He knew the exact degree of pain that each one of these rods could inflict.

"To work, my boy!" commanded one of the men, getting up and leaving the cards scattered over the table. "No work, no pay."

Johann watched him stretch his limbs. He wore a close-fitting white sweater and appeared sleepy. The second guard put out his cigarette and looked at Johann.

"Well, what about telling us today who sent you here?" The guard spoke calmly. He might have been asking Johann for a match to light his cigarette. When he had finished speaking he yawned and stretched his arms just as the other man had done.

"Nobody sent me," Johann answered.

Simultaneously, the two men turned toward him. They started as if they had been touched with a red-hot poker. Their eyes flashed with anger. Johann began to tremble. One of the men came up to him and dealt him first one blow to his jaw, then a second. Johann's jaw lost all sense of feeling. The other man caught hold of him by the shoulders and laid him out face downward on a bench near the rack. Then he straddled his back and sat down astride. Every time the guard climbed on his back Johann feared he was going to die of suffocation. But today he wanted to die. He felt pinned to the boards of the bench, his ribs digging into his chest, like so many spikes. His lungs were crushed beneath the weight of the man on his back as though beneath a millstone.

"What did you say?" asked the guard who had hit him under the chin. The other guard did not answer. Johann felt the first blow on the soles of his feet. He tried to draw them up, but the man who was sitting astride his back caught hold of them and pinned them down to the bench. Then came the second blow. It was from one of the thicker rods. His soles were no longer burning. He now felt the pain only in his head. Later on, when the blows began to fall regularly, he felt them not in his head but in his chest. Then in his shoulders. After that he felt nothing. His body seemed to have gone numb. But this did not last long. He began to feel sharp cuts on his soles like slashes from a knife. Those were the fine rods. He felt the repercussions of the blows in his knees and even more in his kidneys. He lost control of his bladder and his stomach. The blows came down as thick as hail. Johann felt sick. A yellow light appeared before his eyes, and he began to vomit the food he had taken. His wet trousers stuck to his skin. The bread and water he had swallowed refused to stay in his stomach.

Johann felt he was merging into the yellow light before his eyes. A bitter greenish fluid had welled up in his mouth. Liquid matter began to leave his body by the nose, the mouth, and the other apertures. The liquids were mingled with a green froth like the spittle of a toad. Johann was now hovering on the utmost verge of life. His mind alone was still conscious. The guard was hitting him with even finer rods, but he no longer felt anything.

His very blood, no longer able to endure the blows, was striving to escape from his tormented frame. It burst forth through all the gates that were open. It abandoned his body through his mouth, his nose, his ears, and it mingled with his urine. It was even breaking out through the pores of his skin. It had to escape. At all costs and by every means.

❦ ❦ ❦

WHEN he came to, Johann remembered yesterday's confrontation with Isaac and Rosa Nagy.

"If only they had told the truth, the Inspector would have let me go. They would not have tortured me so much yesterday."

Never before had he had such a beating up. From the soles

of his feet to the crown of his head his whole body was but one open bleeding wound.

"Isaac Nagy said he did not know me. He looked straight at me and said he had never seen me before. And his wife the same." He remembered how he had cleaned Isaac Nagy's shoes every morning, cut wood, and scrubbed the kitchen floor at Mrs. Nagy's orders. How could they have said such a thing? Johann wondered. They even pretended they had never seen Julisca and had never had a servant by that name.

Johann had reached the limits of his endurance. He knew that he was enfeebled in body and mind and that both yesterday and the day before yesterday he had not been able to remember when and how he had got back to his cell. That was because of the blows. Nevertheless, he was *positive* that he had lived in Isaac Nagy's house. He was positive that Julisca was the servant there. And yet Isaac Nagy had said *no.* His wife had said *no.* He had heard them with his own ears, saying *No, no, no.*

Johann Moritz shut his eyes.

ͳͳ ͳͳ ͳͳ

AFTER a while they came to fetch him yet again. He began to tremble. For the first time he made up his mind to kill himself. These tortures were past bearing. The guard left the door open and remained on the threshold. Through his half-closed eyes, Johann could see him grinning.

"Get up," said the guard.

Johann had a vision of Inspector Varga. He heard his voice. Then he saw the torture chamber, the rack with its array of iron rods, and he felt the whole weight of the guard astride his back. His lips pleaded, half whispering:

"No."

"Get up," ordered the guard.

Johann did not hear him. It was as if he were dead.

The guard came over to his bed and pulled him to his feet. "No, not today. Question me and torture me tomorrow, if you like. And the day after, and every day to the end of my life. But not today."

"Today you're going to be released," said the guard. Johann did not believe him. He had stopped believing anything.

And yet on that day he was released from the prison. But he was not set free altogether. Being a Romanian citizen, he was sent to a labor camp.

🐜 🐜 🐜

BEFORE he left prison he received a letter from Julisca. The guard from Inspector Varga's office had come into his cell and handed it to him just as Johann was going. The letter was written in Julisca's own hand.

DEAR JANOS,

I have been out of my situation for four days. I am writing to tell you not to come and look for me in Petofi Street when they let you out. I am going to the country to stay with my mother in the district of Balaton, in the province of Tisza, where I'll be waiting for you with much love. Do come as soon as you are out of prison.

JULISCA

Underneath, in the right-hand corner, she had scribbled in haste:

Yesterday I went to fetch my things from the Nagys'. Mr. and Mrs. Nagy ask you not to be angry with them for declaring to the Inspector that they did not know you. Jews are beginning to be arrested in town. They were afraid to admit that they had harbored refugees in their house. They send you their best regards. Mr. Nagy gave me a suit for you. It is almost new, and I am keeping it for you till you come. He is very nice, and so is Mrs. Nagy. Don't be angry with them. They were afraid of being arrested, and that is why they said they did not know you. Such are the times. Fear would make one kill one's own grandmother. I send you a kiss.

JULISCA

☙ ☙ ☙

FOR three whole hours the Hungarian Cabinet had been in secret session at Regency Palace. Though the conference was over, the Foreign Minister again rose to his feet.

"The problem of the fifty thousand workers has not yet been solved," he said. "And it is the most important of all."

"The matter has been settled," retorted the Premier firmly. "We have reached a unanimous decision."

The ministers had picked up their brief cases, ready to go. The Foreign Minister appeared not to notice this and went on:

"We must yield somewhere, there can be no doubt about it," he said. "The balance between ourselves and Germany must be maintained. We are not on terms of equality. However unwillingly, we are still compelled to face the fact that Hungary's position with regard to the Third Reich is in practice that of a subordinate and not of an ally. And the only alternative is submitting to military occupation, which would put us in a worse position than ever. In the first instance we were required to furnish three hundred thousand workers. After protracted negotiations this number has been reduced to fifty thousand, but this minimum must be forthcoming."

"My government will not hand over a single Hungarian citizen for slave labor," said the Premier hotly.

"Germany sets great store by her demand," said the Foreign Minister. "It was sent in the form of an ultimatum. Their industry is in desperate need of man power. If we do not furnish at least fifty thousand men our refusal may prove fatal. I have been informed that if the demand is rejected, the military occupation of Hungary must be considered imminent. It is my duty to make this clear to you. The responsibility lies in your hands, gentlemen."

"Couldn't we work a compromise, perhaps?" suggested a minister.

"Were we required to send but one single Hungarian to Germany as a slave, it would in no way alleviate the gravity of the situation; and in addition, history would never forgive such an action," said the Premier. "Our answer must consequently be a categorical refusal. In this field there can be no compromise."

"We might send the Germans fifty thousand workers who are not Hungarian citizens," said the Minister of the Interior. "We have more than three hundred thousand aliens interned in Hungary. Why not send them?"

"I object to this solution," said the Foreign Minister. "It would only complicate matters. It is contrary to international law where political prisoners and internees are concerned. We need the sympathy of other nations. Were we to adopt this solution the honor of the Hungarian Crown of Saint Stephen would be stained irremediably. Furthermore, we should conjure up an undending series of new enemies."

In half an hour a compromise solution was arrived at. It was decided to send to Germany fifty thousand non-Hungarian workers whose nationality was to some extent uncertain. The Minister of the Interior undertook to screen the workers in such a way as to make it impossible to prove that any one of them belonged to a specific foreign power.

"In this way we save our Magyar blood," said the Minister of the Interior. "History will not be able to accuse us of sending Hungarians into slavery. The worthiness and nobility of our aim will induce history to forgive us the means employed to attain it."

❦ ❦ ❦   I

Count Bartholy, chief of the Hungarian press, went into his
office and called for his secretary. He intended to dictate an
official communiqué concerning the decisions taken in the
course of the secret session of the Cabinet.

"Anyone who is denied the right to honor and self-respect
is a slave," said the Count to himself. "But nowadays anyone
who tries to live a moral life signs his own death warrant. Our
society denies man his personal honor and self-respect, that is
to say, his freedom to live. It tolerates him only if he lives as a
slave. But this state of things cannot last. A society in which
everybody—from a Prime Minister to a street cleaner—is a slave
must inevitably collapse. And the quicker it does, the better
for all."

"Did you say something, sir?" asked the secretary coming
into the room.

"No," he said. "Take this down, please: Official communiqué: In the course of yesterday's private session of the
Cabinet it was decided to grant special facilities for visas and
travel to Hungarian workers desirous of going to Germany in
order to specialize in particular branches of heavy industry. The
number of workers to whom special facilities will be granted
has been provisionally restricted to fifty thousand."

The secretary got up.

"Dispatch it to the papers," said Count Bartholy, "with instructions to have it printed on the front page."

❦ ❦ ❦

That evening Count Bartholy dined with his son, who was also
his principal private secretary. Over coffee the Count asked
his son:

"What do you think about this business of sending workers to Germany?"

"A real K.O. in the political ring," said Lucian. "A masterly performance. Instead of sending the Germans Hungarian workers we merely pack off a few thousand foreigners, scraped together from prisons and concentration camps. What a first-rate smack in the eye for German arrogance. A stroke of genius."

"Did you know that in exchange for these workers we are getting certain advantages from the Germans?" asked the Count. "Or to put it more clearly, did you know that we are to receive payment for these fifty thousand men?"

"That goes without saying!" said Lucian. "Do you expect us to hand over workers to the Germans without asking for something in return?"

"And don't you feel insulted at your father's having been a party today to the sale of human beings?" asked the Count. "This kind of transaction is the last stage on the road to moral decadence."

"You are funny, Father," said Lucian. "Is that why you have been in such low spirits all evening?"

"Don't avoid the question," said the Count. "Do you or don't you admit that today I have been a party to white slavery?"

"If you choose to look at it that way, all right then, you were a party to white slavery," said Lucian, smiling.

"And it doesn't disturb you?"

"It would be idiotic to let it disturb me," said Lucian. "Anyway, I'm sure there must be something else upsetting you besides. The whole business is far too insignificant to worry over, even for a moment. We were forced to send workers to Germany. If we had not acted the way we did, we should have had to send Hungarians. Now that would really have been serious."

"Granted, it would have been more serious from the Hungarian point of view," said the Count. "From the human point of view, however, there is no difference. We have sold the Germans human beings."

"Nothing but inevitable political necessity, Father. It is bound to happen."

"Europe stamped out the slave trade several hundred years ago. The last slaves to be sold were the Negroes in America. Throughout the world today it is illegal to traffic in slaves. The abolition of slavery is one of the greatest achievements of our civilization. The school textbooks are full of it. And now we have put the clock right back and are once again trading in human beings. We have taken a sudden leap out of the twentieth century back into the pre-Christian era, skipping right over the Renaissance and the Middle Ages."

"One must not take things so tragically, Father," said Lucian. "After all, these workers aren't going to be bound hand and foot. They are only going to Germany to work there."

"They are not put into chains for the simple reason that they have no possibility of escaping. Contemporary society has methods of keeping a tight hold on its slaves that the Greeks never dreamed of. I don't only mean machine guns and electrified barbed-wire fences, but all the other methods at the disposal of modern technocracy—ration cards, permits to live in hotels, to travel by train, to walk up and down the streets, to move from one place to another. Neither the Greeks nor the Egyptians would have put their slaves in chains if they had had the automatic means of control at the disposal of modern society. But the slavery itself remains unchanged."

"I wouldn't worry too much," said Lucian. "There is nothing we can do about it. We have no alternative—almost every country in Europe has sold slaves to Germany—Romania, Yugoslavia, France, Italy, Norway. The only thing we personally could do would be to withdraw from the government and fight against Germany because she purchases slaves and forces other countries to sell them. Upon which, another government would come into power and slaves would be sent to Germany just the same. And even supposing we could destroy the German Reich, the problem would still remain unsolved. The Russians would take the place of the Germans, and the Russians are the biggest slave traders in the world. In Soviet Russia every man is the recognized property of the state."

"And you are not appalled by this state of affairs?" asked the Count.

"No."

"That is even more serious," said the Count. "It means that you have lost all respect for human beings. And you yourself are a human being. This means that you no longer respect yourself."

"I respect every man according to his worth," said Lucian. "I trust you are not going to reproach me on that score."

"You respect man just as you would respect a car in proportion to its precise market value."

"What's wrong with that?" asked Lucian.

"But do you respect man as man, for his intrinsic human value?"

"Of course I do. I should never be able to hurt anyone without feeling sorry and guilty."

"But then you wouldn't hurt a dog, either, without feeling sorry for it, because you know that if you whip it, it will suffer. That is pitying man as you would any living animal. What I want to know is whether you respect man as such, as of value in himself, unique, and irreplaceable, even when the individual in question has no utility value and when he arouses neither your pity nor your love for him as an animal."

"I have never asked myself that question," said Lucian. "I know that I respect man in proportion to his social value and as a living animal. Everybody thinks and feels the way I do."

"Are you sure, Lucian, that nowadays everybody thinks and feels the way you do?"

"Quite sure," said Lucian. "It is the only possible logical

conclusion. Man is a unit of social value. Everything else is pure hypothesis."

"That is extremely serious."

"What's so serious about it?"

"Our civilization, Lucian, has disappeared. It had three qualities; in the first place, it loved and respected the beautiful, a habit acquired from the Greeks; in the second place, it loved and respected the law, a habit acquired from the Romans; in the third place, it loved and respected man, a habit acquired very late and with much difficulty from Christianity. It was only by respecting these three great symbols, man, the beautiful, and the law, that our Western civilization achieved what it did. Now it has lost the most important heritage of all, the respect and love for man. Without this respect and love, Western culture must cease to exist. It is dead."

"In the course of history man has been through much blacker periods than ours," said Lucian. "He has been burned alive in public squares and on altars, broken on the wheel, sold and treated like a thing. We have no right to be so hard on our own age."

"Very true," said the Count. "In those dark times man was disregarded and despised, and human sacrifice was celebrated out of barbarism. But we had conquered barbarism; we had just begun to appreciate man; we were just starting out on a new epoch. But the emergence of a Technological Civilization has meanwhile destroyed what we had achieved and won through centuries of civilization. Technological Civilization has reintroduced human sacrifice and the disregard for man. Today man is reduced to the single dimension of his social value. . . . Shall we go?" asked the Count. "It is late."

Lucian looked at his watch.

"My watch has stopped," he said. "Can you tell me what time it is, Father?"

"It is twenty-five o'clock."

"I don't understand," said Lucian.

"I can well believe it. No one wants to understand. It is the twenty-fifth hour—the 'now' of European civilization."

🌱 🌱 🌱

"THEY'VE sold you to the Germans, old man," said the foreman, grinning broadly at Johann. "I wonder how much the Hungarians got in return for your hide? You aren't worth much, you know. About one case of cartridges, I should think. I heard the Germans don't pay cash. They send arms and ammunition instead. I don't suppose they'd have given more than one case of cartridges for you. One case of cartridges for the lot: skin, bones, flesh, and all." The foreman slapped him on the back and laughed. "Not a bad price. The Russians wouldn't have paid as much. Their scale of prices for human beings is even lower."

Johann did not appreciate the joke. But he said nothing. The foreman was a student from Bucharest. He, too, had been interned by the Hungarians, and they had been working together on the defenses for eight months. Johann knew the student was fond of making caustic remarks, but he was not a bad fellow at heart.

"So you don't believe you've been sold, eh?" asked the student.

"Of course not," answered Johann. "Men can be shut up in concentration camps or prisons, put to hard labor, tortured, or killed, but they can't be sold."

"None the less, they've sold you, Moritz," said the student. "I'll swear by all the gods the Hungarians have sold us to the Germans; you and me and every Romanian, Serb, and Ruthenian in the camp. They even drew up a deed of sale for fifty thousand heads."

The student walked away. Johann thought over what he had just heard. "He must be pulling my leg," he said to himself. "It can't be true." But all day long the student's words preyed on his mind. He could not stop thinking that the Germans had bought him and had paid for him with a case of cartridges. But on thinking it over he decided that it was stupid of him to believe such a thing.

Their camp was on the frontier between Hungary and Romania. They were digging trenches, and more than half the work still lay ahead. According to Antim, the student, the Hungarians needed at least another ten months to complete the defenses in this sector. To speed up the work they kept bringing in more and more internees. They even sent along some convicts branded with a red-hot iron. The shortage of labor was acute. Nevertheless, one day they received marching orders. All the Romanians and Serbs from Johann's camp were packed into a train and taken away. The Hungarians, it was rumored, were dissatisfied with the way the Romanians and Serbs had worked and were replacing them with Ukrainians in order to polish off the job quicker.

Antim maintained that they were being sent to Germany because they had been sold. A few other Romanians backed him up, but the majority—including Johann—refused to believe it.

One morning Johann got out of the train during one of its halts. There were no lavatories on the train, and they all had to wait till the train stopped. Then they would scramble over the embankments and relieve themselves while the sentries stood guard over them. This time the train had stopped in the open country. It was raining. Johann did not climb straight back in, but hung about for a while beside the train. Looking more carefully at it, he noticed that something had been chalked up on every car. He went up close to the first one and read in German: HUNGARIAN WORKERS SALUTE THEIR COLLEAGUES OF THE GREATER GERMAN REICH. On the second car was written: HUNGARIANS ARE COMING TO WORK FOR THE VICTORY OF THE AXIS.

Johann began to fear that they were indeed being sent to Germany. Further on, the inscription read: HUNGARIAN WORKERS ARE HELPING TO BUILD THE NEW ORDER IN EUROPE. Johann called Antim over and showed him the slogans.

"Now aren't you convinced at last that the Hungarians have sold us to the Germans?" asked the student.

"No, I'm not," said Johann. "It is impossible to believe such a thing."

"You'll find out soon enough, just you wait."

Johann waited. The train remained stationary till evening. At sunset the sentries dispersed into the fields and picked flowers. He had never seen sentries with fixed bayonets being ordered to gather flowers. There was even an officer with them picking flowers, too. Then they returned with their bunches and decorated every car with green leaves, branches, and garlands, as for a wedding.

By the time they had finished it was dark. The train moved off. Johann wanted to try to stay awake to see what was going to happen, but he fell asleep. When he next opened his eyes it was day. The car doors had been locked, and there was noisy coming and going outside. The train had stopped in a station. So far it had always halted out in the country or on the outskirts of towns. Through the windows came the sound of puffing engines and bustling crowds. Johann pricked up his ears and heard someone talking in a loud voice just as he was passing their car.

"They are speaking German," he said, convinced at last that Antim had not lied. They had been sold to the Germans. "Perhaps the Germans really did exchange me for one case of cartridges—bones, flesh, skin, and all."

"We have all been sold as slaves for life," said Antim. He himself had just learned that they had reached German territory. He made a speech to which all the others listened. Johann alone did not listen. One phrase had stuck in his mind: "Slaves for life." He saw himself spending his whole life in concentration camps, toiling and sweating on canals and trenches and fortifications, half starved, beaten, and crawling with lice.

Then he imagined himself dying in a camp. The thought that he would die in a camp brought tears into his eyes. He had seen many prisoners die. He had even helped to dig their graves. Once they were dead, their clothes were removed and they were buried naked. Like dogs, he thought. Dogs are stripped of their hide before they are buried, to make gloves. Prisoners are stripped of their clothes. When they find out how to make gloves out of human skin, they will skin them, too. Perhaps they will have started skinning dead men before my turn comes. He leaped to his feet.

"They can keep me in camp all my life," he said to himself. "But just before I die I want to be set free. I want to be released, if only for an hour, before I give up the ghost, so as not to die shut up. It is a great sin to die shut up. But if they've sold me to the Germans, I shan't ever be set free, not even for an hour before I die."

M M M

"WITHIN ten days at the outside I must get away," said Eleonora West. "If I don't leave the country, they will issue a warrant for my arrest. Ten days is the absolute maximum. Perhaps even that is too much."

She looked at Leopold Stein, who was sitting opposite her in his usual armchair. To convince herself that she was not exaggerating she went over the whole situation again in her head.

The latest date fixed for citizens of Jewish origin to register at a branch office of the Ministry of the Interior had already gone by. Those who failed to comply were liable, by decree, to ten years' imprisonment. She had not reported for registration. Following a denunciation, the Attorney General had instituted an inquiry. In his files there were documents that she had not known existed, which provided conclusive proof of her Jewish origin. There was no way of getting rid of that dossier. All attempts to proceed in the usual way and buy over those charged with the inquiry had met with no success.

"We are beaten this time," she said. "I shall have to abandon the struggle and flee. It is the only thing I can possibly do. For two and a half years I have held out against every attack. It was not easy, and yet I succeeded. But fate does not protect the bold forever."

"The battle is not yet lost," said Stein. "But ten days' notice is too short. We shall have no difficulty in selling the printing press, the paper, and the house, and in getting relatively good prices for them. And there will be no lack of buyers for the furniture, books, and pictures. I will see to all that. The proceeds can be deposited at a Swiss bank in good time. But to obtain Mr. Koruga's appointment and the passports within ten days is completely out of the question."

"The only persons permitted to leave Romania are members of official missions," she said. "My husband must at all costs be appointed Director of the Romanian Cultural Institute at Ragusa, as I told you. On the strength of this appointment, I, as his wife, shall be granted a passport and diplomatic visas. But it must be done quickly. The Attorney General has let me know that the best he can do for me now is to hold up the proceedings for another ten days. After that he declines all responsibility. He will be forced to issue a warrant for my arrest."

Leopold Stein had a sudden vision of Eleonora West in prison. He thrust it aside, in horror.

"And your husband still knows nothing about it?" he asked. "That is a mistake. He is bound to find out sooner or later in any case, and it might happen that if he knows one hour sooner he may be able to help us out. What is he going to say when he is faced with an appointment and passports he never even applied for?"

"I daren't tell him yet!" she said. "I know it's utterly pointless to go on hiding a fact that will be public property in two weeks' time. He will find out soon enough that I am Jewish. But I still can't bring myself to tell him yet. I am worn out. I can't stand any more upheavals. I can't make any more efforts, and to tell him the only secret I have kept from him in two years would need an immense effort. I have been under a strain for too long, and it is too much. I am tired, tired, tired."

She leaned her head on her hands, propping her elbows on the desk. He fixed his eyes on her. She looked really tired. The old man was moved to pity. But there was nothing he could do for her. He opened his brief case so as not to have to look at her; he could not bear to see her with her head buried in her hands, a broken woman. In the brief case, among deeds of sale for Eleonora's house, estate, printing press, and paper, there was a wallet with Traian's initials engraved on it in gold. He took it out and laid it in front of her. She glanced at it and then picked it up.

"Tomorrow is the second anniversary of your wedding," he said. "I know you have been too busy with other things to have had time to buy anything for your husband. I've brought you this wallet for him. I am sure he will like it: it is beautifully worked."

"So tomorrow is the second anniversary of my wedding!" she said. "I had forgotten completely. Thank you, Mr. Stein, for remembering it for me. I know Traian will be delighted."

She looked at the wallet, passing her hand over it caressingly.

"I don't know why I don't tell Traian. Perhaps because I love him too much. He would help me if he knew, I know it. But I won't tell him. I am too scared of losing him. I know I am being absurd, but every time I make up my mind to tell him fear suddenly sweeps over me, and so I keep my horrible secret. Traian is the only thing that holds me to life. If I were to lose him, I should lose myself." Suddenly she put down the wallet and said:

"Do you know what the Attorney General told me? He said I was not married." Her voice was shaking. "And he's perfectly right. I married after the laws forbidding marriages between Romanians and Jews had come into effect. The law was promulgated in April. I was married two months later. Officially my marriage is null and void. All marriages between Christians and Jews effected after that date, with or without full knowledge of the facts, are automatically decreed null and void."

She was silent. The Attorney's words were still ringing in her ears: "Mr. Traian Koruga is not your husband. According to the laws at present in force he is unmarried. Your marriage certificate is null and void. Mr. Traian Koruga at any moment is free to go off and marry another woman without committing bigamy. If you were to have a child, it would be considered illegitimate and would bear the name West, not Koruga. You yourself are guilty of forgery every time you sign the name Eleonora Koruga. You are Miss Eleonora West."

"Pay anything, Mr. Stein," she said. "As soon as possible we must get hold of the passports and visas, passports in the name of Mr. and Mrs. Koruga."

❦ ❦ ❦

FIVE days later Leopold Stein came back, bringing Traian's appointment and two diplomatic passports bound in red leather.

"This time too, Mrs. Koruga, we have won," he said happily. "You have sleeping-car bookings as far as Vienna. You leave on Monday. I am very glad you will be able to leave."

He was wiping his spectacles. Eleonora, who had been examining the passports, looked up at the old man. She noticed that he had grown much thinner. She would have liked to ask him whether he was not leaving too, but he said:

"I don't know whether we shall ever meet again. This very night four thousand Jews were transported to Trans-Dniestria.

I am glad you are going. If ever you come back, you won't find a single Jew left in Bucharest. I shan't be here. Old men don't live long in the concentration camps beyond the Bug."

🐾 🐾 🐾

TRAIAN was in his study. Nora never came to disturb him while he was working. But today she walked straight in, holding the passports. Traian was at his desk, his head between his hands.

"I've brought you a present for the second anniversary of our wedding," she said. "I've managed to get you appointed Director of the Institute of Romanian Culture in Ragusa." She handed him the decree of nomination, and added:

"The Dalmatian coast is one of the most beautiful in the world. You will be able to go on working there in peace and quiet."

"How and when did you manage to do all this on your own?" he asked. "How could you keep it all so terribly secret?"

Traian kissed her.

"Nora, you're marvelous!" he said, and went on: "If you only knew how delighted I am with the appointment! I badly needed a change of climate to carry on with the novel. I felt I could not write the next chapter here. It had to be written elsewhere. I have a feeling it will turn out to be the strongest chapter of the whole book."

Eleonora kissed him on the mouth to stop him from telling her about the next chapter. She was afraid of what she might hear.

(BOOK THREE)

"WE HAVE been advised to put you to light work," said the factory official. "You are still on the sick list. They keep on sending us sick-list men."

He shot a look of hate at Johann. But after he glanced down at the paper in his hand, his look became one of suspicion. Throughout the two years he had been in Germany, Johann had been continually aware of the same distrust in people's eyes. He was constantly being suspected of crimes he had not committed, but which, beyond doubt, he was certain to commit sooner or later.

"Hungarian?" asked the official. "I've had Hungarians before. They were highly unsatisfactory. Perhaps it will be different in your case." He smiled ironically and then began to read aloud:

"Moritz, Janos, Hungarian, thirty-two, unskilled worker, arrived in Germany June 21, 1941." Johann, who in the course of the last two years had come to understand that he was a Hungarian citizen, because it said so in his papers, followed the official's movements as he read through the list of factories, works, and labor camps of the Greater German Reich where he, Johann Moritz, had worked to date. It was a long list. All manner of industries were represented. He was proud of having been in so many places. In his mind's eye he reviewed once more the dozens of camps where he had lived behind barbed wire, the factories, the towns, and all his sufferings. He had expected that the official would admire the brave way he had faced his many ordeals before finally turning up here in front of him. But the official's eyes traveled indifferently over the list of places where Johann had suffered and came to rest on the last entry: "8/3/43: Released from 707 General Hospital for Foreign Workers." Johann was astounded that anyone could read through the catalogue of his sufferings and remain unmoved. But the official showed no signs of emotion. He took his pencil and wrote in a corner at the bottom of the page, where there was still a bit of space: "10/3/43. Reported for work at the Schmidt und Sohn button factory." Then he filed the card away in a drawer among a pile of similar cards and looked up at Johann.

" 'Discipline, obedience, work, efficiency.' That is our slogan for foreign workers. There are German workers in this factory— girls. I must draw your attention to the fact that the first sign of fraternization with any German woman is punishable by a minimum of five years' imprisonment. Our director is inexorable on this point. Remember that every German woman carries in her breast a five years' prison sentence for you. If you so much as make a pass at her, that's what you'll get. And don't go thinking you'll get anything else from her. Your Hungarian predecessor is now in prison. I warned him just as I am warning you, but he chose to take no notice. I suppose he thought that, merely because it was dark and he was hiding with the woman under the blanket, he would get away with it. But in the German Reich every single one of your movements is observed— even what goes on under the blanket. You can do nothing without our being informed at once. We can read your very thoughts. We photograph every idea in your head at least ten times a day. And now for the second point: we are engaged in war production. Everything you see and hear is a military secret. The foreign worker must not know what the factory produces, how much it produces, or by what processes. If you attempt to find out, your head will be cut off. Last January an Italian was executed. At the moment a Czech is on trial. They tried to discover the secrets of the Schmidt und Sohn factory."

The official stood up and went toward the door, Johann following.

"I have not been satisfied with the Hungarians we've had to date," said the official. "They are now all in prison. One of them got twenty years' hard labor for sabotage. Let's hope you'll be an exception—not that I believe in exceptions."

The official had stopped in front of a conveyor belt that was bringing up a series of cases. At the end of the belt a workman was lifting them off as they came along and stacking them onto a trolley beside him. As the official drew near, the trolley was just setting off down the track with a load of cases. In its place appeared a new trolley, empty. The workman, apparently unaware of the change, went on lifting the cases off the belt one by one and stacking them on the trolley, exactly as before. The cases were obviously heavy.

"This is your job starting tomorrow," said the official. "It is quite simple. As the cases come from the factory, you lift them down and load them onto the trolley, which carries them out to the warehouse. Rule number one: work efficiently. Have you done factory work before?"

Johann watched the worker bend down automatically, stiffen his arms automatically, and lift the case of buttons onto the trolley without giving a thought to what he was doing. Nor to anything else, either. He was not even thinking of the people standing beside him. He did not even appear to be aware of them.

"Machines do not tolerate any lapse of efficiency," said the official. "They do not tolerate human chaos, laziness, or sloth."

Johann looked round at the official.

"You are not allowed to think of anything else. If you do, the machine will punish you on the spot. And we will punish you afterward. You must concentrate the whole of your attention on your colleague, the mechanical worker who brings the case and passes it to you. You have only to bend down, take it out of his arms, and transfer it onto the trolley." The official was smiling. Johann tried to see the arms of his mechanical colleague, but could not find them anywhere, so his eyes reverted to the official. The latter was still smiling.

"A robot cannot adapt itself to man. So it is up to you to adapt your movements and co-ordinate them with his. That, too, is as it should be," he said, "because he is a perfect worker. Only the machine can be perfect. We must study them and learn from them how to work. When you are able to imitate them perfectly, then you will be a first-class worker. Not that you will ever be a first-class worker. You are a Hungarian, and Hungarians have eyes only for women and not for machines."

Johann wanted to tell him he was not Hungarian, but Romanian. He wanted to tell him the whole story of his imprisonment and interrogation at Budapest, but the official was standing rapt in admiration in front of the machine that was noiselessly and regularly bringing forward the white packing cases. From them his eyes traveled to Johann and filled with scorn. The contempt in the official's eyes struck Johann with the force of a blow. The story of his experience with Inspector Varga died on his lips.

"Men are inferior workers," said the official, "especially eastern men. They are inferior to the machines. And you are not only a man, but an eastern European into the bargain—a Hungarian. And as if that were not enough, you are just out of the hospital. You're an invalid, that's all you are."

Johann could feel that the official was suffering. He was about to assure him that he would do his utmost to work well.

"How dare you set yourself up beside a machine? Just look at you!" The official measured him from head to toe. "It is an insult to the machines. We should not offer them such poor assistants. It is a sacrilege. Follow me now and I'll give you your kit. You are only allowed in the factory in your overalls. They are worn as a priest wears his cassock in church. But that, I know, is beyond you. All you Hungarians ever see in a factory is the women. Barbarians, the whole lot of you."

ꚃ ꚃ ꚃ

AT FOUR A.M. next morning Johann came alone into the shed and went up to the trolley that the official had pointed out the previous day. There were five more minutes before work started. He was excited. He was dressed from head to foot in blue overalls, and as he crossed the cement floor the wooden clogs on his feet resounded like blows from a hammer. He tried walking on tiptoe, so as not to make such a terrible noise all by himself, but it made no difference. Just as he was halfway across, someone called out to him. Although he had not heard his name, Johann knew that the person was calling to him. He was quite sure of it. He turned round. Just then, the voice hailed him a second time. He distinctly heard:

"*Salve sclave!*" *

A shock of black hair, followed by a face with enormous black eyes and white shining teeth, appeared behind a small barred window. It was the face of a young man, drawn as a skeleton's and with feverish burning eyes. The rest of his body was not visible. As their looks crossed he said, as if they had been old acquaintances:

"*Salve sclave!*"

"My name is Janos Moritz," said Johann under the impression that the young man had mistaken him for someone called

* Hail, slave! (Translator's Note.)

Salve Sclave. The factory siren sounded. The machines started up. Johann went to his post behind the handrail. For a little while longer the dark-haired young man could still be seen behind the window, smiling warmly at Johann. He had heard what Johann had said, but none the less, before he disappeared, he called out once more, looking straight at Johann:

"Salve sclave!"

Johann lifted the first few cases off the moving belt and piled them on the empty trolley. Had the cases not been so heavy, a seven-year-old child could have done the work. He knew that the cases contained buttons. He would have liked to take a look at them. But the cases were nailed down. And even if they had been open, he would not have dared to lift up the lid and look inside. "In January an Italian was executed. Now a Czech is being tried."

He thought of the Czech at that moment standing before his judges, begging their forgiveness for having tried to fathom the secrets of Schmidt und Sohn's button factory. Then he thought of the Italian who had been beheaded. He had met many Italians, and they had all been lighthearted and gay. And so he imagined that the one who had been executed must likewise have been lighthearted and gay. He imagined the severed head, with a fine black mustache, still smiling as it rolled down at the feet of the executioner.

He made a solemn vow that he would never, never look at the buttons, even if a case should break open by accident. It really wasn't worth risking one's head just to look at some buttons. He decided the buttons must be for military uniforms. As he picked up the wooden case and put it down on the empty trolley—he had not even noticed that the loaded one had gone —he wondered again what kinds of buttons were inside. There would be buttons for the navy, the infantry, and the air force. Some gilt, some black, and some matching the color of the uniforms. He liked to believe that the cases he was handling contained gilt buttons. They were the most beautiful of all, like gold coins. Sailors wore that kind on their uniforms. Perhaps in his cases there were buttons for the navy.

The official's words suddenly flashed across his mind: "We can read your very thoughts. We photograph every idea in your head." He forced himself to stop thinking of the buttons in the packing cases. It was a secret, and he had no wish to find out secrets.

After a while, he caught himself wondering what the Germans could be doing with so many military buttons. All the soldiers and officers he had ever seen already had buttons on their tunics and overcoats. The buttons that were being made now must therefore be intended for new uniforms. He gazed at the cases that were drifting up to him one after another in a regular stream and said: "They must contain millions of buttons. Enough for the entire German army. Perhaps there has been an order that all the soldiers are to be issued new uniforms, and that is why they are making so many buttons."

It occurred to him that these new uniforms might perhaps be meant for a victory parade at the end of the war, when the men would march down the main street with flags flying and bands playing. "All the soldiers will wear shining gilt buttons, bright as the sun." He smiled and pictured himself in the crowd, taking part in the march past, proud of the fact that the buttons that the soldiers and officers, why, even the generals, were wearing on their tunics had passed through his own hands. "Perhaps the very buttons I am holding now," he said to himself, "will be sewn on a general's uniform. And all the general's overcoats and uniforms will have buttons from this case. A general might need a whole caseful all to himself."

Johann was so deeply lost in the train of his thoughts that he forgot to lift up the case that stood before him. The conveyor first pushed against it and then brought it crashing to the floor. He rushed to pick it up. By this time the next case had appeared in its place and he was not there to receive it. Crash-

ing against the cement, it made even more din than the first. He
tried to pick this one up too, having managed to wedge the first
one under his arm. But at this point a third case struck him in
the small of the back. He dropped the first two cases in a fit of
panic, a panic the like of which he had never known before. A
fourth case came thundering down onto the cement. Then a
fifth. He went back to his place on the platform. Abandoning
the cases that had come off the conveyor, he began to load the
trolley with the ones that were now coming up. He looked
beseechingly at the machine, at the moving belt, to persuade it
to stop till he had picked up the fallen cases. But one after another the cases came on and on. He glanced anxiously about,
fearful lest he should be punished. But there was no one around
to take him to task.

At midday the machines came to a standstill. Till that
moment he had been quaking for fear of being caught. He
stepped off the platform, picked up the scattered cases and put
them on the trolley. He was thankful no one would ever find
out that he had done wrong.

But the trolley, which had started automatically, had
stopped with the rest of the machinery and now stood motionless with its load of five cases. He thought of pushing it forward, but found he could not move it. It only worked automatically. He then thought of taking the cases under his arms
and carrying them to the warehouse. But he saw he would not
be able to pass through the door in the wall that was made
specially to fit the trolley. So he stood there with a case under
each arm, not knowing what to do next. A voice rang out behind him. He put the cases down on the truck and turned round
apprehensively.

Behind the little window with the iron bars the head with
its emaciated face and black hair had reappeared. The young
man who had hailed him in the morning was again looking at
Johann with a friendly gleam in his eyes. Again he said:

"*Salve sclave!*"

Johann forgot his cases and his morning's blunders and returned the smile.

"That is not my name, I am called Janos Moritz. You must be taking me for someone else."

The young man's lips parted in a grin, showing his white teeth. He laughed heartily. Then he disappeared behind the window, calling out for the last time:

"*Salve sclave!*"

Johann went for his dinner, thinking that there must be a really striking resemblance between him and this Salve Sclave, seeing that the dark-haired young man insisted on calling him Sclave even after he had told him his name was Moritz.

In time, Johann discovered that the young man from the window called all foreign workers at the factory Salve Sclave. He was French and called himself Sclave, too. But Johann found out that his real name was Joseph.

❧ ❧ ❧

JOHANN had been working in the button factory for five months, and since that first day he had not dropped a single packing case. As each one came up, he took it off and put it on the trolley, without even looking. He no longer thought of the buttons inside the cases, or of the generals who would wear them, or of the soldiers who would parade through the market square in new uniforms with glittering buttons out of the cases he himself had carried.

He no longer thought at all. He did not even daydream, not even about the head of the smiling Italian rolling at the feet of the executioner. Now and again he had felt curious to know what had happened to the Czech who was being tried the day he himself had arrived at the factory, whether he had been condemned or acquitted. But that was only at the beginning.

Now he no longer cared. In the mornings when he checked in, the Frenchman used to appear at the foundry window and shout:

"*Salve sclave!*"

And Johann would answer "*Salve sclave,*" but without thinking what he was saying. He smiled at the Frenchman without even realizing it. Then he sat down on the platform and waited for the cases of buttons. Once he had tried to simplify the work by picking up two cases at once and putting them on the trolley together. But the conveyor had not allowed it. The chain caught at a corner of one of the cases and the cogs screeched as if they wanted to tear at him. It had made his flesh creep. It was as if all his teeth had been torn out by the roots. After that he had never experimented again. The machine did not want it, and he had to comply with the wishes of the machine. Now, even if he could have taken five cases at once, he would still only have taken one. He had been caught up in the rhythm and could no longer get away from it. The work was neither hard nor easy. Formerly, when he had been working hard, he sweated and got exhausted and swore soundly. Now he neither sweated nor swore. He had the feeling neither of working nor of not working. In the old days whilst he was at work, he used to think of all sorts of things, and the time passed more quickly. But now he no longer thought of anything. Lifting cases from the belt and putting them down on the trolley left him plenty of time to imagine a thousand and one things— but his mind remained as empty as a shell, and nothing came into it. Not a thought, not a dream. He was no longer even conscious of the work he was doing. He was aware that his brain, as well as his arms, lifted the cases, because otherwise his heart and his brain would have been elsewhere. But there they were, with the cases and with the machinery. He could feel his whole being shriveling up, like a plant deprived of water. At night when he climbed into bed he seemed to be merely bending down to lift another packing case; in the morning when he got up it was as if he had just put the case on the trolley and had his hands free for a moment. Even his sleep was now devoid of dreams. He himself had taken on the color of machines instead of that of the earth. Lately he had even forgotten that the cases he was handling contained buttons, and on the rare occasions when he did remember, he smiled. And his smile was dry, like the earth after a drought.

The doctors declared that he was sick and interned him in the camp infirmary.

❧ ❧ ❧

JOHANN was now in the wooden hut that served as the infirmary. There was barbed wire over the windows. He had been there for four weeks. His lungs were affected. His whole body burned like a flame consuming him with its fire. The only thought that ever came into his mind was the button factory, and he longed to be back in it. He lay with his eyes shut. One day there was a sudden commotion. Perhaps it was the doctors making their rounds. Suddenly his nostrils detected a fragrance that he had not breathed for a long time but that was vaguely familiar to him, the smell of freshly scrubbed skin. He smiled and opened his eyes. A woman in military uniform was standing beside his bed. She was young and fair-haired, and her body smelled fresh and clean. She was looking down at him severely, but he went on smiling. Two police guards and the infirmary doctors were standing next to her. While she was looking at him, one of the doctors asked:

"Is that he?"

The woman was reading Johann's medical sheet and looking at him with suspicion. Everybody in Germany looked at him in this way.

"Hungarian?" she asked. "They and the Italians are the most dangerous." Her fingers seized a corner of the blanket in which Johann was wrapped and uncovered his chest. Then she said:

"It's not that one—the one we want had hair on his chest."

On her way out she stopped at every bed, scrutinizing the faces of the men and sometimes uncovering a chest. She did not find the man she was looking for. The guards followed her out.

The smell—which was not made up only of water, soap, and scent—persisted in the room even when she had gone. Johann remembered that the smell of Susanna's skin, and Julisca's, had been the same.

One of the doctors was Dutch. He said:

"Last night somebody here in camp made love to a German girl. That woman caught them at it. They arrested the girl, but he got away. He was a dark fellow and had hair on his chest. The girl wouldn't give his name, but they'll find him all the same. He'll get five years for it, poor devil."

He was now looking out of the window.

"They've got him," he said.

Johann sat up and saw a Serbian being led under the window with his hands tied behind his back and a guard on either side. He was a handsome man with black hair. Johann knew him. He worked at the rope factory and was a cheerful lad. The young woman in the uniform was walking behind him.

"I told you I'd get him in the end," she was saying.

🦋 🦋 🦋

THE only time Johann was not frightened was when he was with Joseph. Ever since he had been in the hospital he had lived in constant terror. At the factory, he had been haunted by the fear of dropping the packing cases, or of not getting them off the belt in time. He was afraid of looking at a German woman. He was afraid of accidentally discovering some secret about the buttons. He was afraid of everything German—of the Germans themselves, of German soil, German words, and even of the air he breathed because that, too, was German. In Romania he had been imprisoned, unjustly treated, starved, and beaten. But he had not been afraid. Nor had he been afraid of the Hungarians, though they had torn his flesh to shreds. They had been human beings. Even Jurgu Jordan was a human being, and Johann had not been afraid of him.

He had never been afraid of people, because he knew they could all be both good and bad. Some were in the main good, others in the main bad—but all men had a little of each in them.

In Romania the adjutant had offered him a cigarette after knocking out two of his front teeth at one blow. In Hungary the guards had given him a drink of water and some tobacco after burning his feet with red-hot irons.

In Germany he had never been beaten. Every day he received half a pound of bread, hot coffee, and soup. The work, too, was easier here than it had been on the canal in Romania or the fortifications in Hungary. But he could not go on living here. He was absolutely certain that the Germans would cut off his head, though he realized that it was foolish of him to believe such a thing. He felt he would be handcuffed and taken to prison even if he did nothing wrong, even if he never discovered the secrets of the button factory. Over here people were as evil as their machines. Perhaps the machines were not really evil—and the German people no more evil than machines. But all the same he could not live with machines; it made him shrivel up. And he was afraid of them. All machines and all people who were like them made him terribly afraid. Between them and the machines he felt lonely. He felt so lonely it made him want to scream. That was why he was so fond of the Frenchman. Joseph now came up to him.

"*Salve sclave*," he said.

"*Salve sclave.*" Johann answered, smiling. Joseph liked his greeting to be answered in this way.

"We are all slaves," he would say. "It is as well to remind each other of it a thousand times a day, lest we forget. If ever we should forget that we are slaves, then everything is lost. Everything. Our consciousness must be kept awake."

It was Sunday afternoon. Johann and Joseph were lying on the grass in the shadow of a hut. Joseph was telling Johann about the woman he loved. Johann knew that her name was Beatrice, that she lived in Paris, had big black eyes, and wept every night because Joseph was a prisoner. He had been told so much about her that he was sure he could have picked her out in the street from among a thousand other women. At times it seemed to him that he heard her voice. Her speech was like music. He was conscious of her as a presence between Joseph and him. And when he was with Joseph he always felt there were three of them. It even surprised him that Beatrice did not join in the conversations.

♯ ♯ ♯

"ALL prisoners return to their huts!" ordered the camp commandant through the loudspeaker.

"Another search," said Johann, rising. Joseph followed him, saying:

"What are they after now?" He was annoyed at the idea of having to spend Sunday afternoon cooped up indoors. The workers left the square by small groups. Outside, the sun was shining and it was warm. Johann and Joseph went to a window and peered out through the barbed wire.

"So it *is* true," said Johann. Three large military trucks had driven into the square and had drawn up under their window. Of late, it had been rumored that they were to have women at the camp. It had happened in other camps; but the prisoners did not believe it. Now the women had come, women for them. Inside the three large trucks there were blondes, brunettes, and redheads—for them.

"So it was true what they said," said Johann. He still dared not believe it, though he could see them with his own eyes. But the women were there. He looked at them. They were heavily made up with lipstick and powder and wore flimsy frocks. They glanced up at the windows crowded with prisoners, and giggled. Soon they were bustling out of the trucks. As they jumped down and the wind lifted their skirts. Johann could catch sight of their petticoats and their colored drawers, which were as thin as cigarette paper, and see right up their thighs. Behind him Johann heard the men laughing, and it startled him. He could not bring himself to laugh.

"No woman is to leave the trucks," came the command over the loudspeaker. "No orders to dismount have been given." The voice was harsh and authoritative. No one could see the commandant. He spoke from his office. The women turned back and climbed into the trucks as quickly as they had tumbled out, piling in one after another. They were afraid because they had left the trucks without waiting for orders. As they climbed back in, the prisoners once again had a glimpse of their knees, petticoats, and colored drawers. The girls were still laughing, but this time it was frightened laughter.

"Ten women to each hut," said the commandant. "They will stay till nine P.M. Hut leaders have received special instructions for proceeding according to program and are held responsible for the maintenance of order and discipline."

The loudspeaker was silent. The women sat quietly in the trucks, waiting for further orders.

"Merde!" said Joseph, grinding his teeth. Johann, thinking the Frenchman was speaking to him, turned toward him. But Joseph was fuming with rage and was looking the other way.

"The women will dismount in orderly groups," said the voice through the loudspeaker. That was what they had been waiting for. They jumped down from the trucks and split up into five groups. Then five men—the five hut leaders—went across and signaled to them to follow. The women were still laughing as they walked toward the huts.

Johann could not conceive how they were going to "proceed according to program." He knew the women had been sent to make love with the prisoners. The Germans maintained that the level of production was increased when the prisoners made love. And the Germans wanted efficiency. The reason why they had sent the women along was so that the men should work more efficiently in the button factory, the rope factory, and in the foundry on the outskirts of the town.

He did not see why this should be so. Nor did he see how all the men would be able to make love with the few women assigned to each hut. The dormitories were large and held many beds. There were many men and few women. Not every prisoner would get a woman to take to bed with him. "Perhaps these women will go from bed to bed." But then he supposed they would be ashamed to be passed from one man to another. He had never thought of women in connection with his hut and its barbed wire. And yet there they were on the threshold, and the hut leader was telling them something, probably giving them final instructions. They were laughing very noisily.

"Shall we go back outside?" asked Joseph. "We can go where we were sitting before."

Johann followed him. Other men were leaving the huts, too. At the door they brushed past the women, who smelled of powder and scent. They ogled Joseph and Johann as they walked out and tittered. They were laughing at them for going outside. Johann felt a woman's hand pass over his cheek as he went through the door. He lowered his eyes. The hand was clammy and scented.

"*Salvete sclavi!*" said Joseph as he passed them. Their only response was a burst of laughter. But Joseph was not laughing. His face was somber.

Back in the open Joseph stretched out on his back on the grass and stared at the sky. He did not utter a word. Johann sat down beside him, thinking of the women. Joseph was also pre-occupied with the women, but Johann could not guess what his thoughts were.

"Go in if you want to," said Joseph.

"I don't want to," he answered.

They were both silent. For the first time the Frenchman sat without mentioning Beatrice.

"Those are all Polish girls from concentration camps," said Joseph. "If they take on this job for six months, they are after-ward set free. But in six months they are utterly ruined. They leave the camps only to go straight into a hospital, an asylum, or a morgue."

"I thought they were women from the streets," said Johann. He now pitied them. "I didn't know they were prisoners like us."

"They are not prostitutes, Jean" (he always called Johann Jean). "These women are slaves making a desperate bid for their freedom. They are slaves trying in sheer despair to break their fetters, with nothing but their bodies to help them do it. Heroic —but unfortunately useless. They only tear their own flesh. The chains of bondage are stronger than human flesh and blood."

At nine o'clock in the evening the women left the camp. Now as they climbed into the trucks there was no more laughter. They were smoking. Joseph shouted to them heartily as they were leaving:

"*Salvete sclavi!*"

That night the Frenchman escaped from the camp.

❧ ❧ ❧

"THE officers require an interpreter for Balkan languages," said the factory official, taking Johann to the office. "And mind how you behave; they are officers of the General Staff."

Johann waited outside the door for over an hour. Then he was shown in. The air was thick with smoke, and there was a strong smell of wine. There were glasses and empty bottles on the table.

No one turned round when he came in. He stood by the door, the fumes choking him. He longed to go back to his packing cases. There at least it was quiet, and there was no cigarette smoke to stifle him. He stared in fascination at the red stripes on the officers' trousers. They were all young. He counted them: there were seven. One of them came up to him and put his hand on the top of Johann's head. He twirled it round to one side as if he were playing with a ball, surveying first his right profile, then his left.

"Turn round," the officer said. He proceeded to examine Johann's head from the back. After that he felt his shoulder, probed under his chin, told him to open his mouth, and examined his teeth. Then he ordered:

"Undress."

Johann took off his overalls and put them down on the floor by the wall. The officer did not take his eyes off him. While Johann was undressing, he followed every one of his movements. The rest, meanwhile, carried on with their conversation, taking no notice of him.

"Gentlemen," said the officer who had ordered him to undress and who was a colonel in the S.S., "gentlemen, I should like to give you a demonstration."

They all stopped talking and gathered round Johann, who stood naked and confused in their midst. He had been summoned as an interpreter, but now the Colonel was talking about using him for a demonstration. Johann had a momentary picture of conjuring tricks as he had seen them at the circus. A man from the audience would be called up on the stage, and the conjuror would whip live cats, rabbits, and fowl out of his pockets. Johann knew what those demonstrations were like. And he knew of no other kind. And now the Colonel was proposing to demonstrate with him. Perhaps it would be like what he had seen at the circus when he had been in the army. He smiled eagerly. He was not afraid of demonstrations. The men whom the conjuror called onto the platform had never come to any harm. They merely stood and gaped. And probably he, too, would just stand and gape while the Colonel pulled rabbits, cats, or fowl from behind his head or his wrists. He went on smiling amiably at the Colonel. He had always liked conjurors. "I could never do tricks and demonstrations, however hard I tried," he would say. He admired the Colonel for his cleverness, but suddenly he remembered his mother's words. She used to say conjurors were the devil's apprentices. He stopped smiling, feeling a little uneasy. He had always been afraid of the devil.

"Gentlemen," said the Colonel, "I set eyes on this individual for the first time in my life ten minutes ago, when he walked into this room. I don't even know why he is here."

"He is the interpreter for Balkan languages, sir," said the official.

"I had forgotten I had asked for one," said the Colonel. "I was struck by this man's face the moment he appeared in the doorway."

The Colonel put his hand on Johann's head; Johann smiled; he could hardly wait for the Colonel to whisk out a rabbit from behind his head. The Colonel kept a straight face. But Johann knew from the circus that all conjurors kept straight faces, even when the audience was shaking with laughter. He expected to hear laughter now and was ready to join in. He had not laughed for a long time.

"Although I set eyes on him only ten minutes ago, at the same time as all of you, gentlemen, and although I have not exchanged one word with him, I am now prepared to give you in considerable detail, basing my conclusions entirely upon scientific observation, the biography of this man and the history of his entire family for the last three hundred years."

Johann remembered having seen this kind of turn at the

circus, too. The conjuror would pick out a man in the crowd and guess his name, his age, whether he was married or single, and a good many other things. People would be amazed at the conjuror's powers. But Johann did not care for such turns. He only really enjoyed those where rabbits and cats kept popping out of one's pocket, and was disappointed that the officer could not do proper conjuring tricks. He would have liked to watch exactly how the conjuror did manage to pull a cat out of his pocket. He had tried to find out at the circus, but there had been a crowd round the conjuror and he had always somehow picked on someone else.

"The science of race has progressed so rapidly under the National Socialist regime," said the Colonel, whose name was Müller, "that we are now hundreds of years ahead of other countries. Merely by looking at this individual naked, I am able to tell you where his ancestors came from, what marriages they contracted, what were his family's habits and occupation, and so on. You will be able to verify my deductions on the spot by addressing yourself directly to the individual."

"Incredible!" said the officers. They came even closer to Johann.

"The shape of the skull, the formation of the frontal, nasal, and facial bones, the structure of the skeleton, particularly the chest, and the position of the clavicle prove conclusively that this individual belongs to a Germanic group which, though numerically reduced, still exists at the present day in the Rhine Valley, Luxembourg, Transylvania, and Austria. There are also some eighteen families in China and the United States, but these have not yet been incorporated into the statistics because their existence was discovered only a few months before the outbreak of war. In the statistics we are to publish in a special number we shall furnish detailed and for the first time complete data about this Germanic group, which bears the name of 'the Heroic Family.' This family has eight hundred members at the most. Their descendants emigrated by series from southwest Germany between A.D. 1500 and 1600. They are Germans of the original stock who have succeeded in preserving the purity of their blood in spite of the monstrous pressure exerted on them in the course of history. The race, gentlemen, has its own instinct of preservation, which is far stronger than that of the individual. The Heroic Family, of which this young man standing before you is a member, has provided ample proof of the tenacity of this racial instinct. What force was it that caused the ancestors of this young man, over a period of three to four hundred years, to go persistently out of their way to marry only women of their own race, when they were probably surrounded by others far more attractive? It was the racial instinct of self-preservation, the call of the blood, that safeguarded the members of this family from the mortal sin of racial intermarriage. Throughout the history of this family there has not been a single instance of it. That, and that alone, explains how it came about that the young man we have here is an exact reproduction of his forefathers. Observe his hair—strong, but silky—it is the hair of the Heroic Family, such as it was four centuries ago and such as we found it preserved in relics that have come down to us. To the expert eye, its identity is unmistakable. It is a shade silkier than the hair of the chief Germanic groups, but the stock is visibly the same. This young man's nose, forehead, eyes, and chin are identical with those on the centuries-old engravings in our museums. In all the intervening years, no change has taken place."

The officers fingered Johann's head and felt his hair, looking at him with admiration. He felt all eyes riveted on him. It had never happened to him before. He was now a hero. But he was afraid of disappointing the officers. He longed to have done something to deserve their praises—praises such as were lavished only on those who received the Iron Cross with Diamonds and Oak Leaves.

Colonel Müller's fingers again strayed over Johann's shoulders with admiration and reverence, as though he were touching the relics of Saint Parasceve the Miracle Worker in her shrine at the Church of the Three Hierarchs. Johann hung his head, filled with shame that he had not been fighting in the front lines and distinguished himself in battle.

"This group which has been entitled the Heroic Family," added the Colonel, "offers the most striking example of racial heroism. Today has been a red-letter day for me because I have had the good fortune to come across this specimen. I should like to mention incidentally that one of my forefathers married a girl of the Heroic Family. Unfortunately, as he was killed on the field of honor three months after the marriage, there were no heirs. But that is beside the point. A photograph of this young man, together with all appropriate anthropometric and historical data will, I hope, appear in the treatise I am now working on and to which, under the supervision of the Reichsführer, Dr. Rosenberg, I have been devoting my attention for the last ten years. It will be the crowning achievement of my work."

"Congratulations," said the officers, clicking to attention. The Colonel flushed with emotion. He lifted his right arm in salute and then shook hands with them each in turn. Johann stood by motionless, watching them.

"Are you from the Rhineland, Luxembourg, or Transylvania?" asked the Colonel.

"Transylvania," answered Johann.

The officers uttered cries of admiration: the Colonel was radiantly happy.

"I will now give you more precise information as to his domicile," said the Colonel, and turning to Johann: "Were you born in Timişoara, Braşov, or the Szeklers country?"

"In the Szeklers country," he answered.

"Wonderful," said the Colonel, rubbing his hands joyfully. "I knew I could not have been mistaken. The moment he opened the door I had the impression of seeing a figure stepping out of the portrait gallery of the Heroic Family. I know those family portraits so well. You will be able to admire them for yourselves in my work. I shall publish them in enlarged colored plates. I repeat, gentlemen, this young man is a perfect specimen of the Heroic Family. He confirms my whole theory."

The Colonel asked the official to bring Johann's papers.

"The wretches," he cried out in a fury, reading them. "No member of the Heroic Family has ever been called Janos. The name is a sacrilege."

The Colonel turned toward Johann, frowning angrily.

"Did your father give you the name of Janos?" he asked.

"No sir. My name is not Janos," said Johann. He was about to say that his name was Jon.

"Of course not—it is unthinkable for a member of the Heroic Family to have baptized his children with names other than those in the German calendar. It has never been known to happen in all those four centuries. It would have been out of the question."

The Colonel beamed at Johann with satisfaction because he was not called Janos.

"Who gave you this name of Janos?" asked the Colonel.

"I don't know," he answered. "They filled it in on my papers when I got to Germany two years ago."

"His name is not Janos," said the Colonel. "This is the sort of infamy to which the Heroic Family has been exposed time and time again. Their names were distorted by the people among whom they lived, but in spite of that their blood was never adulterated. It has remained as pure as crystal."

The Colonel turned to the factory official.

"With effect from today this young man is to be placed at the disposal of the National Institute for Racial Studies. We need him as a specimen."

"Is he to stop working at the factory?" asked the official.

"Yes," said the Colonel curtly. "I will send special instructions later on." Looking at Johann, he thought: "The progress of science has been tremendous, but we are still far from perfection. This specimen of the elite among an extremely interesting racial group should be preserved in an Anthropological Garden, specially set aside for rare and valuable types of the human race. But unfortunately such gardens have not yet been established. In Europe there are parks for the breeding, selection, and preservation of different species of animals, but so far prejudice has prevented us from establishing Anthropological Parks. That is a disaster for science. In this field the Americans hold the initiative: they have special reservations for the Indian races. But eventually we shall build them in Europe, too. First we must have victory. In a future lecture, I will propose the establishment of the first Anthropological Park, where rare specimens will be made available for scientific study. This member of the Heroic Family will be one of the first human specimens to adorn our park, and I shall donate him."

He looked at Johann and smiled. He visualized him in the Anthropological Park, in the Pavilion of the Germanic Race, living there with his wife and children.

"The day will come," he said. "For the time being we must find this young man an occupation worthy of his origin. He would be happiest as a soldier. I know the Heroic Family. Its male members are the fiercest warriors of the Germanic race. Let us give him the chance of becoming a soldier."

The other officers again congratulated the Colonel. They approved of his suggestion. Once more he flushed with pleasure. He asked his ADC for his brief case and wrote out, on a sheet of paper with the letterhead of the General Staff, a recommendation for Johann Moritz to be enrolled in the SS. Then he handed it to the factory official.

"See that all the necessary formalities are completed without delay," he ordered.

The Colonel turned toward Johann and smiled. "Within a month I want to receive a photograph of you in uniform. It will be invaluable to me for my study of the Heroic Family, to which you belong. I'll send a copy to Dr. Goebbels. You'll be able to see your picture in the papers and illustrated magazines."

❦ ❦ ❦

"THIS man is unfit for military service," said the captain, who was medical officer to the recruiting board, when he had examined Johann. "He has several spots on his right lung. A soldier needs sound lungs."

Three weeks had elapsed since the encounter with Colonel Müller. Johann had been told that soldiers received a ration of almost half a loaf of bread a day, that they were issued warm clothes and boots that did not get wet, and that they got extra food and cigarettes. He knew he would be better off as a soldier than as a prisoner. But in spite of that he was glad that they were rejecting him.

"This fellow has been specially recommended by Colonel Müller of the General Staff and of the National Institute for Racial Studies," said another medical officer, looking through his file. "We cannot turn him down."

The three medical officers considered Johann.

"Can you do clerical work?" asked the captain. "What was your civilian occupation?"

"Agricultural laborer," he answered.

The doctors held a whispered consultation and then told him to wait outside. When they called him in again they informed him that he had been accepted and gave him a written order to report to his unit.

"You are to join the Auxiliaries," said the captain. "In view of the fact that you are unsuited to clerical work, you are being posted to a company of military police."

❦ ❦ ❦

THE commandant of the disciplinary camp blew his whistle to assemble the prisoners for their meal. Private Moritz jumped at the signal. He had completely forgotten that he was in the watchtower and had automatically started a frantic hunt for his mess tin. He reddened with annoyance.

"Fool that I am," he muttered to himself, clutching his rifle. "Here I go again forgetting I am a sentry and not a prisoner."

In the three days since he had been made a sentry, the same thing had happened to him every time the whistle had sounded. He could not get it into his head that he was a soldier. At the sight of the barbed wire and the file of prisoners, he forgot all about his present status and felt a prisoner again. After he had spent so many years in concentration camps the idea that he was a prisoner for life had worked itself into his blood. He could not think of himself in any other way. Whenever his successor came to relieve him he started to tremble, thinking a guard had come to arrest him. Now as he watched the prisoners queueing up for their soup he again forgot that he was in the tower and began to wonder why his turn was so long in coming. For an instant he was back again in the queue.

Ever since the first day he had been on the lookout for old friends among the prisoners. He was genuinely surprised not to have found any. He had passed through so many camps in Germany that he felt he was bound to come across at least some old acquaintances in this Straflager. He would have enjoyed meeting an old acquaintance. He was not allowed to speak to the prisoners, but he would have liked to catch a glimpse of a friendly face, even if only from a distance.

Suddenly he again forgot that he was a soldier on guard and started shouting:

"Joseph, Joseph."

The prisoners who were assembled in the yard looked up at him. Joseph looked, too, but then went back to his food. The Frenchman had not recognized him. Johann called again, and this time Joseph stiffened and stared, mess tin in hand. Then he turned away.

"Don't you recognize me?" cried Johann. "I am Moritz Janos."

"*Salve sclave,*" said Joseph with a broad grin. He had recognized him at last. He put his mess tin down and came closer to the fence.

"How on earth did you get there, Jean?" asked Joseph. Johann told him briefly how he had become a soldier. Joseph had learned more German since they had last met, but there was a strong wind blowing and a good distance between them, so that they found it difficult to understand each other.

"And how did you get here?" asked Johann.

"They caught me five days after my escape," he answered. "Could you let Beatrice know? We are not allowed to write from here, and it's four months since I had news from her."

Johann asked for her address. Joseph wrote it on a piece of paper. While he was writing, Johann took out the packet of cigarettes he had been issued by the company that very morning and threw it over the barbed wire into the yard, where it landed at Joseph's feet.

"Tomorrow I'll bring some more cigarettes and some bread," he said. "And tonight I'll send off the letter; I shan't forget."

Joseph stooped to pick up the packet of cigarettes, twisted the slip of paper with the address round a pebble, and threw it back at Johann. It fell into the middle of the barbed-wire entanglement. Joseph was going to write the address again.

"Leave it, I'll get it back," said Johann. "They won't shoot at me if I go near the fence." But just as he was going down the steps from the watchtower, he caught sight in the distance of the corporal who was coming to relieve him. So he rushed back up the steps, shouting to Joseph.

"I can't fetch the address now, the corporal is coming. I'll be back on duty tomorrow at nine. I'll see you then. I'll get that address out. Good-by for now!"

"*Salve sclave,*" answered Joseph. He walked away, lighting a cigarette. He was wearing the same gray suit as before, the worse for four months' wear, and he was much thinner. The food in camp was very bad.

While he was being relieved, Johann watched Joseph out of the corner of his eye and thought:

I'll bring him a whole loaf tomorrow.

᭒ ᭒ ᭒

THAT night Johann had an attack of fever. The following day he was taken in an ambulance to the hospital. He knew Joseph would be expecting him at the fence to receive the bread and cigarettes. It worried him to think that the Frenchman would stand there in vain. "Poor Joseph," he said to himself. "He must have been looking forward to my bringing him that bread in the morning."

But he consoled himself with the thought that he would soon be well again and that then, every day, he would be able to bring Joseph bread, cigarettes, and letters from Beatrice.

Johann, however, had caught double pneumonia. He remained in the military hospital for two months. On February 1 the medical officer said to him:

"At the end of this week you will be able to leave the hospital. You will be granted thirty days' sick leave."

It occurred to Johann that if he went on leave he would not be able to go and see Joseph, and Joseph was still waiting for him to come and fetch Beatrice's address and write to her. He was also waiting for the promised food and cigarettes. Johann decided to give up his sick leave and to return to his company.

"You must get back your strength, my boy," said the MO. "You need good food and a rest. Otherwise you're done for. Where are you going to spend your leave?"

Johann no longer had the courage to say he was not going on leave. But he blushed.

"I understand," said the MO. "You have nowhere to go. I could, of course, send you to a convalescent home, but I don't think that is the right place for you. What you need is a warm, family atmosphere."

Johann was touched. The doctor had guessed his thoughts. He did not want good food, or convalescent homes, or money. All he longed for was a place where he could feel at home.

"What you need is a woman to look after you and help you regain your self-confidence," said the MO. "Without that you will never recover properly. Only a woman can do it. Naturally, there are plenty of women in the convalescent homes, but they are there exclusively for the sexual satisfaction of the patients. For someone in your physical and psychological state, they are totally unsuitable. What you need, my boy, is tenderness, not stimulation."

The MO took a good look round. He had absolute confidence in his diagnosis and knew exactly what the patient needed. His professional conscience told him to prescribe the tenderness, familiar intimacy, confidence, and devotion of a woman. But he was unable to offer his patient any of these medicines. And yet the patient could not recover without them.

His eyes came to rest on the nurse standing beside him with the medical charts.

"Nurse Hilda," he said. "You live in the town with your mother, I believe?"

"Yes, sir, a few yards from the hospital," she answered.

She was looking straight into his eyes with the confidence and discipline of a soldier awaiting his officer's word of command.

The MO smiled. He had found just the very thing.

"I am placing Johann Moritz in your charge; you will treat him as your husband. In a month's time, when he has recovered his health, bring him back here. I want to have another look at him before I send him back to his unit. He needs a woman to be his sweetheart, his sister, and his mother."

"I understand, sir." She was a squat girl, with chubby cheeks and a high color. She was twenty years old. The doctor examined her appearance and was satisfied. She seemed to have all the desirable qualities. Looking at her hair, he thought, It's lucky she is fair. I should not have prescribed a brunette in this case. Blondes are soothing by their very presence.

"For this purpose you will be granted fourteen days' leave," he said to her. "You will devote your entire time to him. You can have your dinner at the hospital, but you must do some cooking at home as well. He needs dishes prepared with love and care, not merely what is dished up out of a tub."

"I quite understand, sir," said Hilda, proud of the mission entrusted to her. She knew that her fellow nurses would all be jealous.

"Have you a room to yourself?"

"Of course," she answered, blushing.

"I think you will like the boy," he said, and before she could answer, he went on, "Have his discharge made out, also leave passes for both of you, and fill in a thirty days' ration voucher for two people with Category A supplements."

"Jawohl," said Hilda, holding the door open for him. The doctor turned round in the doorway, looked at Moritz, and said hurriedly:

"Good-by, my boy, and mind you get well quickly!"

❦ ❦ ❦

JOHANN glanced out into the hospital yard. It was snowing. On the far side he could distinguish the barbed-wire entanglements. For a long time he gazed out of the window. Suddenly two cold hands came from behind and covered his eyes. He turned round —it was Hilda. He had forgotten all about her and what the MO had said.

"Put on your uniform and come down to the pay clerk to collect your pay," she said. "I've got your leave pass and discharge. My leave pass has been signed, too."

She spoke quickly. She helped him into his uniform, slipping her hand under his pullover to smooth it out. Her hand next to his skin on his bare chest gave him a familiar sensation, something he had known before, a long time ago. She dressed him as if, for many, many years, he had been her husband or her child. Hitherto she had always been cold and distant with him, going away as soon as she had brought his medicine and taken his temperature. Now, all of a sudden, she had become familiar and intimate, more intimate than either Susanna or Julisca. He felt that she had fallen in love with him, quite suddenly. Doctor's orders. She loved him. Thereby fulfilling the promise made to the MO. The hand that had touched his skin in arranging the pullover and that had buttoned up his tunic was the hand of a woman in love, of a mistress, of a sister, exactly as the doctor had ordered.

"The MO has authorized us to take a bed from the hospital," she said. "A big white one from the surgical ward, with two woolen blankets. Mine is too small for two people."

She thought of the bed.

"The MO says I mustn't excite you too much," she said. "Naturally. You've been dangerously ill. But after a week's diet of good food and rest things will be quite different."

"What'll be different?" he asked.

She cut herself short and kissed him on the lips.

"You'll see."

He collected his pay, but he was not happy, because he was carrying out an order. It was not an order to work on fortifications, or in a button factory, or to go on guard at the camp. He had been ordered to go with Hilda and make love to her, for one month, in order to recover psychologically and physically. It wasn't a bad order, but it was an order all the same. And no order could ever make him happy.

🌣 🌣 🌣

"DO YOU know, if we got married, I should get an extra fourteen days' leave," said Hilda, after Johann had lived with her for a week. Johann looked at her tenderly for a long time.

"You told me yesterday you wanted to marry me, didn't you?"

"That's true," he confirmed. He remembered that the night before he and Hilda and her mother had drunk five bottles of wine among themselves.

"Why not?" she went on. "If we hurry, I can get my leave extended. And so can you. Then we'll be given a flat, furniture, and a grant of two thousand marks. You won't have to sleep in barracks except when you're on duty. I talked it over with Mother, and I think the best thing would be to get married right away."

Johann said nothing. She thought it was because he did not want to waste his leave on formalities.

"You won't have to do a thing about it," she said. "You can stay at home and rest as you've been doing, and I'll deal with everything there is to be done at the Standesamt, Wohnungsamt, Ernährungsamt, Abeitsamt, and the Politzeiamt * and all the other authorities. I know you don't want to waste your leave trekking about from one place to another."

Johann agreed. Hilda's arguments were logical. Getting married could bring them nothing but advantages.

And so they were married. They were allotted a three room apartment with bathroom and kitchen. They received two thousand marks, and in addition coupons for sheets, clothes, furniture, crockery, firewood, coal, wine, and meat for the wedding, a radio, and all sorts of other things besides.

"We should have been fools not to get married when there

* Registry Office, Lodgings Bureau, Food Office, Labor Exchange, Police Station.

are so many advantages attached to it," she said, helping Johann to get ready to go on duty. "Aren't you better off sleeping at home than in the barracks?"

"Of course," he answered.

"And isn't the food I cook for you in the evening better than what you get in the mess?"

She was delighted.

"In two months' time, probably, when I declare my pregnancy, I'll get more leave, and then you'll be able to eat at home for lunch as well as for dinner," she said. "We'll get even more food. Expectant mothers are entitled to three ration cards. I'll feed you really well. I should love to see you grow fatter."

He smiled and said:

"You're a good girl, Hilda."

🐦 🐦 🐦

THE gendarmery at Fantana received a circular in duplicate to be posted on the door. Sergeant Nicolae Dobrescu read it: "WANTED: THE JEW MORITZ, Jon, alias Johann, alias Jacob, alias Jankl, is wanted by the police. All posts have been warned. Moritz escaped from a labor camp. Any person found harboring him, or possessing knowledge of his whereabouts without disclosing them to the authorities is liable to imprisonment." In the right-hand corner of the notice there was a photograph of Johann taken full face and profile. The Sergeant looked at it and said: "And so the fellow really was a Jew, after all," and sent for a gendarme.

"Take your rifle and go and fetch me the Jew's mother and father at once," he ordered. "Stick the notice up on the door. Do it properly so that the wind won't blow it down."

It was snowing in Fantana. The Sergeant glanced out into the street. Father Koruga was just passing by. He had developed a slight stoop and was carrying a brief case under one arm.

A little while later the gendarme came back.

"I have only brought the woman," he reported. "The old man is ill."

This annoyed the Sergeant. He had intended to interrogate them together.

"If you give the order, sir, I'll carry him here," said the gendarme. "He can't stand on his own feet. I pulled the bedclothes back and took a look at him. His whole body was swollen like a gumboil."

The Sergeant thought it over and gave up the idea of interrogating the old man. He told the gendarme to call in the woman, who was waiting outside.

Aristitza swept into the room, blazing with anger.

"How dare you send a gendarme after me with a gun?" she asked. "As though you hadn't enough thieves and criminals already to round up and fetch here with your bayonets instead of having to come interfering with honest folk. Or do you suppose I'm a criminal?"

She was seething with rage. When the gendarme had come to fetch her she had made up her mind to go and scratch the Sergeant's eyes out.

"You're not a criminal," he said, "but all the police in the country are after your son."

Aristitza looked at the notice he had handed her. When she saw her boy's picture she started crying.

"How thin he has grown, poor soul," she said.

The fact that he looked ill meant he had been maltreated. She wasn't interested in anything else.

"Read," ordered the Sergeant.

"What for?" she said, wiping her eyes. "I can tell from his picture that he is starving and probably crawling with lice, and has been beaten up and kept in prison. Otherwise he wouldn't look so thin. What more do you want me to read? I don't need to know anything else."

The Sergeant started reading the circular aloud. She interrupted him after the first few words.

"Just read that bit again, Sergeant," she said. "Perhaps I

didn't understand. You did say the Jew Moritz Jon, didn't you? If that's what's written there, then that isn't my son. No son of mine is a Jew."

The Sergeant passed her the notice. Her heart ached again on seeing how thin her son had grown.

"Is that him?" asked the Sergeant.

"That's him, all right, poor soul!" she said. "May God never forgive the sins of those who locked him up."

"So you recognize him, all right, eh?" he said. "Then why go on pretending he's not a Jew? We're just wasting time. You'd better listen to what I'm going to read. What you say makes no difference. You are an unauthorized individual. I believe only authorized statements. This is a statement issued by authority and is therefore gospel. It states that your son is a Jew."

"If you dare say that again I'll scratch your eyes out," she said. "Are you trying to drive me wild? Poor lad—he went away as strong and handsome as an oak and now he's nothing but skin and bone."

"Don't insult the authorities," he said. "Or I'll run you in for resisting an officer in the execution of his duty."

"I and my husband, not the authorities, made Jon," she cried. "It was I, not the authorities, who carried him in my womb and gave him my milk. And I know he is not a Jew."

"The Ministry of the Interior lays down in black and white in the circular that Jon Moritz is a Jew."

"Let the Ministry come and say that to my face if he dares! I'll spit in his face if he thinks he knows better than I what I carried in my womb."

"If you are Romanian, then I suppose your husband is Jewish," he said. "One of you must be Jewish—this statement is official. Perhaps you don't know yourselves."

"Are you drunk?" she asked. "Do you mean to tell me I don't know which icon I bow to and who is my God?"

"We're not discussing icons," he said. "You can be a Christian Jew. It is a question of blood."

"My and my husband's blood is Christian. But it's they who imprisoned and tortured my boy who are pagans."

"Are you quite sure your husband's a Christian?" he asked insinuatingly. "Haven't you ever noticed anything in all these years of living together? It is easier to prove with men than with women. Or perhaps there are things about him you don't know?"

"Are you trying to tell me I don't know the man I've slept next to for thirty-five years?" she yelled. "Even a whore knows the sort of man who gets into bed with her, and you are telling me I've been sleeping beside my husband for thirty-five years without knowing him? Do your authorities know more than I about the boy my husband and I made together? Are you and your authorities, Sergeant, going to call me to account for what I bore in my womb and fed at my breast?"

Her eyes had focused on the Sergeant's inkstand. She saw red. The inkstand she was going to pick up and hurl at him was red, too. The walls were red; the Sergeant himself was red. He followed the direction of her eyes and prudently removed the metal inkstand out of her reach.

Her fingers were clutching furiously at her skirt as if they were trying to throttle the life out of the "authorities." When she found that the inkstand had disappeared she felt she had been deprived of her last weapon. She gnashed her teeth. Then, picking up her skirts, she flung them back over her head in one swoop. The full, pleated skirts blew up as if in a gust of wind, even taking her blouse with them. Her body, with its shriveled, olive-colored skin, was naked—her dingy breasts hung like two empty pouches. The Sergeant had a brief glimpse of Aristitza in all her nakedness as she spun round. He shut his eyes. The door banged violently. The walls shook, while lumps of plaster fell on the desk. Aristitza was gone. Her voice still echoed in the Sergeant's ears like a wheezy horn.

"There's my answer for you. . . . Put that in your pipe and smoke it, one after the other, you and your authorities."

WHEN she got home, Aristitza flung off her shawl and crouched down by the hearth. She made up the fire with fresh logs and watched the great red flames leaping and dancing before her eyes. Tears were streaming down her cheeks. "I won't tell my husband anything," she said to herself. "He is sick, and it won't do to worry him."

She looked round. The old man lay asleep on his back. Looking at him through her tears, she thought of Jon, whom the authorities and the police had been torturing for five years because they mistook him for a Jew. If he had been a Jew, he'd have found a way out soon enough. But poor Jon was only a simpleton and believed every word people said to him. If they had thrashed him to make him say he was a Jew, he had probably said it. And the authorities had taken his word for it.

She sat with her head in her hands and wept. After a while she could not bear it any longer. She had to tell her husband that their son's photograph was printed on a green notice like the ones they used for elections and that it had been posted on the gendarmery door. "I won't tell him that Jon is as thin as a rake—it would upset him too much. But I'll tell him how the Sergeant said he was Jewish."

"Jancu," she said, "wake up, or you won't be able to sleep tonight." The old man did not answer. He never answered when she woke him. He would lie there with his eyes closed, hearing everything she said but too lazy to answer.

"Jancu," she said, "the Sergeant has just told me you are a Jew—what do you think of his cheek? He got what he was asking for, all right."

She thought she saw a smile on his lips. They had had many quarrels during their thirty-five years of married life, but she had always been fond of him. She was often at him for being too soft and kindhearted—everybody cheated him. But she loved him, with all her heart, and now more than ever.

"Jancu dear, if you are not better by tomorrow I'll go to town to fetch a doctor," she said. "I'll sell the pig to get enough money. As soon as you are better we'll buy another pig. But you've got to get better."

The old man still did not answer.

"Open your eyes, Jancu, I've got a cigarette to give you," she said. "I've been keeping one specially for you."

She got up and went to fetch the cigarette she had hidden on the beam.

"The matches are beside you, aren't they?" she asked, coming to him. She was going to put the cigarette in her husband's mouth as she sometimes used to do in the mornings in the early days of their marriage. She knew he would not open his eyes, but his lips would part when he smelled the cigarette.

But this time the swollen lips were still. They did not part, even when she touched them with the cigarette.

"What's the matter, Jancu?" she said. She shook him by the shoulders. Touching him with her hand, she felt his skin cold through his shirt. She touched his forehead, and it was as cold as ice.

The old man had died.

She began screaming. She started to rush out of the house, but stopped and turned back to the dead man. Taking the match with which she had intended to light his cigarette, she lit a candle instead and set it at the head of the bed.

She was weeping loudly, knowing that now not a soul would hear her.

❧ ❧ ❧

ARISTITZA went on wailing till she was hoarse. Then she began to sob quietly. In the end the sobbing died down from sheer exhaustion. But inside her, as she sat by her dead husband, the weeping continued silent and tearless. Her grief was no less for her silence.

But eventually her mind, too, began to tire. Her weeping ceased altogether. At that moment she suddenly realized she was alone. All the while she had been crying, it was as if there had been somebody with her. She tried to start again, but the tears would no longer flow. It was dark in the room. She lit the lamp, wondering how she had failed to notice earlier that night had fallen.

She put the water on to boil for the evening meal, as usual. Then she drew the curtains. But when everything was done she felt all the more lonely. She was dazed and tired out. She looked at the dead man's face. She was not afraid of the dead. That night, and on the following three nights till he was buried, she would sleep in the house alone with the dead man.

The Sergeant's words came back to her: "Maybe your husband is a Jew."

She was standing in the middle of the room, with her arms folded on her breast, not knowing what to do next. The water was boiling, but she did not feel hungry. The bed was unmade, and she could have got into it, but she did not feel sleepy. She had to find something to do. Her mind and body were shaken and harassed with grief and would not be calmed. Somehow or other they had to be occupied. And then there was her loneliness. She gave a further tug at the curtains and moved across toward the bed. The Sergeant seemed to be standing beside her, saying: "Maybe your husband is a Jew."

Aristitza looked at the dead man. She drew back the bedclothes. The body was swollen. She looked at the shirt and at the thick canvas trousers she had so often washed and darned with her own hands. She unfastened the belt and pulled the trousers down to his knees. The dead man's skin was purplish blue.

"Why should I be ashamed?" she said aloud. "He is my

husband, after all." She remembered the days when they had both been young and she used to see him naked at her side. Now his body was almost blue.

"Maybe your husband is a Jew." The words re-echoed once more in her ears. Her fingers traveled down her husband's belly and then further down still. Here, too, he had turned blue, as had eyelids, his nose, and his lips—blue and cold. She drew back her hands, started, and hastily pulled up his trousers and drew the bedclothes back over him. Then she stood up and made the sign of the cross. She was trembling from head to foot.

"Merciful God, I thank you for stopping me in time." She crossed herself again. "If I had looked I should have gone straight to hell. It would have been a great sin. But I didn't look, I didn't see anything. I don't even want to find out whether he is Jewish or not—I don't want to."

She looked at the dead man.

"Forgive me, Jancu," she cried, weeping. "I swear I didn't see anything—I didn't even want to see. I would never have been so wicked, Jancu, you know me well enough for that. The Sergeant and his authorities put the idea in my head. May they perish in hell-fire, both of them."

🐾 🐾 🐾

PRIVATE MORITZ was marching through the town, escorting five prisoners. It was seven A.M. As he passed in front of his home Hilda appeared at the window and waved to him. She held Franz, their child, in her arms. Johann heard her say: "That's your father over there. Look, he's got a gun and a helmet."

Franz was only three months old. He could not see that Johann had a gun and was escorting prisoners through the town. But every morning Hilda showed him the same picture to make him proud of his father. As proud of him as she was herself.

The rest of the way, Johann kept thinking about the child and Hilda. When they had left the town behind them, the prisoners crossed a meadow. Johann walked behind them silently, with his rifle slung over his shoulder. Then they all went down a bank and halted under a bridge over a river. That was where they worked every day. Johann followed them. As soon as they reached the dry bed of the river the prisoners turned toward him, bursting into gay chatter. Here no one could see them.

"*Salve sclave!* Did you sleep well?" asked one of the prisoners, warmly shaking hands with Johann. It was Joseph.

"*Salve sclave!*" Johann answered. He shook hands with the others. Then, propping his rifle up against a boulder, he opened his coat and pulled out a loaf and five packets of cigarettes.

"I still owe you fifteen marks," he said, handing Joseph the cigarettes. "I couldn't get any soap. I'll try again tomorrow." He took another loaf out of a bag that hung from his waist under his overcoat and gave it to Joseph. The prisoners sat down and started smoking. Johann lit a cigarette, too. Every morning since they had begun work on the bridge they spent the first half-hour sitting about and joking with Johann. Then they set to and worked till noon. Both for him and for the prisoners alike, it was the best hour of the day. He would hand out the letters from France that came to his address, and would give them cigarettes, bread, and the things he had bought for them in town. After that they had to start work.

More often than not, Johann would lend a hand surreptitiously. He enjoyed helping them, although the prisoners did not like it. He felt sorry for them. All five were intellectuals and were not very good at this sort of work. He used to pick up a spade and show them how to do it. He was accustomed to manual labor, and it came to him easily.

"Jean, there's something I want to discuss with you," said Joseph.

The other four got up and started work. There began the regular sound of picks and spades hacking into stone.

"We are going to escape," said Joseph, when he and Johann were alone. "Not now, but one of these days we are going to escape, all five of us."

Johann looked at him. He thought Joseph was pulling his leg, but he was serious.

"What harm have I done you or the others that you should escape?" asked Johann. "Do you want me to spend the rest of my days in prison?"

He was pale with anger.

"You know I wouldn't have the heart to shoot if you ran away," he said. "I couldn't. And if I don't shoot, I'll go to prison. You must be joking."

"Far from it," said Joseph. "We are definitely going to escape, but you won't go to prison."

Johann had heard enough.

"I'll ask them at the company to put me on some other duty," he said. "As from tomorrow I shan't come to the bridge with you any more. Not if you're going to escape. I'm not going to kill you and I'm not going to prison, either. I've never yet shot at anybody. And I've had enough prison already to last me a lifetime. From tomorrow I won't come with you any more. Once I've gone, you can escape as much as you like."

"Why don't you listen and let me tell you our plan?" asked Joseph. "You must escape with us."

"There's no need for me to escape," said Johann sharply. "I have a wife and child. I am not a prisoner. If I were, I might try to escape."

"But you are a prisoner, Jean," said Joseph. "You are a slave with a gun, and we are slaves without one. Apart from that, we're all in the same position. You must escape with us."

"As from tomorrow morning I shall not come with you again," he answered, lighting a cigarette. He was red with anger.

"We are thinking of your own good, my dear Jean," said Joseph. "The war is almost over, you know. The Allies are advancing. Don't you realize that if you are caught in an SS uniform you'll be in for it? They'll imprison you for ten or twenty years."

"Don't be silly," said Johann. "There's no reason why the Allies should put me in prison, if they do come. I've done no harm. On the radio it says the Allies are just people."

"You are their enemy, Jean. You are the enemy of my own country, France, and of all the Allied Nations."

"Me the enemy of France?" Johann fired up. "What do I buy you bread for and cigarettes, why do I do everything I can for you—because I am France's enemy?" He threw away his cigarette. "I didn't know you called me your enemy. I thought we were friends."

"You are a friend of the Germans and you are fighting on their side," Joseph replied. "You are Hitler's soldier, and don't you forget it."

"When I have a bottle of beer, where do I go and drink it? With the Germans at the barracks or here with you all under the bridge?" asked Johann in violent indignation. "Answer me, Joseph. With whom do I smoke the tobacco I get? With whom do I sit and talk over what's on my mind? Not with the Germans; you are the only friends I've had. And now you go and tell me I'm your enemy. Have you ever seen me on friendly terms with Germans? My friends have been you and no one but you."

His hands were trembling as he lifted a cigarette to his lips.

"You were saying the Allies would give me twenty years' imprisonment. It might even be the French, I suppose, mightn't it?"

"That's right," said Joseph. "If French troops come here, they will arrest you."

"If that is so, it means there's no more justice left in the world. I shouldn't be sorry if they shot me. What's the sense of living when there's no justice left on earth, or when you and the others call me your enemy. I'm not coming to the bridge with you again. Escape if you like, go ahead. It's none of my business. I am not going to stop you. If I can help you without risking my neck, I shall. It's always a good deed to help a prisoner escape. I'll do that. But I'm not running away with you and I don't want to spend my life in prison for your sake, either."

"You mustn't look at it that way," said Joseph. "We want to save you, too. That's what we call friendship. We want to take you with us to France."

"My wife and child are here," said Johann. "I can't go with you."

"In a few months' time, the Allies will be here. Then we'll get your wife and child over to France with us. I have a farm just outside Paris. You could live there. You're a farmer. You could look after it and make some money. When you've saved enough you could buy some land and a house of your own. France is a beautiful country. The people are good and kind. What would you do here in Germany when the war is over? Let's escape together."

"I'm staying here."

"We'll leave your wife enough money to live on till we come and get her. We've already collected the money for her— five thousand marks. We'll come for her in a month or two. France will be grateful to you if you save five French prisoners. What have you to say now?"

Johann did not answer. The whole day long he dreamed of the French farm. He tried to imagine the land he would buy, the house he would build, and the life he would lead over there with Hilda and Franz. "There'll be other children, too," he said to himself. "I'd like to have a little girl and call her Aristitza like my mother." He smiled at the thought of this future. Then he frowned and said: "I am not going to escape!"

卐 卐 卐

HILDA met him on the doorstep. She was dressed to go out to the pictures.

Johann did not even notice what film they had seen. His thoughts had been elsewhere. He remembered nothing but the weekly newsreel. It had shown the latest battle scenes on the front. Shattered tanks, burned-out houses, dead bodies. It also gave a map. The front line was now closer than ever to the German frontiers. When they came out of the theater he was silent and thoughtful. Hilda noticed that he was not his usual self and asked him if he felt ill. He did not feel like talking. Before getting into bed he looked at his child in the cradle. But even after he got into bed, he could not sleep.

"Hilda, what will happen to us if Germany loses the war?" he asked.

"Germany will not lose the war," she answered. Johann remembered the battle scenes he had seen on the screen, the map, Joseph, the child in the cradle, then said:

"Hilda, I know Germany won't lose the war—but just supposing she does, what are we going to do? I shall be taken prisoner. What are you and the child going to live on?"

"We shall either win or die, every one of us," said Hilda. "No true German will go on living in an occupied Germany."

"And supposing we don't die?" he asked.

"We'll die fighting," said Hilda. "Those who are left alive when everything is lost will commit suicide."

"That'll happen to the men," he said. "But what will the women do?"

"The women will do the same. I shall be the first to commit suicide with my son if we lose the war. I shall not outlive the hour of defeat. But Germany won't lose the war—she will never be conquered. How could you even think of such a thing? And now good night." Hilda pulled the bedclothes over her head.

Johann thought of her and Franz. He imagined them dying. All night long he dreamed that the Allies had entered Germany and that their tanks were drawn up outside his house. He dreamed that Hilda had taken his rifle, shot Franz in his cradle, and then shot herself. He cried out in his sleep and woke up in a cold sweat. Light was coming in through the window. It was already morning. He crept out of bed so as not to wake Hilda, who was still fast asleep. He dressed and went to the barracks. He did not apply for a different duty, as he had intended to do the day before. The Frenchmen made no comment, but they were glad to see him. Their eyes twinkled happily. They had been very much afraid that he would not be coming any more.

When they arrived under the bridge, Joseph said, as usual: "*Salve sclave*. Did you sleep well last night?" This reminded Johann of the nightmares about Hilda committing suicide and killing Franz.

"Joseph," he said, "will you swear you'll bring my wife and child to France if the Germans lose the war?"

"As soon as the Allied troops get here, we'll come for them and bring them back to Paris. We swear it."

Johann laid his rifle aside and told them of the discussion he had had with Hilda after the pictures.

"But supposing you arrive too late, after she has shot the child and killed herself?"

The Frenchmen promised they would ride in with the first Allied column. Johann's eyes shone with gratitude.

"If you promise me that, then I'll come with you," he said. "When are we going?"

"Tomorrow morning," said Joseph. "We'll come out to work as usual, but we'll never go back to camp. This is a glorious deed you are doing for France. France will always be grateful to you."

"I'm not doing anything for France," Johann answered. "I know Hilda—she always keeps her word. If we don't get to her in time she will kill herself with the child in her arms. She has a heart of stone."

"Nevertheless, at the same time, you are rendering France a great service," said Joseph.

"Why do you insist on believing that you know more about what goes on inside me than I do myself?" said Johann. "How should I escape for the sake of France? What do I know about France? All I know is that I have a wife and child. They are in danger. It is for their sake that I am coming with you."

ฬ ฬ ฬ

Letter from Traian Koruga to his father:

FATHER

    I am sending this letter by the diplomatic bag. Please reply without a moment's delay. All the alarm bells are ringing inside me. I am afraid that something may have happened to you. Laugh at my panic if you like, call it hysteria, but please, I beg you, answer immediately. I want to know if you are alive.

    My novel is progressing. I have reached Chapter IV— the fourth hour after the death of the white rabbits. At the moment, all over the world, the mechanical slaves are smashing up everything in their path, and one by one the lights are going out. Men are wandering about in a darkness bordering on death.

    Our love to you and Mother.

TRAIAN AND NORA

Ragusa, Dalmatia, August 20, 1944

(BOOK FOUR)

ᔕ ᔕ ᔕ

FATHER KORUGA answered Traian's letter immediately. He informed him that he and his wife were in perfect health and that in Fantana nothing had changed since his departure. Only Johann Moritz was still missing, and nobody knew what had happened to him.

Just as the old man was reading the letter through again, George Damian, the attorney, walked into the yard. He had come to spend a day or two in the country with the old man. He came almost every week. The two men set off together to post the letter.

"Traian is terribly worried about us," said the priest, showing the attorney the letter he had just received.

The attorney read it, smiling.

"Traian is a poet. He exaggerates," he said. "And if you ask me, he is overwrought into the bargain."

There were crowds of people about in the village square. The postman's cart had not yet left. The old man tried to give him the letter, but he refused to take it.

"No more mail can be accepted for abroad," he said. "At six o'clock this evening Romania capitulated. The country is being occupied by the Russians. The King spoke over the radio."

The priest put the letter back in his pocket.

⚐ ⚐ ⚐

THAT evening the peasants gathered together in the priest's yard. They had come to ask for his advice. The Russians were already in the neighboring town. The townspeople were fleeing into the villages. Rumors of appalling atrocities were circulating: of women raped and hanged, of men shot dead in the streets.

Father Koruga came out on the veranda. The peasants all seemed troubled and uneasy.

"Strangers have become rulers in the land," he began. "They are even worse than their predecessors, because they are foreigners. But true Christians know that all dominions on this earth are hard to bear. The only real kingdom is the kingdom in heaven."

"Should we take to the forests and continue the struggle against the invader?" asked a young peasant. "What do you advise us to do?"

"The Church can never exhort men to fight for the conquest of worldly power."

"Does the Church, then, advise us to stretch out our hands in readiness for our chains?" demanded the peasant. "Does the Church expect us just to fold our arms, and stand and watch while our women are being raped and our homes burned down? Surely the Church cannot ask that of us? And if it does, then we are no longer with the Church."

The young peasants agreed with him. The priest remained calm.

"Jesus Christ taught that men should submit to temporal authority. You will answer that the new rulers of Romania are cruel and foreign. I know that. But the strangers who governed the land where the Son of God was born were cruel pagans, too. Remember the thousands of children slaughtered in Judæa on King Herod's command after the birth of Jesus Christ. That dominion was indeed cruel, no less, perhaps, than the Communist regime. But Jesus did not rebel against it, nor did he incite others to rebellion. He said: 'Render unto Caesar the things that are Caesar's and strive to attain the kingdom of God.' "

"And you, Father, will you say prayers in church for Stalin?" asked the young peasant. "If you do, it means that you are praying for Antichrist. And we will never set foot inside your church again."

"If the rulers of the country command me to pray for Stalin, as I have been doing for the King, I will comply. Stalin is an atheist, I know. But atheists are human beings, for all that. Their souls are heavy with sin because they have strayed from the paths of Christ. It is the duty of a priest to pray for the salvation of men's souls and above all for the souls of great sinners."

"You can pray for Stalin if you like, but you'll never see us in church again," said the peasant, whose name was Vasile Apostol. He went on in a hostile tone: "And if we go into the forests to fight for freedom and humanity, against the Bolsheviks, will we, too, be prayed for on Sundays?"

"The priest shall pray for those who fight in the forests and in the mountains, not only on Sundays, but morning and evening, every day of the week, because the lives of those who fight are always in danger and therefore they stand in need of the prayers of the priest and of the mercy of the Holy Mother of God." A hush fell on the crowd.

"If you ever pray for us in church, you will be shot," said Vasile Apostol.

"That is not a reason why I should stop praying for you. Christians have no fear of death."

"We are going into the forests," said Vasile. "Before we

leave we should like you to bless us and celebrate Holy Communion for us. We don't know whether we'll ever come back. We are going to fight for Christ and the Church."

"If you fight for Christ and the Church with the sword you will be committing a great sin," said the priest. "You would do better to stay at home. The Christian Church and faith are not upheld by the might of war."

"We are going to fight for Romania, which is a Christian country," said Vasile. He began to divide the peasants into groups. Most of them, the best men in the village, had decided to take to the forest. There were also some women and boys among them. They knelt down on the grass in Father Koruga's yard. He read out a prayer from the veranda and then came down and blessed them one by one.

"Please give me your blessing, too," said George Damian, kneeling before the priest. "I am going with them to fight for humanity and freedom."

"The Church bestows its blessing upon all who ask for it," said the priest.

"Even upon those who are deliberately going to do wrong?" asked George Damian. "Or are you convinced of the justice of our cause?"

"Do what you will, provided only you have love," said the priest. "So long as your deeds spring from true love, you need have no fear of sin. You are on the right road."

George Damian kissed Father Koruga's hand, as the peasants had done, and then joined the groups which were heading for the forest.

Inside the house the priest's wife was weeping.

❧ ❧ ❧

TWO hours had gone by since the peasants had left the village. The priest tried to regain his composure by reading. But two peasants who were not from the village came striding into his library without even knocking. They were wearing nationalist-colored armbands and held revolvers. The priest pretended he had not noticed their weapons and smiled up at them.

"I think I am wanted at the village hall," he said, raising his voice so that his wife should hear him in the next room and not be frightened.

"We have instructions to summon you before the People's Tribunal," said one of the peasants loudly.

The priest glanced toward the other room. "She may not have heard. I only hope she hasn't," he thought. He put the book down in the armchair and went out. Before leaving the yard he looked back. It was a look of farewell.

The two peasants escorted him, one on each side. He passed through the gateway, holding his head high. His walk was not that of a prisoner. His brows seemed to touch the sky. So he walked through the village street all the way from his house to the hall.

🐾 🐾 🐾

THE People's Tribunal was presided over by Marcu Goldenberg. He sat in the mayor's chair in the assembly hall. His hair was cropped short like a convict's. A few days before. the Russians had released him from the prison where he was serving his sentence for the murder of Langyel.

On his right, at the mayor's table, sat Aristitza, Johann's mother. Marcu had picked on her because she was the poorest "citizen" in Fantana. On his left was Jon Calugar. He had killed a gendarme with his hatchet fifteen years before, in consequence of which he had now been made a judge.

Father Koruga greeted them. Marcu stared straight at him without answering. The other two lowered their eyes and pretended not to see him. They had already passed sentence on many people. The hall was now empty except for the three judges and the two peasants with the colored armbands. Marcu asked the priest for his name, age, and profession.

"Being a priest is no profession," he said. "A shoemaker makes shoes, a tailor makes clothes. Every worker produces something. What does a priest produce?"

Aristitza and Jon Calugar kept their eyes on the ground. The two peasants with the armbands laughed behind the priest's back.

"You have no profession." said Marcu. "It is a crime that at your age you should still be without a profession. You have lived as a parasite on the backs of the workers."

Marcu's face was a lemon yellow. His lips were thin and blue. The priest remembered that old Goldenberg, Marcu's father, had had the same thin lips, but they had been smiling. Marcu's lips were tightly drawn.

"Do you know why you have been brought before the People's Tribunal?" asked Marcu.

"No," answered the priest.

"The typical answer of a reactionary," shouted Marcu viciously. "The reactionary always claims he doesn't know why he is up for judgment. Do you admit that you organized Fascist bands which subsequently took to the forest?"

"I have not organized bands," said the priest. "I admit to having said prayers in the yard of my house for the young men of the village who asked me to do so."

"And were they not Fascist bandits?" asked Marcu. "Why is it you prayed for them, if you are not their confessor?"

"I knew that the young men for whom I prayed were faced with a momentous decision," said the priest. "They needed the help of the Holy Mother of God, and I prayed that she might aid them and enlighten their ways with the light of knowledge and justice."

"The People's Tribunal condemns you to death by hanging," said Marcu. "You are found guilty of conspiring against the public safety by organizing armed rebellion."

Aristitza and Jon Calugar lifted their eyes in fright and looked at Marcu. He was writing and paid no attention to them. They turned their eyes to the priest. Father Koruga smiled at them serenely.

"The execution will take place in public tomorrow at daybreak," said Marcu. "The session of the People's Tribunal is now adjourned."

🐝 🐝 🐝

FATHER KORUGA was seized by the peasants with the armbands and locked up in the stables attached to the hall. There he found George Damian, the attorney, who had been captured on his way to the forest, the Sergeant of the gendarmes, and Vasile Apostol, with eight other peasants, the most prosperous in the village. They had all been sentenced to death and were to die before dawn on the following morning. The People's Tribunal had ordained it.

During the night the prisoners were taken out of the stables one by one and shot on the edge of the manure pit. Marcu had received orders not to hold executions in public, so as not to stir up the masses against the Red Army. He shot all the prisoners himself with a bullet through the neck.

🐝 🐝 🐝

SOON after midnight Aristitza heard a knock at her window. It was Susanna, Johann's wife. Hearing her wailing, Aristitza jumped to the conclusion that the Russians must have occupied the village and raped her daughter-in-law. She leaped out of bed in a fury. She knew that a Soviet patrol was expected in Fantana and that the Russians were in the habit of raping women, but she could not tolerate the idea that the first woman they laid hands on should have been her daughter-in-law, the daughter-in-law of a judge of the People's Tribunal.

"What's happened to you?" she asked, opening the door.

"Father Koruga has been shot," said Susanna.

"That's not true," said Aristitza. "Goldenberg wants to hang him tomorrow in the churchyard. But he won't be able to do it. He isn't the only judge in the village; I am one, too. Tomorrow we'll give the priest another trial and set him free. I've spoken to Jon Calugar. Go and tell his wife to go to sleep quietly and not worry."

"Father Koruga is dead," said Susanna. "Some men who watched him being shot came and told me."

Aristitza refused to believe it. However, she did not go back into the house. Together with Susanna she set out toward the village hall, still wearing nothing but the clothes in which she had slept. It was a clear night. The two women walked quickly, keeping to the middle of the road and not talking. Susanna was crying quietly. From time to time she wiped away the tears with a fold of her skirt. Aristitza was snorting with irritation. Several times she turned round to Susanna and shouted:

"Are you sleeping or walking? What's flowing in your veins, blood or whey?"

Susanna quickened her step, certain none the less that all their hurry was in vain. The priest was dead, and no one could do anything for him now.

The lights were still burning in the village hall, but there was no one about.

"Let's go to the stables," said Aristitza. "I'm a judge and I have a right to ask and be told what's going on."

Inside the stables it was pitch-dark. The door was shut but not locked. As they went in, Aristitza suddenly got scared.

"Haven't you any matches?" she asked Susanna.

"No, Mother."

"You never have anything," said Aristitza angrily. "Even when you got married you had nothing. No one but a fool like my son would have taken you naked as you were."

Susanna did not take offense. She knew Aristitza was venting her anger on her only because she was afraid to find out that the priest really was dead.

"Anybody here?" cried Aristitza, standing in the middle of the stables.

"There's no one here, Mother," said Susanna. "Marcu came and fetched all the prisoners from the stables and shot them outside by the manure pit."

"You're dreaming," said Aristitza. "How could he have done without consulting us other judges first?"

Susanna was silent. The two women went out into the yard and began to search for the bodies in the dark.

"There's nothing in the yard," said Aristitza. "I told you you were dreaming. Perhaps they were locked up somewhere else and the reactionaries in the village spread the rumor that Marcu had shot them."

Susanna left Aristitza and started hunting on her own. She searched carefully all over the yard round the manure pit. She was certain the priest had been shot. The villagers who had watched it happen had told everybody that the prisoners were taken out of the stables one by one and shot in the back.

"We'll go and find Goldenberg," said Aristitza. Susanna gave a little scream and collapsed on the grass. Aristitza came up to her furiously.

"What's up with you now, you good-for-nothing?" she cried. "Did you catch sight of your shadow and trip over it?"

But the words stuck in her throat. Near Susanna, in the grass on the edge of the pit, there were other bodies.

First of all Aristitza made out the body of a man in a white shirt who was lying at Susanna's feet. Another, all in black, lay a few paces away. And there were more beyond. Aristitza crossed herself to regain her courage.

"Get up. I need you," she ordered. She was not afraid of the dead, but at that moment she did not want to be alone.

Susanna stood up, trembling. Aristitza took hold of her hand. The two women started to scrutinize the bodies, bending down over each one. They peered close into their faces to make out who they were. Nine of them were lying on the edge of the pit. Three had fallen in. Aristitza was bending over a corpse and examining it attentively.

"This is Nicolae Ciubotaru, the former mayor," she said. She went down on her knees and put her ear on his chest to see if his heart was still beating. She got up and said:

"Dead."

A little way further on, she bent down over another man, listening for his heartbeat.

"Their bodies are still warm, but their hearts have stopped beating. This was Constantin Solomon, God rest his soul," she said. "He asked me to marry him when I was young."

To hold back the grief that was overwhelming her, she shouted angrily at Susanna:

"Help me, can't you! See if any of them are still alive. Don't stand there whimpering like a ninny."

"I can't, Mother," said Susanna. "I'm frightened."

"What are you frightened of?" asked Aristitza. "Keep your ear to their chests, hold your breath a moment, and find out if the heart is still beating. If it isn't, pray God rest his soul and cross yourself. If it is, there'll be more to do than making the sign of the cross. Understand?"

"I understand, but I'm frightened," said Susanna.

"You wretched good-for-nothing, you!" said Aristitza furiously. "What possessed my son to marry you?"

Aristitza was bending over another body.

"This must be that young lawyer who used to come to

Father Koruga's," she said. "He was a friend of Mr. Traian's, a real gentleman."

She pulled his jacket aside and listened for a moment. Then she got up and said:

"May God forgive him. He's dead, too. I shouldn't wonder if the poor man hasn't got a wife and children expecting him home."

Then suddenly she forgot about Susanna. She had found the priest's body and was bending over it with more reverence than she had shown toward the others. She drew his cassock aside and listened. Then she whispered:

"Father Koruga's not dead, girl."

Hearing that the priest was not dead, Susanna began to weep even more.

"Have you lost your senses?" asked Aristitza. "Instead of being glad, you start crying. Come over here and see for yourself how nicely his heart is beating."

Susanna knelt down beside the priest, but did not put her ear to his chest. Aristitza took the priest's hand in her own and said:

"He is still warm, girl. Feel how warm he is."

Aristitza's ears and eyes and hands were longing to find more evidence still of the life left in the priest's body. But apart from the warmth of his hands and cheeks and the sound of his heart, her senses could not ascertain any further signs of life in the man at her side.

"So that's all life is—a few heartbeats and a little warmth given off by the body." It seemed to her that it was too little.

"If that's all there is in a man's life, then it truly isn't very much," she said.

There was silence everywhere around them.

"Father Koruga smells so beautifully of musk rose and incense. His body is like a church; it has such a lovely smell. Like a real church."

The rest, except for the priest, were all dead. Some, those who had not died at once, were still warm. They had been in agony for some time. Their corpses showed how they must have writhed about in the grass before finally death relieved them of their suffering. The others were stone-cold. They had been killed on the spot the moment the bullet had entered their bodies.

Aristitza wiped her hands on her skirts. It was the fifth or sixth time that she had wiped them without realizing exactly why. Now her knees were wet, too.

"It must be their blood," she said. "In the dark I must have put my feet and hands into the blood. It is a great sin to trample on a man's blood. But God will forgive me. It was only because it was dark."

While Aristitza was down in the pit examining the other bodies, Susanna rubbed the priest's forehead.

"Where's the wound?" asked Aristitza, scrambling out of the pit and wiping her hands again.

"I don't know, Mother."

"You never know anything!" said Aristitza. "The wound must be stopped up at once. If we don't put something over it, all the blood will drain away, and life with it."

She found the place, which was sodden with blood. The priest was wounded in the back above the right shoulder.

"Give me some rags to tie up his wound," Aristitza ordered.

Susanna tried desperately to think where to find some rags. Aristitza lost patience. She lifted her skirt to tear off a strip of her petticoat. Her hands fumbled frantically between her skirt and her skin, but could not find the petticoat. She lifted the skirt to her breasts.

"Where the devil's my petticoat?" she said. Then she remembered that in the morning she had been in such a hurry to get to the Tribunal that she had forgotten to put it on. "I've only got my skirt on and no petticoat," she said.

She took the priest in her arms, undid the cassock and uncovered the wounded part of the shoulder.

"Give me your petticoat, Susanna," she ordered. She wiped the blood from his wound with the palms of her hands.

"How beautifully he smells of musk rose and incense—his body smells exactly like a church."

Aristitza turned round to Susanna, who had removed her dress and was now taking off her petticoat. She was naked.

"Are you out of your mind?" cried Aristitza. "Aren't you ashamed of standing naked in front of the priest and the dead men?"

"How am I to take off my petticoat if I don't take off my dress first?" asked Susanna.

"Strumpet that you are," said Aristitza without listening to her. "Parading about in your nakedness before the dead and the priest."

She spat on the ground.

❦ ❦ ❦

ARISTITZA and Susanna stopped by the side of a corn field and laid the priest's body on the grass. They had carried him there all the way, wrapped up in his cassock as if in a tarpaulin. To begin with, they had each taken hold of one end of it and had slung it between them like a hammock. But he was too heavy for them. Sweat ran down their cheeks. Every time they paused, Aristitza would bend down to see if the priest's heart was still beating. Then they picked him up and went on. But by now they were no longer carrying him slung between them, but dragged him behind them.

"May God grant that he doesn't die on the way," said Aristitza. "We must hurry. There'll be time enough to rest tomorrow and the day after."

Aristitza had not dared to take the priest to her own house.

The Communists might have found him there. "He may have escaped once, but they'll make sure he doesn't get a second chance," she said. "It would be safer to take him to our boys in the forest. They'll look after him and put him on his feet again. The Communists will never find him once he is in the forest."

"The district medical officer is with them," said Susanna. "If only we could find him. He has the first-aid box and bandages from the village."

"We'll find him all right," said Aristitza. But gradually as they drew nearer to the forest, their hopes dwindled. The forest was immense, and they could not possibly have found the district medical officer; they might as well have been looking for a needle in a haystack.

"If we don't find our boys," said Aristitza, "we'll have to take him ourselves and hide him from the Communists. At least that'll be something. After that we'll see. You'll have to stay beside him in the forest while I return to the village. I'll be back before daylight with food and water and maybe with some old woman who knows how to heal wounds."

Susanna started weeping. She was afraid of being left alone in the forest at this hour, in the middle of the night. Silently she prayed that God should make them find the boys.

❧ ❧ ❧

SKIRTING the edge of the forest ran a main road. Before crossing it Aristitza listened to make sure no one was coming. There was a convoy of trucks moving slowly up the road. The muffled sound of the engines could be heard in the distance like a humming of hornets. The convoy was climbing the hill toward them. The two women laid their burden on the grass and crept up to the road hiding between the corn stalks.

"It's a Russian convoy," said Aristitza. "But it doesn't matter. We'll wait till they've gone by. They can't see us."

The vehicles were drawing closer. When they had reached the top of the hill, not far from the women, the whole convoy halted. The drone of the engines ceased, and the crickets could be heard. A few soldiers jumped down from the trucks. They spoke in whispers.

"They are Germans," said Susanna.

Aristitza pricked up her ears. She and Susanna crept closer to the convoy, keeping just inside the corn field, and listened again.

"They are Germans," said Aristitza. "What about asking them to give us something for the priest? They're bound to have a doctor or a medical orderly with them."

The two women came out of the corn field.

"Don't you know a word of German?" asked Aristitza. "Not one word? If we don't say something to them they'll think we're enemies and shoot us."

"I don't know one word," answered Susanna.

They went a few steps nearer the convoy and stopped. They stood on the highway side by side, pressing close together. Aristitza caught hold of Susanna's wrist and clung tightly.

"You're younger than I am," she said. "Try to remember a German word. You must have heard Germans speaking sometime or other. Your father used to speak German. When you're young you have a better memory."

"I can't remember a single word," said Susanna. "Let's say something in Romanian."

"What can we say to the Germans in Romanian?" said Aristitza crossly. "They won't understand, and they'll think we are Communists."

"Let's shout 'Christ,' Mother," said Susanna. "The Germans are all Christians. If they hear us say 'Christ' they'll realize we're not Communists. 'Christ' means good and honest thoughts."

"You try it," said Aristitza. "If the Germans understand you, then you can't be as stupid as you look."

"I daren't do it alone," said Susanna. "Let's shout together."

The two women pressed even closer together and began to call out softly at first, then louder and louder:

"Christ, Christ!"

"Who's there?" came a hard voice from the first truck.

The women did not understand what the German had asked and answered in chorus:

"Christ."

Two soldiers came up to them. Aristitza was trembling all over, more even than Susanna. The Germans could not make out what they wanted. The women went into the field and returned with the priest. They put him down right in the center of the road, just ahead of the convoy. The Germans switched on the headlights and looked at Father Koruga's face.

"Is he a priest?" asked an officer.

"Christ!" answered Aristitza.

"Did the Bolsheviks shoot him?" asked the officer. Thinking the officer had asked whether the wounded man was a Bolshevik, she replied with conviction:

"Christ!"

The German convoy was retreating. The officer who had been talking to the women gave the order to move on. He signaled to Aristitza to remove the body so that the trucks could pass. Aristitza caught him by the hand and begged him for a doctor or orderly to bandage the priest's wound.

Hearing the engines start up, she became desperate. She did not want to let the Germans go before they had tended the priest's wound. Going down on her knees in front of the officer, she kissed his hand. No other doctor, she knew, would ever come their way again.

"What does the woman want?" asked the officer in charge of the convoy.

"They want us to take a casualty with us to the town," said the other officer. "He seems to be an Orthodox priest."

"Why not?" said the officer in charge. "We are a civilized

people, even when we are in retreat. Put the casualty into the ambulance, but hurry, the convoy must proceed."

The priest was wrapped in a blanket and lifted on a stretcher into a military ambulance. The column of vehicles began to move on.

Aristitza tried to climb up beside the priest, but the soldiers laughed at her and slammed the door of the ambulance. The convoy got under way. Susanna watched it disappear into the night and began to weep as though she were crying out for help.

"What's the matter now, woman?" asked Aristitza, shaking her by the shoulders. "Do you want the Russians to hear you screaming?"

"God will punish us, Mother, for the sin we have committed," said Susanna. "We ought never to have handed him over to the Germans. Heaven knows what they'll do with him."

"They'll take him to the hospital," said Aristitza. "He'll be better off in the hospital than in the forest."

But a few moments later she, too, started weeping. She was sorry for what she had done.

"We shouldn't have given him to the Germans," she said. "We've done a great wrong, and God will punish us. We'll go to hell for it. We handed poor Father Koruga over to the Germans, and it's all your fault."

The two women would have liked to run after the convoy and take the priest back. But the road was empty.

They began to make their way back to the village.

🙟 🙟 🙟

THE next morning Aristitza was arrested. At the village hall she was lashed with the end of a thick rope dipped in water. She confessed to having taken the priest away during the night and handed him over to the Germans. At nine A.M. she was shot at the edge of the manure pit. Susanna fled from the village with her two children. When Marcu's men came to arrest her, they found Johann Moritz's house empty.

⚑ ⚑ ⚑

"THAT," said Joseph, getting into bed, "was the greatest day of my life." The French prisoners who had escaped with Johann's help had reached American territory a few hours before.

Johann and Joseph were now lying in a beautiful room in an UNRRA hotel. They had eaten a whole array of delicacies, drunk wine, and smoked expensive cigarettes. They had been given parcels of food, clothing, and a host of other things.

Johann looked at the parcels neatly stacked on the carpet by the wall. He felt honored as never before. The Americans had given him new shirts and a suit, a razor, shoes, soap, and cigarettes. They had showered these gifts upon him, Johann Moritz, almost as soon as they had set eyes on him. He was proud of it. Now, for the first time, he felt that he, too, had made a great contribution to Allied victory.

"If I hadn't done something important, the Americans wouldn't have given me so many things," he said to himself. He remembered that they had not even asked him his name, and so he supposed they must have heard about the escape even before their arrival. All the Americans had smiled at him as if to show him that they knew what he had been through and what courage and bravery he had displayed.

He was tired, but he did not feel like sleeping. He looked round the room, unable to believe that it had all been prepared specially for him. All the things that lay scattered about on the chairs and the table and the carpet belonged to him. The Americans had given him all these things because he had saved five prisoners from a concentration camp.

"We made a perfect escape," said Joseph.

Johann remembered how he had marched off the camp parade ground one morning with the five prisoners. They had gone right through the town. Hilda had been at the window with the baby as usual, saying: "Look, that's your father with the gun and the helmet." Johann had smiled his daily smile at them. However, they had not halted at the bridge. The prisoners had marched on beyond it, and he had marched on behind them, with his rifle slung over his shoulder, as far as the forest. Everyone he met on the way thought he was a soldier escorting some prisoners. But, in fact, the escape had already begun. One woman, he was convinced, had stared at him intently. His heart had started thumping with fear. Others, too, had seemed to glance at him suspiciously, but he had pretended not to notice.

As soon as they had reached the forest, he had changed into the civilian clothes the Frenchmen had brought for him. Joseph had taken his rifle and smashed it against the trunk of an oak. At the sight of the splintered gun Johann had felt something break in his heart. But he was determined not to show it. After that the Frenchmen had put a match to his uniform and burned it. Seeing his uniform in flames had made him want to cry, but he had controlled himself so as not to annoy the Frenchmen. All the time, they had kept on cursing Hitler, but he had no idea what they were talking about.

Then they had walked for a whole week, keeping to the forest all the time. One fine day, emerging into a clearing, they had spotted some American jeeps on the road. The Frenchmen had burst out singing. Oblivious of their exhaustion, they had sung wildly till the forest rang with the sound of their voices. They had stuck red, white, and blue ribbons in their button-holes and in his. Then they had come down to the jeeps. The Americans had given them cigarettes and had taken them to UNRRA, where their rooms stood waiting for them, and the food was ready on the table, as though they were expected.

Ever since that moment the Americans had done nothing but give them parcels and food. He felt it must all be a fairy tale. But looking at the parcels and at Joseph, he realized that it was all true. These things had really happened to him, because he had made a great contribution to the Allied victory.

Joseph had fallen asleep. Johann lay and thought how, from here, he would be going on to France. He thought of the house he was going to build, of Hilda and Franz. "When the war is ended I'll get Father and Mother over to France, too," he said to himself.

Then he fell asleep, still dreaming of future happiness. He went to sleep on the edge of the bed, fully dressed, and did not stir again till morning.

❦ ❦ ❦

JOHANN had been at UNRRA for a whole fortnight. He had given the Americans a description of his escape with the five French prisoners. They had congratulated him and had made him write down exactly how it had all happened. They were going to publish his story in the papers. Everybody praised him and wanted to talk to him. As the days went by he became more and more convinced that he had helped the Allies to win the war. He was happy and proud of having done something for the Allied Nations, proud that they were pleased with him.

One day the director of UNRRA had him called to his office. The director had already sent for him several times before and had made him tell the story of the escape. Johann came gaily into the room. The director invited him to take a seat in an armchair and smiled and handed him the box of cigarettes. Johann was amazed at the honor shown to him. Every time he had come he had met with the same reception, but he still could not get used to it.

"You are no longer entitled to receive food and lodging from UNRRA," said the director, when he had lighted Johann's cigarette with his lighter. "As from tomorrow you will not have the right to feed here and you must vacate the room you are at present occupying in the hotel."

Johann turned very pale. He was wondering what he could have done to make the Americans so angry with him. "I must be guilty of something dreadful if they suddenly throw me out of UNRRA and turn me onto the streets!" he thought.

Until that day he had been receiving a stream of presents from them. He had five parcels full of things he had been given for himself and for Hilda. They had even given him toys and clothes for Franz when they had found out that he had a child. They had asked for a photo of Franz and had all looked at it.

"And now, all of a sudden, these same gentlemen throw me out. I must have done something very bad," he said to himself.

"UNRRA is only responsible for the protection of citizens of the Allied Nations," said the director. "You are an enemy of the Allied Nations."

Johann thought of the presents received in return for his great deed. Every one of them had told him how much he had helped the Allied cause. For fourteen days he had been treated like a hero—and now these same men maintained that he, Johann Moritz, was an enemy of the Allied Nations.

"You are an enemy alien," the director emphasized.

"I've done nothing against the Allied Nations," said Johann. "I swear it, sir, I am not guilty of anything against them."

"You're a Romanian, aren't you?" asked the director harshly. "Romania is an enemy of the Allies. You're a Romanian, consequently you must be our enemy. UNRRA does not exist to provide food and shelter for enemy nationals. You must vacate your room by tomorrow."

Johann went out of the room, hanging his head. His rifle, he remembered, lay in fragments in the forest and the Frenchmen had set fire to his uniform. He could not go back to his company without his rifle. "And where shall I go now?" he asked himself.

❦ ❦ ❦

IMMEDIATELY after Johann was posted as a deserter, Hilda was taken into custody. At the military-police post she stated she knew nothing. Two days later Hilda's mother was also arrested. They were interrogated and then beaten, but the special investigation officers could get nothing out of them. In the course of the search they made at Johann's house they came across Colonel Müller's letters.

"He's a friend of Johann's," said Hilda. "Colonel Müller used to send us two hundred marks a month. At Christmas and Easter and on our birthdays he always used to send us food and cigarettes."

The military police informed Colonel Müller of Moritz's desertion, in the hope of eliciting further information from him. Two days later a telegram a whole page long came back from General Staff. This is what Colonel Müller wrote to the police:

IN COURSE OF FOUR CENTURIES NO SINGLE CASE DESERTION RECORDED IN ANNALS OF HEROIC FAMILY OF WHICH JOHANN MORITZ IS MEMBER STOP ABSOLUTELY INCONCEIVABLE THAT JOHANN MORITZ SHOULD HAVE DESERTED STOP AM CONVINCED HIS DISAPPEARANCE RESULT OF ABDUCTION OR ASSASSINATION STOP PROCEED WITH THOROUGH INVESTIGATIONS ON THESE LINES STOP DISAPPEARANCE OF JOHANN MORITZ CONSTITUTES IRREPARABLE LOSS HEROIC FAMILY STOP HE MUST BE FOUND AT ALL COSTS STOP DO NOT CAST SUSPICION OF DESERTION OVER ONE OF BRAVEST AND MOST HONORABLE FAMILIES OF GERMAN BLOOD STOP DO NOT USE WORD DESERTION IN YOUR INQUIRY STOP WIFE AND CHILD OF JOHANN MORITZ TO COME UNDER OFFICIAL PROTECTION OF INSTI- TUTE GERMAN STUDIES AND RESEARCH STOP UNTIL JOHANN MORITZ FOUND WIFE AND CHILD TO RECEIVE FOOD PENSION FROM INSTI- TUTE STOP LOCAL POLICE REQUESTED WATCH OVER SAFETY OF WIFE AND CHILD STOP ANY FURTHER INFORMATION CONCERNING JOHANN

MORITZ TO BE COMMUNICATED TO ME TELEGRAPHICALLY AT GEN-
ERAL STAFF STOP MÜLLER COLONEL HQ GENERAL STAFF GERMAN
ARMY

"If the Colonel finds out that we arrested Moritz's wife, within twenty-four hours we shall be posted to the front lines as a disciplinary measure," said the provost marshal in command of the military police. "We had better ask the woman not to tell the Colonel that she was taken into custody."

"And what about that inquiry?" asked the lieutenant in charge of the legal branch.

"Close the dossier at once. We don't want to get entangled with the OKW," * said the provost marshal. "Not that I'd be fool enough to believe that this is anything but desertion. But periodically those brass-hats go and make bigger blunders than the ordinary private. Colonel Müller is a scholar. I've read his articles in reviews. He has published some books, too. But he is too much of a fanatic. How on earth does he make out that Moritz isn't a deserter?"

Hilda was driven home in the provost marshal's car.

"Any time you need a car, just give me a ring," said the provost marshal. "My Mercedes stands at your disposal day and night. Anything else you need, just let me know. I would ask you not to mention to Colonel Müller that you were arrested. It was done simply as a matter of example for the other men, a mere routine formality."

"So my husband is not a deserter, then?" asked Hilda. "Has he been sent on a special mission?"

"We cannot tell you everything," said the officer. "But your husband is not a deserter. The rest is secret."

Hilda flushed with pleasure. Thereafter her life became one continuous dream out of *The Thousand and One Nights*. She was convinced that her husband had been sent on a special mission by the General Staff. "Otherwise, why should the police have put a car at my disposal?" she argued.

* Oberkommando Wehrmacht.

She spent hours on end daydreaming at the window, imagining Johann in all kinds of treacherous and mysterious situations such as she had seen in adventure films.

"He never told me anything about it," she said to herself. "He considered me inferior. But I will strive with all my heart to live up to my husband." She kissed her child, saying: "Never, never, in all my life, have I been so happy. Only the wife of a Johann Moritz can know the utter bliss of being the wife of a hero."

❦ ❦ ❦

"I JUST can't believe it's all over," said Hilda. "Everyone has left town and fled into the forests or out into the country. The Russians are said to be only a few miles off. All the neighbors have gone. But I don't believe it. It's all enemy propaganda, to provoke a panic. I'm staying here. Germany cannot lose the war."

"Bring me a basin of water," said the officer to whom Hilda had been talking. He took off his leather coat and put it on a hanger. His suitcase was on the chair. Then he took off his tunic and hung it over the back of the chair. He was left wearing his pullover. Hilda was watching his every movement. She could have gone on looking at him for hours, watching him take off his leather coat, hang it on its hanger, and unbutton his tunic.

"And bring some hot water for shaving," he ordered. He turned his back on her and opened the suitcase. Hilda went out of the room, leaving the door open. From out of the kitchen window she gazed at the military car that was drawn up outside the gate. It was the car in which the officer had arrived. Hilda looked at her watch. He had been there hardly fifteen minutes. "And it's as if I had known him for years," she said to herself.

The officer had knocked at the door, and she had opened it. She was alone in the house. He had said harshly—as if he were giving orders to his orderly—that he wanted to wash and change. Without waiting for an answer, he had walked in, brushing straight past Hilda in the doorway. She had caught the smell of his leather coat mingled with the smell of wind, dust, and war. She had followed him in like one intoxicated.

The newcomer was tall, a real giant. He had thrown open the living-room door as though walking into a room of his own house. He had started undressing with the door open, while Hilda had stood on the threshold, awaiting his orders. But the giant just went on undressing, without taking any notice of her. As he removed his helmet, Hilda saw that he had silvery-white hair. Then he had taken off his coat. She noticed he wore the shoulder braid of a lieutenant.

"He is an officer in the Reserve," she had said to herself.

Several times the giant had glanced in her direction. But his eyes had looked unseeingly straight through her. She started to talk, saying anything that came into her head. The giant did not answer or even look at her again. When he had finished taking off his tunic, he simply ordered her to bring him water and a basin. Hilda thought of inviting him to wash in the bathroom. But he had asked for a basin, and she dared not contradict him.

As she was filling the jug with water, Hilda took another look at the car standing outside the gate. It was covered with dust, like the giant's leather coat. When she went in with the basin, he was in his shirt sleeves.

"Get me a mirror!" he said. He was immersed in his own thoughts and seemed very tired. She thought he might like to sleep. She would gladly have made up the bed in the bedroom and left him there to rest.

During the last few days column after column of troops had passed through the town. Soldiers and officers alike had knocked at the door, demanding shelter for the night, or water to wash in or to heat their cans of food. She had always done everything she could to help them, thinking of her husband. She knew that Johann was on a special mission and she wanted to prove herself worthy of him by doing her duty toward the Fatherland.

For these soldiers and officers, she had made up a bed in the living room. But for the giant's sake she was prepared to sleep on the sofa of the living room and let him have the bedroom. She hoped secretly that perhaps he would sleep, not in Johann's bed, but in her own. This thought sent a shiver down her spine. She fetched the mirror Johann always used for shaving and brought it to the giant. He was pacing up and down the room, with his shirt unbuttoned at the neck. He took the mirror out of her hands, looked for a place to hang it, and could not find one. He was tall, and if he had set the mirror on the table, he would have had to stoop all the while he shaved. Without a word he thrust the mirror in her hands and started lathering his face.

"Higher!" he ordered.

His face was tanned by the sun and the wind. A sandy-red stubble had grown over his cheeks. She was holding the mirror level with her mouth. At his command she lifted it higher, up to her forehead. When he bent close to it she could feel his breath. Her hands were trembling, but she only gripped the mirror tighter, forcing herself to keep it steady.

"Higher still," he said gruffly.

She raised the mirror above her head. Her arms were beginning to ache, but she did not mind. She longed to say something, but the regular scraping of the razor shaving the giant's soft and lathery beard forced her to keep quiet. She closed her eyes and listened to the sound of the razor. Her dilated nostrils were inhaling the scent of the soap, and with it, not soap only, but the smell of war and valor and distant travel. His coat smelled just the same. He did not notice that she was swaying. He was shaving with meticulous care so as not to cut himself.

When he had finished, he scrubbed his hands with soap in the white washbasin.

"Roll up my sleeves!" he said.

She turned up the sleeves of his shirt, afraid to touch his skin. But accidentally her hand brushed his, and she shivered again. The smell of the wind and the forests that the giant had brought with him was permeating the house. It had impregnated the furniture and the carpets and the walls, and she knew it would never come out. She felt that it had penetrated her clothes and her pores, her hair and her blouse, and that, however much she washed, it would never again leave her in all her life.

"Now I want to be left alone."

As she turned round to shut the door behind, she caught sight of him stripped to the waist. He was in the act of pulling off his shirt, and it hid his head. She saw only his chest. As a nurse, she had seen thousands of naked men. But never had she beheld such a chest as this.

She went into the kitchen and looked out of the window at the car. The baby was asleep. She wondered whether the officer would leave at once or have a rest first. She would have liked to prepare him a meal. She was on the alert now, ready to answer the minute he called her.

"The Russians are only two miles away!" said a neighbor passing under her window. "Are you staying behind?"

"Yes, I am," Hilda called back to her. She was wondering why the giant did not call her. She could not bear the suspense any longer. She knocked at the door and walked in. He had put on his full-dress uniform, and his chest was covered with decorations.

Hilda stood in the doorway, dazed. He smiled at her. It was the first time she had seen him smile. The scent of wind and war and leather had gone now, and instead the room was filled with the scent of flowers.

"I want to know if you are a true German woman," he said. "I want to ask you to do me a service that only a German woman could do for me."

"I am," she answered, "and not only am I a good German woman, but my husband has been sent by the Greater Ger . . ."

She was just going to tell him the secret of her husband's departure. But she suddenly broke off. On the table there now stood the framed photographs of two beautiful women. As she looked at them she found she no longer had the courage to reveal the secret that she had never before disclosed to anyone but that she would willingly have revealed to him. Now that she had seen the photographs of the two women she regretted the impulse she had had to reveal her secret to him.

"My wife and daughter," he said. "They are both dead. I loved them very much, but they both betrayed my love. They both disappointed me. My wife is buried. My daughter is somewhere in the world, I don't know where. She married a wastrel, and since then she has been as good as dead to me."

Hilda looked at the photographs of the two women. "I should never have betrayed him if he had loved me," she thought.

Beside the photographs of the women stood one in a leather frame—the Führer.

"And now the Führer is dead, too," he said. "And Germany no longer exists. These were all that I lived for. When I was young I loved horses, too. But that was only a passing phase. One by one I have watched the ideals of my life collapse before my very eyes—my wife, my daughter, the Führer, and the Fatherland. Now my turn has come. In half an hour's time the Russians will be here. Before their arrival I should like to fulfill the last duty of my life."

Hilda had tears in her eyes. She had been hoping he would sleep in her own bedroom, that he would say he was hungry, and that she would be able to give him food. And now, instead, he stood before her dressed in his parade uniform.

"I will do everything you ask me," she said. "Do you wish to go anywhere?" She was looking at his uniform.

"I am not going anywhere," he answered. "This is my last journey on earth." He was laughing now.

"You thought I was going somewhere because I have shaved, washed, and put on my dress uniform?"

He gave her a pat on the shoulder. She felt humble and inferior beside him, just as she had felt beside Johann when she had heard that he had been sent on a secret mission.

"Listen carefully to what I am going to tell you," he said. "It is perfectly simple, really. Yet no woman but a German woman could do it. My wife would have been incapable of it. But you, you'll be able to do it. She was too much of a *Weib*, too weak-minded. I wouldn't even have asked her. But with you, it's different."

Hilda felt proud that the giant should have asked her to do something he would not even have asked his wife.

"When I am dead," he said, "drag my body into the courtyard and burn it. You will find me lying dead here on this groundcloth."

He had already spread an army groundcloth out on the floor. It was new and covered the whole floor.

"All you have to do is to catch hold of the corners of the cloth and drag me down into the courtyard," he said.

He pulled out two cans full of gasoline from underneath the table.

"Here's the gasoline. It's aviation fuel. When you've got me into the yard, wrap the cloth round me and pour the gasoline all over it. Then set fire to it with this lighter."

He was smiling as he took a gold cigarette lighter out of his pocket and handed it to her.

"Here's the lighter to start the fire," he said. "When the first blaze dies down, pour on the second can. After that I don't think there will be anything left to burn. The Russians will find nothing but my ashes. No soldier worthy of the name shall allow even his dead body to fall into enemy hands. Such, throughout the course of history, has been the tradition of the German warrior. When everything was over he embraced death and his body was destroyed. The foe never found more than a heap of ashes."

The giant rubbed his hands. Hilda was looking at the photographs in silence.

"If you want to burn the photographs, wrap them in the ground cloth with me and let them burn together. If you'd rather keep them, you can—but I don't see why you should want to. I've never lived here. I'm from Romania."

She stood motionless, trying to imagine the giant lying dead on the cloth. She could not bring herself to believe that it was possible. To her it seemed that he could never die, that he was eternal.

"Are you afraid?" he asked. "A German woman is never afraid, above all when she has work to do for the Fatherland. I hope you understand that you are serving your country by fulfilling the last wishes of one of her soldiers."

"I know," she said. "I'm not at all afraid. But I can't believe that it is all true. I don't believe the Russians will ever get here. I don't believe Germany is defeated."

"Everything is over," he said. "Everything is irretrievably lost. Don't forget to put the revolver back in its holster and to set fire to it so that it may burn along with me. A soldier must be buried or cremated with his weapons."

There was a moment's silence. He was gazing somewhere into the distance, lost in his thoughts as in fathomless waters.

"Now it's all over," he said.

Hilda raised her eyes. She thought he was going to shoot himself there, in front of her. She would not have been able to stand it. But he was not going to do it now. He turned to face the Führer's photograph. Springing to attention, he saluted with outstretched arm.

She was just behind him, looking at his shoulders and waist tightly pulled in by the uniform. She saw his outstretched arm.

He stood as still as a statue. The salute seemed to last an eternity.

At last he brought down his arm, turned about, took one pace forward, raised his arm again, and saluted her.

"Good-by, my friend, and thank you," he said. "I am Lieutenant Jurgu Jordan, but there is no need to tell anybody. Be proud of what you are going to do. It is an honor for a German woman to fulfill the last wishes of a soldier."

He shook hands with her. It was the strong handshake of a final farewell.

"Now I wish to be left alone," he said in a tone of command. "Come in as soon as you hear the shot. Farewell."

THE first Russian trucks appeared at the end of the road. Hilda first heard the hum of their engines and then saw them from the kitchen window. She rushed back toward the room where she had left the giant. He had told her not to come in until she had heard the revolver go off. She had not heard anything and dared not disobey his order. The Russian trucks rumbled along the street and made the walls of the house shake. She could not wait any longer. She was terrified now. She knocked on the door and burst in.

The giant lay on his back on the cloth in the middle of the room.

"How is it that I never heard the shot?" she asked herself.

His body lay stretched out full length, as if he had died standing to attention to salute the Führer's photograph. His peaked cap was on his head. His face was a violet blue and seemed to be powdered over with ash. His right cheek, his mouth, and his nose were stained with blood, but there was not much of it, only a thin trickle.

She picked up the revolver lying by his side and put it back in its holster. She was still wondering why she had not heard the shot.

She lifted the corners of the groundcloth and covered the body. Before covering his face, she looked at him for the last time.

"I don't feel as if I were standing beside someone dead," she said to herself. "I am not afraid of death. I don't even see it when it is close to me. Perhaps it is because at the hospital I saw men die by the thousand."

She covered his face without touching it. Now he was dead, he was no different from all the other dead men she had ever seen. Alive, he had been so unlike the others. But now she could hardly remember the time he had been still alive, when he had shaved and put on dress uniform. When she had been near him then, every fiber of her being trembled.

But now, now all that seemed to have happened many years ago. She had almost forgotten it.

From outside came the rumbling of Russian trucks and tanks. Suddenly Hilda was afraid. She wanted to take the child in her arms and flee into the woods through the little gate at the back of the garden. But she remembered the promise she had made to the giant.

"I wish I hadn't promised to burn him," she said to herself.

She could not carry the corpse into the garden. The Russian soldiers passing in their trucks and tanks might see her.

"I'll have to wait till tonight," she said to herself. "I'll carry him down then, set fire to the groundcloth, and run away into the woods with the child."

She went on standing beside the body, thinking of nothing. Then it occurred to her that if anyone were to find the body in her house, she might be arrested. She fetched the child in from the next room and sat down on a chair with it beside the body.

"I cannot break a promise given to a soldier before his death," she said to herself. She locked the door, resolved to wait till dark. There was only an hour or two till then. She did not have her watch on, but she remembered noticing a big one on the giant's wrist. She drew the groundcloth aside and looked at the dead man's watch to see how much longer she would have to wait. At that moment there was a bang on the door.

She pressed the child to her breast and did not answer. She could hear them speaking Russian outside the door. There was more thumping. She opened the window that faced onto the garden.

"I can't run away without first keeping my word," she said to herself. "Johann, my husband, is a hero. I have no right to behave like a coward."

She unscrewed the cap of one of the gasoline cans and poured it over the groundcloth. By now they were using the butt ends of their rifles on the door. She unscrewed the second can, but only poured half of it out. She was afraid the Russians would break down the door any minute and she was hurrying desperately. She picked up the child and went toward the window.

"I'll jump out of the window and then throw the burning lighter into the room. It will start the fire. Then I shall have kept my promise," she thought.

There was a strong smell of gasoline in the room. The child started coughing. She hurried still more. As she climbed on the window sill to jump into the garden, the Russians started to burst open the door with their shoulders, but the door was strong. From the window to the flower beds in the garden was only a short jump. She could easily have done it. But at that very moment three Russian caps appeared from below the window ledge.

There were other soldiers in the garden. It was too late to jump through the window. She glanced toward the door. The child, choking with the gasoline fumes, was screaming. She decided to jump out of the window after all and make a dash for the woods past the Russian soldiers. At that moment a hand came after her through the window and grasped her foot.

She screamed. She wanted to defend herself, but she had nothing but the lighter in her hands. Without thinking she pressed the catch like someone pressing the trigger of a revolver when his life is in danger. For a fraction of a second there was a great light. Then there was darkness, a darkness deeper and blacker than night. And after that there was never light again. In the same flames that consumed the body of Jurgu Jordan perished Hilda, the wife of Johann Moritz, and their child, Franz. And the same fire destroyed the house from cellar to attic and everything in it, including the photographs the giant had brought with him and put on the table: those of Susanna's mother and of Susanna, Johann's first wife.

The giant's gasoline sent long flames shooting up into the night sky.

❧ ❧ ❧

TRAIAN KORUGA and Eleonora West were seated side by side, facing Major Brown, the American military commander of Weimar.

"And that is all, Major Brown," said Traian. "On August 23, when Romania was occupied by the Russians, my wife and I were interned by the Croats at the same time as members of the Romanian Legation. We were interned in a hotel and were treated in accordance with international law as diplomatic representatives of enemy countries. After that, Croatia was occupied by Tito's Partisans. We were interned in Austria, then in Germany, finally in Czechoslovakia. When Germany capitulated and there was no one left to keep us interned, we set out for the west. We abandoned everything we possessed and started walking toward the west."

Eleonora's thoughts traveled back over the hundred and fifty miles they had covered on foot. Her legs were swollen, and the soles of her feet were covered with calluses.

"We have abandoned everything and fled through fields and woods in order to reach territory occupied by the Americans, the British, or the French," Eleonora went on. "We did not want to fall alive into the hands of the Russians or the Partisans. We would have committed suicide rather than be caught by them."

"Why are you so afraid of the Russians and the Partisans? No one need be afraid of them—except Fascists! The Russians and the Partisans are our allies. They have been fighting for the victory of the United Nations."

"You are not a Fascist either, Major Brown, but I don't think you would be prepared for your wife to remain in territory under Bolshevik occupation, were it only for twenty-four hours," said Traian. "Not for political reasons, but simply because of the cruelty and terrorism of the Russians. I don't believe that you yourself would have the courage to penetrate into a Russian or Partisan zone unless you were in uniform and under heavy escort. Is it fair, then, that you should ask us, two defenseless persons, why we fled before barbaric hordes armed with automatic rifles of the latest American type?"

"And what is it you want now?" asked Major Brown. "You are not allowed to leave Germany. And while you remain you will be treated as enemy citizens. You will be subject to the same obligations as the German population and will have the same rights. Nothing more."

"In other words, no rights at all," said Traian. "Every German woman in Weimar is obliged to clean out the lavatories of the concentration camp at Buchenwald and wash the linen of the liberated inmates at least once a week. Do you wish to send my wife to do the same?"

"We are not enemies of America and the Allied Nations," said Eleonora. "For over a year it was the enemies of the Allies who kept us interned. We have come now to ask you for permission to occupy a room somewhere in this region; or, if we are not authorized to stay, for permission to leave. We are both homeless. We don't know where to sleep or eat, we have no-where to wash, we are not permitted to stay, and we are not permitted to go."

"You are enemy citizens," said Major Brown. "I am not interested in your personal misfortunes. You hold Romanian passports, don't you? You are therefore enemies."

"But Romania has already been in the war for ten months against Germany, on the side of the Allies," said Eleonora. "You know that as well as we do. Eighty thousand Romanians have already laid down their lives in the Allied cause. Do you consider those who fight shoulder to shoulder with you as your enemies?"

"Romania is an enemy state," said Major Brown again. He took a printed sheet out of a drawer and read out: "Enemy countries: Romania, Hungary, Finland, Bulgaria, Germany, Japan, Italy. That's clear enough, isn't it? You are enemies of the United States."

Traian stood up. Eleonora looked beseechingly at the Major.

"Haven't you ever read in the newspapers that Romania has been fighting on the Allied side for almost a year?" she asked. "Aren't our identity papers, showing that we have been interned by the Germans, sufficient proof for you? We are not your enemies."

"True or not true, I just am not interested," said Major Brown. "In the instructions I have received, it lays down that Romanians are enemies of the United States. I've already wasted too much time arguing with you. You, madam, are my enemy, my enemy, you understand? If I had fallen into your hands, you'd have had me shot there and then, not sat and talked to me as I am talking to you. All this is illegal anyway, and will not happen again. One does not argue with one's enemies."

Major Brown was livid with anger. He did not even ac-knowledge Traian and Eleonora as they took their leave.

"That is the West for you," said Traian as they went downstairs. "They are no more interested in man than they are in facts. They have no eyes for the individual. They have generalized everything and bow only before rules and regulations."

"I can't walk any further," said Nora. He took her arm. She leaned against his shoulder and started weeping.

"We almost ran for a hundred miles. We ran as people run toward Mecca."

"Don't regret it, Nora," he said. "We've escaped from the savage terror of the Russians. And we're lucky to have done that. There is ho place on earth where people are happy today. The earth has ceased to belong to men."

❦ ❦ ❦

FOUR days later Traian and Eleonora went to see Major Brown again. They needed a permit for a further week's residence.

Nora's feet were swollen, and she could scarcely walk. She had put on the best silk dress she had and wore a hat and high-heeled shoes. After telling the sentry on duty that they wished to speak to Major Brown, Traian said to her:

"You're all dressed up as for an official reception." She smiled. The last time she had worn that dress was three years before, one morning when she had paid a visit to the Finnish minister.

"Major Brown requests you to wait a moment," said the soldier politely.

A few minutes went by. Eleonora was pleased. Then another soldier appeared.

"Are you the Romanian diplomats who wish to speak to Major Brown?" he asked. "Would you be good enough to wait a little longer, please." And he vanished.

Eleonora began to think that Major Brown was a gentleman after all and knew how to behave. That was the second time in five minutes he had apologized for keeping them waiting.

Military government headquarters had been set up in a large building with a vast entrance hall. Nora looked at herself in a mirror. She was thinner now and the pleats of her dress hung better than when she had worn it last time at the Finnish Legation.

"This way, please," said the second soldier, coming toward them. Eleonora walked away from the mirror, smiling. Traian took her arm. They followed the soldier, who was not going up the stairs toward the Major's office where they had been the last time, but toward the exit. He asked them to get into a jeep that was waiting outside the gate.

"Where are we going?" asked Traian.

The soldier at the wheel shrugged his shoulders. There was a strong wind. The car sped through the streets of the town. Traian leaned over to the second soldier and shouted in his ear:

"Where are we going?"

He shrugged his shoulders, just as the other one had done.

Traian turned toward his wife. She was holding onto the brim of her hat with both hands and was laughing. She had always loved speed.

The jeep drew up outside a stone wall at the other end of the town. A doorkeeper in a peaked cap opened the gates, but the car did not drive in. One of the soldiers handed the doorkeeper an envelope. Then he signaled to Traian and Eleonora to get out of the jeep.

"Where are we?" she asked.

The Americans stood waiting for her to climb out, but did not answer.

"Where are we?" she asked the doorkeeper in German.

"The town jail," he answered, and took her by the arm.

She had meant to have a word with the soldiers, but it was too late. The jeep had disappeared as quickly as it had come. She turned toward Traian. He was white. The iron gates slammed behind them.

They were in the prison courtyard.

🐝 🐝 🐝

TRAIAN was locked in cell No. 5 on the ground floor and Nora in cell No. 26 on the third.

"There is obviously some mistake," said Traian to himself as soon as he had been left alone. He tried to guess what had gone wrong. But remembering that at that very moment Nora was locked in a cell exactly like his own, he lost his nerve.

As they were being separated, he had tried to kiss her and speak some words of love to her. The guard had caught him by the shoulder and had forbidden him to go near her. Nora had turned imploringly toward the guard, but he had pushed her brutally round the corner of the corridor. That was how they had parted in the hall of the prison.

"I suppose they must have mixed me up with heaven knows what criminal with the same name who looks like me. But why have they arrested Nora?"

Traian started banging on the door with his fists, to summon the guard.

"I would have expected the Russians to arrest me," he said to himself. "For them clean hands is good enough grounds for an arrest. In fact, it wouldn't have surprised me in the least if they had arrested me even without looking at my hands. I was prepared for anything from the Russians. I did two hundred kilometers on foot to escape a form of society where 'absence of a cause' constitutes adequate cause for arrest, murder, or deportation."

Though his fists were sore, he went on drumming on the door of his cell. He was no longer doing it to make the guard come, but to punish himself for running a hundred miles in vain, dragging Nora behind him. Nora with her swollen legs and bleeding feet.

"I expected the Germans to arrest her because they are Nazis and anti-Semites."

"What do you want?" asked the guard in the doorway.

"I want to speak to the prison governor at once," said Traian. "My wife and I have been arrested by some stupid mistake."

"I know, I know," answered the guard ironically. "Everyone says he was arrested by mistake when he first gets here."

"Don't trifle with me," said Traian. "I wish to speak to the governor immediately."

"There is no governor here," answered the guard. "You've been arrested by the Americans. We're only responsible for the prison administration. We're not even supposed to speak to the prisoners. In a way we're prisoners, too."

"Then I want to speak to the Americans."

"The sergeant comes only once a week—on Mondays."

Traian remembered that it was Monday.

"Do you mean to say I'll have to wait till next Monday?" he asked. "Do you expect my wife to stay in prison for a whole week?"

"It's no use your telling me all that," said the guard. "You can bang away at the door for hours and hours, but it won't do any good. The sergeant doesn't come again till next Monday, and there's nothing I can do about it." He shut the door.

"All right, pass it on or keep it to yourself, just as you like, but until I am allowed to speak to the governor to find out the reason for my arrest, I shall not touch food or water. It is my only means of protest, and I shall adopt it."

"Hunger strike, do you mean?" asked the guard.

"Yes, and I shall not drink, either."

The guard stood on the threshold for a moment, keys in hand.

"Pity," he said. "You're still so young." He turned the key twice in the lock.

♯ ♯ ♯

NORA spent half an hour banging at the door of her cell with her fists. Eventually, a guard came to the door but did not open it. He peered into the cell through the grille.

"If you go on banging on that door, you'll be punished," he said. "Prisoners are not allowed to bang on cell doors."

The guard went away. Nora stretched out on the bed. A second later she leaped to her feet. "There are probably lice," she said to herself. She was frightened. She would have liked to start banging again on the door and ask for another mattress or at least to find out whether there were lice in her bed, but she had now been told she was not allowed to bang on the door. She paced up and down in her cell.

In her heart of hearts Nora was conscious of a sense of guilt. Fundamentally, she knew that her arrest was justified. Ever since she had faked the documents proving her racial origin, and had paid for the theft of the birth certificates from the archives, she had been haunted day and night by the thought of prison. Every day she had been expecting to see the police coming to take her away. She had known she would be found out and arrested sooner or later. All the way across Germany she had trembled at the sight of every policeman because her papers were forged. These last years of her life had been spent in constant dread of the hour of her arrest.

"That hour has come," she said. "They have found out that I am Jewish, and there is no salvation now."

Every particle of her body was quivering with fear.

"It is absurd of me to think that the Americans have arrested me because I concealed my Jewish origin and forged some papers in Romania. Yet I am sure that that is the real cause for my arrest. The only one. It isn't logical, but it is true. I am guilty. For five years I got away with it. This time I'll be punished, punished severely and cruelly, but justly."

She felt cold. Her underwear, frothy and light as soap bubbles, her dress, thin and airy as a veil, could afford her no protection against the chilly dampness of the stone walls. It penetrated to her skin and beyond, to the very marrow of her bones. Till that moment she had never felt cold in her kidneys. Anatomically speaking, she did not even know exactly where they were or what they looked like. But certainly they were freezing. And not only her kidneys. Her intestines were freezing as well.

She wrapped her dress over her knees, but that did not help. She was afraid to sit on the bed. The icy coldness of the cement floor was rising through the thin soles of her shoes, rising to her knees and above her knees, spreading all over her body. She began to shiver, and her teeth chattered.

Outside it was warm; but that meant nothing to her while her teeth were chattering and she was shivering as though it were midwinter. To get warm she squatted down on her heels in the middle of the cell. At that moment she suddenly realized she had to go to the lavatory. She had to go that very instant. Hundreds of needles were piercing her bladder, and she was losing control of the muscles.

She remembered having read in novels that in prison cells there were buckets instead of lavatories. But in her cell she could see nothing but the bed, the table, and a small barred window; and the door. She went over and lifted her fist to bang on it.

"Surely they can't refuse permission to use the lavatory," she argued.

And then, suddenly, she remembered the harsh words of the German guard: "If you bang on the door again you will be punished." Her arms dropped to her sides. She was afraid to bang again.

"I am guilty because I banged on the door when it was not allowed," she told herself, and started pacing to and fro again across the cell.

Again she stopped in front of the door and lifted her

clenched fists to it. But even now she dared not bang. "If you bang again you will be punished."

While these words were ringing in her ears, an electric current seemed to shoot through her body—a warning signal. Suddenly her muscles refused to obey her any longer, and she lost control completely. She felt the wet spreading, first her drawers that were so fine and brief, then her girdle, then her stockings. Something warm and wet was oozing down her thighs and along her stockings, right into her shoes.

She made one last effort to restrain herself. But it was as if her muscles, her flesh, her whole body were no longer hers. She squatted down further. As her drawers grew warmer and warmer, there overcame her gradually a sensation of pleasure and relief, such as she had never known before in all her life. It was as if every muscle, every pore, and every fiber in her body was relaxing. It was more than just pleasure. It was delight. Even stronger, perhaps, than delight: it was sheer ecstasy. It enabled her to break right away from everything earthly. She was floating in space. This moment of complete detachment and ecstasy seemed to last forever. It was beyond time: her whole body was liberated.

She felt she had been urinating for hours on end without stopping. But when her eyes fell on the wet cement all around her she became terror-stricken. She stood up and ran into a corner of the cell, in an attempt to hide. It was the most dramatic instant of her life. The cement floor of the cell was wet all over. Streams were trickling under the bed, under the table and up to her very feet.

She knew she had done something that was not allowed and that she would be found out and severely punished. The guard's voice echoed sharply and threateningly in her ears: "You will be punished."

She wanted to tear up her dress and use it to mop up the floor, but obviously it was useless. There was too much liquid to be absorbed by the silk dress and the scanty underwear she had on, which was in any case too dainty and fine, too beautiful for wiping. And all the time there was an insistent voice at her ear: "You will be punished."

Now fully aware that she would never be able to hide, that she would be found out, and that it was futile to attempt to escape punishment, she covered her eyes with her tiny fists, from which she had not yet removed the lace gloves, transparent as spider webs, and began to weep in sheer despair.

🌷 🌷 🌷

"THIS has all been a most regrettable accident," said Sergeant Goldsmith, the NCO in charge of the prison. "Allow me to tender my apologies. I am extremely sorry that your case was not brought to my notice sooner."

A week had passed since Traian and Eleonora had been arrested. Traian was now lying on his bed, too weak to move. He had touched neither food nor water for seven days.

Sergeant Goldsmith had brought their belongings in his car and was now helping Nora to unpack. He kept offering them cigarettes and was evidently deeply embarrassed.

"Tomorrow morning you will be set free," he said. "I personally will find you somewhere to live and will drive you there in my car. I feel most sincerely sorry for what has happened."

Neither Traian nor Eleonora uttered one word.

"Mr. and Mrs. Koruga are not under arrest," said Sergeant Goldsmith to the chief guard. "They have been brought here by mistake. They are staying till tomorrow because they have no other living quarters. They will both sleep in this room. See that they are given clean sheets and blankets. They are to be treated as our guests."

The Sergeant went away and returned half an hour later with a parcel. He had brought food for them both and oranges and grapefruit for Traian. As he was taking his leave, he apologized again, shook hands with Traian, and departed.

The chief guard had watched the scene with wide-open eyes, like a man witnessing a miracle.

"I knew all along the Americans would come and apologize," said Nora. "The United States is a great and civilized country."

Traian had fever and fell asleep right away. During the night he dreamed he was on the submarine and that the white rabbits were all dead, every one of them. He woke up in a cold sweat, his pajamas drenched, saying: "Once the white rabbits are dead there is no more hope." He had shouted in his sleep with all his might, but the sailors refused to believe him.

🐇 🐇 🐇

THE following day Sergeant Goldsmith did not show up. Nora waited for him all day.

"He might have been detained by something or other important," she said in the evening. "Tomorrow, though, he'll turn up, all right."

The chief guard was of the same opinion. Nevertheless, Sergeant Goldsmith came neither the second nor the third day. A week later a new sergeant appeared.

"I have no knowledge of your case," he said. "Sergeant Goldsmith has gone back to the States. He left me no instructions with regard to you. But I will make inquiries and inform you of the results next Monday."

Then he went away.

He was a red-haired young man with freckles all over his face. He had refused to disclose his name even to the chief guard. His signature was illegible and he was always nervous.

The following week he returned to the prison, but only spent a few minutes in the office. When the Korugas came to see him he had already gone. They had to wait another whole week.

This time the sergeant was in a bad temper.

"I have made inquiries about your case," he said. "You are arrested under the same conditions as anyone else. We have had no special instructions to justify our giving you preferential treatment."

The sergeant turned his back on them.

"They are to be locked in separate cells," he instructed the chief guard, "and to receive exactly the same treatment as the other prisoners. I will tolerate no exceptions in this prison."

The guard opened his eyes wide. He was staring hard at the sergeant, to make sure he had not misunderstood. Then he said:

"I understand. Separate cells. Ordinary treatment. No exceptions."

The guard's voice quivered.

卐 卐 卐

"THEY are coming to separate us," said Nora, hearing the guard's footsteps in the corridor. She hung on Traian's neck with both arms and started sobbing violently.

"I'd rather die than be locked up again all alone in a cell."

The chief guard stopped in the doorway and jingled his keys. Nora. however, did not turn round. She knew why he had come, and Traian knew, too. Traian looked at him steadily. He would have liked to beg him to leave them together at least five more minutes. But he did not speak. He knew it was useless.

"This summer I shall be relieved of my duties," said the guard. "I am too old. At my age, I can no longer learn to play hide-and-seek. And I don't even want to."

The guard paused. He was mustering all his strength as if to lift too heavy a burden. Then he said:

"You will remain as you are. Together and with the door open."

"Has the sergeant revoked his order?" asked Nora.

"The sergeant has not revoked his order," said the guard, walking away jingling his keys. The door of the cell remained wide open.

☙ ☙ ☙

"WHAT have the Americans got against us?" asked Nora in desperation. "Why have they kept us under arrest for six weeks?"

"The Americans have nothing against us," answered Traian. "They are not even aware of our existence."

"And how much longer do they need to discover they have arrested us and are keeping us in jail?" she asked. "I can't bear it any longer."

"They never will become aware either of your existence or of mine," he said. "Western civilization, in this last stage of its progress, is no longer conscious of the existence of the individual. And there are no grounds for hoping that it ever will become so in future. This society understands only certain aspects of the individual. As far as it is concerned, man as an entity, as an individual, does not exist. You, Eleonora West, who are in prison though guilty of nothing, and I and others like us, are simply not there. We exist only in so far as we are infinitesimal fractions of a category. You, for example, are an enemy citizen arrested on German territory. These particulars are the maximum amount of detail concerning you that Western Technological Society is able to register. It is enabled to recognize you exclusively by these characteristics, and it treats you, therefore, according to the laws of multiplication, division, and subtraction, whichever happens to suit the case, as a unit in the category to which you belong. You are identified with the

[251]

Romanian fraction. That fraction is arrested. The fault or crime that leads to the arrest is a general property of that category."

"And yet I am sure the Americans had reasons for arresting us," she said. "They have something against us; someone must suspect us. Otherwise they would have let us go. I suffer agonies through not knowing the reasons for the arrest. For there must be reasons."

"There are indeed very good ones," said Traian. "They are absurd from the point of view of a human being, but perfectly justified from the point of view of a machine. The West today evaluates man exclusively according to technical standards. Man, as a thing of flesh and blood, capable of joy and suffering, is nonexistent. And that is why the fact that they have arrested us, locked us up, and tomorrow may execute us cannot be considered criminal. It would be criminal if it bore reference to man as a thing of flesh and blood. But Western society is incapable of registering the existence of the living human being. When this society arrests or kills a person, it does not arrest or kill a living thing but an abstract conception. Like any other machine, it cannot be held responsible for such acts. No one can expect a machine to treat men according to their individual characteristics."

"And what might they be, these justified and perfect reasons for which the Americans arrested me?" she asked.

"I have no idea," he answered. "All I know is that to subject man to mechanical laws and standards—which are excellent so far as machines are concerned—amounts to murder. Any man forced to live under the conditions and in the environment suited to fishes will perish within a few moments, and vice versa. The West has evolved a society that is analogous to a machine. It is now forcing men to live in it and to adapt themselves to its new laws. For the time being, the West still has hopes; at times even, it deludes itself with the mirage of success. But men who are treated according to laws governing motorcars or chronometers must inevitably perish. 'People are not alike.

. . . *Nations are not alike. Everybody is not the same or as clever or strong as everybody else!'* * Only machines can be perfectly alike; only machines can be replaced, taken to pieces, and reduced to a few essential parts or movements. When men and machines will be identical, then there will cease to be men on earth."

Nora sighed.

"As a human being, you do not exist," Traian went on. "Or if you like, you exist, but only through the eyes of a machine. For the technocrats of today, as for the barbarians of old, man has no value. Or if he has, it is negligible.

"Your arrest is an infinitely small fact. Infinitesimally small. If it is unjust, then the injustice of it is likewise infinitesimally small. But fundamentally, you are not even arrested."

"We are not arrested?"

"Hardly," said Traian. "We, that is to say, you and I, are not arrested, although we have been in prison for six weeks. The categories to which we belong are arrested. For Western Technological Civilization our persons do not exist as separate entities. Therefore, they could not be and are not arrested."

"To be thrown into jail and then be told you are not under arrest is very cold comfort indeed."

"But it is a comfort none the less," said Traian. "The only one possible at this late hour of history."

❦ ❦ ❦

"WELL, it's all up now," said the chief guard, coming into the Korugas' cell. "Read the communiqué. Thuringia and the city of Weimar have been handed over to the Russians. Soviet troops have already entered the town. Trucks loaded with troops have been moving in all night. The Americans have withdrawn. They are retaining only the government building,

* Jawaharlal Nehru.

the prison, and a certain number of houses. No one is allowed to leave. A cordon of military police has been thrown round the town."

Nora read the communiqué in the newspaper. She looked at Traian and then at the guard, who was leaning against the door.

"And when will the prison change hands?" she asked. "Are we to be handed over to the Russians with it?"

"I am afraid so," answered the guard. "The Russians are expected to take over this morning or this afternoon, or, at the latest, this evening. We have not been informed of the exact time of the handing over."

Traian buried his face in his hands. For an instant his thoughts went back over the past. Flight. One hundred and fifty miles on foot. Russia. Terror. Rape. Siberia. Nora's swollen blistered feet. Political commissars. Handed over in a cell, as formerly slaves were handed over in fetters.

"We must concentrate on essentials, for the times are upon us," said Traian. "It is no longer the moment to keep secrets or cherish illusions. The chief guard may listen. I know the Americans intend to hand us over to the Russians, locked up in our cells. That is a crime. But from their point of view, the Americans are innocent. They are as innocent as the railway engine that seems to be smiling as it crushes a man's body on the track. The West has reduced sin itself to a single dimension. It has minimized it to the extreme. I might even say that it no longer knows the meaning of sin. The Americans are not guilty; it is their civilization that is guilty. But that doesn't matter now. I brought it up only to keep us from deceiving ourselves.

"Any minute now we may be handed over to the Russians, that is to say, to the most bloodthirsty terrorists that have ever operated through the state anywhere on the face of the earth. And even if I could still stand the idea of man mechanized and reduced to the function of a robot, I could never face the mechanized wild beast. I cannot and will not do so. Before I am handed over to the Russians I shall attempt to escape. If I fail, I shall commit suicide."

Traian turned toward the guard.

"Will you help us to escape?" he asked.

"I will do everything in my power," answered the guard. "I want to get away, too. I'm an Austrian, and I want to go home to Vienna. But I shall go later."

"And what will happen to me?" asked Nora. "I'd be too scared to attempt to escape. You had better kill me, Traian."

"We'll commit suicide together," he answered. "But it is worth trying to escape first. It should be possible. The prison wall has been bombed down. The main thing is to get into the courtyard. From there it'll be child's play."

❧ ❧ ❧

"I haven't the courage to climb down a rope from the third floor," said Nora. "You're a man and can do it, but I am much too scared."

Traian was knotting sheets and blankets together to make a rope.

"Don't be afraid," he said. "You won't have to do anything. I'll fasten the rope round you myself and lower you through the window. Once you're in the courtyard, all you have to do is to creep along the wall and wait for me at the other end under the tree I showed you."

She had been holding one end of the rope while he was tying the knots. Now she dropped it.

"I can't escape. All the time you're lowering me down on the rope, I'll be afraid they'll shoot at me. That alone will be enough to make me faint. Are you sure they won't shoot at me while I am climbing down?"

"It's possible," he said. "But we've got to try. They may not shoot. In any case, we have a better chance of survival if we try to escape than if we just stay and kill ourselves."

"Supposing we stayed here for the Russians," she asked. "Perhaps the devil is not so black as he is painted. Communists are human beings, after all. If they can manage to exist, why shouldn't we?"

"You're right," he said. "In the Soviet state there must be human beings. Life there may be no harder than it is in the West. There are no objective standards of judgment, and there is no objective truth. Everything is subjective. None the less, I refuse to live even for one hour in the Red Paradise. Others may think my obstinacy absurd, but from my own point of view it is justified. And for a human being, things can be just or unjust only from a personal point of view. I, personally, do not wish to fall into the clutches of mechanized beasts from the banks of the Volga.

"That is my particular phobia.

"I am ready to surrender my life at any time. But until such time as I do surrender it, I want to live as I choose. It may be argued that my conception of life is not the right one. I am open to conviction. But I will not allow others to organize my life for me or compel me to follow what they consider is the right path. My life is my own. It belongs neither to the kolkhoz nor to the community nor to the political commissar. Therefore, I have the right to live it in whatever way I may choose and to co-ordinate it with the commissar's only if I so desire. Actually, I have no such desire. But even if I had, no one would have the right to blame or praise me. It is my life, and I shall do what I please with it. And I refuse to live this life of mine in the Soviet fashion.

"That is why I am committing suicide."

Nora began to cry. He went on tying the sheets together. She held on firmly to the other end.

"Look and see whether the Americans have moved out of the watchtowers," said Traian.

Nora went out into the corridor and looked at the watch-towers over the prison gates to see if there were any signs of Russian sentries.

"We must check every five minutes," he said. "The best moment to make the attempt will be when the Russian and American sentries change over. After that it will be too late."

All morning they went on working at the rope. They tried it out to see if it was long enough and sufficiently strong to take their weight.

And every five minutes one or the other would go out to look at the watchtowers and would come back, saying:

"Still Americans."

And that made them both happy. They had the illusion that as long as the Americans remained on guard in the towers of the prison, everything was still not lost.

☸ ☸ ☸

AT SIX o'clock in the evening Traian and Eleonora were escorted out of their cells and packed into an American truck together with other prisoners. Traian looked pale, Nora was crying.

"They must have chosen some other spot to hand us over to the Russians," he said. "We are heading east."

The streets of Weimar were jammed with Russian troops and vehicles.

"What about jumping out of the truck?" he asked her. "We are certainly being taken to a Russian prison."

They had left the town behind. Nora looked at the green fields and then at the sun. She could see for herself that they were traveling eastward.

"We are just coming to a forest," he said. "You jump first, hide in one of those thickets, and wait for me. I'll jump straight after you."

She was crying.

"Get ready," he said.

"In a minute," she answered. "Not just now, I'm too frightened."

"We shall never get such a good opportunity again," he said. "Look at those bushes all along the road. We can hide easily. Can you do it now? Look, the truck has slowed down."

He grasped her arm. She gripped the bench tightly with both hands.

"No," she said. "You jump if you want to. I swear I won't hold it against you if you leave me and escape alone."

He sat down again beside his wife and closed his eyes so as not to see the dense bushes that would have made such an ideal hiding place. He knew they would never again have such a chance.

When he opened his eyes the sun was shining straight in his face, blinding him. It was no longer behind him as it had been before. They were heading due west.

"The Americans are good chaps, after all," he said, holding Nora's hand. His face was radiant with happiness. "They are not handing us over to the Russians."

"Where are they taking us, then?" she asked. Traian's face clouded over.

"To an American prison," he said. He was ashamed of his sudden wild happiness.

"Forgive me for having been so gay, Nora. One must be mad to rejoice at having been transferred to one prison rather than to another. But the people of Europe have reached that stage. The only choice open to them is between two prisons."

🖎 🖎 🖎

"YOU'RE Johann Moritz, aren't you?" asked the American officer. He smiled amiably and went on, "The commandant of the town wishes to hear about your escape. It was you, wasn't it, who saved five French prisoners from a concentration camp?"

Johann flushed with pleasure. He never would have believed that one day American officers would come to fetch him by car and ask him to tell them all about his exploits. "Even the commandant of the town has heard of me," he thought, and he gave his name with more pleasure than ever before in his life:

"Yes, I am Johann Moritz."

"Let's go!" said the officer. "I've got my car here."

Johann wanted to go and put on his jacket. He was wearing only his shirt and trousers. And he wanted to put on some socks, for his feet were bare inside his shoes.

But the officer was in a hurry.

"The commandant is waiting for us," he said. "Come as you are. You'll be back in half an hour. I'll bring you back by car."

They both climbed into the jeep and drove away. Johann made up his mind to tell the commandant his story without embroidering on the facts. He was already choosing his words and his cheeks were red with excitement. He tried to imagine what the commandant would look like and how he would sit opposite him and tell his story.

In the meantime the car had drawn up outside a stone building. The officer turned toward Johann.

"You stay here," he said.

Johann climbed out. He was sorry the officer was not coming with him. It would have given him more courage to tell his story. But the jeep had driven off. The sentry on duty at the gate led him into the courtyard, where two German policemen came to fetch him. Glancing to the right and to the left, he found it hard to believe that the commandant of the town lived in such an ugly building, but he did not dare ask questions.

When he stepped inside he noticed that all the windows were barred as in prisons, and so he asked:

"Is this where the commandant of the town lives?"

The policemen burst into roars of laughter. They could not

stop. They locked Johann into an unlit cell in the basement. As they turned the key in the lock, they were still laughing at the prisoner's question.

❧ ❧ ❧

CORINA KORUGA, the priest's wife, was summoned to the village hall. It must have been about midnight when the two peasants with colored armbands knocked at her window and told her to follow them. It was a moonlit night. She locked the door carefully and kept the key in her hand.

At the village hall there were a dozen or so Russian soldiers carousing with the peasants. The priest's wife was led in front of them. They gave her a glass of wine and eyed her up and down.

She lowered her eyes and silently prayed to Saint Nicholas. The soldiers forced her to drink, but she went on with her prayer, neither looking at them nor even touching the glass with her lips. One soldier poured wine down inside her blouse; another lifted her petticoats and splashed wine up her thighs. She seemed not to see them or to hear what they were saying. She sat with her eyes closed, saying her prayer and thinking of Saint Nicholas, who looked like Father Koruga, her husband. The Russians and the peasants emptied further glasses of wine over her head, down inside her blouse, and up her petticoats. Her skirt and her blouse were drenched. Then they dragged her down on the floor. Her dress and her body felt as wet as if she had fallen into the river. And then she felt herself sinking down and down and drowning. Saint Nicholas had stayed on the bank and was praying for her.

The following day, after what had happened at the village hall, Corina, the wife of Father Koruga, the priest, hanged herself in the henhouse.

ψ ψ ψ

Nora West's first night in the Ohrdruf concentration camp. "There must be some definite reason for our arrest. Otherwise they would not torment us like this," she said to herself.

She was lying on bare boards without pillow or blanket. Her hips, her elbows, and every bone in her body were all hurting.

When she had reached the concentration camp a few hours before, it had been already dark. As soon as they had got down from the truck that had brought them from Weimar, she and Traian had been separated. Traian had been taken somewhere else, and she had been sent here.

The women's camp was a group of wooden huts. In the room where she was lying there were about thirty other women. She had not seen their faces when she walked in, because of the darkness, but they all seemed very young. She had stretched herself out on the boards and had started crying. Then she had fallen asleep.

"It must be about midnight," she thought. "I wonder what sort of women can be shut in here with me."

From the far corner of the room came a stifled laugh. It seemed to her that it was a man's laugh. But there couldn't be men in a women's camp. She pricked up her ears. It was a man. There was no doubt about it. He had stopped laughing, but he could be heard making love. The movements of the couple were clearly audible. A man laughed again, but this time the laugh came from another part of the room. Nora took fright.

"Why should I be afraid of men who are making love?" she asked herself. But she could not quiet her anxiety. In spite of herself she was afraid.

She stopped up her ears. She could no longer hear anything. Yet she seemed to see them even with her eyes shut. The planks of her bed rattled. She opened her eyes and saw that the door had been flung wide open. More men had come in. They stood talking to each other in the middle of the room. A woman in a nightdress was standing beside them.

Nora broke down and started to scream. She shut her eyes and screamed at the top of her voice.

She could not have told herself why she had first started. But she went on because she was frightened of the men and women in the room. They would come and thrash her till she was black and blue because she had screamed and had prevented them from making love.

"It's stupid of me," she thought. "I shouldn't have screamed. Now they are all going to set on me and beat me to death. They have every right to kill me because I screamed."

The men rushed out of the room. Many of them were dashing toward the door. Some had been lying on the floor. She had not heard those. One had been in the bed next to hers. She had not heard him, either. Now as the men hurried out they looked like ghosts.

They all seemed to her to be very tall and black, blacker even than the night.

A few women left at the same time as the men, but soon they came creeping back into the room on tiptoe and slid onto their beds.

Everything grew quiet at last. The women were all back, each one in her own bed. Only two of them were still in the middle of the room. They were standing in the dark in their flimsy nightdresses. Their thickened silhouettes stood out in the darkness. They were silently pressing close to each other. Nora noticed that they were eating something. They were nibbling chocolate.

She lay and waited for the two women still standing in the middle of the room to go to bed, afraid lest they should strike her or even kill her in her sleep. But the women went on munching their chocolate in silence.

"Who was it screamed?" whispered one of them. "Wasn't it that red-haired foreigner who came in this evening?"

"I don't know," the other whispered back. "I'm not sorry she screamed. I'd had enough of my fellow and didn't feel like starting all over again."

They went on eating their chocolate and said nothing more. Nora watched their movements closely. Eventually they separated, making for different corners of the room. They got onto their beds. The boards creaked. Soon they were both asleep.

But Nora felt stifled and could not calm down. The men had all gone now, and the women were asleep, but there was a smell of sweat and wine and love-making. Though the windows were wide open, the smell would not go. She felt she could not breathe in such an atmosphere.

"There must be a reason for our arrest," she kept on saying to herself. "Otherwise I could not have been shut up in here to suffocate."

She wanted to cough, but put her hand over her mouth and stopped herself. She was afraid that her coughing would wake up the women and that they would beat her.

※ ※ ※

THE first morning in the concentration camp. When Traian opened his eyes he saw Johann Moritz.

"We must have slept side by side all night," said Traian, shaking hands warmly with him. "How did you get here?"

Johann told him, beginning at the end with the officer who had fetched him to tell the commandant the story of his escape with the Frenchmen.

"Instead of taking me to the commandant of the town they put me in prison," he said. "For eight weeks they left me in a cell with no windows and without a ray of light. I went on expecting the commandant to send for me. He never did. Then they brought me here. That is all."

Johann cut his story short and asked:

"And how did you get here?"

Traian shrugged his shoulders.

The prisoners who had been sleeping on the ground were waking up one by one. The concentration camp of Ohrdruf was a meadow enclosed by barbed wire. Fifteen thousand prisoners had been herded in there together, just open sky, earth, and men.

At each of the four corners of the barbed-wire perimeter were stationed tanks and guards carrying automatic rifles.

"Have you any news from Fantana?" asked Johann. He looked at Traian and said:

"I can't bring myself to believe you are here. How did we manage to come up against each other face to face like that, and sleep alongside each other all night? I just can't understand it."

꽃 꽃 꽃

THE camp commandant at Ohrdruf was a Jew. Eleonora was glad.

"A Jew will have a greater understanding of my sufferings. He will help me to get out of here as he would help a relative," she said to herself.

She had made up her mind to tell him everything. To plead with him and implore his help. She would speak to him as to a brother.

The walls in the commandant's office were lined with photographs of German concentration camps. Nora looked at them. They were as big as the walls themselves. They showed men hanged or starved to death, prisoners in striped suits, gallows, piles of corpses, trucks stacked high with dead women.

Nora had totally lost her bearing. She saw herself in an extermination camp for Jews in Nazi Germany. She looked at the red-haired lieutenant sitting behind his desk. Her eyes pleaded with him to rescue her from extermination, starvation, torture, and the gas chamber.

"I am your sister," she thought. "I implore you to help me." But she did not say it.

Never before had she felt so strongly that she was Jewish.

"Lieutenant," she said.

Her voice shook, and she felt a lump in her throat. Her sobs choked her, preventing her from speaking.

"You are not to speak except to answer questions," the officer said sharply.

Nora bit her lip and was silent, waiting for the questions. The officer read without looking at her.

"Your name is Eleonora West Koruga?" he asked severely. "That's you, isn't it? Your husband has been arrested, too, hasn't he?"

The officer's manner of address was familiar, but it was not exactly the familiarity of a brother.

"Your husband was an official of the dictator Antonescu, wasn't he?"

"My husband was an official of the kingdom of Romania," she replied.

The officer blushed till his freckly, pale face was blood-red. His lips quivered. "There were terrible pogroms in Romania, weren't there?" he asked.

"There were," she answered.

"In Romania there were concentration camps for Jews, and camps where they were exterminated in gas chambers, hanged, beheaded, shot . . ."

The lieutenant had risen to his feet. Nora was about to tell him she was Jewish herself, and that she had had to procure forged papers and then flee, and that she had lain trembling night after night.

"Answer my question!" roared the officer. He came up to her with clenched fists. She was sure he was going to strike her in the face. She shut her eyes and waited for the blow. Her body was shaking, and she was too terrified to bring out a single word.

"Answer me, you criminal!" he roared. "How many Jewish women did you kill with your own hands? Answer. If you don't speak, I'll tear you to pieces. How many Jewesses did you murder with your own hands?"

Nora could not say anything.

"So you aren't telling, eh?" he said. "Now it's you who're afraid. Now it's you who're trembling and wetting your little drawers from fright. But you weren't frightened when you were out murdering!"

"I myself am a . . ." said Eleonora.

"Get out, you bloody Nazi bitch!" he shouted. "Get out!"

His fist loomed up threateningly before her eyes. She went out of the office.

(BOOK FIVE)

Traian was writing. Johann stood beside him, watching how his fingers gripped the pencil and how he carefully traced the letters as though he were threading pearls.

Johann had not patience enough to write himself. He did not like it. But while Traian was writing he could have kept on watching for hours on end.

"When Master Traian writes, it's just as if he were praying before the icons," he thought. "You forget he is a prisoner when you watch him. You don't notice that he's barefooted and unshaven and that his trousers are torn. When he is writing Traian Koruga is a gentleman. You feel you ought to take off your hat in his presence and speak in a whisper."

"Have you ever heard of snake charmers?" asked Traian, pausing for a moment.

"Yes, I have," said Johann.

"Daniel was thrown into a lions' den, and the lions did not devour him," said Traian. "He tamed them. Human beings can charm snakes and tame lions. Mussolini kept in his study two tigers which he had tamed. Human beings can tame all wild animals. But recently a new species of animal has appeared on the surface of the earth. These animals are called citizens. They do not live in the jungle or the forests, but in offices. Yet they are more ferocious than the beasts of the jungle. They are a bastard breed of man and machine—a degenerate breed, but today the most powerful on earth. Their faces are the faces of men, and outwardly they are indistinguishable from human beings. But soon enough it becomes obvious that they don't behave like human beings. They behave exactly like machines. They have chronometers in place of hearts. Their brain, too, is a kind of machine. They are neither machines nor men. Their appetites are those of wild beasts, but they are not wild beasts. They are citizens . . . a strange mongrel type. They have gone forth and multiplied to the ends of the earth."

Johann tried to imagine what these "citizens" were like, but he could not. He had a fleeting vision of Marcu Goldenberg, but Traian broke into his train of thought.

"I'm a writer," said Traian. "To my way of thinking a writer is a tamer of men. By revealing unto men the beautiful— in other words, truth—you make them gentle. I am going to try and tame citizens. I had started writing a book and I had got as far as Chapter IV. At that point the citizens led me away into captivity, and I was no longer free to write. Chapter V still remains to be written.

"There is no more point in writing it now. I shan't publish any more books. Instead of Chapter V, I want to write something to tame the citizens.

"If I succeed, I shall die at peace with myself. I'll read out to you what I write. It won't be a novel, or a play. Citizens don't like literature. To tame them I shall adopt the only form they approve of. I shall write petitions. Citizens do not read poems, novels, or plays. They only read petitions."

✄ ✄ ✄

PETITION No. 1. *Subject: Economic (Fats)*

I intend to submit several petitions. To begin with, here is one on an economic subject. I know that your Western Technological Civilization is built up on a materialistic basis. Economics is your Bible. I am a writer, and every writer is a witness. The first qualification required of a witness is impartiality. Therefore, my petitions will bear evidence of authentic truth.

The problem I wish to lay before you seems to me to be one of the utmost importance. It is on the subject of fats.

You are all fully aware that there is at the present time a world-wide shortage of fats. When I arrived at this camp I found the prisoners sleeping on the floor, side by side. I could hardly find room enough to wedge myself in. I had just got out of prison, and the surrounding fields seemed very big to me. I could not understand why you had not made a larger enclosure for the men.

The 15,000 persons in the camp are packed tight. Standing up, there is a certain amount of room. But lying down, there is so little that they have to pile up on top of one another. All night I was unable to stretch out my legs. My neighbors, however, stretched theirs by putting them on my head. Their legs were warm and kept me from feeling cold during the night.

I realize now why you made the enclosure so small— to save the grass in the fields. Grass is expensive. It would have been a pity to let the prisoners trample on it. It is far better to let a cow chew it because cows produce milk, and prisoners produce nothing.

Secondly, had you made a larger enclosure you would have required more barbed wire. Steel is expensive. Obviously, it is not worth spending money on wire merely so that the prisoners should have more room for their legs at night.

Thirdly, I reckon that a large proportion of the prisoners will die during the coming winter. Some even earlier, probably. Those who are left will then have sufficient room to lie down full length. I presume that you took this factor into account when you built the camp. I cannot but express my admiration for the efficiency of your planning methods.

Before going to sleep I listened to a lecture. I could not avoid it. The lecturer, who claimed to be a professor from Berlin University, spoke on fats. In this petition I should like to summarize and discuss this lecture.

The professor made a daily check on the number of beans in the soup we eat in camp. For thirty consecutive days both at midday and in the evening he counted every bean that appeared in his mess tin. He added up the total and worked out an average. He is now able to state that a prisoner receives ten beans a day from the two soups. The professor's assistants also counted their beans over a period of thirty days and confirmed his calculations.

Next the professor kept a record of the potato peelings and the quantity of flour in the soup. This calculation was, of course, only approximate, because he was not allowed into the cookhouse.

As you are no doubt aware, the Germans are experts at anything to do with measurement. It may therefore be assumed that the beans were accurately counted. The Germans are a painstaking and scrupulous people. After thirty days' work the professor had collected all the necessary data and made his research the subject of a lecture, which was much appreciated by the audience. The Germans enjoy listening to lectures on any subject under the sun. It is a habit they formed during the Middle Ages.

After explaining his method of counting the beans by straining his soup every day, he gave the number of calories contained in each bean. I don't remember the exact figures. Then he worked out the total number of calories contained in ten beans and added the number of calories in the potatoes and flour that the prisoners could not identify in the soup but whose presence the professor assumed. He concluded by stating that each prisoner in the camp received an average of five hundred calories per day. On some days they received much less. It had happened that on several consecutive days the professor himself had been unable to locate a single bean in his soup, and on those days there had been nothing for him to record. On other days, however, he had found fifteen, sometimes as many as eighteen beans. The average is therefore correct.

A man who is asleep consumes a thousand calories a day. The prisoners in the camp do not sleep the whole day long, therefore their consumption is greater. Nevertheless, the professor put their consumption at a thousand calories a day, which is an absolute minimum.

The prisoners receive five hundred calories in beans. The remaining five hundred they consume daily have therefore to be drawn from their own fat reserves; i.e., the capital accumulated in their bodies. Because they spend five hundred calories of the reserves they had when they arrived in camp, the prisoners lose six pounds per month per person. This, too, of course, is an average. The weighing was carried out daily by the professor's assistants with improvised weighing machines and weights. However, the instruments seem to have been fairly accurate.

By working out the total of the six pounds of fats that every prisoner loses by transforming them into calories, it can be proved that there is, in this camp of Ohrdruf run under your very competent administration, a monthly wastage of forty tons of fats. Every month, five wagonloads of fat evaporate and vanish into thin air. Consider the enormity of such waste.

I am not an economist and am therefore not in a position to offer a solution. But I am certain that, with the technical resources you have at your disposal, you should be able to avail yourselves of this living fat. Why should it be wasted?

This is the object of my petition.

I am sure you will appreciate my point. You are members of the most advanced branch of Western civilization. You might perhaps send back home a report to the Institute of Science. It is barbarous to allow forty tons of fat to be squandered every month. Besides, there are other camps—several hundreds, I believe, in Germany alone. You could collect mountains of fresh fat every day.

Ever since that lecture given by the professor from Berlin, the whole atmosphere seems to me to reek of human fat. Your camp is a gigantic crushing machine for extracting fats from human beings . . . I can sniff it in the air. Do you never find yourself noticing this smell of living human fat when you sit in your office with the window open? And yet your very clothes must be permeated with it. Ask your wife or your mistress who sleeps with you if your hair and skin does not smell of human fat when you get into bed next to her. Women have a more highly developed sense of smell than men. They will tell you. As for me, the very thought of it turns my stomach. And now allow me to assure you of my deepest admiration and respect for your civilization. In view of the technical resources at your disposal, I have no doubt that you will not fail to find a way of making use of these vast stores of human fat. Don't forget, I myself have six pounds a month to offer you fresh from my own body.

THE WITNESS

❦ ❦ ❦

PETITION No. 2. *Subject: Beauty, Human (Ideal of in Western Technological Civilization)*

Last night I discussed aesthetics with a German professor. We had an argument. The Germans, like all other Europeans, have never really got beyond classicism. That is why their social organization has collapsed. A healthy and progressive civilization like your own must evolve its own modern art as Western technology has done.

This professor showed me the prisoners walking about on the camp parade ground. Although, as you know, they are now mere bundles of skin and bone, he declared that they were ugly. He was bogged down in the Greek ideal of beauty. In my opinion, human beings reduced to skeletons enclosed in skin are magnificent—real works of art. They represent the type of human beauty most characteristic of Modern Technological Civilization.

I tried to persuade the German that your civilization has an esteem for and appreciation of beauty far higher than any other civilization on earth and that your practice of extracting fat from the human body is inspired purely by aesthetic motives, for the embellishment of the universe. He did not understand. These Germans are always very slow on the uptake. That is why people say they are bulletheaded. Tomorrow I shall give a lecture on the modern Western ideal of human beauty.

There is a Swiss sculptor, Alberto Giacometti, who, in his own field, has been inspired by the same principles and achieved the same ideals of masculine and feminine beauty as you have achieved in practice by eliminating fat and flesh from the human body. Here is what has been said of him:

"*Restless Artist Giacometti was troubled by the fact that he could not do all his job at once. If he started on the tip of the nose, the rest of the face would lose shape and perspective. 'The distance between one side of the nose and the other,' he wrote, 'is like the Sahara.' Later, in an effort to grasp the whole, his sculptures began to shrink until they became so small that they would fall apart at the touch of his knife. Finally, his figures began to seem real to him only when they were long and slender. 'And it is almost there,' says Giacometti, 'where I am today.' 'For him,' wrote Existentialist Jean-Paul Sartre in a catalogue introduction, "to sculpt is to take the fat off space.' "*

And that is precisely what you are doing here in camp. I have always known that your entire civilization was founded on aesthetic principles. How beautiful it will be when, in this universe of tomorrow, the whole world shall be peopled with beings whose bodies are built according to the harmony of the new aesthetic canons as they are seen in Giacometti's art—and in yours.

THE WITNESS

ὗ ὗ ὗ

"WELL, Moritz, old fellow," said Traian, "I have already written at least forty petitions trying to reveal the truth and to persuade them to stop torturing human beings. I know that what I wrote was right. Every petition was skillfully composed. But it was all in vain. I wrote in various styles—legal, diplomatic, telegraphic, cookbook-recipe, even advertising. I was alternately sentimental, vulgar, and beseeching: I cried out for justice, using every means taught me by my despair. I received no answer.

"I told them the most uncompromising home truths, but they did not get annoyed. I went down on my knees to write to them, but they were not moved. I insulted them grossly, but they did not take offense. I tried to make them laugh, I tried to excite their curiosity—all to no purpose.

"I could arouse neither their higher feelings nor their baser instincts. I failed to provoke the slightest reaction. I might have been talking to a brick wall. They simply have no feelings. They do not even know the meaning of hate. They don't understand revenge. They don't understand pity. They work automatically and exclusively according to plan. If I were to tear off a strip of my body and write a petition on it in warm blood they would still not read it. They would throw it into the wastepaper basket, exactly as they did with the others. They wouldn't even notice that it was a strip of flesh still warm from the human body. They

arc indifferent to man. It is the indifference of the citizen toward the human being, an indifference that has gone further
than that of the machine."

"Poor Master Traian," said Johann compassionately. "What
are you going to do next? Perhaps it might be better to stop
writing petitions."

"I shall go on writing," said Traian. "I shall not stop until
I am dead. There is not a beast under the sun which mankind
has failed to tame. Why shouldn't we succeed in taming the
citizens?"

"Perhaps you should try some other way," said Johann. "I
don't think you'll get anywhere by writing."

"Every victory won by man, from the time of his appearance on earth till the present day, has been a victory of the
spirit. It is through the spirit that we shall tame the citizen in
his office.

"If we fail, they will tear us to pieces. We must teach them
not to destroy man when they meet him. Until we have taught
them this we cannot go on living on the same earth, in the same
towns and streets, with them. It will be harder than taming
tigers. And yet I have never felt more optimistic than at this
moment. It is doubtless the optimism of man before death.
The chapter of *The Twenty-fifth Hour* wherein are written my
'Petitions' will be the final spasm of my death agony. But I shall
write it."

🜚 🜚 🜚

PETITION No. 3.   *Subject: Economic (Prisoners Retaining*
only one half or one third of their Bodies)

A colleague of mine who is an accountant and myself
spent four days working out the total of prisoners in the camp
who possessed only one half, two thirds, or four fifths of their
body. My friend is still busy with the statistics. He is good at

calculations. I am hastening to write to you because, from the economic point of view, the problem seems urgent. You could save thousands of marks every day.

The point is this: Of the fifteen thousand prisoners shut up with me, three thousand no longer have whole bodies. About two hundred have no legs at all. They drag about camp like reptiles. Twelve hundred prisoners have only one leg, others are one-armed. A few have both arms missing. So much for the external parts of the body.

Many, on the other hand, are short of certain internal organs, a lung, a kidney, fragments of bones, etc. Forty prisoners possess no eyes.

All these prisoners were arrested automatically, as I was. To begin with, I felt sorry for them. My friend Johann Moritz shuts his eyes every time he sees the most seriously crippled and maimed men in the camp. But Johann Moritz is uncivilized. He doesn't understand that if the arrest is automatic and if one belongs to a category that is to be interned, one can't get out of it merely by being short of a leg, an eye, a nose, or a lung.

Automatic arrest does not admit of exceptions for those whose bodies are not in working order. And this is as it should be. Justice must be the same for all, and no exceptions.

There is a professor here who has no arms, having lost both at the front. You gave orders for the arrest of all professors, and it would have been unjust to make an exception for my friend merely because he had no arms. What connection is there between a man's arms and automatic arrest? None. He is a professor, therefore he has to be arrested along with the rest of his category. And that is precisely what you did. You never make mistakes. That is why my admiration for you knows no bounds. At any moment I would be prepared to lay down my life for your great and magnificent civilization. You are the incarnation of justice and precision.

To come back to my subject: These fractions of men who retain only a given proportion of their bodies receive the same quantity of food as prisoners in possession of their full quota of limbs. This is a great injustice.

I propose that these prisoners should receive rations in proportion to the amount of body still in their possession. Your government makes great sacrifices to pay for every morsel of food consumed by the prisoners. But by a prisoner you mean a whole man. If you were to assemble the three thousand maimed men in the camp and if you were to count their hands, feet, eyes, and lungs, you would see that the whole lot taken all in all do not make up more, in flesh and bone, than a maximum of two thousand men. You could therefore economize to the extent of a thousand rations per day.

Why should you spend money to feed parts of the body that the prisoners no longer possess? Such generosity on your part is entirely uncalled for. Considerable satisfaction would, I am sure, be caused in higher quarters if you were to draw attention to this fact. You might even receive a decoration for saving the state unnecessary expenditure. And money, as we all know, is the only thing that counts. With the above words of wisdom I shall now respectfully close.

THE WITNESS

🙚 🙚 🙚

PETITION No. 4. *Subject: Military (Sex, Change of)*

As a result of starvation, certain prisoners in this camp undergo general transformations that you might find of considerable military interest. Here in outline is the point in question. Prisoners who have been interned for a long time and who have been living on five hundred calories a day, no longer find it necessary to shave. Men who normally shaved once or even twice a day came first to shave once every two or three days, then once a week, then twice a month, and now they no longer shave at all. Their beards grew gradually sparser and silkier till they were like down; finally, they vanished altogether. Their cheeks and chin became soft and smooth like that of a woman. But that is not all. Their voices, too, became more feminine. Their breasts developed till they were as marked as those of a thirteen-year-old girl. Their skin is as soft as a woman's. Even their ways have become feminine. I don't know precisely what is happening to their sexual organs, but I believe that if you maintain their present diet, or particularly if you reduce the rations still further, their phallus and the adjoining male organs will eventually wither away altogether, and with that their transformation into women will be complete. The doctors maintain that all this is due exclusively to starvation. This is what they say: *"Lack of food had sharply cut the production of both androgen, the male sex hormone, and estrogen, the female hormone. In addition, the impaired liver failed in its task of hormone regulation. It was able to destroy excess androgen as usual, but not estrogen. Thus the hormone balance swung gradually in the female direction."*

These facts can be of the utmost military importance for your civilization. Consider the eternal peace that would reign in all the world if you were to put all your male enemies into camps—as you have in fact already started to do—and keep them on a few hundred calories per day till they all turned into women. Any nation that chose to be your enemy would thus be totally deprived of males. There would be no one left to wage war against you. I think your great General Staff will know how to put this discovery to good use. In view of the practical and inventive genius of your civilization, I am certain you will even attempt the inverse operation—the systematic overfeeding of women who are willing to enlist as volunteers, and their transformation into males. Your man power would thus be considerably increased.

In conclusion, I submit that the present rations of five hundred calories issued to prisoners of the camp under your administration be still further reduced. By this means, prisoners might be more rapidly transformed into real women.

THE WITNESS

❦ ❦ ❦

PREPARATIONS for departure. The fifteen thousand prisoners were to be transferred to another camp. It was two A.M. Tanks and trucks were massed round the camp. All the searchlights, including those on the tanks, were turned full on and made it as light as day. The sentries had been doubled, and the barrels of all the automatic weapons were trained on the flood of prisoners surging toward the gate like a mighty river. Traian and Johann moved forward side by side. It was a cold night, and they felt the warmth of each other's bodies. Johann's teeth were chattering.

At the gates were stationed two squads of soldiers armed with truncheons. They counted the prisoners as they came through the gates and divided them up into groups.

"They want to pack seventy of us into a truck normally meant for ten or twelve men," said Traian. "How will they do it? Did you know there was a law governing the interpenetration of human bodies?"

Johann did not answer. He was shivering. Traian watched the troops loading the first truck. First of all, twenty men climbed in. That made it apparently full to bursting point already. Then the soldiers started hitting out at the men in the truck with their truncheons until they pressed closer together. Ten more were packed in, and truncheons began to lay about this batch. They crowded over those who were already in the truck, and again there was made room. Ten more men were driven in. Now there could not have been room even for a child. The troops reversed their rifles and started belaboring the men with the butts. Ten more climbed in. Out of the entire batch of seventy, not one man was left below. They were all in the truck. The blows ceased. The truck was ready to move off.

Traian climbed into the truck, keeping hold of Johann's hand. They did not want to lose each other.

"There is no such thing as an absolute law, Moritz," said Traian. "Not even the laws of physics are invariable. According to physics two bodies cannot occupy the same area in space at one and the same time. Here, however, is a case where seven men are occupying the area of one. Can you go on believing in physics after that? Have you ever heard of Picasso?"

"No, Master Traian." Johann's voice sounded stifled. Traian was tall and could get some air. Johann was small. His head was wedged between the chests of his neighbors. His lungs were so crushed that they could not absorb a breath of air.

"I'm suffocating," he said. He was panic-stricken and almost in tears. He could not move. His nostrils sought air, the least little bit of air, and could not find it.

"I'm suffocating, Master Traian, I'm going to die," he said.

"Answer me, have you ever heard of Picasso?"

"No. I haven't," said Johann. "I don't know anything. But I'm suffocating. I'm sure my end has come."

Traian wanted to raise Johann's head, but he could not move his arm. He could not move a single muscle. His body was crushed and pulverized and reduced to a minimum volume. But his head was free and towered above the others.

"This Picasso is the greatest painter of Western civilization," said Traian.

"I can't hear a thing," said Johann. "If only I could just get my nose free, even just one side of it. Help me, Master Traian, please help me. I'm dying."

Traian tried to make a little room for him. Johann's head was pressed against his chest.

"Picasso has painted your portrait just as you are now in this truck, old man."

"My portrait?" asked Johann. "I can't hear. My ears are blocked."

"Your portrait," said Traian. "The likeness is as good as a photograph. Seven men occupying the same area in space at the same time. One has five legs, another three heads, but no lungs. You have a voice but no mouth, while I have nothing but a head, a head floating in space over a truck. The first time I saw this particular painting—it was in Paris—I liked it very much, but I didn't see what it was meant to represent. Only now can I understand that it was a picture of our truck, painted with astonishing accuracy. Not a detail escaped him. He has painted our camp, too. He paints as if he were taking photographs. Nothing but real life. He is a genius."

The truck moved off. Traian looked at the people all round him. He looked down at them from above. Not one was still a human being made in the image and likeness of God. There were no longer any living beings in the truck as it wound through the village streets in the darkness. However, the men in the trucks were not dead, either. They were hovering between life and death. One second they came alive, and the next they were dead again. At times they were simultaneously alive and dead. At this particular point in space which they were occupying, space itself had ceased to exist; space had been eliminated. It was dead. At this particular point in space, time also had ceased to exist. Time was dead. And material reality was dead.

Existence was reduced to spasms. Eyes were spasms. Flesh, blood, air, time, thought—all were spasms. Men had lost their shapes and their spirit; they were spasms.

"Can you still breathe?" asked Traian.

"I don't know. I think so, but only with one side of my nose, and at that only from time to time," said Johann. "Through your chest and ribs."

"One side of your nose will have to do," said Traian. "Now listen, I have to tell you something of tremendous importance."

"I can't listen to anything. . . . Please forgive me."

"You must listen," said Traian, quoting T. S. Eliot. "It is very important.

" 'Every horror had its definition,
Every sorrow had a kind of end:
In life there is not time to grieve long.
But this, this is out of life, this is out of time,
An instant eternity of evil and wrong.
We are soiled by filth that we cannot clean, united to
    supernatural vermin,
It is not we alone, it is not the house, it is not the city
    that is defiled,
But the world that is wholly foul.' "

"Louder, please. I can't hear," said Johann.

Traian went on as loudly as he could:

" 'Clear the air! clean the sky! wash the wind! take the
stone from the stone, take the skin from the arm, take
the muscle from the bone, and wash them. Wash the
stone, wash the bone, wash the brain, wash the soul,
wash them, wash them!' "

"I don't understand a thing," said Johann. "How lucky you are, Master Traian, with your head up there. You aren't suffocating."

In camp, the small men had suffered less than the large from hunger. But in the truck with its load of seventy men, threading its way through the streets of Ohrdruf like a phantom, the smaller prisoners were on the point of death through lack of air.

"Master Traian, don't go on talking, I can't hear anyway," said Johann.

"If you don't hear it'll cost you your life."

"Hear what?"

"The German professor was wrong," said Traian. "He has sinned grievously and will die for it."

"What German has sinned?" asked Johann.

"The professor who weighed our living flesh and fat," said

Traian. "To gauge the standard of our suffering, he weighed it while it was still warm and living. But the suffering of man can be measured neither by the pound nor by the ton. . . . Life cannot be weighed. He who attempts to do so is guilty of mortal sin."

"I can't hear," said Johann.

"Never mind," answered Traian. "You don't need to hear in order to perish. Our truck driver can't hear anything, nor can the sentries, nor can the soldiers with the truncheons, nor those with automatics who can hardly wait to shoot you down. Not one of them can hear a thing. And yet they will all perish together with us, at the same time and in the same way. Can't you see them perishing?"

"I'm blinded," said Johann. "I can't see a thing."

"Can't you feel anything, either?"

"Nothing," said Johann. "Save that I can't breathe."

"You can feel the only thing that really matters, don't you see?" said Traian sadly. "Why do you say you can't feel anything? Everybody has the same feeling, but they refuse to admit it."

🐾 🐾 🐾

THE prisoners were packed into cattle cars. Into each car, with a sign outside that read 24 horses, they herded one hundred and forty men.

One by one, the doors of the cars were slammed and locked. In the rear of the train they packed three thousand women.

The train was long. Traian thought he would have liked to see the whole of it from the distance.

"This train of ours is like the procession that climbed up to Golgotha, except that it is mechanized," said Traian. "We are mechanically propelled up to Golgotha. Not like Jesus, who went up on foot with the two robbers. Do you know why Jesus was crucified between two robbers?"

"No," said Johann.

"To punish an innocent person, judges would sometimes put a guilty man on either side of him. The dodge is classical. They dared not crucify Jesus alone, so they placed him between two famous robbers in order to distract the attention of the crowds during the execution.

"You and I, my wife, and many others have each of us a guilty person on our right or on our left. It's just the same dodge as the one used at Golgotha, only the proportions have changed. On that occasion there was one innocent man between two guilty men, whereas now there are ten thousand innocent men between two guilty ones. But that is only a minor difference; and so is the fact that we are being crucified automatically and mechanically. The principle remains the same. But the dodge is childish. As soon as the execution is over, the multitude forgets all about the two guilty men who were killed with Jesus; they remember Jesus and Jesus alone. This has always happened, and it will happen again this time. Even if the crucifixion takes place automatically and even if we are carried up Golgotha by railway."

Traian moved over to the barred window of the car. The train had halted.

"Can you see anything?" asked Johann. His eyes did not come up to the level of the window.

"We've stopped at a station," said Traian. "There's another train drawn up alongside."

"Is it full of prisoners, too?" asked Johann, whose curiosity was aroused.

"It is full of ex-prisoners. They are foreign slave workers liberated from what used to be Germany," said Traian, looking at the throng of men and women milling round the neighboring train.

"They are all smoking cigarettes," said Traian.

Johann swallowed.

"There's a woman getting out of a carriage, eating a sausage and white bread," said Traian, and he, too, swallowed.

"I do wish I could see," said Johann. "I may know some of them. What nationality are they?"

"Mixed," said Traian, looking at the flags chalked on the outside of the cars and the colored ribbons in buttonholes. "There's a woman eating white bread and butter, and her legs are as white as the bread. She must be Danish. Behind her there is a Frenchwoman. She is attractive. Black eyes."

"Are there other French?" asked Johann.

"There is a whole crowd of them just next to our car," said Traian. "They are with some Belgians and Italians."

"I want to see the Frenchmen," said Johann impatiently, his old passion for the French now fully awakened.

Traian lifted him by the arms till he could see.

"They are French," said Johann. "The one standing by the Italian looks the living image of Joseph. Can you see him?"

"Which Joseph?"

"My friend Joseph," said Johann. "Didn't I tell you about him? He is the one I helped to escape. If I didn't know for sure that he was in France I'd think it was him. He looks exactly like him. Won't you say something to him?"

"What do you want me to say?" asked Traian.

"Anything you like," said Johann. "He is so like Joseph. I don't know French, but I should love to say something to him. Say hello and wish them good luck on their journey home."

Johann could not pass by a Frenchman without saying a friendly word or smiling warmly at him.

"Look, he's standing just close to us," he said. "Say something now."

Traian was still silent. Johann could no longer restrain himself and cried in German:

"Good luck to you on your way home!"

He had spoken gently. His face was radiant with joy; he had

had the chance to speak to a man who was dear to him because he was French.

On the platform the hum of voices ceased abruptly. The crowd under the window looked up at Johann in silence. Traian heard the one who looked like Joseph ask in French:

"What does that swine of a Nazi want?"

All eyes on the platform were fixed on Johann Moritz, who was still smiling warmly at the men and women from behind the bars of his window.

"The Nazi swine probably wants a cigarette," a woman said.

The young man who looked like Joseph began to put his hand in his pocket, but suddenly he stopped short. He picked up a stone and hurled it straight at the window where Johann stood smiling. The stone went between the bars and fell into the middle of the car, hitting one of the prisoners.

"Take that for a cigarette!" said a woman. "So you feel like a smoke, eh? I've spent three years in Germany because of you."

A second stone came crashing into the side of the car, then a third. A shower of stones was now raining down on them. The prisoners threw themselves on the floor, with their heads away from the window. Stones were pelting down as thick as hail. From outside came shouting and swearing, as if the car were being taken by storm.

There were voices of men, women, and children, voices of rebellion. They were shouting in French, Italian, Russian, Danish, Flemish, Norwegian, in every language in the world. They were all shrieking the same curses, the same words of hatred broken loose, and the words that followed the hail of stones raining on Johann were the same in all languages: Nazi swine, Nazi criminal, Nazi murderer, Nazi, Nazi.

All the DP's had got out of their train and joined the others in throwing stones at the cars full of prisoners. The guards and the military police were trying to restore order, but the attack was too violent to be calmed. It merely increased in fury. The police began shooting, firing over the heads of the crowd. From the hearts of the liberated slaves there surged one long cry of revolt against the police trying to protect the Nazis from being lynched.

Even after the first stone had come whistling past his ears, Johann still stayed at the window. At the height of the assault, he had neither moved nor ceased smiling. He just did not understand what was happening round him. And even if he had understood, he would never have believed that the Frenchman who looked so like Joseph had actually thrown stones at him and tried to smash his face in.

He was still there, standing with wide-open eyes watching the crowd hurl volleys of stones at him from below, when the prisoners in the car caught him by the ankles and tore him away from the window, bringing him to the floor. Hundreds of hands sought him, clawing the air, ready to tear him limb from limb. Hundreds of feet were trampling him down and stamping on him with hatred, with despair, with uncontrolled brutality, while from outside a steady hail of stones came rattling against the walls and through the window.

The prisoners could not forgive him for unleashing the hatred and provoking the attack of the liberated slaves on the platform. They wanted to tear him to pieces. He was no longer surrounded by human beings, but by a mob, by the thousand-footed Beast of the Apocalypse trampling on his body, and crushing his warm, living flesh. And outside, the same thousand-footed Beast of the Apocalypse was hurling stones at him.

Blood was pouring out of his nose and mouth. Johann was sure he was going to die. Once he had reconciled himself to this thought he no longer felt the boots trampling on him nor the fury of the fists that were striking him. He no longer felt any pain at all; he was aware of nothing, save that the end of his sufferings was at hand. He remembered Father Koruga, the church in Fantana, and the icon of the Holy Mother of God. His body and soul were filled with peace. He heard the stones battering against the sides of the car, and he knew now that they were meant for him—and for him alone.

Everyone desired to crush him. Everyone sought the death of Johann Moritz. He knew it now. He felt that mankind could not go on living, that there would be no more progress in the world as long as he was still alive. He was responsible for all the evils of the world. He, Johann Moritz, was guilty. And that was why all these people wanted to kill him. That was why the prisoners were trampling on him; that was why the ex-prisoners were pelting him with stones; that was why the soldiers had kept him prisoner. As long as he was alive, nothing would quiet the multitudes. The military police could do nothing with the DP's until he, Johann Moritz, was killed; until he was dead, the prisoners in the car could not be controlled; as long as he was left alive, none of the troops with their tanks and automatics could go home across the ocean.

He had to die. He was Man. He could not be forgiven. Lord, wherein have I sinned? he thought. I love the French and I wanted to say a friendly word to one of them. That is why they are killing me. They killed Jesus, too, because he loved men.

He remembered what Traian had said: "We are being taken up Golgotha by rail. We are climbing a mechanized Golgotha." Johann had the feeling that he was on the Cross and that night was come. It was dark, dark, dark.

☙ ☙ ☙

IT WAS late the same day when Johann came to. His head and chest were bandaged. He was propped up against Traian's shoulder, and he could feel the contact of Traian's bare skin against his cheek. Traian had no shirt on.

He would have liked to ask Traian why he had taken off his shirt, but he lacked the strength.

"I'm thirsty," said Johann.

Traian pretended not to hear.

"I'm thirsty," repeated Johann, who, for several hours, had lain unconscious in Traian's arms. During that time Traian had dressed his wounds with strips of his own shirt, had found room for him, and had stretched him out on the floor.

Johann had not spoken all the while. From time to time Traian had put his hand on Johann's chest to feel the faint beating of his heart. Now and again he had removed his hand and applied his ear to the bandages to listen, because he could no longer feel anything with his hand. Even by gluing his ear to Johann's chest he had scarcely been able to catch the sound of the heartbeats.

And now Johann had spoken.

Traian was filled with joy, as though it were himself who had risen from the dead. But Johann wanted water. He was thirsty, like Jesus Christ on the Cross. And there was no water in the car.

The prisoners had spent twenty hours locked in without food or water and without permission to get out and relieve themselves. The atmosphere in the car was foul and stifling, and there was an acrid stench of decaying excrement. Urine had seeped all over the floor, and Johann was lying in it. He himself had urinated on the floor boards without realizing it. He had still not opened his eyes, but only his lips.

"I'm thirsty," he said.

"I am very sorry, but there is no water. There is nothing to drink," said Traian.

He tried to think what he could give Johann to moisten his lips. He remembered having read somewhere that, while Genghis Khan's warriors were riding through the steppes and had nothing to eat or drink, they used to dismount, open a vein in the horse's heel with a knife, and suck a drop or two of the blood. Then they bandaged the wound and rode on. For days on end the soldiers of Genghis Khan would eat or drink nothing save these drops of warm blood.

Traian was obsessed by this picture. He would willingly have given Johann some of his own blood to quench his thirst. The blood would have done him good.

"I'm thirsty," said Johann in a pleading tone.

"There is nothing to drink, old man," said Traian. "The only drinkable liquid—and I'd gladly give you a drop or two—is my own blood. But you must not drink blood. A man who drinks human blood turns into a vampire. He keeps the shape of a man, but he isn't one: he is a machine, a devil, a mob. He has every characteristic of man, except a soul."

"I'm thirsty," murmured Johann.

"I can well believe it!" said Traian. "But in spite of that you must not drink blood. And there is nothing else I can offer you. You are the only man around me who has never yet touched human blood. Do you hear? All the others have drunk it and have become vampires. They are no longer men. Among all these prisoners and guards and ex-prisoners who stoned you, there is not one who is a man. You are the only one who is still a man because you still love men."

"I'm thirsty."

"I believe you. I believe that you are thirsty and that you will die unless you drink," said Traian. "But it is better to die than live as a vampire. You must not drink human blood. Do you understand what I'm saying?"

"I'm thirsty," Johann whispered once more.

ǂ ǂ ǂ

PETITION, *by Johann Moritz*

I, the undersigned Moritz, Jon, native of Fantana, in Romania, submit this petition to the authorities of the country in which I am at present confined, to require them to inform me why they are keeping me imprisoned like a thief, and why they are torturing me as only Christ was tormented on the Cross.

I have not put this question to you before, as I might well have done, because I am a patient man. I work on the land, and people who work on the land know how to wait.

I therefore waited a whole spring, I waited a summer and then a whole long winter.

Now it is spring again. I am nothing but skin and bone. My soul is black with sorrow and distress, as black as coal or ink. I can wait no longer. And therefore I ask you: why are you keeping me prisoner? I have not stolen; I have not killed; I have deceived no one, and I have committed none of those things which are forbidden by the law or by the Church.

If I am neither a thief nor a criminal nor an evildoer, why do you keep me in prison?

You stoned me and tortured me till there was nothing left of me but a shadow wandering over the face of the earth.

I have been interned in fourteen camps. I think the time has come to ask you what you hold against me. I take a long time to make up my mind. But now my mind is made up.

I am sending this petition by post to the authorities in the land. I shall send it via the guard at the gates of the prison. It shall reach the ears of the authorities, though first it may travel all round the world. The authorities must be made to listen to my appeal, even if their ears are stopped up. I shall post this my petition on every door of the prison. I shall cast it into the street with a sling. I shall catch the birds as they fly over the camp and tie my petition to their feet, that they should carry it to the ends of the earth.

From this day forward I shall not cease to cry out for justice. You will shut me away in deep dungeons so that I should not be heard. But wherever I may be I shall not hold my peace. If I have neither pencil nor paper, I shall scratch the petition with my nails on the prison walls. When my nails are worn down to the quick I shall wait till they grow back and begin anew.

If you shoot me, I shall go neither to hell nor to heaven nor to purgatory. My soul will remain here on earth to haunt you like a shadow wherever you shall go. A hundred times shall I rouse you from your slumber and proclaim to you and to the mistresses at your side that I was in the right. And you will not be able to shut your eyes. To the end of your days you will not be able to listen to music or to words of love or to anything at all, for my words, the words of Johann Moritz, will be echoing in your ears.

I am a man, and if I have done no wrong no one has a right to imprison and torment me. My soul and my life belong to me alone, and whoever you may be and in spite of all the tanks and machine guns and planes and camps and money you may possess, you still have not the right to touch my life or my soul.

Throughout my life I have desired but little: to be allowed to work, to have a home for my wife and children, and to have enough to eat.

Is that why you imprisoned me?

The Romanians sent the gendarmes to requisition me, as they requisitioned property and animals. I allowed them to requisition me. My hands were empty, and I could fight neither against the King nor against the gendarmes, who were armed with rifles and pistols. They insisted that my name was not Jon, as my mother had christened me, but Jacob. They interned me with the Jews in a camp behind barbed wire—like animals— and put me to hard labor. We had to sleep in a herd like cattle; we had to eat in a herd, drink tea in a herd, and I supposed that we should be taken to the slaughterhouse in a herd, like cattle. The others went to the slaughterhouse. I escaped.

Is that why you imprisoned me? Because I ran away before being led to slaughter?

The Hungarians maintained I was not called Jacob but

Jon. They arrested me because I was a Romanian. They tortured me and made me suffer and then sold me to the Germans. The Germans maintained my name was neither Jon nor Jacob but Janos, and tortured me once more because I was a Hungarian. Then a colonel came along and informed me my name was neither Jon nor Jacob nor Jankl nor Janos, but Johann. He made me a soldier. But first of all he measured my head, counted my teeth, and put drops of my blood into glass tubes. And all that to prove that I had a name other than that my mother gave me. Is that why you imprisoned me?

As a soldier, I helped some French prisoners to escape from the camp. Is that why you imprisoned me?

When the war ended and I thought that there would be peace for me, too, the Americans came and fed me like a king on chocolate and American food. Then, without another word, they put me in prison. They sent me to fourteen camps, as if I were one of the most dangerous gangsters the world has ever known.

And now I want to know: Why?

Is it because you don't like my name: Janos or Jon, Johann or Jacob or Jankl? Would you like to change it, too? Go ahead. I know that men no longer have the right to bear the names they received at baptism. But I warn you: I cannot wait any longer. I want to know why I am being imprisoned and tortured.

Awaiting your answer, I am yours respectfully,

Moritz, Jon, Johann-Jacob-Jankl-Janos
Agricultural laborer and head of a family

"Why are you crying, Moritz?" asked Traian when he had finished reading out the petition.

"I'm not crying."

"But I can see tears in your eyes."

"I don't know why."

"Are you afraid of sending in the petition?" asked Traian. "Isn't everything I've written true?"

"It's not that I'm afraid," answered Johann; "it's all true."

"Then why are you crying?"

"That is exactly why I am crying," said Johann, "because it is too true."

❦ ❦ ❦

TWO days after the petition had been sent off, Johann was summoned for an interview. Traian lent him his own shirt and trousers.

"We've won," he said. "Our petition has had an effect."

Johann's eyes shone. He already saw himself free.

"We've won. And I owe it all to you," he said. "Everything you wrote in the petition was so true."

"Don't be afraid," said Traian. "It's they who ought to be afraid, because it's they who are guilty."

Johann went off to the interview with a smile. At midday he was back. Traian stood waiting for him outside the door.

"How did it go?" he asked. "Have they told you when you will be released?"

Johann kept his eyes on the ground. He always put on a mysterious air when he was asked a question.

"I'll tell you later," he said. "I can't now."

"Are you crazy?" said Traian. "I've spent hours out here waiting for you to hear what happened, and all you have to say is that you'll tell me later?"

Johann had picked up some cigarette butts off the floor in the office. He now took them out of his pocket, unwrapped them slowly, and made two equal little heaps of tobacco, one for him and one for Traian. Then he started rolling a cigarette in newspaper.

"I'd rather tell you some other time, Master Traian."

"Did they say they weren't going to release you?"

"No, they didn't say that."

"Did they swear at you?"

Johann went on rolling his cigarette.

"No, they didn't swear at me."

"Did they beat you up?"

"No."

"Then, why don't you say anything?" asked Traian. "Evidently nothing bad has happened."

"Nothing at all," said Johann, lighting his cigarette.

"Didn't your turn come?" asked Traian. "That doesn't matter. They'll call you tomorrow."

"My turn came."

"Did they question you?"

"Yes."

Johann's tongue seemed paralyzed. Each word had to be dragged out by force. Traian lost patience.

"Tell me everything they asked you," he said. "Start at the beginning when you walked in."

"I went in first," said Johann. "When I got inside the office he told me to sit down. There was a chair in front of the table."

"That's at least a good beginning," said Traian. "If they asked you to sit down, it's a very good sign. They must have looked up your file and found out that you were innocent. I don't think they invite everyone to sit down. Go on."

"A sergeant questioned me."

"Was he polite?"

"Yes."

"What did he ask first?"

"First he looked through the files," said Johann. "Then he asked me: 'Are you Johann Moritz?' I answered 'Yes.' He glanced at me, looked back at the files, and asked: 'How do you spell "Moritz," with a *t* or a *tz*?' I told him I spelt it either way. In Romania I spell it with a *t* and in Germany with a *tz*."

Johann stopped. He looked into Traian's eyes with despair.

"Go on," said Traian impatiently. "Why have you stopped?"

"Then the sergeant said: 'Thank you. You may go.'"

"Was that all?"

"That was all," said Johann.

"And you didn't try to say anything else?" said Traian. "Why didn't you say what I told you?"

"I tried," said Johann. "But the sergeant wouldn't listen. He didn't even look at me and said: 'Call in the next man!'"

"And what did you say?"

"Nothing."

"How absurd!" said Traian, burying his face in his hands. "How utterly absurd! And so you went away?"

"Yes, I went away."

"And that was the interview we've been waiting for all through this year in prison," said Traian. "Wasn't there anything else, anything at all? Perhaps you've forgotten something."

"Nothing else at all," said Johann. "I went out. As I shut the door behind me, my hand was shaking. They called the next man. It was Thomas Mann."

"What did they ask him?"

"They asked him if he spelled Mann with one *n* or two."

"Nothing else?"

Two large teardrops rolled down Johann's cheeks.

"You must resign yourself to it, Moritz," said Traian, patting him on the shoulder. "Once the white rabbits have died there is no other way out."

🐾 🐾 🐾

PETITION No. 5. *Subject: Justice (Interviews, Mechanization of)*

I am aware that you have received instructions to interrogate each prisoner in this camp individually. This order is patently senseless. Since all the inmates were arrested automatically and en masse, it is absurd to interview them individually.

However, I fully appreciate the reason why this order was issued. Your civilization is capable of occasional gestures of courtesy toward native customs. It is a concession for the sake of appearances and politeness.

One of your officials is obliged to interview five hundred prisoners in the course of the morning and a further five hundred in the course of the afternoon. I have noticed that you put the same questions to all of them, and that you don't listen to the answers. What could a prisoner have to say that could be of any interest? Nothing.

But I am worried about all the energy wasted in asking the questions. It requires a colossal effort to ask the same questions a thousand times a day. I should imagine that the officials detailed for this duty must suffer every evening from pains in the jaw and lips.

I therefore suggest that the questions be recorded. The routine would then operate as follows: The officer in duty sits at his desk. He must do that, because it is laid down as part of the procedure for individual interviews. He pushes the button that puts the needle on the record. As the prisoner comes in, the record says, "Sit down." The prisoner sits down. The record goes on revolving. The first, second, and third questions follow. Then the record announces: "Thank you, you may go!" The prisoner gets up and goes out. At the exact moment he reaches the door the record comes to the last sentence: "Next man in." That is the end of the interview. The next man comes in. The record starts again from the beginning, automatically. The same record could be used to interrogate from four to five hundred prisoners.

Meanwhile the officer in charge sits at his desk and reads a detective story. At lunchtime he will be able to eat normally and his jaws will not ache from unnecessary strain.

It must be remembered that these interviews are held

for the purpose of asking questions and not for that of listening to the answers. The work can therefore be performed by a machine. It is perfectly logical. Formality must be respected, but at the same time the interviewers must not be overworked. Justice cannot but gain by this procedure. In a civilized society, justice must be automatic and should not proceed as in the days before the discovery of electricity. What on earth is the good of so many technical inventions if justice can't even make use of electrical recording?

THE WITNESS

卐 卐 卐

FIFTEENTH internment camp: Darmstadt. It was exactly the same as all the other fourteen, except that it contained an Orthodox church, small and improvised. Traian and Johann took off their service caps and went in.

The church was set up in a tent with the altar at the far end. The icons were sketched on cardboard with carbon and colored chalks. There were no boards even for a floor; nothing but bare earth.

It had rained during the night. The water had seeped under the tent flaps, turning the earth into mud.

In the middle of the church there was a crucifix the size of a man. Traian kneeled down in front of it. Jesus was made of cardboard. The thorns of His crown were of tin from the cans of food rolled and cut into thin strips.

Traian lifted his eyes to the wounds made by the nails in the hands and side of Christ. The painter had had no red chalk for the blood. To represent the wounds he had stuck bits of red paper off packets of Lucky Strike cigarettes. The black lettering had not been effaced and was clearly visible.

"Never yet have I seen Thee, Jesus, so painfully crucified," said Traian. "I had come to pray for my own wounds. But I cannot do it. Forgive me, Jesus, if I pray first for Thy Lucky Strike wounds, which stain with blood Thy sides and Thy hands and Thy feet. They are more painful than my own wounds of flesh and blood. Let me pray first for the food-can thorns of the crown on Thy head."

Traian's eyes, traveling over the body of Christ, discovered the letter *M* written in printer's ink on the Saviour's breast. It was the *M* from the ration cases of "Menu Unit," from which the crucified body of Christ had been cut out.

Traian stood up and kissed the feet of Christ.

"Now I feel I have truly partaken of Thy body, O Jesus, our Saviour, our eternal 'Menu' of hope. Lord, my only 'Menu Unit,' I have never understood more clearly that Thy body is our nourishment. How did the artist prisoner conceive the idea of cutting Thy body out of cardboard 'Menu Unit' cases? Thou art at last the all-embracing symbol of my thirst for divinity, for bread, and for liberty."

Traian was in a state of ecstasy. He was unconscious of everything around him.

Johann was examining the angels made out of the silver paper from cigarette packages, and the icons of the Holy Mother of God adorned with necklaces cut out of the gilt-lined lids off canned puddings.

He made the sign of the cross before the icon of Saint Nicholas, who looked like Father Koruga. Then he came over to Traian and knelt down beside him, looking at the red wounds of Christ.

"Lord," said Traian, "I am not asking Thee to dash this cup from my lips. I know that that is impossible. But I beseech Thee to help me drink this cup. For a year I have held it close to my lips. For a year I have dwelt on the borders of life and death; for a year I have stood between dreams and reality. I exist outside time and yet I still live. Life has drained away from me through every pore of my body, and there is none left in me. Yet I breathe still, and still crawl from place to place sustaining my body with bread and water, though I have the desire neither to eat nor to drink.

"And all this suffering is my lot because I cannot understand whether I am a prisoner or whether I am free. I can see that I am in prison; and yet I cannot bring myself to believe that I am in prison. I can see that I am not free, and yet my mind tells me that there is no reason why I should not be free. The torture of not understanding is infinitely harder to bear than slavery.

"The men who have imprisoned me do not hate me, neither do they desire my punishment or my death. They simply want to save the world. Yet they are torturing and killing me over a slow fire. They are inflicting slow torture and death upon all mankind. I know well enough that I am not alone.

"The rulers of the world say fine things about liberty. I know they are not lying when they claim to seek freedom for mankind. Yet, speaking of freedom and the fight for freedom, they are building prisons. The earth is full of prisons. In their speech there is good: but when they come into contact with the flesh of man, their touch is lethal, like that of poisoned arrows.

"The rulers of the world have started building gigantic hospitals, that they may heal the wounds of man. But prisons, not hospitals, rise out of the bricks to which they have set their hand.

"They seem to be enchanted by evil.

"It passes my understanding.

"That is why I want to die. Help me, Lord, to die.

"This hour is too much for me. It is beyond my strength and my endurance.

"This present hour is not of life. I cannot pass through it with my flesh and blood. This is the twenty-fifth hour, and it is too late for salvation, too late for life, too late for death. It is too late.

"Let me be changed into a rock, O Lord, but leave me not as I am.

"If Thou wilt forsake me now, I shall not even be able to

die. Behold! My flesh and my spirit are dead, and yet I live. The world is dead, and yet the world lives. We are neither the quick nor the dead."

Traian covered his face with his hands. Johann stroked him timidly on the shoulder, but he felt nothing.

A priest came into the church. He was wearing American army clothes marked with the letters PW like all the other prisoners. Johann went up to him and kissed his hand. Traian was still kneeling in front of the crucifix.

The priest asked Johann where they had come from and what nationality they were. When he heard that Traian's wife was a prisoner, too, he folded his arms across his chest and prayed for her. Then he blessed Traian, who was still unaware of his presence.

"We hold a service here at six o'clock every evening," said the priest. "I am the Metropolitan Paladius of Warsaw. My council of priests is here with me. We were all arrested. The services are very fine. Do come. There is a Romanian priest, too, who celebrates Mass sometimes, but at the moment he is in the hospital."

Johann looked intently at the Metropolitan.

"I'll send word to him at the hospital," said the Metropolitan. "When he hears there are Romanians here he will come and give you his blessing."

☙ ☙ ☙

AT SIX o'clock a council of priests began the evening service. They all wore their stoles over their PW uniforms.

Traian and Johann stood next to each other. The Metropolitan had put on his chasuble and miter. The precious stones that usually adorned them were missing. The Metropolitan's voice, by its gentleness, was reminiscent of a cello.

Traian went up toward the altar. But as he reached the crucifix he suddenly collapsed on the ground. Johann thought Traian had missed his footing and slipped. He ran to help him up. But Traian's body felt limp, as if all the bones in it had dissolved. His cheeks were the color of wax.

Apart from the priests, there was no one else under the tent of the church. Johann lifted his eyes to beg them for help. At that moment he understood why Traian had fainted.

"Father Koruga," was all that Johann could say. He fell on his knees before the priest as if he would kiss his feet. But Father Koruga no longer had any legs. He came up to them supporting himself on his crutches.

Johann stood motionless.

The priest's hair was even whiter than before. He smiled with infinite kindness and joy. Through his eyes and his smile shone a glimpse of heaven.

"Traian, my beloved son!" said Father Koruga, but as he tried to bend down to him, one crutch slipped from under his armpit and fell. He propped himself upright on the other crutch.

Then, deliberately, he dropped that one, too. He stood straight as an arrow beside Traian on what was left of his legs. He had let go of his crutches to free his arms, that he might throw them round his son.

Johann picked up the crutches and stood holding them beside Father Koruga and Traian.

❦ ❦ ❦

JOHANN, Father Koruga, and Traian now lived together under one tent in the Darmstadt camp.

After a whole year's delay, the prisoners were at last allowed to receive mail. Johann was the first to get a letter. Hilda's mother wrote:

DEAR HANS,

On May 9, 1945, your house was burned down. *I know
you have not yet heard about it. It caught fire in the afternoon,
just as the Russian troops were coming into the town. Hilda
and Franz were indoors at the time. The first few weeks I did
not even know that they had been burned alive. But one day
when I was hunting about in the debris to see if by any chance
something might have escaped the fire I found their charred
bodies. Hilda died with the child in her arms. I don't know why
she did not run away as soon as the house caught fire. She must
have been asleep. I find it difficult though to believe that she
could have been asleep at that hour and especially on the very
day when the Russians entered the town. Everybody had fled,
particularly the women. And in any case Hilda never went to
sleep in the afternoon, as you know. After lunch, when she came
back from the hospital, she would always start right away with
the housework.*

I collected their charred bones and buried them together in one coffin in our cemetery. I could not get hold of two
separate coffins because they are very expensive and no one
wants to make them. Nowadays people here are burying their
dead without coffins. You can't get boards, let alone nails. I had
to take the nails out of the walls and the picture frames and give
them to the carpenter for Hilda's coffin. Even then he wouldn't
make it. He said the nails were too fine and too short for a
coffin. I gave him one of your hats to persuade him. Please don't
be angry with me for not asking you first, but without the hat,
nothing would have induced him to make the coffin, and their
bones had to be buried somehow or other. As it was, I had had
to keep them at home for a whole week. I also had a wooden
cross made. When you come you'll be able to order a stone one.
All our family have beautiful stone crosses in the cemetery.

Among the ruins of your house they found the corpse
of an officer, completely charred. He must have been one of
those who had sought hospitality or who came to change out of

their uniforms into civilian clothes. All our officers and men did that when the Russians came. He was buried in our cemetery at the town's expense. In his brief case, which was not completely destroyed, I found his papers. His name is Jurgu Jordan, and he came from Romania like you. I thought I would mention this to you because he may have been a friend or relation of yours who had come to see you.

ᛒ ᛒ ᛒ

"THINGS have perhaps turned out for the best," said Father Koruga. He had put his hand on Johann's shoulder and was trying to console him.

"Supposing Hilda were still alive and you were to be set free one day, you would not have known where to go. You would have had to abandon one woman and return to the other."

"So Susanna didn't divorce me, then," said Johann. That was the first time he had heard that Susanna had remained faithful to him.

"And is she waiting for me at home?"

"Susanna is waiting for you and will go on waiting for you to the end of her days," answered the priest. "She is still your wife. She only signed the divorce certificate under duress in order to be able to keep the house instead of being thrown out with her children onto the streets. She acted out of despair. But never for one moment did she consider herself legally separated from you."

"So all this divorce was a fraud!" said Johann. "And I, like a fool, thought Susanna had married another man. That's why I married Hilda. I thought Susanna had deserted me. How was I not to believe it, when I read the divorce certificate with my own eyes? But I have committed a great sin. I know. God will never forgive me."

"This sin will be forgiven you," said the priest. "What has happened is very serious, Moritz. But neither you nor Susanna is to blame. The state and the law alone are responsible. And the state will not be forgiven. God will punish it even as he punished Sodom and Gomorrah. Retribution will fall, not only on our particular state, but on all states of this our civilization, on account of their sins, which cry out to heaven."

卐 卐 卐

TRAIAN was summoned for his first interview.

"Are you trying to tell me you don't know why you have been arrested and interned for over a year?" asked the officer. "There are twenty thousand prisoners, and not a single one who admits knowing why he was arrested. Every one of you maintains that we swept through Europe, arresting right and left indiscriminately; but you are mistaken. Every arrest was made in conformity with a decree."

Traian smiled. The officer intercepted his smile.

"Do you mean to tell me that our laws do not conform to the eternal principles of justice? I hear this reproach day after day. It's utterly ridiculous the way you all rail against the absence of inherent values or of universality in the laws by virtue of which your arrests were made. Firstly, every country has the right to decree whatever laws it wishes and to be governed accordingly. Laws made by ourselves in our own country are exclusively our own business. Secondly, there are no eternal principles of justice. Justice is made by man. And nothing that is human can be eternal. In the great sphere of the universe one law is as good as another. All are equally and at the same time ephemeral and eternal. To maintain the contrary is to deceive oneself.

"According to the laws at present in force in the zone of American occupation, you are under arrest as an official of an enemy country. That is the law. Your wife is under arrest by virtue of the same law, which provides that wives of high-ranking enemy officials shall be arrested automatically. In addition, your father is subject to automatic arrest, as an official of an enemy state.

"I am prepared to admit that this may seem hard to you, but that is the law. Throughout the course of history laws have always been hard. After all, you couldn't have expected us to come and ask for your approval at the time we were making these laws, could you?"

Traian stood up. He wanted to go. He had known from the moment he had started to write *The Twenty-fifth Hour* that the time would come when there would be laws depriving men of the right to live their own lives. At the time of his arrest he had had an intimation that these laws had already come into force, but he had gone on hoping vaguely that he was mistaken.

Now he had received official confirmation of the fact that these laws were rigorously applied and universally respected. There could be no possible mistake. Men who had done no wrong could be and were being legally arrested, tortured, starved, stripped, and exterminated.

"I know that you personally are not guilty," said the officer. "I've already sent in five applications for your release and that of your wife and father, in spite of the fact that officially we are not permitted to apply for the individual release of prisoners arrested automatically. I have had no reply. Release orders cannot be granted to individuals, but only to categories of individuals."

"Is the question of the individual's innocence or guilt of no interest to you whatsoever?" asked Traian. "Not even out of curiosity?"

"No, we are not interested in that aspect. However much it may offend your susceptibilities as an educated man with an individualistic, theological, aesthetic, and humanitarian upbringing, there is nothing I can do about it. In any case, I don't see the necessity of making any changes in the existing order. Our system may perhaps appear dry, technical, and mathematical, but it is just. The universe itself functions in a mathematical way, and no one would take it into his head to change its course or direction."

"So the interview you have just granted me does not interest you and might just as well never have taken place?" asked Traian. "Does nothing that concerns the individual interest you?"

"Nothing," said the officer. "All we want to know from an individual is his personal data—that is to say, his full name, date and place of birth, occupation, etc.—which will be noted and card-indexed in our files and statistics.

"As a matter of fact, individual interviews are only granted in order to verify data and to make it possible to put prisoners in the appropriate categories. Orders for continued confinement or for release are thereafter made only by categories. Our job is to place everyone in his appropriate category. It is mathematical precision work."

"Don't you consider it inhuman to liquidate man as an individual and treat him as a fraction of a category?"

"No, I can't say I do," answered the officer. "This system is practical, quick, and above all fair. Justice can only gain by this procedure. Justice has adopted the methods of mathematics and physics—that is to say, the most precise and accurate methods possible. Only poets and mystics object to them.

"But modern society has done with poetry and mysticism. We are now in the era of mathematics and exact sciences, and we cannot put the clock back for sentimental reasons. Besides, sentiment is the invention of poets and mystics."

The officer indicated that the interview was over.

"Take it easy," he said.

Traian opened the door. At that moment he heard the officer who had interviewed him say coldly:

"Next one in."

Ⱶ Ⱶ Ⱶ

JOHANN wanted to escape. Ever since he had found out that Susanna had not divorced him and was waiting faithfully for him with the children, Johann could not keep still.

"It isn't even worth trying," said Traian. "The minute you get near the barbed wire the Poles will shoot you down."

Johann glanced at the Polish sentries in their American uniforms dyed blue. Their eyes were fixed on him as if they had guessed his thoughts, and their rifles were held at the ready.

"And if by some miracle the Poles were to miss," Traian went on, "the American or German patrols would get you. Before you got to Romania you'd have to deal with Austrian, Czech, French, and Hungarian patrols on every road, and in the end you still wouldn't get home. They'd catch you en route. If you escaped the bullets of one nation, the next one would get you. Between you and your family, my dear Moritz, between you and your house, all the nations of the world stand armed and determined to bar your way. Between each man and his intimate private life there is this international army. Man is no longer allowed to live his own life. If he tries, he is shot. That is what tanks and machine guns, searchlights, and barbed wire are for."

"I'll run for it, all the same," said Johann.

The Polish sentry in the tower eyed him even more closely.

At that moment two American officers appeared on the parade ground and headed toward the infirmary. Johann watched them pass.

Suddenly, without another word, he left Traian, ran toward them, and stood blocking their way. The officers stopped. For a moment they looked at Johann and Johann at them. Then one of the officers who was middle-aged and rather fat put his arms round Johann and hugged him. The prisoners gathered round in amazement. They had never seen an American officer hugging a prisoner.

Johann accompanied the American officer, who still had his arm round his shoulder, toward the infirmary. They all went into the building together.

Traian went over to the infirmary and waited at the door to find out what had happened. He expected Johann to come back and tell him all about it, but Johann was a long while coming.

After a while Traian heard Johann's voice. He had stuck his head out of the window of the infirmary office. His black eyes were aglow with excitement.

"The American officer is my friend, Dr. Abramovici," he said. "I recognized him at once. It was him I escaped from Romania with. Now I am sure to be set free."

He shut the window. His friend had called him inside to talk.

❧ ❧ ❧

BOTH in Romania in the camp and in Hungary Johann had always spoken Yiddish to the doctor. And they spoke Yiddish now. Lieutenant Abramovici, Army Medical Service, was sincerely glad to have met Johann and listened carefully to every word he said.

Johann told him everything that had happened from the time they had parted up to that very day. Dr. Abramovici nodded his head in sympathy, particularly when Johann told him all he had suffered in the fifteen camps where he had been interned for the last few years.

"I have to go now," said Dr. Abramovici, looking at the gold watch on his wrist. "I know you need help, my dear Jankl. Of course you do. Tell me everything you need, and I'll help you. I haven't forgotten that we've spent a few awkward moments in each other's company."

He gave him a hearty slap on the back.

"I'm in power now," he said. "Whereas you are still out of luck. What do you need? Cigarettes, food, clothing? Just tell me what you want."

"I want to be set free," said Johann. "I want to go home to my wife and children."

"Don't ask for the impossible, my dear Jankl," said the Doctor in annoyance. "Ask for something in my power to grant you. Your release can only come automatically. You mustn't even think of it. You must be patient."

"But I am not guilty," said Johann. "Why should they keep me shut up?"

"Your guilt and your release are in no way connected," said the Doctor, who was becoming irritated. "Has anyone ever maintained that you, Johann Moritz, were guilty of anything? I very much doubt it. I know you and I know you're a decent fellow. But there is no connection between a prisoner's guilt and his release. Absolutely none. Your release is merely a matter of waiting patiently."

"I have waited long enough."

"That's what you think," said the Doctor. "Obviously you're still a simple-minded peasant. Do you imagine that a prisoner can be released by any old official who happens to be there merely because he is innocent? If that were the case, then the camps would be emptied overnight. Every Nazi in them would concoct some proof of his innocence. Releases are only granted on the order of HQ in Frankfurt. From there the papers are sent to Washington for approval and then referred to Wiesbaden. A special commission checks them through at Esslingen and sends them on to Berlin. The release order is issued in Berlin, and passed on to Heidelberg. The moment the order reaches Heidelberg, the card is removed from the files in hundreds of offices—and it is only then that you can be set free. The whole machinery is exceedingly intricate and works automatically. Every prisoner has his own card. The Americans have vast record offices, as big as that barracks over the way. As soon as the order is issued and sent to Heidelberg to be dealt with, the card is removed automatically from the record offices in Washington, Stuttgart, Ludwigsburg, Munich, Kornwestheim, Paris, Berlin, and Frankfurt.

"Your name is indexed all over the world. At the Federal Bureau of Investigation in America, at Allied GHQ, at European Command in Paris, at the Control Commission in Berlin, in all the concentration camps and prisons, and in all the offices of CIC, CID, MP, SP, SOS—in fact, everywhere.

"Every one of your movements—even if it is only your transfer from one camp to another—will be recorded by an alteration on your card in each one of those record offices. Did you know that?"

Johann saw his name spelled out in every city in the world, relayed by an immense electrical apparatus, first lit up and then plunged into darkness, like the searchlights above the wire entanglements of the camp. He now knew that his every movement was photographed and flooded with light.

"I didn't know."

"If you had known, you wouldn't have asked me to have you released. That's why I'm not angry with you for asking me. Did you really believe that I could extricate you from this stupendous apparatus all by myself?"

Samuel Abramovici roared with laughter.

"Not even the President of the United States in person could do it," he said. "You'll just have to wait your turn."

"But if I am innocent why should I be kept behind barbed wire?" asked Johann. "What has the apparatus got against me? I've done no harm. This apparatus of yours is probably meant for thieves and criminals and evildoers."

"It's time you stopped reasoning like a country bumpkin, my dear Jankl," said the Doctor. "You make a personal issue out of every problem, out of everything. Great and civilized countries just aren't interested in the personal problems of individuals. The fact of your guilt or innocence is your own personal affair. It might possibly interest your wife or your neighbors or the other peasants in your village. They are the only ones who still bother about personal questions. Civilized countries operate on a large scale—not on an individual one."

"But why was I arrested?"

"We worked on a system of preventive arrest according to categories. And you belonged to one of them. Whenever we want to pick up a suspect—a war criminal, for example—we know we have him handy, and we don't have to start combing the villages and the forests to hunt for him. Too much time would be wasted. As it is, all one has to do is to press the button marked with the appropriate letter in the index, and in the twinkling of an eye, the card of the individual in question appears before you, complete with photograph, height, weight, color of hair, date of birth, place of birth, number of teeth, and everything you want to know about him. Then all you have to do is to pick up the microphone and radio across the details of the camp or prison in which he happens to be, and a few hours later you have him standing in the flesh before the judges of the International Tribunal at Nuremberg. It's stupendous! It's the result of the scientific method. Everything is automatic. Everything works by electricity. How can you expect them to set you free? It would mean releasing you before your turn. It would be madness. You are like a thread in a loom. Once it has been put in, no one can get it out again. You just have to wait until its turn comes to be taken off the loom, interwoven with the other threads. It can't be done any other way. Machines work with precision. You must be patient with them.

"And by now you are thoroughly caught up in the machine. You can bang your head against it and get worked up as much as you like; you can't get out. The machine is deaf. It doesn't hear, it doesn't see, it just operates. It operates with admirable efficiency, and achieves a degree of perfection that no man can ever hope to attain. You only have to wait long enough and you may be dead certain your turn will come. The machine does not forget, like a human being. It is accurate. You understand?"

Johann shrugged his shoulders.

"So there is nothing you can do to get them to release me?"

"Haven't I explained to you, man, that you are right in the heart of the machine and that nothing can be done about it?"

"But if you would only put in a word for me it might help quite a lot," said Johann. "Commandants are human beings like us; they'll understand. Perhaps they'd set me free when they heard I have a wife and children and that for years on end I have been tormented in camp after camp without ever having done any harm to anyone."

"I'll never get you to see straight," said the Doctor irritably. "You keep on bringing everything back to personal and private issues. You are incapable of leaving yourself out of the picture. That is characteristic of primitive and uncivilized man. You had much better tell me what you need. I have to go. Do you want any cigarettes, or food, or clothing?"

"I should have liked to have justice," said Johann. "But I see that human justice is dead all over the earth. I don't want anything else."

"You might as well take a cigarette, all the same," said Dr. Abramovici, smiling and offering Johann his pack of Luckies.

"We were fellow sufferers, after all, my dear Jankl."

Johann stretched out his hand for a cigarette. The pack was empty. The Doctor felt his pockets, but could not find any more.

"I'll offer you a cigarette next time I come round, my dear Jankl," he said. Then he departed.

꟞ ꟞ ꟞

FATHER KORUGA, with his crutches on his knees, sat in front of the officer who was interrogating him.

"What were you doing in Germany if you were neither a Nazi nor a collaborator?" asked the officer. "Your tale about waking up in a German military hospital without knowing when or how you got there is good for the nursery. Such things may happen in your Balkan fairy tales, but not in real life. For an American interrogating officer the story simply does not ring true. It smacks too much of the fairy tale—it is too märchenhaft. Why should the Germans have kept you in their hospital if you were not their friend or collaborator? Why did they look after you for half a year and amputate your legs? Because you were their enemy? Purely from humanitarian motives? Since when have the Germans become humanitarians? The Germans put all their enemies away into concentration camps and then sent them to the gas chambers. You were their collaborator. That is why they looked after you. You must be very sorry that Hitler did not win the war. Am I right?"

Father Koruga was silent. He was pale. Beads of perspiration fell from his eyebrows. He found it painful to sit on a chair. Ever since his legs had been amputated he could only lie down. On top of that he was running a high temperature. He wished that the interview might come to an end at the earliest possible moment so that he might be allowed to get down off that chair.

"You would have been very glad if Hitler had won the war, wouldn't you?" the officer went on. "Hitler would have made you Metropolitan of Romania if he had won the war. You would have been very pleased with a Nazi victory."

"No, I should not have been pleased," said the priest.

"Then were you pleased when the Allies won?"

"That did not make me happy, either," said the priest.

The lieutenant's face clouded over. The priest smiled and said:

"No victory won by force of arms will ever make me happy."

Even as he answered, the priest was looking at the photographs of concentration camps on the office walls. He remembered the corpses of George Damian, the attorney, of Vasile Apostol, and of the other peasants in Fantana who had been shot by Marcu Goldenberg at the same time as he, and who had been thrown in the manure pit behind the stables. He thought of the children's corpses in Dresden, Frankfurt, and Berlin, the bodies of Dunkirk and Stalingrad. And he was unable to rejoice at a victory achieved at their expense.

"In order to achieve victory the earth has been strewn with the bodies of innocent men, women, and children:

" 'Even in victory, there is not beauty,
And who calls it beautiful
Is one who delights in slaughter.
He who delights in slaughter
Will not succeed in his ambition to rule the world.
The slaying of multitudes should be mourned with
    sorrow.
A victory should be celebrated with funeral rites.' " *

"That is a very fine poem," said the officer. "Did you write it?"

"It was written by a Chinese who lived two thousand years ago."

"Write it down for me," said the officer. "I'd like to send it to my people back in the States."

The officer smiled, thinking of his family. Suddenly his smile turned into a frown. He looked suspiciously at the priest.

"Are you sure the lines you recited just now were written by a Chinese?"

"Quite sure," said the priest. "But if you like them, it's immaterial who wrote them. They are beautiful. The rest doesn't matter."

"On the contrary, it matters a great deal," said the officer. "I'm glad the author is Chinese. China is an ally of the United States. My family will be very pleased. If the lines had been

* Lao-tse.

written by an enemy poet I could not have sent them. Copy it out for me by tomorrow morning. I'll give you a pencil and paper. Did you ever study anything else apart from theology?"

"I learned all that my leisure permitted and that it pleased me to learn."

"You don't happen to know Chinese, do you?"

"No."

"What a pity," said the officer. "I should have got you to write out the poem in Chinese characters. That would have been a surprise for my family, who certainly don't expect letters in Chinese from me. But never mind, if you don't know Chinese, write it in English. The Chinese who wrote that poem has a sense of humor. And, moreover, he is an ally of the United Nations."

Back in his tent, the priest felt broken with exhaustion. Johann helped him to lie down on the bed and put cold compresses on his forehead.

"Did he say anything about setting you free, Father?"

"Nothing," answered the old man.

"What did he ask you?"

"He asked me to copy out a poem by Lao-tse. He would have liked to have had it in the original and was quite upset that I could not write Chinese characters."

"Was that all the interview was about?"

"That was all," said the priest.

🏵 🏵 🏵

Traian received a letter from Nora.

"I knew Nora had been arrested," said Traian, gripping the envelope marked *Prisoner of War* between his hands. "But I had hoped she had been freed in the meantime. Now I can cherish my dreams no longer. I know for certain that she is a prisoner like us, in a camp like ours, suffering as we do. Like us, she is ordered about and transferred from camp to camp. Like us she is guarded behind barbed wire by Poles armed with automatics. My very being revolts and can stand it no longer."

Nora had not known Traian's address when she had written. On the envelope she had put his name and the numbers of all the internment camps in the American Zone. Her letter must have passed from camp to camp before finally reaching him.

"They would not tell her where I was," said Traian. "And they refused to tell me in which camp they had put her."

The priest, who was lying on the bed with his head swathed in compresses, tried to comfort him. Johann was standing beside him. Traian remained unmoved by his words of consolation.

"There is a limit to human endurance," said Traian, standing up. "I think I have reached it. No human being can go beyond this limit and yet remain alive!"

Traian went out of the tent.

"Master Traian is going to kill himself," said Johann, frightened.

The priest was lying on his back with his eyes shut. He did not hear Johann's words. He was praying. He was praying not only for Traian and Nora, but for Johann and for all the other human beings whom Western Technological Civilization had brought to that limit beyond which all life was unthinkable.

"Master Traian will kill himself if I leave him alone," said Johann.

The priest opened his eyes. He touched Johann's hand and then let him go.

🦋 🦋 🦋

"LET me hold your hand, please," said Father Koruga. He was lying as before, with his eyes half closed. His forehead was pallid and the blood had drained out of his cheeks. The old man took

Traian's hand and held it between his own. Not a word was spoken. The two hands now had the same warmth. The blood seemed to flow from one to the other. They felt close to each other, as only father and son can feel. Their hearts beat in the same rhythm. But the priest's heartbeats were growing fainter and fainter.

Johann asked the priest if he might change the compress, but the priest shook his head to indicate that it was no longer necessary. And he smiled.

Johann sat down on the edge of the bed.

The priest said:

" '*I warm'd both hands before the fire of life;*
    It sinks, and I am ready to depart.' *

"I feel at this moment as though I were warming my hands, not with your warmth, but with the fire of life!" said the priest. "You are afire with a fierce heat that can only be the flame of life itself."

Traian gripped his father's hands still more tightly. They were cold, but the priest was smiling.

"I dreamed two great dreams on this earth," he said. "Living, to be a priest in America, and dead, to be buried in the graveyard at Fantana. You know the place, Traian. There are no walls or fences round it and, overgrown with high grass and wild flowers, it is like a meadow. There I felt I should most happily have rested in peace forever.

"And now both my dreams have come true, but in how strange a way. I never went to America, but America came to me. I shall die in this prison above which flutters the star-spangled banner of America.

"I shall not be buried in the graveyard of Fantana, but that graveyard has grown and grown, until finally it has engulfed the whole of Europe.

"Fantana and Romania and the whole of Europe are now nothing more than a black blot on the map of the world. Like

* Walter Savage Landor.

a blot of ink. The whole Continent is as silent and joyless as the graveyard at Fantana. The time is at hand when the whole world will be a flowering wilderness like our graveyard.

"Wherever I am buried in this continent of ours, I shall feel I am resting in the unwalled graveyard of our little village. Let me quote a passage from T. S. Eliot:

> " 'History has many cunning passages, contrived corridors
> And issues, deceives with whispering ambitions,
> Guides us by vanities. Think now
> She gives when our attention is distracted
> And what she gives, gives with such supple confusions
> That the giving famishes the craving. Gives too late
> What's not believed in, or if still believed,
> In memory only, reconsidered passion.' "

"Why are you telling me all this?" asked Traian. "You would do much better to rest."

"You are right," said the priest. "But I have something more to tell you. I quote from Keyserling: 'Life has no objective aim, unless it be death. Every real and true aim is always subjective.' The technocrats of Western civilization attempt to impose an objective aim on life. That is the best way of annihilating it. They have reduced life to a series of statistics. But 'Statistics in evitably leave out of account the case that is unique of its kind. The more humanity develops, the more decisive will be the particular uniqueness of each individual person and each individual case.' Contemporary society is moving in precisely the opposite direction. Everything is reduced to generalities. 'It is attempting to generalize and to seek or find all values in generalities that Western man has lost all sense of the value of the unique, of that which takes individual life as a starting point. Hence the great danger of collectivism, whether interpreted in the Russian or the American way.'

"And thus it is almost inevitable that this society should collapse, as you said yourself one evening in Fantana. Technological Civilization has grown to be incompatible with individual life. It stifles it. And mankind is dying like the white rabbits in your novel.

"We are all perishing in the poisoned atmosphere in which none but mechanical slaves, machines, and citizens can live and breathe; it is all just as you were going to describe it in your book.

"Thus men have sinned grievously against God. *'It is not sufficient to say that an injustice has been committed in the eyes of God. God is never offended by us except when we act against our own good.'* * At this moment we are pitting all our strength against our own good and therefore against God. It is the lowest stage of degeneration that any human society can attain. And therefore it will perish in the same way as so many other societies in historic and prehistoric times.

"People are trying to bring about its salvation by a logical order, whereas this very order will bring it to perdition. Here is what the English, poet W. H. Auden, says:

> " *'O foolishness of man to seek*
> *Salvation in an ordre logique!*
> *O cruel intellect that chills*
> *His natural warmth until it kills*
> *The roots of all togetherness!*
> *Love's vigour shrinks to less and less:*
> *On sterile acres governed by*
> *Wage's abstract prudent tie*
> *The hard self-conscious particles*
> *Collide, divide like numerals*
> *In knock-down drag-out laissez-faire,*
> *And build no order anywhere.'*

"Herein lies the crime of Western Technological Civilization. It kills the living man, sacrificing him to plans, theories, and abstractions. Here we have the modern variant of human sacrifice. The stake and the auto-da-fé have passed away, but

* Saint Thomas Aquinas.

in their place stand bureaucracy and statistics, the two present-day social myths whose flames consume the sacrifice of human flesh.

"Democracy, for example, as a form of social organization, is undoubtedly superior to totalitarianism, yet nevertheless it represents human life only in its social dimension. To consider democracy as an end in itself is to kill human life by reducing it to a single dimension. This is the very mistake that the Nazis and the Communists have made.

"Human life has no meaning unless it is conceived as a whole. We can only grasp its ultimate purpose if we bring into play the same senses that help us to understand religion and to interpret or to create art. In the search of the ultimate end of life reason plays only a secondary role. Mathematics, statistics, and logic are as ineffectual, as guides to the comprehension and organization of human life, as they are to the appreciation of Mozart or Beethoven.

"But our modern Western society persists in trying to arrive at an understanding of Beethoven and Raphael by means of mathematics and calculations. It is relentless in its efforts to improve men's lives by resorting constantly to statistics.

"These attempts are both ridiculous and tragic.

"The most that man could achieve under this system would be an acme of social perfection. But it would not help him in the least. Once his life has been reduced to its social and automatic element and subjected entirely to the laws of the machine, it will simply have ceased to exist. These laws can never under any circumstances give life its meaning, and if life is deprived of its meaning—its only meaning and one that is totally free, and above and beyond the bounds of logic—then life itself will finally become extinct.

"Contemporary society has long since discarded these truths, and now, with breathtaking speed, with all the energy of despair, is striking out along new trails.

"And that is why the waters of the Rhine and the Danube and the Volga are already flowing with the tears of slaves. These tears will flood the rivers of Europe and all the rivers of the world until the seas and oceans are overflowing with the bitter tears of men enslaved by science and the state, by capital and by bureaucracy.

"Then in the end God will take pity on man and save him, as He has done in the past time and time again. And meanwhile the handful of men who have remained human will float on the surface of the waters like Noah in his ark; they alone will not be dragged to the bottom by the chains of slavery. They will be saved, and because of them human life will survive on the earth, as it has survived before.

"But salvation will come only to men as individuals. It will not be granted according to category.

"There is no church, no nation, no state, and no continent which can save its subjects en masse or by category. Salvation will come to them as individuals, independently of their religion or race, of their social or political category. And that is why man must never be judged according to the category to which he belongs. The category is the most barbarous and diabolical aberration ever begotten by the human mind. And let us not forget that our Enemy himself is a being and not a category."

The priest paused, and Traian took advantage of it to ask apprehensively:

"Why are you telling me all this now, Father? Wouldn't you do better to rest?"

"That is what I shall do," said the priest. "I shall rest. But before I do, I wanted to tell you these things. You know and feel them, as I do. Everyone knows and feels them. Johann Moritz does. But it did me good to repeat them. I could not have rested if I had not said them to you."

"Your hand is cold, Father," said Traian.

"I know, Traian. It is because there is in me a strange state of restlessness that I cannot control. An unquiet stronger than the flesh."

"I don't understand, Father," said Traian. "What do you mean? Are you feeling ill?"

"No," said the priest, "But remember what Cardinal Newman wrote:

" *'I can no more; for now it comes again,*
That sense of ruin, which is worse than pain,
That masterful negation and collapse
Of all that makes me man: as though I bent
Over the dizzy brink
Of some sheer infinite descent
Or worse, as though
Down, down, for ever I was falling through
The solid framework of created things
And needs must sink and sink
Into the vast abyss. And, crueller still,
A fierce and restless fight begins to fill
The mansion of my soul.' "

The priest's lips contracted as if an agonizing pain had shot through his body. Traian bent over him. Suddenly the priest's face was illuminated by a smile of warmth and infinite love, as if a powerful searchlight had been turned on somewhere inside his skull. His lips murmured some barely audible words. Traian thought he could make out these lines of Cardinal Newman:

I went to sleep; and now I am refreshed.
A strange refreshment: for I feel in me
An inexpressive lightness, and a sense
Of freedom, as I were at length myself,
And ne'er had been before. How still it is!

Traian understood that this was the end and knelt down beside the bed. He began to sob.

Johann stood up and asked:

"Should I call the doctor?"

Traian did not answer. He was still clasping his father's hand between his own and weeping with a despair that he had never known before.

Johann understood. Taking off his cap, he knelt at Traian's side and made the sign of the cross.

A few seconds later he rose to his feet. Prisoners had poured in from neighboring tents. The space between the beds was jammed with people.

Johann edged his way through the crowd of prisoners, who had removed their caps and were all standing in silence. He came back a few moments later with a candle made out of wax scraped off the outside of chocolate boxes. He lit it and set it at Father Koruga's head, using an old empty can as a candlestick.

❧ ❧ ❧

THE camp PW medical officer, followed by two stretcher-bearers, came into the tent where Father Koruga had just died.

"What do you want?" asked Traian.

"To carry out the corpse. Corpses must not be left in the tents," said the doctor.

"Where are you going to take it?"

"Out of the camp," said the doctor. "We don't know where. We inform the authorities, and the Americans pick it up in a truck."

"I wish to know first where you intend to take the mortal remains of my father."

"There are many things we would all like to know, but, unfortunately, it isn't possible," replied the doctor harshly.

The two orderlies came up to the bed to lift the priest's body onto the stretcher. The doctor stopped them.

"First I must certify that he is dead," he said. "For all I know, he may still be alive."

He took the priest's hand and held it for a minute. Then he applied his ear to the old man's chest.

"Take him away," he told the orderlies.

"No," cried Traian.

"What's the use of setting yourself against us? We are ordinary prisoners just the same as you, and we must obey orders."

"I demand to know first where you are taking my father's body. That is the least I can ask since I am not allowed to be present at his funeral. I want to be sure he will receive Christian burial. It is my right, even though I am a prisoner. The moment my father died, he ceased to be a prisoner and is consequently entitled to be treated with the respect due the dead, regardless of what they may have been while alive."

"Who told you the dead were not respected?" asked the doctor suspiciously.

"That is not what I said. But my father is an Orthodox priest, and I want him to be buried according to the rites and ceremonies of the Church which he served in his lifetime."

"You can send in a written application to the American authorities tomorrow," said the doctor.

"Can you guarantee that tomorrow will not be too late?"

"I can't guarantee anything," said the doctor. "I'm a prisoner like yourself."

"Then I will not permit my father's body to be removed. Before I part with it, I must have an assurance that he will be buried in accordance with the ritual of the Orthodox Church."

"It's no earthly good objecting," said the doctor.

"But I am going to, all the same."

"We are obliged to remove the body. We have strict orders to the effect that no corpses should be allowed to remain within the camp."

"You can take him away by force, if you like. But you'll regret it."

The orderlies seized Traian by the arms and pushed him

violently aside. The priest's body was lowered onto the stretcher. Traian struggled in the grip of those who were keeping hold of him. As the stretcher passed close by him, all he could see was his father's high forehead, smooth and clear as the disk of the moon.

Behind the orderlies, bareheaded and with lowered eyes, walked Johann, still holding the candle in the old can that served as a candlestick.

"You will pay dearly for this sin," shouted Traian. "There are deeds that bring their own inevitable retribution. Do not forget, Doctor, that you refused me permission to accompany my father's body as far as the camp gates."

"It is not my doing. It is camp regulations."

"Control yourself," said the camp leader, coming up to Traian. "If they hear you shouting they'll put you in the padded cell."

"From now on, nothing can keep me quiet," said Traian. "No cell will ever stifle my cries. From now on I shall go on a hunger strike until I die in the midst of these twenty thousand people. I want to die by degrees, hour by hour, as a symbol of protest. My death shall be a cry of revolt that shall pierce the very ears and eyes and flesh of those who are imprisoned with me and those who are keeping me imprisoned. It will be heard in the four corners of the earth. No one will escape its wrath. Never, not even when I am in my grave."

❦ ❦ ❦

"DO YOU really want to die?" asked Johann. "Die of hunger and thirst?"

It was the fourth day of Traian's hunger strike. It was warm. Traian was lying on his back in the shadow of the tent. Walking exhausted him; speaking exhausted him. Standing and listening to people talking, looking at the sky, everything exhausted him. Life itself and his very existence were an intolerable strain.

The signal for the midday meal had just gone. Johann made a further attempt to persuade Traian.

"Shall I bring you your meal?" he asked.

He was holding Traian's mess tin in his hand.

"They'll only be glad if you die," he said. "But it is wrong to want to die."

"If you like you can eat my share," said Traian. "I don't want it."

Johann went away and came back with his mess tin full of soup. He put it down on the ground, sat down, took a spoon out of his pocket, and wiped it with his hand. Then he propped the mess tin between his knees. The soup was hot, and his nostrils dilated as he inhaled the steam.

Traian's mess tin lay empty beside him.

"Why didn't you take my share?" asked Traian. "What you get isn't enough. It isn't enough for anybody."

"I couldn't eat your share," said Johann. "God would punish me if I did. How can you expect me to eat your share while you go hungry? It would be wicked, and I couldn't do it."

When he had set the mess tin between his knees, Johann lifted his eyes to the leaden gray sky and remained thus for a few moments, with lips slightly parted, looking up at it. Then he made the sign of the cross.

Traian watched each movement. Johann dipped the spoon into the soup with the slow deliberation of a man performing a sacred ritual. When it was only half full, he raised it to his lips with a slow sweeping gesture, as though he were partaking of communion. Having swallowed the liquid, he paused for a moment, still keeping the spoon steady, as though it were full.

His black eyes gazed intently somewhere into the distance at some point that he alone could see and that lay beyond the bounds of heaven and earth.

Then once more he dipped the spoon into the soup, still

only half filling it, and once more lifted it to his lips with the same deliberate sweeping gesture that was so inviting that Traian had to swallow.

And again the spoon went down. He never filled it to the brim, never swallowed more or less than half a spoonful at a time. He completed the cycle with the same slow rhythm and profound gravity.

Johann ate with the solemnity of a priest celebrating High Mass, with a scrupulous and voluptuous rhythm. Eating was for him a sacred rite, the ritual of nourishment reinstated in all its primeval grandeur. Like every essential ritual, it precluded haste and was performed with concentration and solemnity. Not a drop was left on the lips or strayed to the ground or remained in the spoon.

These gestures, verging on the sacred, with which Johann took his food paralyzed all skepticism and commanded silence. There was nothing theatrical about them, nothing superfluous.

At this hour of his meal, Johann became integrated into the mighty rhythm of nature. He took nourishment as the trees draw their sap from the depths of the earth. His whole being became absorbed in the ritual he was performing, and, at that moment unaware of anything going on around, he recaptured the fullness of his true individuality, returning to nature with the essence of his being and becoming one with her.

When he had finished eating and had caught the last drop of soup in his spoon, he remained for a minute absorbed in the spectacle unfolding before his eyes, which he alone could see. Then joining the tips of three fingers of his right hand, he made the sign of the cross yet again.

Turning toward Traian as if he had come out of a dream, he said:

"It is a great sin to eat another man's food."

Then he stood up and went to wash out his mess tin.

Traian was gazing into space. He did not see anything. Before his eyes was the image of Johann performing the divine service of nourishment, the solemn act that he himself had now renounced.

☙ ☙ ☙

"I REFUSE any form of medical assistance," said Traian.

It was the evening of his fourth day of fasting. The Camp Commandant, Lieutenant Jacobson, had been informed that a group of American journalists who were touring the prison camps of Germany had recently arrived in Stuttgart. He had instructed Burgomaster Schmidt and the chief medical officer to remove Koruga temporarily from the camp. His case was not to come to the notice of the press. It was far too scandalous. Traian Koruga was not a Nazi. His father, who had just died, had been a priest and had had both legs amputated. He had a Jewish wife. All this would be a scoop for a reporter. Jacobson had no wish for that kind of publicity. If a press campaign were launched he would be recalled to America forthwith, just when he was on the point of completing an important collection of German porcelain. He had bought most of it at the cost of a few packs of cigarettes. Some of the packing cases were in a cellar in the British Zone, ready waiting to be shipped to the U.S.A. If he could manage to buy up the whole collection, which was scattered abroad throughout various German towns and villages and cellars, he would be able to live comfortably on the proceeds of their sale for the rest of his life. But for this it was imperative to stay there until he had completed the collection.

If it had not been for the journalists and the threat of a scandal, the Koruga case would have been passed over in silence. He would not even have mentioned it in his report. In the camp prisoners died of hunger every day, and, when so many died because they had not enough to eat, it made no particular difference that one should die because he did not want to eat.

But under the present circumstances, an open scandal would have spoiled all Jacobson's plans. He was out to avoid that at all costs. Much was at stake.

Burgomaster Schmidt, who had been a colonel in the S.S. and was now chief of the Weimar police, promised Lieutenant Jacobson that he would use his discretion in dealing with the matter within the shortest possible time.

"Every doctor is in duty bound to assist a patient, with or without that patient's consent," said the Burgomaster to Traian. "You are running a high temperature, and you will be removed to the camp infirmary."

It was ten o'clock in the evening. Johann was sitting on the edge of Traian's bed. Whenever he heard the Burgomaster's voice he started. It seemed to him that his voice was the voice of Jurgu Jordan. They were almost identical.

"I refuse to move from here," said Traian. "You want to get me out of this tent, not because I am ill but because you are terrified of a scandal. But you can't hush it up. I suppose I am dying too quickly. That's the real trouble, isn't it? The twenty thousand corpses you keep imprisoned in this camp don't worry you in the least. All the others are dying slowly. There is nothing sensational about that, and gradual death provokes no scandal. Why don't you send them to a hospital?"

"My duty as a doctor is to send you to the infirmary," said Professor Dorf, the PW medical officer. "Your condition is extremely serious, Mr. Koruga. We cannot allow you to spend another night in this tent."

Two orderlies lifted Traian and put him down on the stretcher as if they were handling luggage. Johann clenched his fists and gnashed his teeth. He wanted to defend Traian, but the fight was lost before it began.

"It is the greatest of crimes to do a just thing for an unjust reason," said Traian.

The doctor ignored the remark.

"Go ahead," ordered the doctor.

The orderlies carried the stretcher out of the tent. The prisoners made way for them without a word. They were all awake and silent.

It was the silence that accompanies death. They were aware that something unusually serious was happening, but none of them could have said what it was.

It was a moonlit night. Johann walked behind the stretcher, his eyes fixed on the ground, as if he were following a funeral procession. He was carrying Traian's clothes, shoes, glasses, and pipe. Tears had come into his eyes. Then suddenly he realized that the man on the stretcher, his friend, was still alive.

When they reached the infirmary doors, Johann was turned away.

"You are not allowed to come any further," said the Burgomaster. "Those are the orders. No one is permitted to speak to Traian Koruga or to see him. I'll take his clothes and shoes to him myself."

That night Johann walked up and down alone outside the barbed-wire fence round the infirmary. He could not bring himself to desert Traian.

🦋 🦋 🦋

TRAIAN was confined to one of the infirmary wards. There were six beds in it, and all of them were empty. The ward had been cleared specially for him. Two young orderlies had been assigned to watch over him.

Traian lay on the bed and turned his face toward the wall. His lips were as dry as ash. Dreams flashed through his mind, like reels of colored film.

Though his eyes were shut he found himself blinded from within by some sort of powerful neon light. It was hot and burned into his eyelids. All his thoughts were colored and illuminated by it. Even his body seemed made of light and was as fiery and unsubstantial as his dreams. He had the feeling of floating in space.

"Now I can understand why ascetics and mystics fast," he said to himself. "By the process of starvation, one can so easily shed the burden of the earth. God is very close. It is as though one's forehead were touching the skies."

But this state of ecstasy did not last long. Suddenly he became aware of the presence of food. One of the orderlies had placed a tray of food on the chair beside his bed. Traian had his back toward it, but, even without looking, he could tell exactly what was on it.

First of all he detected the smell of potatoes fried in butter. Then he was conscious of the smell of coffee. He was sure of the presence of the food on the tray as if he had seen and tasted it. His sense of smell had been sharpened. In the past he would never have been able to distinguish one smell from another with such precision.

On the tray there was also a jug of hot milk. The steaming milk had the same intensity of smell as the coffee. The smell of meat was equally insistent. It struck his senses like an excessively garish color in a painting. The smell of the butter and the roast meat merely enhanced the irritating effect of the other dishes. It permeated the bedclothes, his shirt, and his hair and the walls around him.

He felt the smell of slightly burned meat, of butter, milk, and coffee, sticking to him like an ointment. Every time he breathed it penetrated deeper into his lungs and even seeped down into his stomach. This gave him the sensation of eating and therefore breaking the intended austerity of his fast. He tried to eliminate the smell of food from the air he breathed, but it was impossible. With every passing moment the smell grew more insistent.

Traian began to analyze it consciously, as if he were dividing a ray of light into the colors of the spectrum.

"It is as good a way as any other of testing the accuracy of my sense of smell," he said, abandoning himself to the excitement of this experiment which allowed him the illusion of being fully in control of himself and of having succeeded in reducing the food to a mere subject for scientific analysis.

One of the first discoveries he made was that the meat was neither beef nor pork. In spite of the fact that it was canned meat and that therefore many ingredients had been added in its preparation, he was able to establish definitely that it was poultry, probably turkey. He longed to turn round and check his deductions, but restrained himself and kept his face to the wall. The milk was slightly burned. It was powdered and probably highly concentrated, which was why it must have boiled over too quickly. There was also some canned fruit on the tray. It was the faintest smell of all. His nostrils could hardly detect it; it was as insipid as an almost neutral color.

But the fact that he had detected the presence of stewed fruit gave him a feeling of intense intellectual satisfaction, as if he had broken a record or made some discovery in a laboratory. The only question he could not answer was whether or not there was bread on the tray. If there was, then it must have been white bread made out of American flour, refined down almost to pure starch, and it must have been stale.

"I should eat right away if I were you," said the orderly, coming over to the bed. "Once it gets cold, it won't taste of anything."

Traian did not answer. He wanted to proceed with his analysis of the contents of the tray, but he now found it impossible. He had been interrupted and could not regain the necessary calm and concentration. All the smells had now merged into one, just as all the colors of the rainbow may merge into white. The orderly's words had broken into the scale of smells as a stone thrown into a pond will shatter the harmony of the succession of the waves.

Traian felt disappointed and saddened because he could no longer analyze and appreciate the smells from the tray. Then he fell asleep. The next morning the tray was still there. Still he did not look at it. The smell was now hardly perceptible, as if the food were no longer alive, as if it had died or frozen during the night.

He was tired. He did not turn round and did not even open his eyes. Several times he moistened his lips with saliva, but found to his disappointment that his lips tasted bitter and felt rough.

The orderly brought another tray of food and put it down in place of the first one. This time there were eggs fried in butter. They had a garish and striking smell, like the colors of an advertisement. Beside the eggs were marmalade, milk, coffee, and butter. All these smells were now like so many piercing arrows to his flesh. He shut his eyes tightly in pain. "Lord, help me to reach the end more quickly," he whispered pleadingly. "It is so hard to resist temptation when one has a human body."

He comforted himself with the thought that in two or three days his body would give way.

"In two or three days' time, I'll be dead," he said to himself, and fell asleep again.

❧ ❧ ❧

TRAIAN sat upright in bed, propped up by the pillows, and looked out of the window. It was midday. Outside, the prisoners were paraded in three ranks. They were naked. The entire parade ground was full of naked men.

Right under the window of the infirmary there was a jeep surrounded by a group of soldiers armed with rubber truncheons. They were all chewing gum. One by one, the prisoners approached the soldiers unsurely and awkwardly. Naked men always walked unsurely. Traian knew the feeling. He, too, had walked like that when he had had no clothes on.

"Another search on?" he asked. "I wonder what they are hoping to find this time."

These searches took place several times a month.

An old man had just appeared before the soldiers.

"There's Paladius, Metropolitan of Warsaw," said Traian.

The Metropolitan was tall, though he walked with a slight stoop. He was so thin that his ribs could be counted from a distance. A skeleton covered in skin. He had a white beard. It was the only white thing on the whole square. Its soft heraldic white was reflected in the eyes of those who beheld it. As he approached, the soldiers started laughing.

But the Metropolitan appeared to be unaware of their presence. He was looking over their peaked caps into the sky. On that day the sky was as blue as the cupola of a Byzantine church.

The soldiers examined the Metropolitan's fingers.

"Spread them out," ordered the interpreter.

The old man spread out his fingers. The soldiers searched carefully. The prisoner wore no rings.

"Arms up," ordered the interpreter again.

The old man lifted his arms, first to the level of his chest, as though he were giving benediction, then above his head. He glanced neither at the interpreter nor at the soldiers, but they were scrutinizing him carefully, searching his armpits for hidden jewelry. Then they examined the hair on the nape of his neck. The Metropolitan had long white hair that might well have concealed rings. The soldiers parted his hair strand by strand, first with the tips of their truncheons and then with their fingers. They inspected the white hair on the crown of his head and on his neck. Then they felt his beard to see if there were no rings there.

"Turn round," said the interpreter.

The old man turned his back on the soldiers.

"Bend down."

He bent down as though he were bowing before the icons. But this was evidently not enough.

"Legs apart."

The Metropolitan opened his legs wide. They were white and slender. The interpreter and the soldier bent down to make sure the Metropolitan had not hidden rings or other gold objects between his legs. But they found nothing. One of the soldiers said something to the others. The old man was still bending forward, with his legs apart and his back to them.

"Dismissed," said the interpreter.

The soldiers searched the next man. The Metropolitan went back to his place in the ranks with the same hesitant gait. His hair and beard fluttered in the breeze like the silken folds of a white flag. To Traian it seemed that, unlike the rest, he was not naked.

Traian's eyes followed him till he had regained his place in the ranks of naked men. Though he was in the midst of all the rest, he did not form part of the general throng. Something about his head caught and held Traian's eye. It was perhaps the whiteness of his hair or his beard that attracted the attention, or maybe it was the way he carried his head. Something that compelled the reverence with which one contemplates an icon.

"Now I know what I am seeing," said Traian, starting. The orderlies turned and stared at him, but he, oblivious, went on gazing out of the window.

"The Metropolitan's head is encircled with light. It is a halo. There is a blinding light emanating from behind his forehead, more powerful than arc lamp or neon, and it sends out rays of golden light around his head."

After he had regained his place in the ranks, the old man looked up toward the infirmary windows. The rays of light around his head shone even more brightly.

"The halo was not simply invented by the icon painters," said Traian. His eyes scanned the other prisoners. A few others had halos, too. He did not know them all. But the Rector of the

Vienna Academy had one, and so had a young journalist from
Berlin. A Greek minister, the Romanian Ambassador in Berlin,
and several others all had halos. Rays of light flashed from their
foreheads as though from blazing flames or arc-lamp reflectors.
But they were more beautiful than either fire or electricity.
These rays emanating from their brows might have illuminated
the whole world, and night would have been banished from the
earth.

🐾 🐾 🐾

"WHY won't you eat?" asked Lieutenant Jacobson, the Camp
Commandant.

He had come to visit Traian in his ward. He had sent the
Burgomaster and the doctor out of the room in order to be left
alone with him.

"What is it you want?" asked the Lieutenant. "What's the
point of all this buffoonery in camp?"

"I won't eat because I don't feel hungry," said Traian. "I've
suddenly lost my appetite. And I feel sick, terribly sick. My
stomach is turning. Don't you ever feel sick, Lieutenant?"

Jacobson was silent. He wished he had not decided to stay
alone with Traian. The prisoner seemed to have gone mad. His
eyes were burning. "He might easily jump at my throat and
strangle me," thought the officer. He glanced toward the door
and then smiled:

"Relax, Mr. Koruga," he said. "You're overexcited, and it is
quite understandable. This is the sixth day that you haven't
taken food or drink."

"Don't go away, Lieutenant. I am not mad," said Traian.
"Don't be afraid. That was a stupid question of mine about feeling sick. Of course you wouldn't be feeling sick. If you start right
away by shutting your eyes and holding your nose, there is no

further danger. People get used to feeling sick. It's merely a question of will power. I have no will power and that is why I couldn't help feeling sick. There are workmen who eat their breakfast, lunch, and dinner in manholes over sewers or in latrines. They don't feel sick because they are used to it. I've seen them with my own eyes eating salami and bread and butter a couple of paces from the latrine holes. They were licking their lips, laughing and joking. Even with the keenest sense of smell you can get used to it.

"The Germans used to burn the corpses of prisoners from the concentration camps and, as soon as they had shut the doors of the cremating ovens behind them, go off gaily and have lunch without the slightest feeling of repulsion. There are men here who own mattresses stuffed with the hair of women killed in concentration camps, and on these same mattresses they have made love to their mistresses, and begotten children with their wives—on these mattresses stuffed with the hair of murdered and burned women. They were not squeamish. They did not feel sick. They were perfectly happy.

"I was in the same prison as a woman in whose bedroom and drawing room there had stood lamp shades made of human skin. They gave the light a sensuous and yellowish quality. By the light filtering through these lamp shades of human skin, she made love, ate, danced, drank, abandoned herself to her lover's embraces. She was happy. Anyone can get accustomed to nausea. It is merely a question of habit and will power.

"The Russians used to rape eighty-year-old women, ever so many of them. They queued up and took turns to rape them, ten Russians to one woman. And after that, instead of being sick they simply drank vodka.

"You wouldn't do that, I'm sure. You don't rape women. You give them chocolate and use contraceptives when you make love to them. You don't do what the Germans do, either. Every people has its own customs. But don't get worried. You'll never feel sick, whatever you do. You are in no danger, I'm sure of that. I say danger because, believe me, nausea is a great danger. I know what I have had to suffer from it.

"My intestines turn inside out like a glove and I taste the ends of them in my mouth. All the bile turns back, and my stomach heaves with sick disgust. And I am swept with pity for mankind, with an immense pity. How do you expect me to eat under those circumstances? How do you expect me to feel hungry? Do you see now that I shall never again be able to eat?"

Lieutenant Jacobson had edged toward the door. He wished he had not come. Neither the Burgomaster nor the doctor had warned him that Traian was mad. According to them, the patient was wholly sane. The facts, however, proved that they were wrong.

"You are quite right, Mr. Koruga," said the Lieutenant. "In the circumstances you couldn't possibly be expected to feel hungry."

"Don't go," said Traian. "It is very hard for me to sit up. Please look out of the window and tell me if the search is over."

"Not yet," answered Lieutenant Jacobson.

Traian was amazed. How could anyone watch the search that was going on outside without losing his appetite? Jacobson was going straight off to lunch. It was twelve o'clock.

"You say it isn't over yet?" he said. "Of course, it couldn't be over so soon. It has scarcely begun. First you searched for gold in suitcases, houses, clothes, pockets, and shoes, in pants and in the linings of suits. Now you are looking into mouths and armpits and up men's bottoms, everywhere. They are stripped naked already: but it's not good enough. Tomorrow you will start ripping off strips of skin to look for gold, and tear the muscles away from the bones to look for gold. And next you will pound the bones to see whether perchance there be not some gold coins hidden inside. You will squeeze men's brains and rummage among their intestines. You will carve them up into slices to find gold. Coins of gold, rings of gold, golden wedding rings; gold, gold, gold. Today we have hardly even begun. We have reached the skin. But the skin will be stripped off. The search must go on. . . ."

Lieutenant Jacobson was no longer in the room. Traian turned his face to the wall.

卐 卐 卐

PETITION No. 6. *Subject: Economic (Prisoners,*
Valuables Found on)

In the course of search carried out on the persons of prisoners, rings, bracelets, watches, fountain pens, coins, and all other objects of value were confiscated. But in spite of the care taken to search the bare skin, the method of search is still far from efficient.

Today I had the occasion to observe that certain prisoners wore a crown round their heads, similar to those worn by saints painted on icons. It is a matter of common knowledge that saints have crowns of gold. Those of the prisoners could not have been of gold or of any other precious metal. If they had been, obviously these crowns, or halos, as they are sometimes called, would already have been confiscated. Nevertheless, their value is by no means inconsiderable.

I am no scientist, but I understand that these crowns are extremely valuable. They are caused directly by certain radiations emanating from the spirit of the prisoners concerned.

It is interesting to note that such phenomena do not occur in the Technological Civilization of the West. It would appear that they are a property peculiar to primitive civilizations. But that is beside the point. Inasmuch as these crowns are valuable, they must not be allowed to remain in the possession of the prisoners. Standing orders expressly forbid any prisoner to retain any object of value in his possession.

I seem to remember that history provides a precedent

for the confiscation of such crowns (halos). Even barbarian conquerors, such as Genghis Khan, appreciated the true value of similar ornaments discovered on certain prisoners, and confiscated them. In those days, however, mechanized transport was not so highly developed as it is today. Genghis Khan, so as to avoid spoiling the shape and luminosity of those halos which he wished to have at his court, gave orders that the heads of the prisoners should be confiscated at the same time. These haloed heads of prisoners from China and Arabia were threaded on a string, tied to saddles, and taken to Mongolia. But on the way, probably because of atmospheric conditions and sudden changes of temperature, the halos vanished and the heads had to be thrown away. They had even begun to rot.

In order to avoid similar wastage, it would be better not to cut off the heads, as Genghis Khan did. Instead, prisoners in possession of these precious crowns could be kept at a constant temperature in air-conditioned tanks and dispatched to your country. Our civilization has the unrivaled advantage of having at its disposal all the necessary technical resources, and we are therefore enabled to obviate the wastage incurred by the barbarian conquerors. The chronicler records that half a million of these precious halos were thus lost.

Yours with undying admiration. Keep smiling.

THE WITNESS

🙖 🙖 🙖

"IN FIVE minutes' time you will be transferred to the hospital," said the Burgomaster.

He was pacing up and down the ward, with his hands behind his back.

"There you will be forcibly fed. I am very sorry about it. We have tried everything in our power, and so has Lieutenant Jacobson. But you have refused to co-operate. We want your good, and all you do is to bite the hand that feeds you."

[341]

Traian was lying on his bed with his face toward the wall.

"Your behavior shows a complete lack of *esprit de corps*," said the infuriated Burgomaster. "You are causing the doctors, Lieutenant Jacobson, and myself to waste our time on your personal affairs. By making us waste our time like this you are acting against the interests of your fellow prisoners. That cannot be tolerated. You are one, and they are twenty thousand. Your own personal problems must be laid aside. Every one of us has a wife and family. What would happen if we all took it into our heads to act like you? But you never even consider the community. You are just plain selfish. I have followed the advice of Lieutenant Jacobson, who is a romantic and believes in democracy like all Americans, and have wasted at least five hours in the course of the last few days on one single camp inmate, thus neglecting the twenty thousand others. I was mad even to have thought of it."

"You don't look after anyone in camp," said Traian. "All you look after is an administrative machine, which is something impersonal. The men in camp must not be confused with this machine, which means card indexes, typewriters, and figures. That is your work. No, sir. You have never been concerned in the slightest with the twenty thousand inmates of this camp. These twenty thousand prisoners are composed of flesh and blood and soul. They are made up of suffering and faith, longing and hunger, hope and despair, and dreams.

"You, on the other hand, are concerned neither with their flesh and blood, which are particular and individual, nor with their hopes and disappointments which are even more individual. Your domain is with files and figures.There is not one single prisoner whom you know personally. How dare you claim to be looking after twenty thousand when you aren't even looking after one? It is ridiculous. You concern yourselves with ideas and abstractions, you and Jacobson, and not with people. Even I, here and now, am anything to you rather than a human being. To you I am nothing but a fraction of twenty thousand.

That is why you are annoyed about wasting your time. You've never yet thought of me as an individual, and you never will. You have probably never even looked upon your wife as a person. She is your wife all right, or the mother of your children, or your housekeeper, but never a human personality. And yet outside the entirety of her essential personality, she has no real existence. And you don't know your own self any better than your wife or your mother.

"You have never really known a single being on this earth. If you had, you would never feel that you were wasting time by looking after any given individual, for all human beings are more precious than time. You have seen in men nothing but a single dimension; but men looked at thus are no longer human beings, any more than a one-dimensional cube is still a cube."

The orderly came in to announce that the ambulance was waiting in the yard.

"I should like to say good-by to my friend, Johann Moritz," said Traian.

"You are not allowed to communicate with the other prisoners."

Traian turned his back on the Burgomaster. The orderlies wrapped him in a blanket and carried him like a parcel down to the ambulance.

The blind was drawn down over the ambulance window, but Traian knew Johann would be at the gate to watch the ambulance drive away. Traian smiled at him mentally and said: "Good-by."

❦ ❦ ❦

"TWO Americans have brought in a mad prisoner from the camp."

The chief medical officer of the Karlsruhe prison hospital got out of bed, switched on the light, and looked at his watch.

It was one o'clock in the morning. The orderly who had brought him the news helped him to dress. The doctor left the room in a bad temper.

Prisoners were always brought to the hospital in batches. In the camp patients had to wait until there were one hundred of them before they were sent to the hospital. Even serious cases were often held for three or four weeks until the required number was made up and the whole batch could be delivered together. In the course of a whole year there had only been two exceptions. This was the third.

"What sort of madman might this be that they should send him to us alone and at this unearthly hour of the night?" asked the doctor, going into the office.

"I should think it's pretty serious," said the orderly. "I haven't seen him yet. He was asleep in the ambulance. But if two Americans brought him here at such an hour it must be pretty serious."

It was cold outside. The doctor had just left a warm bed. He was still shivering as he signed the prisoner's admission card.

The two Americans climbed back into the ambulance and drove away. The doctor went back to bed, giving up the idea of examining the prisoner right away. It was far too cold. But he gave instructions that he should be locked up immediately in the appropriate ward.

Traian did not know he had arrived at his destination. He did not know that the ambulance had had a puncture on the road and that it had delayed them till midnight. He was not even aware of the time. He had opened his eyes just as they had been carrying him through the hospital yard on a stretcher; and he had beheld a blue sky studded with stars. "The Milky Way," he said, smiling at the great white road up there in the sky. Then he remembered the words of the Burgomaster: "We are transferring you to a hospital where you will be forcibly fed." Traian made up his mind to refuse all medical assistance. "As long as I am conscious I intend to go on refusing all food and drink."

The orderlies who had heard him say "The Milky Way" started chuckling. They put the stretcher down. One of them bent over him and said ironically:

"Here we are—here's the Milky Way."

Traian did not appreciate the joke. He shut his eyes and felt himself being lifted in someone's arms and put down on a bed.

🐾 🐾 🐾

TRAIAN glanced all round the room in which he was lying. The lamp on the ceiling was protected with wire netting. The window had heavy iron bars. There were four beds in the ward. Two patients were sitting talking to each other. They wore German army uniforms. When Traian had been brought in, they had not even turned round and had gone on talking. They were both young. The third patient lay in bed with the blanket drawn over his head. Nothing was visible save his heavy shoes, which stuck out at the other end of the blanket. Traian wondered why the patient slept with his shoes on.

By the door sat a guard in a white hospital uniform. He had a square, massive head like Burgomaster Schmidt's, a wooden head whose facial muscles seemed paralyzed or dead. His eyes, too, were lifeless and glassy. It was not the head of a dead man, but that of a man who had never been alive.

The guard came toward him.

"And what story are you going to tell us?" he asked, pinching Traian under the chin as if he were scolding a child. Traian turned away without answering.

"So you aren't going to tell us a story," said the guard. "One of the silent ones, eh?" He patted him on the cheek.

"Have it your own way!" he said.

Then he went back to his chair by the door.

※ ※ ※

"THEY have shut me up in a madhouse because I went on a hunger strike." Traian bit his lips. All the weariness had gone out of him, and he was left with a strong will to fight.

"I'm in a madhouse," he said to himself. "That was a brain wave! I never came across it before, not even in novels describing tortures in Russian prisons. All the doctors and professors among the prisoners have certified me a madman. They want to prove that my hunger strike is an act of madness. But in real life certain things do not work out as simply and as quickly as all that. I'm not done for just yet."

Traian clenched his fists.

"The first step is to prove to them that I am in my right mind," he said to himself. He went up to the guard. He was unsteady on his feet and had to support himself against the wall.

"So you've come across with your little story, have you?" asked the guard. "I knew you'd have one, all right." He was grinning.

"Everyone who comes here has a little story. But I've no time to listen to you now, sonny. You just wait and tell me tomorrow, or the day after, or next month or next year maybe. You'll tell me your story lots of times. There's no hurry."

The guard had a newspaper in his hand and wanted to go on reading it.

"That's your bed over there in the far corner. Go along now and lie down quietly. Don't get into another bed, understand?"

"I should like to ask you something," said Traian.

"I know you want to ask me something," answered the guard in a bored voice. "But I've no time for you now. Go and sit down on your bed. You must be a good boy here, otherwise you'll get a hiding with the whip."

He took a riding whip out of the table drawer, showed it to him, and put it away again.

Traian realized that words would be useless. Whatever he might say would receive no more attention than the ravings of a madman. He went back to his bed.

⊌ ⊌ ⊌

"IT WAS not enough to put me in prison. Now they've put me in a prison madhouse." Traian shut his eyes.

He would have liked to work out a plan of campaign for the following day, but he wasn't equal to it. He fell asleep still clenching his fists.

"Get up."

Traian started. He had only just dozed off. One of the orderlies who had carried him in on the stretcher—the one who had made the joke about the Milky Way—was now standing beside his bed. Traian recognized his voice.

"Give me everything you've got in your pockets."

Traian stood up. He put his hand in his pocket. It was shaking. He drew out his handkerchief and handed it to the orderly. From another pocket he brought out his pipe and handed that over, too. In his breast pocket he had a little icon —the icon of Saint Anthony. He looked at it and finally handed that to the orderly as well.

"Have you nothing more in your pockets?"

"No," answered Traian. "That's all I have."

"Raise your arms," commanded the orderly.

Traian raised his arms, but only to the level of his chest. There was a mist in front of his eyes, and he could not lift his arms any higher.

"Raise your arms," repeated the orderly.

"I can't," answered Traian. "I am ill. I feel giddy."

The orderly caught hold of his hands and raised them over his head. Traian strained under the weight of his own arms, which felt as heavy as stones. Never before had his arms seemed so leaden. They rose up as stiffly as drainpipes above his head.

The orderly searched his pockets. Traian was conscious of unfamiliar hands wandering about, not in his pockets, but beneath his skin and in among the flesh itself.

"Drop your arms."

The orderly pushed his hands down to his sides.

"Take out your shoelaces."

"Leave him alone," said the guard of Traian's room. "Look at him; he's gone as yellow as wax."

Traian was made to lie down on the bed. His shoelaces were removed. Then they pulled down his trousers, unlaced the army drawers he was wearing, and took away the laces. Then they took his glasses off his nose.

"Don't take away my glasses," pleaded Traian. He was very shortsighted.

"I suppose you want to cut open your veins with them?"

"I can't see anything without my glasses."

"There is nothing for you to see here."

The orderly made up a parcel out of Traian's glasses, handkerchief, pipe, and icon. It was all that was left of his earthly possessions. Then he picked up the parcel and walked away.

❧ ❧ ❧

"GET up and eat."

It was Traian's first morning in the lunatic asylum. He looked at the bowl of soup that the guard was holding out to him.

"I am not going to eat."

"If you think you can do as you please here, you're mistaken," said the guard. He set the bowl down on the floor beside him and crossed over to the next bed.

"I've been on a hunger strike for the last six days," said Traian.

"Everybody here is on a hunger strike, my poppet. You're not the only one."

The guard had reached the bed of the patient sleeping with the bedclothes over his head and his hobnailed shoes sticking out beneath the blanket. The guard pulled back the bedclothes. Underneath there lay an old man with a white beard. He peered up timidly at the guard and then hid his face in his pillow.

"What do you want?" he asked, and again buried his head under the pillow.

"Up you get, Grandpa," ordered the guard. "Time for you to be fed."

Two young lunatics came up to the old man's bed and stood shoulder to shoulder, pressing close to each other as though afraid of being separated. The guard called them "the Bulldogs."

"Jump on him, Bulldogs," cried the guard as if he were encouraging dogs.

One of the Bulldogs caught the old man under the armpits from behind. The other raised his head and made him sit up.

"Go easy, don't break his bones," said the guard laughing.

The old man was weeping. He had tucked in his chin and kept his eyes on the ground.

"Open your mouth, Grandpa," said the guard. "Nanny's come to give you the bottle."

The old man pressed his chin into his chest and clenched his jaws with all his strength.

"Open up his snout for him, but take it easy."

The Bulldogs knelt on the bed, thrust their fingers in the old man's mouth, and pulled his jaws apart. With one hand the guard caught hold of his nose, stopping up his nostrils, and with the other he poured soup into his mouth.

The patient spat out the soup all over the Bulldogs' chests. They burst out laughing. The guard poured the second spoonful into the old man's mouth. This time he did not succeed in spitting it out. The food had stuck in his throat, and he was forced to swallow it to avoid choking. He could not breathe through the nose because the guard's hand was squeezing his nostrils.

"I'm choking," he said.

The procedure was repeated indefinitely. From time to time the old man screamed out that he was suffocating and started struggling in the grip of the Bulldogs. But they kept hold as hard as they could.

"You're doing all right, you see, Grandpa, aren't you?" said the guard.

The old man's face had turned yellow and beads of perspiration stood out on his forehead.

Traian covered up his eyes to shut out the sight.

"Scared, eh?" asked the guard. "It'll be your turn in a minute."

"Are we going to feed him, too?" demanded the Bulldogs in chorus.

"Sure, unless he behaves himself like a good boy."

The Bulldogs took no further notice of the old man: their eyes had fastened on Traian's neck and jaws. Traian bent down, picked up the bowl of soup, and started swallowing very quickly without chewing. When he finished he said:

"You're right—anyone who has been locked up in a lunatic asylum and still refuses to eat must really be mad. Lunatics can't go on a hunger strike, since they are not responsible for their actions. But I am not mad; that is why I decided to eat. Which doesn't mean to say that I've given up the struggle."

❦ ❦ ❦

"SOMEHOW, I've just got to prove to the doctors that I am sane," Traian said to himself. He had a headache. The food he had just gulped down lay like a lump of lead on his stomach. But he forced himself to stand upright. He tried to smile. Then he went up to the guard.

"I should like to speak to the doctor in charge of this section," he said.

"You'll have to wait for his visit," said the guard. "You'll be able to speak to him when he comes round."

"Couldn't I see him before that?"

"Patients in this ward are not allowed to call the doctor."

"Of course," said Traian. "The doctor isn't going to come just because some lunatic wants him, but I am not a lunatic."

"If you're not mad, then what do you think they sent you here for?"

"To make me break my hunger strike," said Traian. "I've told you that already. But now I've had something to eat. There are therefore no further grounds for treating me as a madman. If I had refused to eat, my behavior might have been interpreted as an act of madness instead of as a gesture of protest. But now there is no excuse for that."

Traian suddenly realized that, all the while he was speaking, the orderly had been reading the paper. He had not paid the slightest attention to what he was saying.

"You still think I'm mad, even now that I have had something to eat, don't you?" His voice shook.

"Go back to bed and let me read my paper," ordered the guard.

"But I'm telling you, man, I'm not mad."

"All right, all right," said the guard. "Now go to bed and be quiet. You must be a good boy here. Naughty boys get the whip."

⁂ ⁂ ⁂

THAT morning the doctor did not come on his rounds. Toward midday one of the Bulldogs left the room, escorted by a guard. Half an hour later he was brought back on a stretcher and set down in the middle of the room. His nostrils, which were stuffed with cotton wool, were quivering. His forehead was pallid. Greenish foam, like that of a mad dog, was trickling out of the corners of his mouth. His lips were trembling.

"What's happened to him?" asked Traian.

The other Bulldog sniggered at the sight of his friend's stiffened body, which was twitching convulsively. The leg and arm muscles twitched up and down independently, as though disconnected from the rest of the body. His skin had taken on a different hue. It was no longer the skin of a living person. His spinal column was still, with the rigidity of dead things. Even the convulsions that shook him were not those of a living being; they were automatic, like the jerks of a mechanical doll. The only living thing about him was the whitish-green foam dribbling out of his mouth, over his chest, and onto the canvas of the stretcher.

"What's happened to the Bulldog?" Traian again asked.

"Nothing," answered the guard. "Only injections."

"What kind of injection? Why is he struggling like that?"

"Don't be inquisitive, my pet," said the guard. "You'll try them, too. Tomorrow, probably."

"Tomorrow?"

Traian stared at the stiffened body writhing on the stretcher.

"What's so funny about that?" said the guard. "You don't believe me? Everybody here has to have injections." He put fresh cotton wool in the Bulldog's nose and pinched his cheek. The Bulldog did not react.

"You could cut slices out of him with a knife and he wouldn't feel it, not while the fit is on. You all need injections. They stimulate the nerves. Just look what fine exercises they can be made to do."

Traian sat down on the bed and buried his head in his hands. The door opened. He gave a start, but it was not the doctor. It was an orderly, who had come to fetch the other Bulldog. He took him by the arm and led him out of the room.

Shortly afterward he, too, was brought back on a stretcher and set down beside his friend. He, too, had cotton-wool plugs in his nose and greenish foam dribbling out of his mouth like the spittle of a mad dog. His limbs jerked about on the stretcher.

Then they came for the old man, and he in turn was brought back on a stretcher.

Traian looked at the three bodies, which, though unrelated to each other, were jerking in rhythm.

"What kind of injection?"

"Cardiazol," said the guard. "Shocks for the nervous system. It shakes up your brain and clears out the cobwebs."

The guard laughed.

Traian turned his eyes back to the three human bodies. Their movements were mechanical, like the jerks of robots. Their nostrils inflated and quivered at the same intervals, and with the same rhythm and intensity. Their chests rose and fell like piston rods.

All that was left of life in the three bodies was the automatic jerking of the muscles. Will, instinct, intelligence—all alike were dead. Nothing remained but the mechanical reflex, and this had been intensified until it had developed into a spasm, an automatic spasm.

What he was watching now had ceased to be just three human beings with lives reduced to bare reflexes, leaving them no better than robots—instead, he found himself watching all the peoples of the earth. It was a foolish, fantastic illusion, but it obsessed him. It seemed to him that Burgomaster Schmidt was leading the whole camp at Kornwestheim in the same diabolical dance rhythm as the three men at his feet. And there was not only the Burgomaster. Jacobson and Major Brown and Samuel Abramovici and all the others seemed to be jerking to the same mechanical jazz rhythm, the shock rhythm of cardiazol injections. A whole civilization was threshing about in wild spasms. Traian covered his eyes and cried: "I won't, I won't."

💥 💥 💥

"YOUR record card makes no mention of a hunger strike."

The doctor looked at Traian suspiciously.

"If you had been on any sort of strike it would have been entered here," he said. "All it says on your card is 'serious mental disorders, suicidal mania, fits of violence, persecution mania.' Nothing whatsoever about a strike. A strike is a sane and conscious act. But there's not a word about it here. The certificate is signed by two university professors, two of the leading names in the German medical profession. Whom do you expect me to believe? You or the two professors?"

The doctor was convinced that Traian had made up the whole story from beginning to end.

"Are you sure your wife is arrested?" he asked. "I shouldn't be surprised if you weren't even married. Where is your wedding ring?"

"It was confiscated during a search at the camp."

"That may be so," said the doctor, "but I have no proof of it. I can only go by what is down on your case paper. Don't be annoyed, but until the contrary is proved, I must start from the following premises: your wife has not been arrested, you are probably not even married, your father did not die in camp, and finally you were not arrested without reason. I am obliged to disregard everything you have told me."

Traian was thinking: "How can anyone prove his own sanity? Every word and movement that hitherto have always seemed perfectly normal appear upon closer analysis to be the typical characteristics of a madman. The same words, phrases, and opinions that in everyday life seem normal and even intelligent become symptoms of advanced madness inside an asylum. It is impossible to ascertain the borderline between sanity and insanity with any degree of precision. And yet I must prove that I am not mad."

"I beg you to help me, Doctor," he said.

"What can I do?"

"Believe me."

"That won't get you anywhere," answered the doctor.

"I am not asking you to tell me you believe me, but to believe me really," said Traian. "And I would also ask you to give me a thorough medical examination."

"That is entirely superfluous. Your first request I cannot grant. I am a scientist. I can only believe what I can establish as a fact. I can't believe without proof."

"Believe me as a human being."

"I am a scientist," repeated the doctor emphatically. "My professional conscience does not allow me to believe anyone's word unless it is supported by concrete evidence."

❦ ❦ ❦

TRAIAN was put through a medical examination. Blood was taken from the veins of both arms. Then a second sample was taken from the tips of his fingers. He gave with resignation. Man must be ready to give away his blood—always and everywhere. But blood was not enough. The first evening they jabbed a syringe into the back of his spine to extract a few drops of the fluid from his brain and spinal cord. He bore the pain, which was agonizing. The process was repeated. Traian endured it without complaint. He knew that man has to pay, not only with his blood, but with his brain. Otherwise he forfeited the right to live.

They stimulated his glands and extracted the innermost secretions, placing them afterward between glass slides and holding them against strong light to examine them. His urine, his saliva, the juices of various glands and internal organs were all examined under the microscope, put in test tubes, weighed, and distilled in the prison laboratory.

The doctors X-rayed his chest and then his skull. They checked his skeleton bone by bone and joint by joint under the X-ray apparatus.

They were searching for the wound that had provoked the desperate outcry of man for justice. The wound was elsewhere, but the doctors were determined to locate it in Traian's body, in his lungs, his brain, his blood, his bones, and in the very marrow of his bones. He let them search.

One by one they tested his muscles and reflexes; his knees, his hands, and his stomach.

They listened to his heartbeats, to the pulsations of his blood, they tried to detect the slightest abnormality in the structure of his lungs.

He was put on the scales and weighed. They measured his height, his waist, his chest, his wrists and ankles. They opened his mouth and inspected his teeth, counting and tapping them. They inspected his tongue as though it were some unsavory dish on a plate. His whole body was examined like an article suspected of being undermined by some hidden flaw. Was it or was it not serviceable?

Then the psychiatrist set to work on him. The doctor talked to him morning, noon, and night, at times into the early hours of the dawn. His answers to the most harmless questions were carefully taken down. The doctors hunted for traces of madness as detectives test for fingerprints at the scene of a crime. He was encouraged to speak of his childhood, of his mother and sisters, his father, and the women he had known. Traian knew well the secret paths hidden in the darkness of the subconscious and did his utmost to help the doctors to penetrate them.

His soul was laid bare, turned inside out like a cupboard full of old clothes and dirty linen. Nothing was withheld from them, and without the slightest compunction or disgust they poked their nose into the most secret recesses of his private life.

The examination finally came to an end.

"You are perfectly sane," said the doctor. "A few complexes, of course, undernourishment, avitaminosis, and subnormal weight. Apart from this, everything is in order. Slight anemia, swollen joints resulting from insufficient nourishment, teeth affected for the same reason. The pulse is somewhat irregular, owing to weak general condition, one or two harmless spots on the lung, and slight rheumatism. But these are all common complaints and are of no importance."

"Are you therefore finally satisfied that I am not mad?" asked Traian.

He was tired, as tired as Jesus on the Mount of Olives.

"I should like to be released from the hospital immediately," said Traian.

"You are going to be interned in the medical ward," said the doctor. "You are physically very weak."

"I wish to return to camp," said Traian.

"That is very unwise of you."

"I want to return to camp at the earliest possible moment."

Seven days later Traian was back in camp. He had brought with him all the medical certificates proving that he was not, and never had been, mad. His eyes were shining with the joy of victory. But his whole body trembled like a shadow with exhaustion and suffering.

ひ ひ ひ

"automatic arrest may be justified as a method, but it cannot in itself constitute sufficient reason for arrest," said Traian. "Before a man is thrown into prison, treated like a criminal, and murdered more or less speedily, there must be a reason. That man must have been guilty of something. Yet, what have I done? Or my wife? What wrong did my father do? What crime has Johann Moritz committed? But when I asked you this question in a very natural fit of despair—after fifteen months' imprisonment—you considered my cry an attack of insanity. The moment that man's cry for justice and liberty is labeled insanity, man ceases to exist. He may belong to the most advanced civilization history has ever known, but it will be of no avail to him."

Lieutenant Jacobson lit a cigarette. Immediately after Traian had returned from the hospital, Jacobson had sent for him, and was already regretting it.

"All you Europeans take things too tragically," he said. "It is a peculiar characteristic of yours."

"You may be right," said Traian. "It is one of our failings. But it is infinitely more serious to stand by and watch the tragedy, the death writhings of man, with a smile on your lips. That is much more than a mere fault or failing."

"I tried to do something for you," said Jacobson, "but I couldn't manage it. I asked the authorities to release you."

"I am sure you have done your best," said Traian. "But you cannot and never will succeed. Never more will any man succeed in freeing either himself or anyone else. Man is in a minority, and his hands are tied. The shackling is done automatically. You, too, are chained. The shackles of technocracy hang from your wrists and ankles. Western civilization has but one gift left to offer us: handcuffs."

"Go back to camp," said Jacobson. "Have a rest. Take it easy. And don't go making a fool of yourself again."

"I shall do the only thing a man is still allowed to do at this late hour of history."

"There you go, off the deep end again," said Jacobson. "I don't like to see you looking so gloomy. Have a cigarette?"

"With pleasure."

Traian lit the cigarette and then asked:

"Don't you ever get the feeling that we are all spectators who have insisted on remaining behind after the show is over? This obstinacy of ours is pointless. We'll all be thrown out eventually. The hall must be aired and the chairs cleared away. The continents must be aired. Another show is due to begin.

The show of history must go on. Yesterday *The Petitions* were billed. The 'Petitions' of man to be allowed to live, his appeal to the bureaucrats of Technological Civilization. The appeal against his sentence was rejected. It wasn't even read. The entertainment had an unfavorable reception. There was no 'happy ending.'

"Tomorrow there will be the première of a show called *The Mechanical Ballet*. The cast will contain no human beings. Only robots, machines, and featureless 'citizens' will appear on the stage. I shall not be present at the performance. The curtain rises too late for me. There is a box reserved for you, however, but only for the first performances. Do go and enjoy yourself. Don't forget you have seats only for the beginning of the season."

Traian left his unsmoked cigarette on the ash tray on the lieutenant's desk and went out of the room.

☩ ☩ ☩

TRAIAN found Johann at the camp entrance near the gates. Johann was depressed. At the sight of Traian his eyes filled with tears.

"Is it really you? I thought I would never see you again."

"Would you have been sorry?"

"To my dying day," said Johann, shaking him eagerly by the hand. "I couldn't even say good-by to you when you went away. They wouldn't let me in to the hospital, although I tried time and time again. Where did they put you?"

"In the madhouse," said Traian. "I've brought back something to smoke."

He untied his handkerchief, which was wrapped round the shreds of cigarette ends he had collected.

"They locked you up there? Poor Master Traian."

They sat down on the scorching earth by the camp gates and started rolling cigarettes.

Johann had not yet got over his surprise. But he dared not ask questions.

"You always admired my pipe, didn't you?" said Traian.

"With a pipe you can be sure of having something to smoke," answered Johann. "You can stuff it with dottle and all sorts of odd bits of rubbish that would never make a cigarette. That's why I'm sorry I haven't got one. It's a hard life in camp without a pipe."

"I'll give you mine," said Traian, handing him his pipe, which he had carried around with him for eighteen months, and which had always stuck between his teeth, though he scarcely ever had anything to fill it with.

"You can't do that," said Johann. "A pipe's worth its weight in gold in camp. And how are you going to smoke?"

"I'm going to give up smoking. This is my last cigarette."

"Did the doctor tell you to give it up?"

"No, he didn't, but I don't want to smoke any more."

Johann took the pipe and began stuffing it with tobacco.

"Thank you," he said. "But if you find you can't give it up, I'll give it back to you, I will: I'll only accept it on condition that you really do give up smoking."

"I shall certainly give it up."

Johann smiled.

"I often said I'd stop smoking, but I could never hold out. It isn't easy to give it up."

"I know," said Traian. "But this time it's for good."

Traian lit his cigarette, and Johann lit the pipe. They smoked in silence. Traian then took off his glasses and gazed at them affectionately. It was as if he were saying good-by to them.

Of all the personal belongings he usually carried about with him, only his glasses had remained. Tobacco pouch, watch, wedding ring, wallet, fountain pen, and pencil had been confiscated one by one. The only things he still retained were his glasses.

When his father had died, he had placed the cross that he had worn round his neck until recently upon the priest's breast, so that it might be buried with him. Orthodox priests were always buried in their chasubles, with an icon on their chests. His father had not been buried in a chasuble. He had worn an American jacket with "PW" printed on the back and sleeves. Underneath he had not even been wearing a shirt. Johann had washed it that same morning, and it was still drying when the priest had died. He had been removed from the tents so quickly that there had been no time to fetch the shirt and put it on him. But Traian had slipped the little cross from his neck and laid it underneath the jacket, next to his father's skin. His father had been buried with it. Perhaps he had been cremated with his little cross.

And now Traian had nothing left but his glasses. It was his only personal possession apart from his body: this body and these glasses were the only material things that he had managed to rescue from his former life. Now he looked at the glasses, turning them over in his hand with a pang of regret. Then he handed them to Johann.

"Will you keep them for me?"

"Can you see without them now?" asked Johann, who had always considered it a great burden and punishment for anyone to have to wear glasses all his life. He was sincerely glad that Traian no longer needed them.

"No, I still can't see without them," said Traian. "But it is more restful not to wear them. I shall never wear them again."

"It always surprised me the way you wore them all day long," said Johann. "You only took them off at night. I've never seen you without them."

"If you are released before me, I should like you to take these glasses to my wife," said Traian. "You may not be able to find her right away, but keep them on you all the time. You never know when you may come across her. You may meet some day in Romania. Be careful not to smash them."

Johann took the glasses and looked at them. He felt that Traian was keeping something from him. The fact that he had given him first his pipe and then his glasses was significant.

"Don't be alarmed, Moritz," said Traian. "I only want you to keep the glasses. I shall never wear them again, but I don't want them to fall into unknown hands. I've seen so many things in life, thanks to them. Do you understand why they are so dear to me?

"It was through these glasses that I first beheld my wife. Through these I have seen thousands of beautiful girls; I have seen paintings, statues, museums, cities, and countries. Through them I have gazed at the sky, the sea, and the mountains, and read countless numbers of books night after night.

"With these glasses I watched my father die, and I have looked at you and at all my friends.

"With these glasses I have seen the collapse of Europe. I have seen men die of starvation, suffer imprisonment, torture, and slow death in concentration camps. Through these glasses I have seen saints and lunatics.

"I have watched a whole continent die, with its burden of inhabitants and laws, its faiths and hopes—die without realizing it, imprisoned in camps and hemmed in by the technological laws of a civilization that has reverted to the automatism of a barbarian age.

"These glasses, my dear Moritz, are as my very eyes. At times I scarcely know which is which! They are inseparable. With them I have seen everything there was to be seen till this very hour.

"But henceforward I wish to see nothing more. I am tired. The performance has gone on too long.

"If I were to keep my glasses on any longer, I should see only the ruins of towns and the ruins of people, the ruins of countries, of churches, and of faiths. I should behold the ruin of my body—the ruin of all ruins. I am not a sadist and I can't bear to look at them. It is more than I can stand to behold nothing but ruins everywhere, as far as the eye can see.

"Over the ruins the advance of the new pioneers has begun. They are citizens of a new world rising in history. They are building at furious speed. In building their civilization, they have started with the prisons. That is their concern. But I have no wish to join them. And so I should have to sit aside and watch for the rest of my life. But to live the life of a spectator, a witness, means not to live at all. Technological Civilization has nothing to offer man except a spectator's seat.

"The irony of it is bitter: the only things they did not confiscate in their searches were my glasses. That was their way of dictating to me the attitude I must adopt toward life. I used to think it generous of the soldiers to leave me my glasses. But it wasn't generosity—it was sadism. For not only did they force me into the position of a spectator, but they even settled what I should see: camps. I am not allowed to see anything but camps, lunatic asylums, prisons, troops, and barbed wire—miles and miles of barbed wire. That is why I've given up wearing glasses.

"They were the last things I was allowed to keep here on earth. Glasses, like eyes, are wonderful things, not to be compared with anything else in the world; but only provided that one is alive. When one is no longer alive, or when one is scarcely alive, or when one is allowed to live only in part, then glasses are nothing but a gruesome jest. Have you ever seen a dead man wearing glasses?"

"But you are not dead."

"That is our only hope—that we are still alive. But hope can't take the place of life. Hope is a weed that grows even among the graves."

"But we are alive, Master Traian," said Johann.

"We hope we are."

Johann looked hard at Traian. He reminded himself that he had just come from the madhouse. Traian had said so himself.

"Don't be frightened, Moritz, old man," said Traian. "I'm not mad. I should be very hurt if you, too, were to think me mad like the rest. You say I am still alive because if I weren't you would see me dead. You would see my eyelids close, my heart stop beating, and my body grow cold. You would see a corpse. But there are some deaths, Moritz, that do not leave a dead body behind. Continents die, leaving no corpses. So do civilizations, religions, and countries. And men, too, sometimes die before their death can be certified by the presence of a corpse. Just because you can't see mine, that is no guarantee that I am alive. Do you follow me?"

Johann started sobbing.

"What's the matter with you, Moritz?"

"You're ill, Master Traian."

"What you mean is that I'm raving and going mad, isn't it?"

"Oh, no. How could I say such a thing?"

"You think I'm insane," said Traian. "That's why you're crying. But you're crying for nothing. I'm not mad, my dear Moritz. I'm saner than ever before."

"Are you, Master Traian?"

"Of course I am."

"I didn't think you were mad, but I thought you might have a headache," said Johann. "You've had nothing to eat for so many days. . . . Very likely they tortured you in that place. . . . You're so pale. It never even crossed my mind that you could be . . ."

Johann avoided saying the word "mad."

Traian reflected that those who suffered spiritually from the disintegration of European civilization were dying with it. And those who remained alive were forever onlookers to the tragedy. Either they belonged to a mechanized civilization like Jacobson or else they were simple souls like Johann Moritz who had never outgrown the phase of instincts and superstitions. Europe had nothing to do with either: both took for a lunatic the man whose spirit had drained the very dregs of suffering.

The only person who, realizing that it was not madness but rather the utmost agony of suffering, could yet survive was Nora, thought Traian. For she had the inherited background of thousands of years of slavery and humiliation. Her people had already grown accustomed to slavery and suffering in Egypt when the pyramids were built. Her people survived the Spanish religious persecutions, the Russian pogroms, and the German concentration camps; and now it would hold its own even against the early stages of Technological Civilization. He was glad for her sake, and smiled.

"Light your pipe, Moritz," he said, "and then go and put away my glasses in the tent. You know I don't want them to be broken when my wife gets them."

"I'll take them at once."

Johann walked away with his measured step and slightly humped shoulders, puffing at his pipe. Traian felt that, as he watched, Johann's steady walk was carrying him, not across the camp parade ground, but through centuries of history; and that as he walked he was entirely oblivious of all that went on around him, his roots planted deep in the earth and his eyes fixed on the blue miracle of the sky, never even wondering what made it so blue.

"Johann and Nora will outlive Europe," he said to himself. "They will find it possible to exist even in the Technological Civilization of the West, though not for long. No human being will be able to live in it for long. They may be in the audiences for the first few performances. But then, finally, the last and toughest of all men will disappear and the robots will spread over the face of the earth from the East and the West, the North and the South."

☙ ☙ ☙

AS SOON as Johann had passed out of sight between the tents Traian stood up, threw away his cigarette, and set out in the direction of the main gate.

Prisoners were not allowed in the area leading to the main

entrance of the camp. Traian was fully aware of this, but nevertheless he walked steadily on. His steps, neither dragging nor hurried, were those of a man who, returning homeward after a day's work, can afford the delicious luxury of dawdling and is yet anxious to get home without too much delay.

The prisoners in the square, of whom there were always several thousand about, noticed that one of their number had entered the forbidden avenue. They crowded toward the fence to take a closer look at him. They thought it must be some clerk from the commandant's office or one of the doctors. These were the only people allowed to go beyond the bounds of their own square.

The prisoners were eager to identify him. In camp not the slightest incident escaped the notice of these thousands of avid eyes. Forced to dwell day in, day out, upon the same objects, they were ever on the alert for any novelty, no matter how insignificant, provided only it was out of the ordinary. This urge to escape from the automatism of routine, to seek out the personal and the original, and to thirst for all that is peculiar and uncommon in life is one of the basic needs of the human soul.

A prisoner walking boldly across a forbidden area was an occurrence meriting close attention. It was an event. Even if, as a company clerk or doctor, he had been entitled to cross the yard, the show was still worth seeing, and the prisoners watched with all the concentrated attention they would have bestowed upon an actor on the stage, simply because he was allowed to do what was forbidden to the general public.

Traian was conscious of being followed by thousands of eyes.

He knew, moreover, that the Polish sentries stationed up in the emplacements that towered above the barbed-wire fences were also watching in amazement, wondering where he thought he was going.

But Traian glanced neither back at the prisoners staring from behind the barbed wire nor up at the Polish sentries in the watchtowers.

He walked straight ahead. His step betrayed more than determination. It was not the measured, uncompromising stride of an angry man determined to overcome every obstacle in his path. It was certainly decided, but at the same time it was springy, like that of a man who took pleasure in walking.

Traian did not in fact take pleasure in walking, but he knew that what he was doing had a purpose behind it, and this gave him a feeling of deep satisfaction. His stride was not the dull and regular movement of an automaton or a machine, nor that of a man driven on blindly by the fury of passion. Traian did not walk like a fanatic.

He walked with open eyes. It is true that without his glasses he could hardly see, but the eyes of his heart and mind were alert and watching, and thus he beheld clearly his way and its purpose, its tragedy and its joy.

He who had eyes to see might have discerned all this in Traian's gait as he strode across the sand toward the barbed wire—all this, and more, a timid and deeply buried sadness. It was the sadness of a man leaving his home behind, of a sailor setting sail for far and alien shores.

He who had eyes to see might have discerned all this in the footprints traced in the sand. But those who were there had eyes to see and yet saw it not.

What the sentries and prisoners saw was Traian drawing nearer and nearer to the wire fence. That was unauthorized. No one was allowed to go within a yard and a half of the barbed wire.

And Traian was actually doing it.

Some of the prisoners shaded their eyes so as not to miss a single one of his movements. Others clapped their hands to their mouths and gaped, waiting for the next move as if it were the most thrilling moment of an exciting football match, an adventure film, or a detective story.

The Pole in the turret was equally astounded. He, too, would probably have shaded his eyes to get a better view if he had not been holding the rifle. As he tried to raise his hand he found he was raising the rifle. That reminded him that a prisoner was approaching the wire fence and that it was his duty to shoot. He pressed the trigger.

As the rifle went off, the Pole realized he had made a mistake: he had forgotten to take aim first. The drill manual said: come into the aiming position; fire. He knew that. It had become a subconscious reaction. Therefore, automatically, he corrected his mistake; before firing a second time he aimed at the target, which happened to be a prisoner who had stepped out of bounds.

Traian heard the first shot go off and, an instant later, the second. Lightning flashed before his eyes, and a feeling of weariness flooded his limbs, warming him through and through, as though he had come into a well-heated room in midwinter and had drunk a good glass of hot toddy. Something warm flowed over his hands. His body doubled up on the scorching ground beside the barbed wire, like an overcoat slipping noiselessly off its hanger and falling on the floor in a crumpled heap.

Traian was filled with intense pity for this body of his which had suddenly given way and become a soft wet mass on the ground. This body had been his best friend. Now, for the first time, he realized how much he valued its friendship. He thought of Nora and of his father, who had also been his friends, as dear to him as his body. The pictures of Nora and his father and mother, of Johann Moritz and George Damian and a few others, rose before his eyes and fell away again suddenly, like pictures on the wall when the cord snaps.

These his most cherished images fell to the ground like his body, piling on top of one another in rapid succession.

His mind could no longer hold them in position before his eyes. All his strength had ebbed away. The last thing to remain upright for a moment longer was his head. His forehead alone was still held high.

But a few moments later even that became too heavy for him.

He laid his cheek on the warm earth and tried to carry his mind back to something. But his memory lay like a flag draped over the images of the past and over his own limp body, from which the blood was oozing out.

Traian knew what he wanted to say, but he said nothing: it was a prayer, one he particularly liked. But, like so many things in life, it was doomed to remain forever unsaid. It was not long. Had he lived a few more moments, he would perhaps have said it:

Erde, du Liebe, ich will . . .
*Namenlos, bin ich zu dir entschlossen, von weit her.**

His cheek and lips pressed closer to the warm earth, tenderly, in a final gesture of friendship and love.

It had all been solemn and perfect, unclouded by the pettiness of man. It had all happened so simply, with the solemn majesty of a dying fire.

In the camp square Johann, who suddenly wanted to scream, put his hand over his mouth and controlled himself. He lowered his eyes and made the sign of the cross.

❧ ❧ ❧

FOUR days after Traian's death Johann received a letter from Susanna.

DEAR JANI,

Probably you thought I was dead. For nine years now we have had no news of each other. I have often told myself

---

* *Earth, you darling, I will!* . . .
  I've now been unspeakably yours for ages and ages.
       —RAINER MARIA RILKE: Translation by J. B. Leishman
          and Stephen Spender.

that you must be dead. I was going to have prayers said for you in church as they do for the dead.

But somehow I always changed my mind at the last minute. Now I am glad I did not have them read for you the service for the dead. It is very unlucky to pray for someone who is still alive as though he were dead.

I got your address from Mons. Perusset of the Swiss Red Cross. He told me you had been interned for several years.

After I had thanked God for keeping you alive, I prayed that He might enlighten the minds of those who keep you in prison unjustly, because I know you are neither a thief nor a criminal and that they locked you up without cause.

I have so much to tell you. So much has happened during those nine years, but there isn't room for everything in a letter.

You'll be angry when you hear that I am now in Germany, that I left our house, land, and all, and that I am bringing up your children among foreigners. That is why I must tell you how it all happened.

It was the second day of Whitsuntide when you left. The people in the village told me that the gendarmes had led you away at the point of the bayonet. I didn't believe them, because I knew you were innocent and that there was no reason why the gendarmes should lock you up and take you away at the point of the bayonet like a criminal.

Four weeks after you had gone I baked a loaf and waited for you. I knew you would come back hungry and thirsty. When the loaf went stale I gave it to the children and baked another so that there should be a fresh one ready for you. I don't know why, but my heart kept telling me you would be coming. I expected you every day. I thought you would come in the evening and I used to leave the gate unlocked so that you wouldn't have to wait till I came to open it. I knew you would be tired and that your feet would be aching and I didn't want to keep you waiting. But you didn't come, my dear Jani. I stopped baking bread for you because I had run out of flour, but I went on expecting you just the same.

One day before Christmas the Sergeant came round and told me you were a Jew and that he had orders to confiscate your house. So that I could go on staying at home with the children he got me to sign a divorce certificate. I signed it. It was winter, and I had nowhere to go. But I never really divorced you, and I went on waiting more impatiently than ever.

When the Russians came to the village they shot Father Koruga and the foremost men in the village. That night your mother and I carried the priest away from the manure pit, meaning to hide him in the forest. On the way there we came across a German convoy and we handed Father Koruga over to them to take him to the hospital. I don't know if we did right. But we couldn't leave him to die. The next morning your mother was shot by Marcu Goldenberg for what we had done. He was going to shoot me, too, but I picked up the children and fled from the village. I worked and suffered in many different places. I was afraid the Russians would shoot me as they shot your mother if they caught me. And I ran away, as far away as I could. But they caught me all the same, in Germany after the end of the war. They didn't shoot me. They were very kind to me. They gave your children bread and sweets and clothes because they were not German children. And they gave me food and clothing, too. I began to be sorry I had fled from Fantana because of the Russians.

This lasted four days. I was waiting till I was well enough to go back home, because I had been ill. One night I heard knocking at the window. It was Russian soldiers. They broke the door down and came into the house. They searched everywhere to see if they could find any other women, and they brought in the landlady's daughter, who was only fourteen. Then they made us drink. They drew their revolvers and said they were going to shoot us if we didn't drink. After that they told us to strip. The children were in the room. I said they could shoot me if they liked but I was not going to take off my clothes in front of them. They tore my skirt and blouse to shreds. All night long the soldiers raped us one after another. They poured brandy down my throat because I wouldn't drink and then into my ears and then they raped me again. Forgive me, Jani dear, but I don't want to keep anything from you. When I woke up the Russians were no longer in the room and the children were crying around me as if I had been dead.

The following evening the Russians came back. They were the same ones. They brought in the landlady's daughter and raped us again.

After that I hid in the cellar with the children so that the Russians shouldn't find me. But the third night they found me even in the cellar. The same thing happened as on the other nights, but I don't know anything about it because I fainted before they began.

This went on for two weeks, night after night. I hid in the garden, with neighbors, and in the attic. But they found me every time. I didn't get away for a single night. I decided to kill myself, but when I looked at the children I hadn't the heart to leave them without a mother. It was hard enough for them to be without a father. What would the poor little things have done all alone in a foreign country, without a soul to look after them? It was for their sakes, Jani, that I stayed alive. But I, inside me, have been dead ever since.

To escape the Russians I fled toward the West. I reached the British and finally the Americans, where I am now. On the way the Russians caught me many times. Whenever they could, they laid hands on me and raped me in front of the children, as they did with all women. Before they let me through to the British Zone, the Russians held me up at the frontier for three days and raped me day and night. The last time I was left pregnant. For five months now I've carried one of their children in my womb.

What am I to do? Please write and tell me whether

*after all that has happened you still consider me your wife and
whether you'll ever come back to me.*

*I am weeping and waiting anxiously for your letter to
know what I am to do.*

SUSANNA

❦ ❦ ❦

FOR a long time after Johann had finished reading the letter his
fingers were still tightly gripping the pages. The signal for the
soup came to him as in a dream, but he did not move. He lay
stretched out on his back on the bed.

The look in his eyes had changed, and his cheeks, and the
way he lay on his bed. He was no longer the same Johann Moritz
he had been just a few moments before, the Johann Moritz he
had always been. He was someone else. The body and the soul
of Johann were like an electric cable charged with a current too
powerful for its resistance. He was now nothing but the dead
embers of what he had been. He, Johann, had ceased to exist.
If someone had jabbed a pin into him he would not have felt
it. He was a man who knew neither hunger nor thirst, who felt
neither sadness nor joy nor yet indifference. . . .

He could have laughed and cried at the same time, because
he no longer was part of anything, because he was no longer
alive.

He got up and went out of the tent without knowing where
he was going.

He stopped at the correct distance from the barbed-wire
fence subconsciously, from force of habit. If he had ventured
into the forbidden zone and if they had shot him as they had
shot Traian, Johann would not have cared. He wished neither
to penetrate the forbidden zone nor to keep out of it. He had
no wishes or desires of any kind.

A little while later two American soldiers came toward him

from the other side of the fence. They held cameras and took a photo of him. He did not move or even glance at them. He stirred only when a third soldier came up from behind. Johann called out to him softly:

"How are you, Strul?"

The American soldier stopped with his camera ready in his hand and stared at him. It was Strul, the office clerk from the Jewish camp in Romania, who had fled to Budapest with Dr. Abramovici and himself. They had seen and recognized each other.

When Johann called him a second time by name, Strul raised the camera to his eyes and pretended to take a photo. Then he turned round and walked away quickly without answering.

Johann stood motionless behind the barbed-wire fence and watched Strul and the other two American soldiers climb into a jeep and drive away.

As the car was moving off, Strul stole a final glance at him, but looked away quickly, ashamed of meeting his eyes. Johann was not angry. At any other time he would have been furious to see that Strul, his former companion through so many hardships, had pretended not to recognize him.

But today it was all utterly indifferent to him: he just did not care. For a long time he stayed by the entanglement.

Someone came up from behind and rapped him on the shoulder. He did not turn round.

"Moritz, get ready to go."

Johann turned round. He thought the order for his release had arrived. A new light appeared in his eyes.

"My release?" he asked the tent leader, who had touched him on the shoulder.

"I'm afraid not, old man."

"Another camp?"

"Nuremberg."

Johann shrugged his shoulders indifferently. He had known

for some time that since he had belonged to the SS he had automatically been declared a war criminal. It was therefore to be expected that he, too, would be sent to Nuremberg along with all the other war criminals, Marshal Göring, Rudolf Hess, Rosenberg, and von Papen.

They would probably condemn Johann to death, too. They would very likely hang him. It made no difference to him now.

And so he went on staring into the distance through the barbed wire.

The tent leader gave him a pat on the shoulder and said:

"Ready to leave in half an hour."

Johann did not stir.

"Get your stuff together," said the tent leader. "There isn't much time left. The assembly is at one o'clock."

"I have nothing to pack," said Johann.

"Aren't you taking anything with you?"

"No."

"Not even your blanket?"

"Not even my blanket."

It occurred to the tent leader that if Johann was not taking his blanket it would give him the chance of having two and thus of making himself more comfortable. But he chased the thought from his mind and said:

"You must take your blanket. The prison of the International Tribunal at Nuremberg is cold and damp. You'll need a blanket."

"I don't need anything."

The tent leader turned to go.

"Be sure you're there on time. You move off at one o'clock."

Still Johann did not go. He stood with the tip of his shoe on the white line that marked the edge of the forbidden zone. The toe of his right foot crept forward, until the white line was half covered. He looked up at the Pole in the watchtower. The sentry was keeping his eyes on Johann and holding his rifle at the ready. But Johann did not venture over the white line.

Half an hour later he was on his way to Nuremberg with the other war criminals from his camp.

Susanna's letter was left behind in the tent, together with Johann's other possessions. The other prisoners tried to read it, but it was in Romanian, and they could not understand a thing. It was written on very thin paper. The prisoners tore it up and made cigarette paper, which they divided among themselves. Then they rolled cigarettes and smoked them.

꙳ ꙳ ꙳

PETITION No. 7. *Subject: Justice. Moritz, Johann*
(War Criminal, Punishment of)

(Petition received at the Bureau after death of witness)

The International Tribunal of Nuremberg, representing the voice of fifty-two nations, has found that my friend, Johann Moritz, was a war criminal.

That's fine. As soon as the sentence is made public, I shall give up walking about with him round the camp square. It is not pleasant, and may indeed be incriminating, to be seen in the company of criminals. Johann Moritz, however, seems unaffected by the decision of the International Tribunal and remains strangely unconscious of the serious nature of his crime.

That is the object of my petition.

Johann Moritz contends that, in all his life, he has never killed any living thing, not even a fly, and that therefore he cannot be a criminal. This is obviously untrue, since the fifty-two nations at an International Tribunal have established that Johann Moritz is a criminal. Furthermore, Johann maintains that he does not know the fifty-two nations and could not therefore have committed crimes against them. His line of argument is, no doubt, naïve. I read out to him the names of the fifty-two prosecuting nations. Most of them he heard for the first time from me. He was not even aware that such countries existed. But that is no excuse whatever.

Johann became indignant when he heard that France and Greece were among the fifty-two nations that accused him. He turned purple with rage and refused to believe it. He claims to have once known five Frenchmen whom he helped to escape from prison. Apart from this he has had no other relations with France. He only met one Greek, who was once a prisoner in the same camp, and to whom he once gave half his bread ration. These were the only relations he ever entertained with Greece.

But these questions are strictly private and personal. These two Allied Nations participated equally with the rest in the verdict that brands him a criminal. The decision is clear and categorical.

In order to convince him of his guilt toward all the Allied Nations, I propose that Johann Moritz be condemned to one year's imprisonment in each one of these countries. This will give him the opportunity of convincing himself that he is a criminal and will eventually break down his indifference.

As it is unlikely that Johann Moritz will live for another fifty-two years, given his weak physical condition, which is common to all criminals, and seeing that his premature death would deprive some of the fifty-two victim nations of their right to keep him a prisoner, I propose that the sentence of forced labor be reduced to six months per nation. This would give him a total of twenty-six years in prison. Should he survive (and it would be a pity if he were to die without having first atoned for his guilt in each one of the fifty-two Allied countries), I suggest that he should be put in chains and sent on tour through the prisons of the fifty-two nations, spending not more than one month in each country. Upon completion of the whole cycle, he should start all over again.

Thus each nation would get its fair share and none would be penalized. Justice is the foundation upon which the Technological Civilization of the West is built. Justice must be done. In view of the fact that certain countries, such as Russia, Poland, and Yugoslavia, do not keep their prisoners in a state of first-class preservation and are sometimes apt to forget about them altogether, I suggest that at the commencement of each tour Johann Moritz be carefully weighed and a detailed inventory be made of all parts of his body. Each nation must sign for Johann Moritz when it takes him over from the International Tribunal and return him to the said Tribunal having the same weight in pounds and in full possession of those parts of his body entered in the inventory.

In this way Johann Moritz would be kept in good working order for the use of each of the fifty-two nations.

It is a principle of the Technological Civilization of the West that nothing must ever be allowed to deteriorate.

It is our duty to require other less civilized nations not to treat after the manner of barbarians objects entrusted to them. We consider it our mission to civilize the entire globe. That is our aim, and we are proud of it.

THE WITNESS

(INTERMEZZO)

⊟ ⊟ ⊟

JOHANN MORITZ was eventually released.

He had been away for thirteen years, during which time he had gone through hundreds of camps. And now he was once again back with his wife and children. It was ten o'clock at night, their first night together. Johann had eaten and was now sitting with his elbows on the table, looking at his children.

Petru, the oldest boy, was fifteen years old. Johann looked at him and rubbed his eyes to convince himself he was not dreaming. He could not believe that the boy standing in front of him was his own son.

Petru was wearing an American windbreaker dyed blue, smoked cigarettes, and had eyes the color of his father's. He, on the other hand, could not believe that this thin spare man with hair graying at the temples, this man who stood before him and whom he had never seen before, was his father. But now that they were going to live in the same room, he was trying to get used to him.

"I'll speak to my boss, he may be able to find work for you in our workshop," said Petru.

Johann smiled.

"I'm sure the boss will take you on if I tell him about you," Petru went on. "He doesn't employ unskilled workmen as a rule, and you are not qualified. But he'll make an exception when he hears you are my father."

Johann looked at his second son, Nicolae, who took after Susanna. He was just as fair and had the same soft velvety eyes.

Then Johann's eyes fell on the third child, who was four years old. It was not his own son. Susanna had had him by the Russians, but Johann had forgiven her. It was not her fault. He lit another cigarette. Petru had welcomed him with a whole pack of cigarettes.

Johann was tired, but he did not feel like going to bed. There were only two beds in the room. Susanna and the youngest were going to sleep in the small bed. Johann was to have the big one all to himself, and the boys were to sleep on the floor.

"This will have to do for the time being," said Petru. "Later on we'll find another room or at least another bed."

The boys spread out their blankets on the floor and began to undress.

Johann was still sitting at the table, resting, propping his head on his hands. He watched Petru and Nicolae undress and lie down. They wished him good night in German. Johann would have liked to hear them say it in Romanian, but the boys had almost forgotten their native tongue.

Susanna put the little one to bed. The child of the Russians, thought Johann. He was a beautiful child with fair curly hair. Johann did not like looking at him. He had written to Susanna from the camp to say that he would consider the child his own. But Susanna did not like it, either, when Johann looked at the fair-haired little boy. She undressed him and tucked him under the bedclothes as if to hide him away.

For a while Susanna stood in the middle of the room, wondering what to do next. Then she sat down at the table, opposite her husband. She knew Johann was tired, but she dared not tell him to go to sleep. She felt responsible for everything that had happened, for her husband's arrest and for all the years he had spent in the camps. It was stupid of her, but she could not help it. And then she felt guilty because the Russians had raped her. That, too, was her fault. She could not bear to look Johann in the face or tell him to go to bed.

She had expected his arrival. She had prepared some food and made up his bed. He had come in famished and had devoured everything she had put before him. Now he was already halfway through the pack of cigarettes Petru had given him.

As soon as the children had fallen asleep Susanna looked up at her husband. Their eyes met, and for a long time neither was able to look away again.

"It's the same dress you had on that night, isn't it?"

Moritz gazed at the blue low-necked frock that Susanna had been wearing on the night Jurgu Jordan had discovered her flight. She had been wearing it still when he had brought her to his parents and when Aristitza had turned them away and they had had to go to Father Koruga's, where Susanna had slept in the little room next to the kitchen. It was the only thing she had brought with her. Apart from that she had had nothing to her name, not even a petticoat. And for the first few weeks after running away from home she had worn only that blue dress. At night she would take it off and sleep naked. Later on she had made herself other dresses, but to her the blue one was the most beautiful, and Johann, she knew, felt the same. She had worn it throughout those first weeks when they had been so intensely happy together.

"I never wore it again after you left Fantana," said Susanna. "The day they took you away I swore I wouldn't put it on again till I saw you back on the doorstep. For thirteen years I carried it about with me and for thirteen years I waited for you. Today is the first time I've worn it."

Susanna lowered her eyes as if she had said something shameful. Then she looked up at Johann and met his eyes. He would have liked to take her on his knees, and say to her: "I longed for you." But the words would not come.

He lit another cigarette and glanced at the children, who had fallen asleep. Then his eyes went back to Susanna. She had scarcely changed. There were a few wrinkles about her face. Her skin was no longer smooth, and her hair not as fair as it had been. It had grown more like hemp. Her breasts now sagged. And yet she looked the same as when he had first set eyes on her. He could hardly believe that the Susanna of Fantana had changed so little in these thirteen long years.

"I'd like to go for a walk," he said.

He did not stand up, but waited for Susanna to move.

"Can I come, too?" she asked.

He did not answer, but sat waiting for her to get ready. Then they both crept out of the room on tiptoe so that the children should not hear them. They felt embarrassed. Going down the stairs, their shoulders touched twice. For some time neither of them said a word.

The sky was dark. Johann wanted to see the main street. She led the way. As they passed in front of a brightly lit shopwindow she took his hand to show him a pair of shoes she wanted to buy for him. Then they moved on, still holding hands, looking into other shopwindows along the street. They did not talk about the camp, or about their house in Romania. For a while the past was forgotten. They were going to have an evening to themselves unspoiled by painful memories.

"I'll rest for a couple of days and then look for a job," said Johann. "I might find something where Petru works."

"You're going to rest for a week or two at least," said Susanna. "There'll be time enough to look for work after that. You're still too weak for the time being. Petru and I earn enough between us to keep us all. I go out washing. I've got good customers."

She squeezed his hand. He liked the way she had told him to take a longer rest.

They had reached the end of the town. On both sides of the road, orchards stretched away into the distance. It was dark.

"You'd think we were in Fantana," said Johann.

"Yes," she answered.

They walked on, remembering the nights of Fantana and the hoot of the owl. They were both sharing the same memory.

"My feet ache," he said. "You wouldn't mind if we sat down awhile?"

They went into an orchard and sat down on the grass.

"It's just like Fantana," he said, stretching out on the grass with his hands behind his head. He turned round and buried his head in the grass.

"Smell the grass, Susanna. It smells just the same as the grass in the garden behind your parents' house. You remember, the garden where we used to meet."

She bent down to catch the fragrance of the grass and felt her heart thumping inside her. She could not answer. Her voice would have sounded too unsteady.

He put his hand on her shoulder. She was still bending low over the grass.

For a long time they remained thus, motionless, separated from each other, save only that his hand was on her shoulder. They dared not draw closer together.

"You know, Susanna, I used to long for you when I was in camp," he said.

A few stars were glittering in the sky. She turned to look up at them, leaning slightly toward Johann, moving gently, so that he shouldn't notice. She felt ashamed.

"Forgive me, Susanna," he said. "In camp I always used to dream of you naked. That's the way it is when you're a prisoner. It's just that I want you to know the truth," he added apologetically. "I used to dream of you naked as I remembered you in the grass behind your house. It was the most beautiful summer we shall ever know."

She edged closer to him and put her head on his arm. He stroked her shoulder and then her back, and finally laid his hand between her breasts.

"You'll crease that beautiful dress of yours, after keeping it for thirteen years," he said.

She was about to say that it did not crease.

"Better take it off and lay it out on the grass, as you used to do in Fantana."

She pulled the dress over her head quickly, as if she were hiding from him. She was quite naked now. Her body gleamed as white as marble against the dark-green grass. She was still not close to him. He put his arm round her waist and said with surprise:

"You're the same as ever. You haven't changed at all. It's all just as it was when we were together in Fantana. How is it that you haven't changed?"

"It isn't true," she said. "I've grown older. But you, you're just the same."

He held her closer. She drew away.

"You draw away just as you used to do," he said. "You wouldn't think thirteen years had gone by."

He had slid his arm round her waist and drawn her toward him, just as he used to, and had pressed his mouth on hers till she almost suffocated. His chest was crushing her like an iron shield. It was all exactly as it used to be.

"Your body smells like the grass in Fantana," she said. "It always had the scent of grass and freshly mown hay. I, too, thought only of you. I swear it. I thought of you night and day. All my thoughts were about you. All of them. You were my sun, my husband, my sky. You alone."

Johann knew she was speaking the truth. She had belonged to him and to him alone. He could feel it from the heat of her body and the thumping of her heart, from the words that burned his ears. He knew he was her sun and her sky and that she had thought of none but him and waited for none but him.

It was as though thirteen years had been swept away at one stroke. They were together again, exactly as they had been in Fantana, the two of them, with life stretched out before them.

Johann was no longer afraid of life.

A little before dawn they got up from the grass. They were both ashamed.

"We're not so young as we were thirteen years ago," she said. "We ought to have gone home sooner."

He laughed. They had agreed to come back to the same spot the following night.

"And every night after that," he said. "We must always meet here, never anywhere but here. Here it's just like Fantana. It feels as if we were really there and that all that has happened since then has not really happened at all."

On the way home they were laughing and chatting. Now that they were not strangers any more, they felt happy and had forgotten their embarrassment. Once or twice he caught her by the waist, and she did not edge away.

"Do you know," he said, "I don't feel tired any more? This very morning I'll go with Petru to look for work. Why wait several days? We'll be able to have two rooms. I'll earn some money, and we'll be happy."

She wanted him to rest first, but Johann had made up his mind.

"This very morning I'll go along with Petru," he said. "I'm used to work. For thirteen years I've been working from morning till night without a break. And it was always heavy, exhausting work."

They stopped in front of a shop whose window was lit up.

"Out of my first wages, I'll buy you a string of glass beads," he said. "What about those red ones? Do you like them?"

She looked at the price and then at him. She could not find words to answer him. The many dreams in which Jani came back and bought her a string of glass beads had suddenly come true.

"We must never never part again," she said.

"If I start work tomorrow, on Saturday I'll buy you the necklace."

By the time they reached their street it was almost light.

He pressed Susanna in his arms and kissed her.

"I can't kiss you at home—the children would laugh at us," he said. "They think we're old. But we aren't really old at all, are we?"

A truck with its lights on had drawn up outside their front door.

Johann's heart began to beat fast. He felt the pockets in which he kept his papers. They were all there and in order, but he was still uneasy. The truck was like the ones he used to see in the camps, and its headlights spread the same glaring light. And yet he knew that the release papers in his pocket were all in order and that all trucks had glaring headlights.

"What's the matter?" asked Susanna.

He did not answer, but, hurried into the house.

On the way up the stairs they met two MP's just coming down from their room. They had awakened Johann's children and told them that at seven o'clock that morning they were all to be ready on the doorstep with not more than a hundred pounds of luggage per person.

Meeting Johann on the stairs, they repeated their instructions to him.

"Ready seven o'clock sharp!"

"Where are you taking us?" asked Susanna.

"All eastern European DP's are to be interned," said the MP. "It's a political measure. Your countries are at war with the Western Allies. But don't worry, you'll be properly looked after. American rations. It's only a security measure. Don't be afraid, you're not under arrest."

Johann decided to run away.

Once before he had been duped into telling the commandant of the town about how he had helped some French prisoners to escape. He had been taken in and that was why he had spent so many years in prison. Now he wasn't to be taken in any more. He picked up the bag with which he had arrived from Dachau eighteen hours before and woke the boys to say good-by to them.

Petru started laughing when he saw his father all ready to go. Petru spoke English fluently and was an ardent admirer of the Americans.

"Where do you think you're going, Father?" he asked. "Don't be so simple. I know the Americans. I've got a whole lot of American friends. We go out together every evening. If the Americans say it isn't an arrest, you can take their word for it. If it is a political internment it means we'll get American food, real coffee, cigarettes, and chocolate. We won't even have to work. It would be silly to run away. You don't know the Americans."

Johann thought of all he knew, all he had suffered and seen. Then he looked at Petru. He did not want to shatter his illusions by telling him what he knew.

He took his bag off his shoulders and set it down on the table. He had no idea where to escape. If he ran away from the Americans he would come up with the Russians, which was worse. But that did not mean he believed the things Petru told him about the Americans. He knew better. Now he felt tired. He no longer had the strength to run away. He had no alternative but to stay and be arrested all over again.

"You're right," he said to Petru. "It would be foolish to run away."

Petru gave him a friendly pat on the shoulder.

"We'll enlist as volunteers in the American army," he said. "When we've beaten the Russians, we'll go back to Romania. This is the war of civilization against barbarism. You, too, must volunteer, Father."

Johann had stopped listening to him. He remembered the barbed-wire fences of Dachau, Heilbronn, Kornwestheim,

Darmstadt, Ohrdruf, Ziegelheim, and the barbed wire of the thirty-eight American camps through which he had passed in the last few years, the camps where Father Koruga died and where Traian Koruga had been starved and tormented. And he could feel each one of the spikes of all this barbed wire stabbing into his heart.

"I shall have been free for exactly eighteen hours," he said. "Now I'm going back to a camp. This time I'm not being arrested as a Jew, Romanian, German, Hungarian, or a member of the SS. This time I'm being interned as having been born in eastern Europe." His eyes filled with tears.

"Aren't you going to pack, Father?" asked Petru, thrilled at the thought of going away.

"I'm ready," said Johann. "For the last thirteen years I've done nothing but move on from one camp to the next. I've been packing and getting ready for thirteen years. You'll get used to it, too. I feel sorry for you, but everybody will have to get used to it. From now on they will see nothing but camps, barbed wire, and convoys. So far I have been in one hundred and five camps. This will make the hundred and sixth. How sad that my freedom lasted but eighteen hours! Who knows if I'll ever be free again before I die?"

Looking at Susanna, he said:

"But it was so wonderful. I am ready to die now. I had never imagined that I would live again through such wonderful hours. It was exactly as it used to be in Fantana, wasn't it, Susanna?"

(EPILOGUE)

cɜ cɜ cɜ

"MRS. WEST, I should like a word with you about a private matter."

Eleonora put down the file she had been reading and looked at Lieutenant Lewis. He was sitting at his desk with his legs crossed, leaning back in his chair and smoking.

Lieutenant Lewis was head of the recruiting office for foreign volunteers. Eleonora was an official interpreter in the same office and had been working under him for the last six months. Why doesn't he wear garters? she thought, looking at his socks, which hung concertinaed round his ankles. Why does he always straddle his chair as if he were on horseback? Only sailors on shore sit that way. And yet Lewis is a young man of good family, with a university education. However emancipated a society may be, it is still not right for a man to sit in his office and show his bare legs to a lady.

Every time he shook hands with her without removing the cigarette that dangled from his lips, every time he threw a file on the table as if he were throwing a bone to a dog, Nora felt she had been slapped in the face.

Lieutenant Lewis never had the slightest inkling that Nora harbored any such thoughts. On the contrary, he firmly believed that she admired him, though her eyes often seemed timid and surprised.

"I am listening," she said.

"Mrs. West, will you be my wife?"

Lieutenant Lewis leaned even farther back in his chair, until it was balancing on two legs only.

"I cannot accept your proposal, Mr. Lewis."

"Have you any other plans for the future?"

"No, I have no other plans, but my answer is: no."

Nora went back to her file, but she could no longer concentrate on her work. She sat bending over the papers, thinking of the past.

She had spent two years in camp before being released automatically in the same way as she had been arrested. When she finally got out of the camp she had lost all her money and dresses, her jewelry, and even her wedding ring. Everything had been confiscated, including the money she had deposited abroad. She was as poor as Job.

Then she was officially informed of Traian's death by suicide. That was all the information she could obtain.

She was not going back to the Russians and she had nowhere else to go, so she remained in Germany, working as a translator in a press bureau. Then came the order for the internment of all persons born in eastern Europe. War was declared, and once more she was automatically interned. But this time it was all different. She now worked in the recruiting office for foreign volunteers.

She had board and lodging in the camp and received a salary. In her spare time she wrote. She was going on with the novel *The Twenty-fifth Hour*, which Traian had left unfinished. She had managed to stow away in a suitcase the first four chapters, which to her mind contained the essence of the book.

She never gave a thought to the future. The only thing she

planned to do was to finish the novel, and that was not so much a plan in itself as a means of escaping from the necessity of making plans. She gave herself up entirely to this work, which she loved, doing her utmost to imitate Traian's style and complete the book as he would have wished it to be done.

Thus, all the while she was writing, she found him near her, sitting at her side, and it seemed to her as if they were writing together. He had told her the whole plot in detail, and she was doing her best to carry it out faithfully.

"O.K.," said Lieutenant Lewis, after a pause. "May I ask why you refuse me?"

"If you really want to know—because of the difference in age between us."

"Nonsense!" Lieutenant Lewis laughed heartily. "You are one year younger than I am. I've seen your papers. Where did you go and dig up that idea from? It's all hooey; our ages are dead right."

"You are mistaken," said Nora.

"You're pulling my leg," said Lieutenant Lewis. "How old are you?"

"Shall we change the subject?"

"Not before you've told me your age."

"It isn't good manners to ask a woman her age," said Nora. "I am nine hundred and sixty-nine years old, but don't forget that women always make themselves out to be younger than they really are. Actually I am much older than that."

"O.K., Mrs. Methuselah!" he said, highly amused.

But Nora was not smiling.

Lieutenant Lewis had firmly believed that she would accept his proposal. But Nora had twice said that her answer was quite definitely no.

"Don't take it too hard, Mr. Lewis," she said. "But I just couldn't spend twenty-four hours under the same roof with you."

"Why not?"

"I've told you already—difference in age," she said. "You are a nice, selfish, charming young man, just like every other young man, whereas I am a woman from another world."

"I don't understand."

"That is precisely why I refused to explain," said Nora. "It is quite natural that you shouldn't understand. I have lived through a thousand years and more. A thousand years of experience that have made me what I am today. You have nothing behind you. You have the present and the future, perhaps. I say 'perhaps' not because I doubt it, but because the future can never be foretold with any certainty."

"Too sophisticated," he said, feeling uncomfortable.

"Look here, Mr. Lewis," said Nora. "After listening to words of love uttered by Petrarch and Goethe, Byron, Pushkin, and Traian Koruga, after having had the troubadours sing to me of love and fall on their knees before me as before God; after watching kings and knights kill themselves for my sake, after hearing Valéry, Rilke, d'Annunzio, and Eliot speak to me of love, how could I possibly be serious about a proposal that you choose to throw in my face mixed up with a puff of cigarette smoke?"

"Do I have to be Goethe or Byron or Petrarch to make an offer of marriage?"

"No, Mr. Lewis," said Nora. "Nor do you have to be Pushkin or Rilke. But you must love the woman you want to marry."

"Agreed!" said Lieutenant Lewis. "Who told you I didn't love you?"

Nora smiled.

"Love is a passion, Mr. Lewis," she said. "You must have heard that sometime or other, or you may have read it somewhere."

"Couldn't agree more," he said. "Love is a passion."

"But you are incapable of experiencing any passion whatever," said Nora, "and you are not the only one. In your civilization no man knows the meaning of passion. Love, the supreme passion, can only exist in a world that believes in the unique value of the individual human being. Your society considers man replaceable. In your eyes the human being, and therefore the woman you claim to love, is not a unique specimen created by God or by nature; a unique copy, as it were. For you every individual is a unit in a series, and one woman is as good as another. This very conception of life precludes love.

"In my world lovers know quite well that if they fail to win the heart of the woman they love, nothing on earth will make good their loss. That is why they often kill themselves for her sake. Their unrequited love can be replaced by no other. A man who really loves me will make me feel that I am the only woman who could make him happy, the only one in the world. He will prove to me that I am a unique being, having no counterpart anywhere on earth. And I shall be persuaded that this is so. A man who fails to make me feel that I am unique and unparalleled is not in love with me. A woman who does not receive this assurance from the man she loves is not really loved by him. I cannot marry a man who does not love me. Could you inspire this feeling in me, Mr. Lewis? Do you honestly think that there is no other woman like me on earth? Are you quite sure that if you tried hard enough you would not be able to replace me? No, you are convinced that if I refuse you, you'll be able to find another woman to be your wife, and if she refused you could always find a third. Am I not right?"

"Yes, you are quite right," he said. "But I should be sorry if you refused me. Honest to God, I would."

"We might just as well get on with the hallowed work of our office, Mr. Lewis."

She opened the file and said:

"Every single person in camp has applied, even the old men, women, and children. They all want to volunteer and fight for your cause."

She smiled. She was thinking of the thousands of people who had fled westward to escape the Russian terror. They had all found sanctuary with the Americans, the British, and the French. They hadn't even stopped to look where they were going; they had simply fled—from the Russians, from barbarism and terror, from torture and death. Their goal was any place where there were no Russians, and they had run toward it with their eyes shut. They knew only that they must not turn back. Behind them were darkness and blood, terrorism and crime. They had kissed the ground where there were no Russians. They had gone down on their knees and kissed it, calling it the Land of Promise and Salvation, without looking to see what it was like. It was a land without Russians. Beyond that fact, they did not care who lived in it or occupied it.

They did not want to see any more Russians.

The Americans arrested the refugees, but they did not mind. They were in the Promised Land. All that they asked of life was to escape from the Russians, and their prayer had been granted. Beyond that they did not care what happened. They had been saved from the Russians, and that was why they did not mind when the Americans arrested them. Even if the Americans had killed them, they would still not have protested.

And now war had broken out—the Third World War. The refugees were exhausted and hungry and shut up in camps. They wanted food and rest, work and freedom, but they had raised no cry when their wishes were not granted. They had escaped from the Russians, and that was all that mattered.

The Americans had promised to release anyone in camp who volunteered to fight in the Western brigades. And so they had volunteered, one and all, not because they wanted to fight, but because they did not want to remain in prison and starve to death.

"These people are terrifically enthusiastic," said Lieutenant Lewis. "The cause that the West is defending against the barbarism of the East has been adopted by all. They all know that the hour has struck when they must win or die. It will be an epoch-making war without parallel in history. The civilized

West against the barbarian East. It will really be a world war, the first world war in history."

Lieutenant Lewis rubbed his hands.

"It is our good fortune and privilege to take part in this war. Victory is already ours. The whole world will be civilized. There will be no more wars, only progress, prosperity, and comfort."

Nora smiled.

"You don't seem very enthusiastic," he said. "I see you are not particularly enamored of the Western cause. Are you pro-Bolshevik? You are the only one to reserve your judgment, the only one who is not wildly enthusiastic."

"There is not a single one who is really enthusiastic," said Nora. "They only appear so to you."

"Aren't all our volunteers anti-Bolshevik, heart and soul?"

"They are all anti-Bolshevik," she said. "But that's as far as it goes. It means that they want to live in freedom. Freedom from terror and death, starvation, deportation, and torture. Their attitude is not political. It is the attitude that man adopts in the face of crime, terror, and slavery."

"What more do you want?" he asked. "That means that they are heart and soul in favor of the Western cause; we are fighting precisely for liberty, security, protection, and democracy."

"Don't be misled by words, Mr. Lewis. This so-called Third World War is not a war of West against East. It is not, properly speaking, a war at all, though the battle lines stretch from pole to pole, covering the entire surface of the earth. This war is nothing but an internal revolution within the framework of the civilization of the West; a mere internal revolution, entirely and exclusively Western."

"But we are fighting against the East, against the whole of eastern Europe," he said.

"You are wrong," said Nora. "You, the West, are fighting against an offshoot of your own civilization."

"We are fighting against Russia."

"Russia, since the Communist Revolution, has become the most advanced branch of Western Technological Civilization. It has taken up all the theories of the West and put them into practice. It has reduced man to zero, in accordance with the doctrine of the West. It has transformed society into one vast machine, in accordance with the doctrine of the West. Russia has imitated the West as only a barbarian or a savage could have done. The only genuinely Russian contribution to Communist society is its barbaric fanaticism: nothing else. Apart from bloodthirstiness and fanaticism, every single thing in the U.S.S.R. comes from the West. And now you are at war with this particular aspect of Western civilization—its Communist aspect. That is why your Third World War is simply a revolution that has broken out and is following its course within the limits of the Technological Civilization of the West. The transatlantic and European aspect of Western civilization is fighting the Western Communist aspect. It is a sort of internecine struggle between two categories, two classes of the same society. It is, if you like, a class revolution, like the revolution of the *bourgeoisie* in 1848. The East has nothing to do with this internal upheaval of the West. No one outside Western civilization has any part to play in it. And since this revolution is typically Western, Mr. Lewis, it is not being fought in the interests of men. Western civilization knows no men."

"I don't understand."

"It is very simple," said Nora. "The interests of Western civilization are not those of men. Quite the contrary. In the Technological Civilization of the West men live, like the early Christians, in catacombs, prisons, churches, and ghettos, on the fringes of life. Human beings are in hiding, for they have no right to appear in public or hold public office. They may not appear anywhere, least of all in offices, for your civilization has substituted offices for altars.

"Men must hide the fact that they are human. They have to behave according to technical laws, like machines. Man has

[396]

bccn reduced to a single plane—the social plane. He has been transformed into a 'citizen,' which no longer has anything in common with the conception of a human being.

"Western civilization recognizes man only as an abstraction —as a 'citizen.' And not recognizing him as a man, how can it make a revolution for his sake? The present revolution, by virtue of its specifically Western character, is utterly foreign to all the interests of man as an individual human being.

"In this your civilization, man has long been a proletarian minority, and whichever side may win the present conflict, his position will remain unchanged.

"The present struggle is a clash between two categories of robots, each dragging in its wake a trail of slaves of flesh and blood. Human beings can no more be considered participants in the present struggle than Roman galley slaves could be said to participate in the wars of their empire. They only bear the chains of war. And those who are in chains cannot take an active part in the fight."

"But the prisoners from this camp are enrolling voluntarily, of their own free will, aren't they?" asked Lieutenant Lewis. "Your contention is very hazardous. I'm not threatening you, but I must contradict you emphatically. Every volunteer comes of his own free will. Do you, perhaps, maintain that we have forced a single one of them to do so? You have witnessed the ensuing scenes of despair when we have had to refuse an application. These people threaten to commit suicide if we don't accept them. Isn't that free choice for you? Isn't that enthusiasm? They are even more fanatical than we are ourselves. The worst punishment that can be inflicted on them is to refuse their applications. Am I right?"

"It's their only way of escape," she said. "They are locked in a dungeon walled in by flames, and there is only one way out. That way out is to enlist in the Western brigades. Hence all these applications pouring into our office. Every one of them represents a last desperate bid for the only gateway to freedom.

They are all applying; not only the refugees from the East, but all the people of Europe."

"You're wrong," said Lieutenant Lewis. "These applications are not the only way to salvation. They can go over to the Russians. Why don't they; why do they come to us?"

"No," answered Nora. "To show them the way to Russia is like showing them the wall of flame beyond which, even if they jump, lies nothing but the very heart of the blaze. Beyond the wall they can hurl themselves into nothing but fire and death. No man will jump into the fire while there yet remains a way out. We are that way out, and so they apply to us. They have no inkling what lies behind the door, and they don't even care. They must get out because they are dying of asphyxiation. A door is at least better than a wall of flame. Even if they knew that beyond it there were only more flames, they would still prefer the door. For one brief moment they can blot out the sight of the fire and cherish one last hope and illusion. That is better than nothing. It is extremely important to hold on to an illusion, however absurd it may be."

"You see everything from a tragic point of view," said Lieutenant Lewis. "The volunteers don't think as you do. They are overjoyed if we accept them. They are prepared to fight to the bitter end to defend our cause, which is theirs, too. They are the best soldiers we have. Just open the door and look at the crowd outside the office. There are hundreds and thousands of them. They all want to volunteer. They all want to fight for the cause of civilization. They all want to sacrifice their lives for our great victory of tomorrow. It will bring happiness and civilization, peace and bread, liberty and democracy, to all mankind. You don't agree?"

"No," she said. "They do not believe in this war. They may not think as I do, because they have suffered too much to go on thinking. They have given it up. But they feel as I do, suffer and despair as I do. Exactly as I do, all over Europe."

"Let the facts speak for themselves, Mrs. West. I will show

you open proof of the enthusiasm inspiring those who enlist. I'll pick a single example, chosen at random."

Lieutenant Lewis rose. He opened the door wide.

"Look!" he said. "Again today, more than five hundred applicants."

He pointed to the queue of men and women waiting outside the door.

"Let us take the first one."

Lieutenant Lewis ushered in the first man waiting outside the door. He was not alone. His wife and his three children came in with him. The man had black hair graying at the temples. His cheeks were somewhat drawn. He had large black eyes with a sad expression in them.

Nora looked at them.

" 'Il y a une mélancholie qui tient à la grandeur de l'esprit,' " *

she said to herself.

The man who stood in front of her was a workman, but the light of his spirit shone in his eyes—the light of a spirit akin to greatness. His sadness was not merely of the flesh but of the spirit.

The woman standing beside him wore a blue dress that hung loosely on her. Her fair hair was streaked with white. She was very beautiful. It was not only her body that was attractive. Her womanhood was like a brightness around her and seemed to radiate from every pore in her body. Nora wanted to smile at her affectionately, but the woman kept her eyes on the ground. She was not sad but frightened.

One of the boys had black eyes like his father. But there was no sadness in his glance. His bold burning eyes examined Nora with curiosity. The other boy kept his eyes lowered. He was fair. He seemed to be far away and in his own world of dreams.

The youngest child had curly hair and blue eyes. Nora was

* There is a certain sadness that is akin to spiritual greatness.

not sure whether it was boy or girl. But it was as beautiful as one of Raphael's angels.

"Here is a whole family wanting to enroll," said Lieutenant Lewis. "Just ask them whether they agree with your ideas. You'll see for yourself that they haven't come in desperation. They come into our ranks because they are athirst for liberty and justice. They want to be accepted in order to fight for peace and civilization. They are fully aware of what they are doing. Ask them anything you like, and you'll see."

"It isn't necessary," said Nora. "I have no need to find out what is in these people's hearts. I know. My own suffering is enough. Don't force me to stir up the despair of others. Carry on with the usual interview. I am not inquisitive."

"Ask them anything you like. I am sure you will change your mind."

"Very well," said Nora.

Lieutenant Lewis's last sentence amounted to an order.

She looked up at the man, who was standing by the door, hat in hand. Their eyes met.

"Your name?"

"Johann Moritz," answered the man. "I want to enlist as a volunteer with all my family. Please accept us all. I need a special age permit—I am over age, but I feel young. The boys are too young. They have not yet attained the age stated on the posters, but they are hard-working, honest lads. We are anti-Bolshevik, as prescribed on the posters. We believe in the victory of civilization, as prescribed on the posters. Only none of us is the right age. That is why we beg you to grant us a special age permit. If you do not accept us we are lost. We cannot bear it any more."

The boy with the black eyes nudged his father with his elbow. He wanted to make him understand that he had said too much. Johann stopped and blushed scarlet. He realized that he should not have said those last words. He had made a blunder.

As a result, the application would probably be rejected. He looked beseechingly at Nora.

"Please accept us," he said. "We are hard-working, honest people."

Petru had taught him many other things to say, but he did not want to say them. He could not bring himself to affirm his belief in civilization, in the West, and all the rest of it. It would not come. His lips refused to pronounce the words. His son would be furious and swear at him as soon as they got outside again, but he could not say them. All he could do was to look beseechingly at the red-haired woman sitting at the desk. She was looking at him.

There was a silence.

The woman at the desk had a warm, kindly look in her shining eyes. Johann's wife raised her eyes and looked at the woman at the desk. The children did the same. Nora went on looking at Johann in silence.

Lieutenant Lewis left the office for a moment. Nora still said nothing and only stared at the man standing in front of her.

"Did you know Traian Koruga?" she asked.

Johann started.

"We were together," he said. He did not want to speak of the camp. Petru had told him to avoid mentioning it. "We were together till the very end, he and I and Father Koruga, too. I was with Master Traian till the moment it happened. . . ."

Johann stopped for a while and then went on:

"He was the best man I have ever known. He was a saint, not a man. Did you know Master Traian, too?"

"I am his wife."

Johann leaned against the door, turning pale. He tried to take his handkerchief out of his pocket, but he had no handkerchief. His fingers touched something made of glass—Traian's glasses.

He had put them in his pocket that very morning to make

a leather case for them. He was afraid of breaking them when he packed them in his suitcase. He took them out of his pocket and held them awhile in his hand, thinking that it would no longer be necessary to make a case for them. They were not going to be in his suitcase.

He placed the glasses on the desk in front of Nora.

"They are Master Traian's." He coughed. His voice was hoarse. "His last words were that I should give them to you. Just before it happened. . . . His last . . ."

Johann's voice was shaking. He could not speak any more. Again he fumbled for his handkerchief. All he found was the piece of leather from which he had intended to make the case for the glasses. He pulled it out of his pocket. He did not know what to do, and in order to do something he put the piece of leather on the desk beside the glasses.

"I was going to make a leather case for them," he said, "so that they shouldn't get broken." He picked up the piece of leather again and was left holding it in his hand. "I'll make it in camp. There is time enough there. Then you could keep them in the case. It is better that way. They won't get broken."

"Well, are you convinced at last that they are genuine volunteers and that they've come here full of enthusiasm?" asked Lieutenant Lewis, coming back into the office.

Nora swallowed the lump in her throat, coughed, and then said decisively:

"I am now convinced that you are perfectly right. These people have begged me to waive the age-limit regulations. They all want to enlist. The whole family."

Lieutenant Lewis chuckled with satisfaction.

"Grant them a permit," he said. "Get out the necessary forms. I'm going to take a photograph of the whole family and send it to the papers."

Lieutenant Lewis went up to the youngest child and patted him on the head. Then he asked Susanna:

"He's anti-Russian, too, isn't he?"

Susanna lowered her eyes. She felt she ought to answer something.

"Yes, he's anti-Russian, too," she said. She was afraid Johann would hear. Johann heard. She bit her lip.

Nora had started making out the forms.

"Come round and see me tonight," she said. "I live in camp, too. We'll sit and chat quietly over a cup of tea. You'll be able to tell me all about Traian." Nora cleared her throat.

"Now answer my questions so that I can fill up the forms. Where have you been from 1938 until today? Tell me everything. Don't worry, your application will be accepted."

The eldest boy smiled. He had won, and he was happy. The youngest boy, too, was happy. He was munching the sweets that Lieutenant Lewis had given him and wore a broad grin.

Susanna kept her eyes on the ground.

Lieutenant Lewis was adjusting his camera. He wanted to take the family just at the moment Johann was filling out the form. Everything was to be genuine.

"In 1938 I was in a Jewish camp in Romania. In 1940 in a Romanian concentration camp in Hungary. In 1941 in a camp in Germany. . . . In 1945 in an American camp. . . . The day before yesterday I was released from Dachau. Thirteen years of camps. I was free for eighteen hours. Then I was brought here."

"Keep smiling," said Lieutenant Lewis.

His camera was focused on Johann and his family.

Johann, watching Nora, remembered the hundreds of miles of barbed wire he had seen, which were now unraveling all along his body.

When Lieutenant Lewis spoke to him, Johann did not glance round. He did not understand English.

"That's how I spent the time from 1938 until today," he said. "Camps, camps, camps. Thirteen years of nothing but camps."

"Keep smiling," said Lieutenant Lewis.

Johann realized at last that these words were addressed to him, and asked Nora:

"What is the American saying?"

"He has ordered you to smile."

Johann looked at Traian's glasses lying on the desk. All over again, he seemed to watch Traian collapse and die beside the entanglement.

He remembered the miles and miles of barbed wire behind which he had been imprisoned. He remembered the amputated legs of Father Koruga. He remembered everything that had happened during those thirteen years.

He looked at Susanna. He looked at the little boy, and his face clouded. Tears welled up in his eyes. Now that he had been ordered to smile he could not bear it any longer. He felt he was going to burst into hysterical sobs like a woman, from sheer despair. This was the end. He could not go on. No living man could have gone on.

"Keep smiling," said the officer, his eyes fixed on Johann Moritz. "Keep smiling. . . ."